THE
DARKEST
DEEP

THE
DARKEST
DEEP

CHRIS BUTERA

All rights reserved. No part of this publication may be reproduced, stored in a retrieval system, or transmitted in any form or by any means electronic, mechanical, photocopying, recording, or otherwise without prior written permission from Podium Publishing.

This is a work of fiction. Names, characters, places, and incidents are either products of the author's imagination or used fictitiously. Any resemblance to actual events, locales, or persons, living, dead, or undead, is entirely coincidental.

Copyright © 2025 by Christopher Butera

Cover design by M.S. Corley

ISBN: 978-1-0394-8878-6

Published in 2025 by Podium Publishing
www.podiumentertainment.com

For Hayley

THE
DARKEST
DEEP

PART ONE
THE TUNNEL

MAW

Ben Breckenridge stared at the tunnel mouth, wondering when he'd become a desperate man.

It loomed before him, the maw of some terrible beast. Tracks rolled from its center like a steel-studded tongue, lights circled the rim sharp as gleaming teeth. Waiting for whatever creature was foolish enough to walk into the depths below.

Waiting for him.

"You my new scrapper?"

A man with a pockmarked, too-pale face was coming his way. He walked with a slouching confidence, an odd, easy grin spreading within his mat of red-gray beard, as if he'd just finished laughing at a joke only he could hear.

"Hey, yeah, think so. Ben Breckenridge. We spoke on the phone." Ben was sweating, hoped it didn't show in the harsh light. "I'm here to fix things."

"Fix?" The newcomer barked a laugh. "Need more than some paint and a soldering iron to pull this place back from the brink. Name's Fontaine, I'm your Ear."

They shook hands. A testing sort of handshake, Fontaine's callused fingertips firm while his eyes searched Ben's face. Ben held the gaze as long as he could before breaking free of the man's grip with a nervous smile.

"You ever seen it before?" Fontaine nodded to the empty station, his overloud voice echoing off the high ceiling. It made Ben wince, like they stood on hallowed ground that called for whispers.

A vast airplane hangar repurposed into a neo-noir Grand Central Terminal. Marble columns and ornate gilding clashed with neon strip lights, every inch designed to be lavish and awe-inspiring.

But that had been *before*. Now, it was disused and decrepit. The shops long shuttered and the transit boards blank, everything plastic wrapped and covered in a sheen of dust. Rain dripped from a crack in the sheet-glass ceiling, thunder pulsed in the sky beyond from a storm that never seemed to end. Storms made Ben nervous.

"Not in person," Ben said, attempting to radiate a nonchalance he couldn't quite muster. "Seen pictures. It's . . . really incredible."

"It's a shithole. Supposed to be some wonder of the world but look at it now. The Transatlantic Tunnel." Fontaine spit on the expensive floor. "Buncha sci-fi nonsense, y'ask me."

Ben only grunted in reply, then noticed Fontaine sizing him up. Gauging Ben like he was a pack mule he was considering buying. It made Ben self-conscious, ill-prepared to start the job interview here and now by sight alone. He straightened, trying for a stance that read casual and self-assured. *Ready.* And Fontaine nodded, seemingly satisfied.

"Come on then, Breckenridge. Let's get you signed and briefed." Fontaine waddled back the way he'd come, heading toward an office set on the station's far side where a sole light burned.

Ben hesitated before following, staring again at the tunnel mouth as terror wormed around his gut and his posture slipped back low. He didn't have to do this. He could turn around, right now. Back out into the pelting rain, his hand-me-down truck, and burn the twelve hours to Chicago. Back to the sad studio apartment where the locks were thick but there was nothing to steal. Back where his bed was always empty, and shadows sat in every corner.

No, he wouldn't turn around. Couldn't. He needed the sun again. He needed her.

Ben Breckenridge followed Fontaine across the station, his steps faltering only a little, knowing how he'd become a desperate man.

Certain the tunnel watched him go.

PRELIMINARY

"Your name sounds like a superhero's. Got that double letter thing." Fontaine leaned his bulk against the office's peeling wallpaper, stretching with an exaggerated sigh as if trying to fill the space. "You know, Bruce Banner, Peter Parker."

"Alliteration." Ben smiled over the paperwork, wanting to seem helpful and hoping to charm Fontaine. He pretended not to notice the food stains streaking the man's company-branded jumpsuit, or how the fabric strained against his girth.

"That's right." Fontaine's eyes narrowed, thin lips curling. "Almost finished?"

"Just about." Ben's pen hovered over a damning line, unwilling to scrawl the words. He skipped the question and trucked through the rest, signing but not reading.

"Where'd we get you from? Older fella like you, probably got a résumé a mile long."

Ben paused, still not used to the idea of being called "older," especially by someone probably only a few years younger. Still, Ben knew he wore forty badly—stress and bad memories carving an extra few years' worth of lines across his face. "Did you want to see my résumé again? I'm happy to—"

Fontaine waved the thought away like it was a fly circling his head. "Not the type I usually get knockin' down my door. Skinny. Educated. You get shitcanned from your last gig or something?" His grin turned wolfish. "What'd you do, piss off your last boss with your ten-dollar words?"

"Nothing like that . . . just out of options, I guess." Ben kept his voice level. Matter-of-fact and professional, like he'd practiced. "Not a lot of jobs anymore for a guy who likes to work with his hands. And that tunnel is fascinating. I'd like to see how it works."

Ben caught Fontaine squinting at him with that appraising stare again. Passing judgment and seeming . . . disappointed. As if sensing a lack of truth in Ben's words. The thought bred panic and he tried to keep his leg from bouncing beneath the table. Beyond the office walls, he heard the rumble of thunder. That *storm*. Pressing in, never giving a moment's peace, rattling about his brain, behind his eyes, tearing—

"Actually, no," Ben sat up a bit straighter. Cleared his throat. "Sorry. The truth is . . . I need this. If I can get this job—if I can *do* this job and see it through—I'm hoping I can prove that I can change. That I can be a better man. It's"—Ben exhaled, forcing himself to meet Fontaine's eyes, to make his words land—"it's my last shot."

Fontaine raised an eyebrow. Scoffed. "Hell, Breckenridge. You could be a stone-cold killer, wouldn't matter to me. S'long as you can walk, take orders, and swing the claw-end of a hammer, I'm happy to have you." He let the chair drop forward, dirty fingernails scratching at his beard. "'Be a better man' . . . *jeeesus*."

Heat flushed across Ben's face, a sour taste growing in his mouth. "I can use a hammer."

"Good." Fontaine leaned forward again, tapping the paperwork with a stubby finger. "Missed a line there."

"Right." Ben forced himself to scratch the words.

Next of Kin/Relationship: *Ellie Breckenridge, wife*

Fontaine took the clipboard, scanning with disinterest. "Won't lie to you, been tough finding people willing to go down into that tunnel."

"Why's that?"

Fontaine blew air out his cheeks. "Take your pick. Hours are shit, food's shit, pays . . . not great." A wink. "Last guy quit on me 'cause he thought the place was haunted."

Ben swallowed a nervous laugh. "You're not exactly making this sound appealing."

A shrug. "Rather give the straight horror stories beforehand so you don't get squirrelly a few miles deep when the walls start to feel like they're pressin' in."

"I'm sure it's far better than the apartment I've been living in the past few years." Ben tried to color the words with another smile, hoping to catch Fontaine's eye over the paperwork. "I should be okay. Tight spaces never really bothered me."

"We'll see." Fontaine put the clipboard down and leaned forward. "This job isn't easy. Doesn't take much for things to go wrong down there and I need you to come back out in one piece, or it's my balls in the vise. I gotta be able to trust you. Can I trust you, Breckenridge?"

"Yeah . . . yeah, of course. You can trust me." Again, Ben tried to stop his leg from jumping, his fingers from worrying at his wedding band and reopening the chafing scabs on the tawny skin beneath. "Does that mean I'm hired?"

Fontaine took a long moment. Again with the stare, the weighing. He checked his watch. "Sure, superhero. Job's yours. Don't make me regret it."

Fontaine stood, and the smile dawning on Ben's face was genuine for the first time since his arrival. Fontaine popped open the door behind him marked **AUTHORIZED PERSONNEL ONLY**, and motioned Ben through.

"Welcome to Steel Glass Ocean."

The command center was dominated by echoes and little else. Three long rows of unused computer stations, their monitors dark and seats askew, facing a massive screen covering the entire far wall. The display showed an active blueprint of the tunnel, blinking with red and green status lights but emitting no sound.

Ben stepped between the cubicles, taking it all in, listening to the rap of his footfalls reverberate against the walls. Awed to be here, where the official teams would have been tasked with overseeing travel, overseeing *history*. A place built for a grand purpose, now vacant. Insignificant. It made him sad to see so much lost.

He stepped up to a terminal at the room's center, the best seat in the house. Imagined himself standing there when the station was operational, the whole room looking at—relying on—him. He wondered what Ellie would think, seeing him here.

A discarded headset sat on a nearby desk, catching his eye. Its microphone bent from where it'd been flung in a hurry. Ben moved closer, stretched a hand toward it, wanting to pick it up and commune with the soul who'd left it behind. To know what happened to them *after*.

The door slammed behind, and Ben pulled his hand away.

"Can't say I won't be happy when this is all done and I can move on," Fontaine said, grunting. "Place is too big for its own good. Takes twenty minutes to get from here to the head. Not exactly convenient."

Ben put his genial interviewee face back on. "Bet it was something to see when it was operational."

"Sure, if you go in for that kind of thing. Looks like a cheap knock-off of that NASA control room, y'ask me. Wasn't around back then myself, and they stopped manning this place a year after shit went south—what eight years back now?"

Fontaine sat himself at a terminal in the back of the room, the only one with signs of recent use, covered in an assortment of creature comforts: yellow notepads scrawled with squiggly text and amateur doodles, a sweat-stained travel pillow half-hiding a candy bar. Two beginner's plastic knitting needles were cradled near the computer's keyboard, a rat's nest of orange yarn spilling loose thread onto the floor.

Fontaine noticed Ben looking. "Not much to do round here but nap and count the hours down. Used to watch the Mets on the big monitor, but my blood pressure kept pushing up. Wife says knitting's supposed to calm the nerves, but I'm startin' to realize I'm all thumbs." He tapped a small portable radio Ben had missed beneath the computer and winked. "Still listen to the games though."

"Gotta pass the time somehow." Ben smirked. He understood now where those calluses on Fontaine's fingers had come from. It softened the Ear's prickly edges some.

But then Fontaine propped his boots—still slick from the bathroom floor—onto the desk, sneering as he pulled the tab on a Coke can. Nodded toward the blueprint displayed on-screen OR on the screen. "Résumé said you studied as an engineer for a spell. What do you think about that?"

Ben looked over the map, studying the lines and functionality like he'd been taught in school, looking for oversights. *Rushed*, was the first word that came to mind. *Inefficient* was another. "Pretty impressive."

"Bet the guys that built it thought the same thing. Didn't stop the clusterfuck from happening." Fontaine slurped his Coke. "Still, small miracles. If this thing didn't go tits up, I'd probably be off breakin' my back on some turbine site or recycling rig rather than sitting here in my own slice of paradise."

Ben turned back toward the display. *Easy*. He had to stay cordial—might have the job now but until he was in the tunnel, he wasn't in the clear. "How's it all work?"

"The tunnel? Shit, figured you might've done some homework before showing." Fontaine jeered, pointed with the can. "Three thousand miles of tunnel and track from here to London sitting about a hundred and fifty feet below water. Broken up into prefab mile-long sections, each connected by double-door bulkheads. The bottoms are lined with this sort of super-buoyant foam that keep them from sinking, then held into place so they don't drift with those . . . fucking, steel lines you see there."

"Tension cables." Ben stared, getting lost in the blueprint. He longed to handle a physical version of it, to know it more intimately. Parse out the hidden details of its construction, trace the cable lines with his fingers as they looped around the tunnel ceiling then arrowed down to the ocean floor below.

"You know a little bit after all."

Ben shrugged. "I did a *little* homework. It's a maglev train, right?"

"That's right. Magnetic levitation, so the whole system's under vacuum. No air, or near to. Least that's what they tell me—won't find me headin' down to test it. Basically, there's no resistance, so you give one of those trains a little push and *woosh*. Bullet out of a gun."

"I've seen schematics for similar setups in Asia and Europe, but nothing like this." Ben couldn't help being drawn closer to the screen, pointing as he spoke. "Those tension cables alert the center here when issues pop up along the line?"

"Yup. Shit goes wrong, computer pings here. But it's the bulkheads you oughta be looking at. You can lose a couple cables, fine, but those doors are where the powers-that-be concern themselves. And now, they're your problem."

Fontaine took his feet off the desk and navigated his screen with a plastic, wired mouse that clashed with the slick tech surrounding it. Ben guessed Fontaine had brought it from home. After a moment squinting and clicking, the blueprint on the wall zoomed in for a closer look at a single section of tunnel. Ben spied the split of miles and bulkheads clearer now, all marked green.

"That's where our money's at, superhero. The interior of each bulkhead is a scavenger's gold mine—copper mesh beneath the flooring, wiring, insulated tubing—you name it. And we're here to pick them clean. Well, *you* are. I sit back here and tell you where the looking's pretty, while you walk down and pull their guts out."

"All of it?"

"To the bones. Strip it down, pile up a nice load on the dolly, then move on to the next bulkhead. Once you're loaded to max, walk the booty on back here and get paid. Simple."

"That . . . it seems wrong to be pulling it all apart."

"Nah we're, uh, *recycling*. The bulkheads still work, not that it matters anymore. We're just grabbing the juicy bits that make them all uniform and pretty." Fontaine leaned back again, a self-satisfied smirk plastering his chin. "I'd really like that steel-glass they use for the tubing, but that's proprietary. Bastards won't let me touch the stuff, but I'll get me a piece of it before I go, don't you worry about that." Fontaine went to drink, paused. "Besides, it's SGO doing the real damage, we're just grabbing what we can before they start the deconstruction. Well, you are."

Ben couldn't believe Steel Glass Ocean would want the tunnel dismantled, not after all the time, money, and materials put into it. It'd be like pulling apart the Golden Gate Bridge. He said as much to Fontaine.

The Ear shrugged. "Hell, they've had nothing but problems with the thing the past eight years. Bankruptcy, protests, lawsuits. The guy that made the damn thing ended up in the nuthouse—'course, that was after the presidential inquiry. Place's just been gathering dust. Figure SGO wants to finally put the parts to good use."

Ben nodded, dazed. Seems he'd come at the right time. "What's your deadline? *Our* deadline."

"Half a year before SGO starts the dismantle, but that doesn't mean you can drag your feet. Travel time from here to the bulkheads is a real bitch, and I wanna strip as many as I can before the hammer comes down. I was lucky. First few dozen bulkheads were quick and easy, my previous crews were in and out in a matter of weeks, but things slow with distance, as you can guess. My last guy stopped at Mile 90, so that's where you'll start." Fontaine lifted his Coke toward Ben. "Here's hoping you'll be my quickest scrapper yet. You do this fast, maybe I can recommend you for another gig."

Ben breathed slowly, watching as the map zoomed back out. Here was a legacy being destroyed. Not the Golden Gate Bridge at all, but the Lighthouse of Alexandria. Something new and wondrous reduced to scraps. He was surprised he hadn't heard anything about the dismantling before now. Unless it was deliberately being kept a secret, or the company's manpower had been so reduced that news didn't register on the networks. It made him notice the silence again. "Where's the rest of the team?"

"You're looking at it."

"Just you and me? I'm going in alone?" A shiver like sparks traveled Ben's spine. Not fear . . . but something else.

"Don't have the money or gear to give you a partner anymore, and like I said, not easy gettin' bodies willing to head seaward." Then, seeing the panic on Ben's face, Fontaine sat up. "Wouldn't worry though, it's safe. I've been running crews through here for almost a year now, problem free. Look at it this way—with just the two of us, we'll both get bigger slices of the pie when it's all over. Besides, you won't be totally alone, I'll be right back here talking in your ear. Technicians used to travel for repairs on their own all the time back in the day, and they didn't have good ol' Fontaine keepin' them company."

Ben turned back to the map, resisting the urge to spit. Heading ninety miles into a defunct tunnel—all alone—was risky. Deadly. Not to mention the travel time, the exertion on the body and mind. This wasn't a job any sane person would sign up for, no matter how desperate.

But then he saw a section at the map's center. Where everything else was blue with operational readiness, near the tunnel's middle a long stretch was different: nearly two hundred miles shaded a bright yellow. The tension cables were missing, leaving only the long tunnel, sagging rather than rising. At its direct center: a single mile section in dark red. Like a warning.

"What's that yellow section?" Ben said.

"The late six- and seven hundreds," Fontaine's watch *beeped* and he stood up with a groan, the swivel chair squealing with strain. "Tension cables broke away and the foam burned off, so the tunnel dips a bit. Drops to, oh, two hundred to two hundred fifty feet in some spots. Too costly to maintain so there's practically no power down there. Barely enough to cycle the bulkhead doors. That means no lights, so it's just dark and cold. We call it the Belly."

Goose bumps raked Ben's arms, standing the hair on end. He rubbed his palms together, swallowed. *The Belly*. He walked over to

Fontaine's station, ignored the wired mouse and Fontaine's scrunching face, and deftly worked touchscreen controls with two fingers, homing in on the Belly's single red mile.

"And that?"

"Mile 781. That's where *The Odyssey* crashed." Fontaine motioned Ben's hands away, eyes daggering with a not so subtle, *don't touch*. "Don't concern you. You won't be anywhere close."

The suit was a better fit for an astronaut than a deep-sea diver. Or deep-sea scrap miner, anyway. Gunmetal black with navy blue accents, smattered with choice yellow toggles and scuffed raw from dozens of previous walks. It was bulky in the chest and sides with small tubes that snaked upward to the place where a helmet would connect.

"Ugly little thing, isn't she?" Fontaine flipped a switch to bathe the "diving" rig in a pool of light, looking for all the world like a sleazy salesman in a showroom. "Rough, but she'll do."

Ben pulled the suit from the rack, surprised at how thin the material was. How light. He rubbed the mesh joints between his thumb and middle finger, thinking how easy it would be for a stray sharp edge to cut the material and leave him gasping for air.

"Rough but tough. Take a lot to puncture that," Fontaine said, as if reading Ben's mind, then tossed him a pair of company branded coveralls to put on. "Try her on."

As he changed, Ben noticed Fontaine staring at the long scar across his bare stomach. Ben quickly covered it up, slipping the suit on over the coveralls. The insides were slick and well creased, like good leather that had been broken in. Fontaine stepped in to assist, but Ben easily pulled the top-heavy chest piece on and—after a quick search—dragged the heavy-duty zipper on the left side. Snug, but comfortable. A weighted blanket.

"You figured that out easy enough," Fontaine said, frowning.

Ben shrugged. "Been scuba diving once or twice. This doesn't seem all that different," He stretched and moved, everything feeling *right*. Like he belonged in this suit. "Whoever designed this ought to be my tailor. Don't think I've ever had something fit so well."

"Better fit. That thing is five times more expensive than my car." Fontaine walked to the equipment shed's far wall, removing a box of palm-sized silver canisters from a drawer. Each cylinder was only a few inches long and tapered at the end with a screw nozzle. They reminded Ben of the CO2 charges for making homemade whipped cream, or whippets found discarded in back alleys.

"This here's your oh-two." Fontaine showed him where it plugged into the suit, just below one of the snaking tubes. "Fantastic little bastards. Air's all compressed to hell, so one little whippet should last you a few days at least, so long as you're not getting too excitable. You won't need to carry very many for this initial walk, but once I get you down on a second or third trip—breaking those triple digit miles—I'll load you up with more."

"I'd rather have more than less right now . . . just in case."

"Figured you might. I'll saddle you with a few boxes then. I've had a few scrappers get all funny on me and burn through air. Not gonna have that problem with you, am I superhero?"

"Not planning on it," he said. Then, seeing Fontaine's face, he added, "really, I'll be okay." He plucked an O2 canister from Fontaine's box, turning it round in his now-gloved hand, the canister glinting in the artificial light. It seemed too small, too inconsequential to act as his life source. "I half expected one of those air tanks clowns use for kid's birthday parties strapped on my back."

"Still got those if you want 'em, but your legs will appreciate these a bit better." Fontaine casually tossed the empty box to the floor. "That suit handles most of the hard labor. Distributing and regulating your air, clearing out your carbon, catching your, uh—what's the polite way to say it? Your *emissions*."

"Really?" Ben chuckled, touching the thick tubing that wound its way down to a satchel at the small of his back like a backward fannypack. "Technology."

"If I could wear one of these on the couch so I didn't have to walk to the head, you better believe you'd find that control room scattered with small yellow bags." Fontaine guffawed at his own joke while Ben winced, certain the Ear was only half kidding. "That's your collection sack at the back, just make sure you don't let it overflow. That, uh . . . wouldn't be pleasant. Starts building up, just swap out a full for an empty. Guy who trained me said you're supposed to treat the tunnel like a national park. 'Leave no trace' and all that. Not that it matters. If you're dropping your shit on the side of the road, it's not like they've got trains burning through that'll smear up."

"And if I wanted to keep it clean?"

Fontaine shrugged. "Clearance chutes in bulkheads, pushes shit to sea. Bags breakdown in the water, so we're not breaking enviro regulations, *God forbid.*"

"Drop bags in the chutes and replace my diapers, got it." Ben gave him a thumbs-up. Seeing his own gloved hand pop-up shot him with the giddiness of a kid playing dress up. Already he was used to the suit, and with it came a faint glimmer of excitement.

Fontaine hoisted up a backpack decked out in the same color scheme as the suit, equally battered by use.

"Life support system?" Ben said.

"Nope, just a backpack. Holds extra oh-two canisters, water, rations, sleeping bag . . . usuals. Used to be this was your air, coolant, health monitor, blah blah. But this ain't NASA. You're gonna be cold, and you're gonna be smelling your own sweat. That's just the reality."

"No tools?"

"Anything you need will be waiting for you at the jobsite where my last guy left it." Fontaine motioned with the backpack and Ben slipped it on. Again, nice and light. "Good?"

"Not too bad," Ben said.

"She'll get heavier every mile, even as she empties. No doubt about that. Those straps are gonna dig in your shoulders too. You can drop your bag on the dolly, but that won't be until you're near 90. Your ass if you break any of this equipment. Like I said—more expensive than my car. I'm not paying for a damn thing."

Ben bit his tongue. He disliked the Ear's crass way of talking, the lack of respect for the tunnel, and the ease with which he was ready send scrappers down into the long dark while he sat back and drank from Coke cans.

Fine. It was all *fine.* Ben was nearly there. All he had to do was endure just a bit longer, then he'd be on the road, job in hand. Alone.

"Surprised you're not coming with me to oversee everything down there, Fontaine. You ever been on this run?"

"Boss gets the choice seat, superhero." A nasty grin split the Ear's mouth. "C'mon. Let's pop that thing off, get back and talk start dates—"

"I'm ready to go now." Ben could hear himself speaking a bit too fast, but didn't care. The briefing and the suit had slipped a little steel in his spine. Now or never.

Fontaine's eyebrows narrowed, tongue greasing one corner of his mouth. "Never had an eager scavenger." He shook his head. "Better to take this slow. Get you properly prepped before descent."

"I feel prepped enough. Everything fits right, I've been briefed, I understand the work and rigors. I'm ready to dive in."

Fontaine paused. Ben watched him glance toward the door and bite his lip. "I don't know—"

"Listen, Fontaine." Ben took a step toward the Ear. "I . . . I can't face going home. Not yet. I need to do this now. I'm ready. Really."

Fontaine's eyes twitched from the door back to Ben, settling on his face. Searching. He rubbed at his beard, the artificial glow giving his too-pale hands a fleshy, washed-out cast. "Awfully anxious to get moving, Breck. If I didn't know better, I'd think you were running from something."

Ben licked his lips, his mouth suddenly dry. "Doesn't matter to you as long as I can take orders and swing a hammer, right?"

Fontaine scoffed, shaking his head at Ben's gall. "Hell, maybe I read you wrong, college boy." He drummed fingers to leg, that odd smile from their initial meeting creeping back onto his face. Bobbed his head back and forth, and finally, nodded. "Alright. Yeah. I like it. About time I had a man with some confidence heading in. Ready to take on the world."

Ben nodded, forcing himself to grin back. He couldn't quite find the emotion. Knowing now what he'd agreed to, knowing what came next. "Ready as I'll ever be."

"Well then," Fontaine stepped over to the door, pushed it open. "No use in waiting, is there?"

ZERO

Ben took his first tentative steps in the suit, wobbling across the room and down the hallway like a newborn colt getting used to unfamiliar limbs. Quickly enough, he eased into a new gait, self-consciousness falling away. Stepping out the door, Ben could almost imagine himself seen from afar, performing a cinematic "astronaut's walk" toward his rocket ship, ready to blast off from the world and feeling ten feet taller.

That was, until he crossed back into the vast train station and spied the tunnel. Waiting for him less than a hundred yards away. Immediately, the fear came back, stomach souring. The suit suddenly felt heavier, constricting rather than comfortable.

"Ask me fifteen years ago, something like this would've been impossible." Fontaine came to stand next to him, hands on hips and following his gaze. "Ask me ten years ago and I'd ask what's the point."

"Why take an undersea tube when you can hop on a cheap flight? I've heard people say the same thing."

Closer to the entrance, Ben noticed stray dollies parked in a haphazard line, each overloaded and spilling copper-colored parts. The tunnel's diseased organs strewn about the floor. Farther away, two utility vehicles, like golf carts without their roofing, sat docked near electric charging stations, one covered by tarpaulin, the other up on blocks.

"Any chance I can ride one of those down to the jobsite?" Ben asked, pointing. "Make both our lives a bit easier."

"The UTVs? 'Fraid not. With the small amount of power the Tunnel gets these days, all the fail-safes are in place to prevent flooding. Means you gotta open each bulkhead door by hand, then close it before the system recognizes you're there and can open the next one. Frustrating process." Fontaine thrust his chin toward the vehicles and grinned. "Those babies are too big to fit in closed bulkheads. You'd never get it past Mile 1. Dollies are barely small enough to fit comfortably but you'll see once you get to 90. College boy like you? I'm sure you'll figure it out just fine."

"Sure. Nothing quite like a little game of Tetris a hundred fifty feet below sea level." Ben rubbed at his chin. He'd figure this little problem out—he'd have nothing but time to plan for it. "How about one of the dollies then? Just give me a nice little push and I'll coast through each mile."

"Hell, in vacuum a little push in one of those would flatten you against the wall before you had a chance to wonder where the brakes were."

"Alright then. Got one of them cartoon pump handcars?"

Fontaine barked a laugh. "That's a new one, I like it. How 'bout you just soar on down there, superhero? Save me the trouble of having to wait for you to reach the jobsite."

Fontaine walked toward the platform, trusting Ben to trail behind. Ben paused a moment, needing to gird his resolve. This close to the start, that need to back out was rearing up again.

But he'd come this far already and if Fontaine was to be believed, this was his last chance before the tunnel was dismantled. His proving ground. *Ellie*. This was it. For her. He fixed Ellie firmly in his mind, knowing what she would say:

"Sometimes you need to do the things that scare you."

Ben followed Fontaine.

High up, rain still pattered on the skylights, the glass dark with obscuring clouds. Ahead, the platform dropped down to tracks, giving way to the open tunnel. The entrance. It seemed smaller, close up—not the grand imposing hole he'd seen from a way off. Just a single tube, thirteen feet round.

"You, uh"—heat flushed Ben's face—"you said the last guy quit because he thought it was haunted?"

"That's right. Said he'd heard voices, started seeing things. Shadows and ghosts." The Ear scowled. "Just some silly bullshit. It's the space, y'know? Days by yourself . . . they do something to a man. Up here." Fontaine rapped on his skull.

"I've done long-distance hikes before," Ben said, trying not to dwell. *Haunted.* "Find them peaceful most times. Boring."

"Hike's different. You got nature. Weather and wildlife. Other people nearby. In there... it's miles and miles of tunnel. Straight on down. Alone. Let's just say some folks don't respond too well to that sort of environment. Last guy practically came out screaming."

Cold pricked Ben's spine straight to his scalp. He scoffed, trying to dispel the tension, like laughing at the scary movie so the real fear doesn't take hold.

"You know, I probably should've asked first thing." Fontaine opened a locker near an operator's stand and pulled out a rounded contraption made of metal finishings and domed glass. A helmet—*Ben's* helmet. "You're not claustrophobic, are you?"

"Would it matter if I was?"

"We'd find out eventually," he said, handing the helmet over.

Ben took it, turning it this way and that. Unremarkable, padded at the neck and sides with a slot and straw for rations. He gripped it in both hands, steeling himself. Took a deep breath. Slipped it on.

It was spacious inside, the glass starting at the chin and enveloping all the way to the crown at the back of his head where it once again became metal and piping. Hot breath fogged the plate visor, making Ben suddenly conscious of its rhythm. Faster than he'd like. Was it fear or excitement?

A *hiss* and *pop* told him the connection to his suit was complete and sealed. The fog retreated. Cool, air filled his mouth, tasting like a dentist's office smelled.

A light flickered on above his forehead as the internal system came online. Readouts crawled along the bottom of his vision, displayed like the HUD of a first-person shooter game. O2 reserve percentage on the bottom left and a progress indicator on his right, scrawled in old school, eight-bit style:

MILE 0

Fontaine knocked on the glass, his voice coming in hollow and muffled from the outside. He pointed to the release valve and O2 connector, making sure Ben was familiar with them. "This helmet here is your life or death. Learn to love her and she'll take care of you."

"I will."

Fontaine stuck out a hand. "Keep your head, Breckenridge. I'll be in touch."

He shook the Ear's hand. This time, Ben maintained eye contact, his gloved hand firm, Fontaine breaking off first with a quick glance away.

Ben turned without another word. Hoping Fontaine couldn't see his face—not the treading anxiety anymore, but a hunger. A smile creeping on his lips. The *need* to dive in. To begin.

Ben Breckenridge hopped down from platform to track, hurrying now before he lost the nerve or Fontaine called him back. He faced the entrance, gripped the backpack straps in both hands, and willed his feet into action. No turning back now, no hesitation. One last deep breath.

And walked into tunnel.

MILE 1 | DESCENT

The airlock cycled closed with a sudden, definite *boom* as he stepped beyond the threshold, shutting out the world behind.

Ben hadn't thought the darkness could be so absolute so quickly. His breathing filled his ears. Ragged, with a slight hitch. Why was it so dark? Was he supposed to bump his way along the walls for hundreds of miles? Fontaine's instructions came back to him with sluggish remembrance: Ben needed to complete the cycle on the bulkhead door before the system recognized he was there.

He groped along the wall, searching for the handle set into the door's face. A vibrating hum shuddered up his arm as his fingers found and gripped the locking cylinder. He primed the lock with his thumb, twisted, then pulled it out like a cartoon plunger.

"Prime, twist, pull."

Ground runner lights burst into life beneath his feet as blue-silver lines on either side of the floor. Ben watched as they poured out from the door and ran the distance of the tunnel, flowing all the way—he figured—to the next bulkhead. Hidden a mile off and down a steady grade, beckoning him onward. His helmet ticked over: **MILE 1**.

Rolling out the carpet, Ben thought.

After Fontaine's talk of doom and claustrophobia, the tunnel seemed to loom before him. Thirteen feet high and round, a perfect circle broken only by the even, level floor. Even with a running jump he wouldn't reach the ceiling. Electric train guidelines were set at ankle height on either side of the tube, marching on and down with the light runners to direct the would-be train's route.

Ben put a hand to the wall, feeling the cold of the sea even through his glove. He could see the slow churn of the water outside and the suggestion of flitting shapes farther in the gloom. It was truly transparent. *Glass.* He rapped on it, feeling just how solid it was. Chuckled and shook his head.

"Didn't name it Steel Glass Ocean for nothing."

"Name doesn't exactly roll off the tongue. Round here we just call it SGO," Fontaine's voice boomed through Ben's helmet, crackling with static.

Ben jumped where he stood, steadying himself against the wall.

"Startle ya? Just me."

"Won't say that didn't just scare the ever-living piss out of me."

Fontaine's laugh cut with static. *"Well, I guess you're getting mighty intimate with the suit's functions pretty quickly then, huh?"*

Ben caught himself nodding, as if the man in his ear could see. Or could he? "Fontaine . . . can you see me right now?"

"Right now, yeah. Got a set of cameras on the main bulkheads, but that's it. No more farther down. Can't visually monitor every inch, that's what we've got the pressure sensors and cables for."

Ben held up a middle finger and turned in place, searching for the camera. "You see that, Fontaine?"

"Might want to put some miles in before you get cheeky."

The downward grade felt like a hand pushing forward, assisting his descent. Ben angled his feet and leaned his center of gravity back, not wanting to tumble ass over ankles right out the gate. Already, the pack was digging into his shoulders in that familiar way he'd felt when out on his all-too-infrequent hikes, the weight like an anchor pinning him to the floor. He was disconcerted to feel the first trickle of sweat teasing his scalp.

Ben looked back up the slope, only to find the bulkhead door was lost to the grade. He wondered how far he'd come . . . couple hundred feet at most. Nowhere close to a mile.

"What sort of a madness would possess someone to do this job?" He whispered as he crept deeper down, the echo of his footsteps running ahead.

"Asking yourself that question already, you may be fucked, friend."

Ben laughed. Readjusted the pack. Felt those straps again.

"It's the view, by the way."

"What's that?"

"Why people dive into that tunnel, besides the bank boost. For the views."

"What view? All I see is tunnel."

"Patience, Breck. Give her a chance to win you over. Once you hit the mile midpoint, might change your mind. You'll see a yellow breaker switch mounted to the side of the wall. Let me know when you're there."

Ben closed the distance a bit slower than he'd expected, a little worried at how winded he was by the effort. Just as Fontaine had said, a small yellow breaker box was stuck to the tunnel's curve, with a metal half-ladder built into the wall just above it leading to a submarine-style wheel-lock hatch on the ceiling. "Alright, I'm here."

"Pop the box open. Flip the switch."

Ben eyed the hatch above. "This isn't a test, is it? Weed out the stupid recruits by having them flood the tunnel on themselves?"

"Just hit it, smart guy."

Ben fumbled the box open, still clumsy with the gloves. Inside sat a simple toggle, white buried in the yellow, unused and rigid. With a little effort, Ben flipped the switch.

Floodlights burst and flared—not inside the tunnel, but *outside* it. Bathing the tunnel exterior in a phosphorescent glow. Ben spied a string of bulbs jutting from the glass like a crown, revealing the sea life in the sudden flash of light: a school of fish rushed by like a shining cloud; an eel banked hard from the harsh glare; an algae-covered boulder stretched waving green hands skyward. An aquarium spread out in a rush of color and movement.

Ben gasped, staring into the blue-tinged oasis, breathing slow, awed breaths. He hadn't known so much marine life could live so close to the shoreline. It was enough to make him feel insignificant.

Then the weight of everything above made his breathing go rapid again. The pleasure souring as flashes of splintering glass and uncorked floodwater seared through his mind. His oxygen gauge blinked, shifting from white to red. Hyperventilating. He stumbled backward, fell ass to floor, staring upward at the wall of blue.

"Easy now. You're alright."

"T-the—" *The water. The fucking water. There's too much of it. Way too much.*

"*Easssssyyyyy,*" Fontaine replied, his voice a soothing drawl.

Ben's breathing deepened, evened. The lights were dimming, erasing the views outside. Just him again. Him and the tunnel.

"*Good? Always find it best to get that out of the way. Everyone has a bit of a . . . let's say—a moment? Would've been weird if you didn't, really. Can't trust a man without a healthy bit of fear. You handled it just fine.*"

"Fontaine, that glass—"

"*Is translucent steel. Three feet thick and supported from beginning to end. It'll take a lot to bust through there.*"

"And if a lot happens?"

"*We'd know. Hell, that's why you're wearing the suit. Glass ever goes, the bulkheads automatically drop into lockdown, preserve integrity all down the line.*"

"Like in *Titanic*."

"*Yeah, well, let's hope the guys who built this thing did a better job.*"

"I, uh . . ." Ben shook his head. Grabbed his left hand with his right, trying to stop it from shaking. "I might have a little fear of drowning."

"*Superhero . . .*" An admonition, but lacking surprise. Fontaine *tsk* tsked. "*Can't say I couldn't guess. Could see you holding somethin' back. Got a sort of skittish look in your eyes. Beyond me why you'd want to take a job surrounded by water.*"

"Glutton for punishment, I guess."

"*Sure, sure. You, uh. You gonna be alright?*"

Ben took a few gulping breaths. *Slow. Slow it down.* Like Ellie had taught him. The thought of her was enough to settle his leaping veins.

"Yeah." Embarrassment got him back on his feet again, adjusting the pack. "Yeah, I'll be able to handle it. Three feet thick?"

"*That's right.*"

Ben considered the switch again. Flipped it. Nothing happened.

"*Lights need time to reset and recover because of the power scarcity. Don't worry, you'll get plenty of chances to shit yourself again soon.*"

"I'll be fine. Really."

"*Better be. No more surprises, Breckenridge.*"

"Don't worry, I'll log a few dozen miles before I spring anything else on you."

Ben set back off down the "road," shaking away the fear of the water around. Here was his new normal, better to embrace it for the adventure it was. His boots clicked off the floor, sending sonar signals to bounce off the walls and down the tunnel ahead. Leading the way.

A light appeared ahead, blue-silver like the ground runners. A singular spot set right in the center of the path, embedded in a steel wall where the runners came to a dead halt.

"Fontaine, I see a light ahead."

"Sounds like you're coming up on the end of your first mile. La-di-da. Congrats, superhero."

Now that he said it, Ben recognized a sealed door. The first real bulkhead. He felt lightheaded, lungs and limbs already taxed. Understanding the miles wouldn't exactly slough away as he trudged farther on. He was going to have to work for each one. But it would get easier. He hoped.

"Not exactly record time, old man. Was expecting a bit more from those string-bean legs of yours. Let's see if we can't make that up, yeah?"

"Fontaine, am I able to turn you off?"

The Ear's laugh eased over the relay. "*My sultry voice not good enough for you? There's a little toggle on the right side of the helmet, but you're really not supposed t—*"

Fontaine's voice cut out as Ben hit the switch. Finally alone.

Approaching the bulkhead door, Ben thought it looked like a gray steel eye: horizontally split by two steel slabs to make the lids with a blue-silver iris at their direct center. The doors and the lock. There were no signs of the previous scrappers on the outside—simply the same locking mechanism back at the start, the retractable plunger no bigger than his hand shining from octagonal housing.

"Prime, twist, pull." The blue eye shifted to green, and the doors parted with a hiss.

The bulkhead was four feet wider around than the rest of the tunnel, wrapping about the tube like a bolt on a screw. But once the doors finished opening, Ben saw just how small the actual interior was: only three feet long before meeting the door to Mile 2.

Fontaine's past scrappers had already been inside, "ripping the guts out," creating a stark contrast from the seamless glass outside. On either side, the wall panels had been removed in square chunks, exposing the electrical wires behind them like tendons, while below, the floor had been reduced to latticework grates mottled in rust and greenish stains. Mostly, Ben noticed what wasn't there: insulation, protective coatings on the wiring, copper pipe linings and more. It gave the space an unfinished cast, like he imagined the interior of a submarine to be—all cramped and prone to snags on stray metal.

Ben *tsk*ed and sighed. These would be his sleeping quarters—damp, ugly, and inefficient. He reached out and engaged the door lock for the next mile, then realized he needed to close the door behind him first before proceeding.

"Prime, twist, pull." That was going to become annoying very quickly.

Once the back door was closed, Ben found himself in near-total darkness broken only by the lock light before him and a blue wash above. He engaged the other lock, immediately not caring for the tightness of the space.

But as he waited for the second door to hiss open, Ben glanced up, following that source of suffused light, noticing the bulkhead's ceiling wasn't the same red-orange mess as the walls. It was glass, like the tunnel, the blue of the ocean twinkling beyond. It was a small thing, but it gave a desperately needed openness to the space. Made him feel like a cave explorer, staring up at a rift in the roof, yearning for a taste of fresh air.

The door finished opening and Ben stepped across the threshold. He cycled the lock and watched the light runners blink on down the tunnel. The helmet readout switched over. **MILE 2**.

Ben shouldered his pack and started toward the next door. And the next mile.

MILE 10 | WAVE HELLO

As the miles settled in, Ben developed a rhythm.
There'd always been a twin side of his mind that leaned toward obsessive compulsion, and the tunnel became the best (or worst) outlet for it. Timing the cadence of footfalls to a beat, counting the number of tethers to a mile section—any distraction from the dawning monotony of the walk.

As he walked, old habits from his life as an engineer came forward: eyeballing each joint and connector, double-checking rivets and hinges, watching for telltale signs of leaks and rust. It became apparent that, even eight years after the last maintenance worker walked through, the tunnel was in working order. He disagreed with the design though. It really needed two train lines rather than the one, and a separate maintenance tunnel underneath. Despite objections, he had to concede it was well constructed.

After fumbling the initial bulkhead, Ben mastered the second, then became bored by the third. *Prime, twist, pull.* Three miles in, the sloping grade had leveled off, leaving him with a straightaway tread, broken only by the next mile marker and its distant twinkling eye. Once past that, just more unbroken road running on and on, already becoming a blur.

He'd brought along his trusty iPod stocked up on music catalogs, but he decided to wait until at least day two before connecting it to his helmet. He needed to have something to look forward to and, for now, he had nothing but time.

As the day waned, he noticed the water darken. The blue diminishing to deeper shades, the tunnel air going cold. Night coming to the North Atlantic. He lifted his arm to check the time, cursing as he realized he'd forgotten a watch, surprised the suit and helmet didn't have one either. He guessed it was sometime past seven, if the darkness and his stomach were anything to go by.

He'd initially decided to put in fifteen miles this first day but coming up on the bulkhead between Miles 10 and 11, he let himself be persuaded to stop.

"Don't wanna overexert myself right out the gate, do I?" Besides, he still had to figure out how to get comfortable enough to sleep in the tiny shoebox of a bulkhead.

Ben cycled the barrier door open, stepped into the space between miles, and closed it behind. The gray steel shut with a reverberating *clang*, sealing him in the close, claustrophobic three-foot space. Suddenly dark, the ocean wash above disappeared, the lock light seeming dimmer than before.

He fumbled about blind, looking for a light switch, cursing himself for not looking when he'd had "sunlight" to go by. Tripped, dashed his helmet against the wall, and bounced backward. He tried to swing back the opposite way, overcorrected, and smashed into the other door directly at his back.

Ben groaned, standing stock-still for a moment and waiting for the bloom of pain in his back to pass. He shook his head to clear the bright flashes swimming across his vision. But . . . the brightness wasn't a trick on his eyes—there was a pen-sized beam of light there. A flashlight set just above the visor on his forehead.

"Would've been good to know about from the start."

He touched the bulb, feeling it depress under his hand, shutting the light off. Pushed again, back on. Grunted with satisfaction, letting the light explore the space.

A small monitor was set against the wall, a dusty LCD screen embedded among the stripped copper. Ben tapped it awake and the display sluggishly lit up with Steel Glass Ocean's company logo before dissolving into two columns labeled **MILE 10** and **MILE 11** along with a series of status readouts colored in green.

Ben scrolled to the bottom, looking but not seeing. Noticed an orange box like a broken pixel at the very end. Tapped it with his thumb. A dialog box appeared with a digital keyboard beneath: ***Please Enter Your Password.*** Ben let his fingers hover over it, considering, before closing the window and palming back to the screen's top.

He noticed a third box in the upper corner he'd missed at first glance stamped with a light bulb symbol. Punched it. Blue-silver lights, the same color as the tunnel runners, lit up from the grate beneath his feet and bathed the bulkhead in shadows and artificial glow. Somehow both harsh and weak at the same time.

"Better than nothing."

Ben dumped his pack, its mass swallowing up the already precious space, and considered leaving it outside the bulkhead at night to open more room for himself. He stepped between the doors, stretching his arms between the two with morbid curiosity. Fully extended, he could touch an elbow to either door and that knowledge made the bulkhead feel even more restrictive. A tall coffin.

"Hey Fontaine," Ben said, switching his relay back to **ON** and clicking the mic.

"*Knew you'd come crawling back,*" Fontaine chuckled in his drawl. "*Where you at, superhero?*"

"Bulkhead between 10 and 11. I don't really need to sleep in these matchstick boxes, do I?"

"*Safest spot, m'fraid. Anything happens in the tunnel, them bulkheads are where you'll want to be. Might be a tight squeeze, but they're sturdy.*" Ben imagined the overlarge Fontaine trying to get comfortable inside. Twisting and shifting his bulk, paunch poked by stray metal.

"Does that mean I can pop off my helmet?" Ben craned his head to stare at the window high above. Not a skylight—an *oceanlight*. All night-dark ocean with undulating hints of current.

"*Means you can sleep easy, not stupid,*" A chair squeaked under Fontaine's weight ten miles away. "*You packin' it in for the day?*"

"Well, I was going to do fifteen miles before punching out, but figured I shouldn't wear myself out too hard just yet." Unconsciously Ben wrung his hands, not wanting to sound lazy or undedicated.

"*I hear that, but let's not let early nights become a habit, yeh? I've got deadlines just like you, bosses breathin' down my neck.*" A pause. "*That said . . . I wouldn't mind takin' off early today. Suits me just fine. This time at least.*"

"I . . . if I have any problems—"

"*You'll be fine. Anything goes funny, just sit and relax. Bulkheads safest place to be and I'm back first thing.*"

"Great . . . great thanks. Listen, Fontaine, don't think I've had the chance to thank you. This job, it, uh." Ben cleared his throat. "It really means a lot."

"*For the wife, right?*" Fontaine chuckled. "*Hell, nothin' to thank. You're doing me the favor. Good dreams, superhero.*"

The line clicked over to empty. Just Ben and the tunnel again.

He rustled through his pack, taking full stock of everything for the first time: ration tubes, water and O2, crack glow sticks, a few colored markers, and his sleeping gear. He was surprised so few items could weigh so much during the walk.

Ben pulled the sleeping equipment out and felt just how thin the sleeping bag material was through his gloves. That, plus no heater or partner, he was going to feel the cold sooner rather than later. At least he had a mat to separate himself from the floor.

He remembered forgetting a sleeping mat the last time he'd gone camping. An October night that turned cold with no pad to keep the freezing earth from leeching the warmth out of his bones. Another flimsy sleeping bag in a ratty tent, nestled beneath the canopy of a thousand-year-old tree. But she'd been there too. Had convinced him they'd be warmer sleeping naked, all bare skin and shared body heat.

He remembered the drape of her arm over his torso. Her hot breath on his neck. The goose bumps spattering his limbs. Turning over to see the star brightness of her eyes in the dark. Opening his mouth and—

There was writing on the bulkhead wall, buried amid the exposed pipes opposite the LCD screen.

Ben sat up, pulled away from the memories. Happy to be distracted. There was a series of handwritten names, too faded and old to make out clearly, save two that were fresher than the rest. The first one was simply a name, RIGBY, in a no-nonsense stamp. The second, just above in a tight, bold scrawl, was a message slashed across the steel in permanent marker. Easily missed at first, but obvious now.

Mile 10—first sleeping hole. Feels like a damn coffin. The journey officially begins! —Holden

There was a date beside it that had been wiped clean. Then, just beside it, more rushed but clearly the same hand:

Slept like shit. Omen for things to come?

Ben caught himself grinning, sensing the sarcasm in the second set. Feeling both a kinship with this wayward soul and better about the close confines, knowing this previous tech had done it first. He recognized the first blushes of loneliness too and pushed that aside.

He finished spreading out his kit and awkwardly ate his first meal, plugging a ration tube into the slot near his cheek, then twisting his head to suck the contents through the short straw, squeezing until it curled like a spent toothpaste tube. He smacked his lips, face souring to a grimace: beef and peas paste which tasted nothing like either or like the worst version of both. After, he switched off the light, lay back and stared up at the dark water in the oceanlight, lazily calculating the miles until his job's start and how much of his various supplies he'd burned through his first day. Waiting for sleep to creep in.

His eyes kept drifting toward the scratched writing. Calling to him. Finally, he uncapped a marker from his pack and scrawled a message below the first by helmet light.

Be sure to turn on the lights—the ocean is beautiful.
—Breckenridge

Satisfied, he lay back to sleep, feeling buoyant, thinking about the possibilities that lay ahead. Wondering if his nightmares from the surface would follow him down here. Turning over Fontaine's words about the previous tech, the haunted walkways, and whatever might be waiting for him, farther on in the dark.

| BULKHEAD 10/11, HER |

Ben couldn't sleep through the night. He'd snap awake in the cold darkness. Afraid. Feeling the tunnel's sway and hearing settling *clicks* along the steel walls. He'd panic, disoriented. Terrified he'd come to after his own burial, that he was mummy-wrapped in a coffin, staring up through a window to an unfilled grave. That once someone heard his screams and realized he was alive, they'd fight to pull him free, only to find the marks where he'd torn his fingernails off trying to get out.

But panic would give way to recognition, helmet readouts, and bulkhead copper. Eventually, consciously, he'd fall back asleep, only to wake up an hour later and do it all over again.

By morning, his legs were stiff and screaming. Heat pulsed between his toes and on the soles of his feet, promising a fresh crop of angry blisters. Ben wanted to get at them but knew he couldn't open the suit. He tried standing but his depleted knees buckled, pitching him forward. He scrambled for a handhold, legs folding to awkward angles. Cursing.

He stared at his backpack with contempt, knowing sooner rather than later he'd have to haul it onto his back again and trudge down that next mile. Then the next. And the next.

"I shouldn't be here," he whispered, hanging his head and watching his legs shake from the effort of standing. "I can't do this. Why the fuck did I think I could do this? Why did I think I was ready?"

He was still close to the entrance. Better to bow out now at ten miles rather than farther down. Ben didn't care about the contract he'd signed, only about the soreness in his legs and feet. Ten miles back, that's all it would take. Forget all of this. Find another way.

Fontaine would have to be told first. The Ear would probably be disappointed, but he'd get another body sooner rather than later to rip the tunnel's guts out. Someone else to stumble into the dark, squeeze into the tiny bulkheads at night and slowly freeze to death. Ben reached for the mic switch.

The shadows shifted on the walls. Lessened.

Ben looked up to the oceanlight, half expecting to see shapes slipping by in the water. Instead, he could *just* glimpse light high above. Bathing the sea and pulling it from dark to bright blue. No storm, but sunlight.

He remembered everything then that led to this moment. This decision. This need to shore up his resolve and put on a brave face. His proving ground. It didn't matter about any sort of payment or reward, not for him. Never just for him.

Ben slung the straps over his shoulder with a groan, cycled the airlock, and watched as the door pulled open to reveal Mile 11, marching on. The pack bit deep into his shoulders, weighing for all the world like an anchor, making his legs scream. He'd get stronger, he'd endure.

For her. For Ellie.

MILE 51 | RHYTHM

Ben flipped the breaker switch and sat below, watching the lights flare and the ocean come to life. Three days in, reaching mid-mile and setting off the flares had become the highlight of the job. Pausing to rest and stretch his muscles, content in knowing the sea was always churning with life even as he trudged along inside it.

The days were quickly bleeding into routine. Ben would wake in the near darkness of the bulkheads and stare up through the glass to gauge the weather—cloudy and dark, or bright enough to see by. He'd eat, dump his waste packs, roll up his kit, and get on the road. Mornings usually filled him with a sense of purpose, calculating how long until he reached 90 and the job's start. Forward progress. He didn't find more notes from Holden or any of the other previous workers, and that was just fine. Ben was enjoying the solitude—the simple pleasure of putting one foot in front of the other. Repetition breeding rhythm. Prime, twist, pull.

Yet at the end of each night, that solitude would start to grate. When Fontaine signed off, the ocean dimmed, and the cold seeped in, the loneliness threatened to overwhelm. He'd toss and turn, slipping into fitful sleep, only to begin again in the morning.

But the mornings were getting easier, his legs and shoulders hardening with the continued strain. Even Fontaine was encouraging him to take it slow.

"*Much as I'd like you to charge through, I'd rather not have to fish an injury out,*" the Ear had said, impatient but resigned. "*Hell, sit! Enjoy the journey a bit . . . that said, you get done earlier than projected, I'll see if I can't scrounge a little bonus for you when you get back stateside.*"

So Ben rested at the light breakers, sipping his water and lighting the sea up, watching the fish float past. On his second day he saw a dolphin pod. On his third, he saw three separate schools of fish blend together to make one surging cloud. He hoped for a big-ticket animal soon. A shark or a whale, but usually it was just wide-eyed guppies and seahorses. That was fine, he had nothing but time and miles.

His media player hung awkwardly by its cord now, hardwired into an auxiliary jack in the helmet. One of the first-generation iPods, scarred from years of use and abuse, clashing with the sleek gunmetal finish of the suit. It had been Ellie's good luck charm for years, one that Ben had borrowed so often she'd eventually "gifted" it to him so he'd no longer feel guilty for taking it. He'd refused her, of course, but she wouldn't hear it.

"Humans need songs like they need water," she'd said, pushing it back into his hands. "Besides, I got myself another one." He'd teased her for that first line, like it was some off-brand poetry recycled for his benefit, but secretly, the words rang true to him. The iPod becoming an extension of himself, of *her*. He held it like a talisman now, a small piece of her in the solitude of the tunnel, journeying with him, allowing him a chance to find his voice.

Ben had fancied himself a singer once, even tried out for the school choir in middle school. He'd been accepted and stood as a tenor for a single recital before teasing from his classmates caused him to drop out. That life seemed wholly not his own anymore, but the singing was still true, if a bit rusty. Alone, under the sea, with nothing but the staccato beat of his steps and the tinny whine of the MP3 player, he let those vocal chords ring. Cycling through his favorite songs and singing along, listening to the echo reverberate on the tunnel walls until he grew hoarse, then just listening. He tore through all his favorites, then the stuff he'd always meant to listen to, then ambiance, then everything all over again. Anything to break the monotony.

". . . 'cause I know nothing, no nothing . . . 'bout love . . ."

He sang now, while lazy in a dreamlike web below the breaker. Watching a manta ray glide over the ceiling, its yawning mouth opening and closing, as the light from the breaker faded. The tunnel swayed beneath him as the ocean bucked and rocked, as the tethers gave sway but no ground. The sensation no longer foreign but fluid. Calming. He could sleep right here, pretending he was on a boat in a harbor, mere feet from dry land.

Ben and Ellie had dreamed about living on a houseboat, years ago. He'd booked an Airbnb in the Amsterdam canals without realizing it was actually a boat. They'd wandered the cobbled roads searching for the address, only to find it belonged to a box-shaped tug sitting permanently anchored between apartment buildings and water.

He remembered Ellie wrinkling her nose at the smell of wood rot and mildew, and Ben had joked about falling off the narrow gangplank when they'd return drunk later, hoping to break the tension and disappointment. The mistaken booking had all the hallmarks of ruining their vacation. But later that night, when Ben sat alone in the steerage cabin drinking a Heineken, watching a pink-orange sunset paint the canal and listening to the soft sounds of Ellie puttering about in the bathroom below, he'd felt a sort of bliss. Removed from all worries and deadlines, simply present.

"You know, if I didn't know any better, I'd say you were relaxing."

Across the years and memories, he could see her look up from below deck, grinning as she toweled off her hair. Here, her ring finger was bare—would stay that way for only a few months more—but her eyes still shone as they always did.

"Couldn't be." Ben sipped at his beer to hide a smile. "Apparently I don't know how to relax."

"First time for everything."

"Actually . . . I think I love it here," he'd said.

"Love? Pretty strong word, Tarzan."

"A gut feeling."

Ellie had climbed up the ladder and came to rest in the crook of his arm, still-damp hair dripping onto his arm. She sipped his beer and he breathed in her scent. Out the window, the nightlife was stirring—the bachelor parties heading toward the Red-Light District, families grilling on their own houseboats, bicycles taking up more of the cobbled streets than cars—the city alight, alive, and on the move. But here, it was just Ben and Ellie. Content and comfortable. Peaceful.

"Now *that* is a sunset," Ellie said, settling in deeper.

The tunnel breaker lights hummed off. Ben punched the switch again, but nothing happened. Needed time to reset. Ben lay back with a sigh, the fathomless melancholy creeping in. He was doing it again.

Wandering a path better avoided before the memories rushed forward toward the present and soured. Best leave them be.

"... 'cause I know nothing ... no, nothing ... about I—"

"*Benny-Boy Breckenridge*," Fontaine cut through the quiet.

The song fell from Ben's mouth like a dropped stone. The once-unwelcome sound of the Ear's voice stirring a smile on his lips.

"Go for Ben."

"*Just checking in, superhero. Not catching you at a bad time, am I?*"

"Just singing to the fish."

A soft laugh came over the radio. "*Getting a little squirrely down there?*"

"No, no. Just keeping the cabin fever at bay. Breaking the boredom. Not much to do just yet until I reach job start."

"*Sounds like you're complaining about an easy workload, boy. I oughta remember that. Try and get you to strip ten bulkheads instead of five. You rather have a mess to clean up?*"

"Maybe . . . make things a bit more interesting."

"*You college boys are all alike,*" Fontaine's voice growled with a lazy contempt. "*Never happy to just sit and let the clouds roll past, always gotta be gunning forward. Noses in books, chasing after expensive bits of paper sayin' how smart you are. Boring is what I'm after. 'Interesting' isn't all that exciting when you're my age. Gotta find your own way to have fun, make things my own personal sort of interesting.*"

Ben resisted the urge to remind Fontaine that he was almost certainly older than the Ear. Instead, he grabbed his pack and set off toward the next mile, running his hand along the wall as he went. "You ever been down in the tunnel, Fontaine?"

"*Once or twice, never more than a mile in. Never learned to swim, if you can believe. Not that I would need to know down there, but the thought's there. Walking under all that water just makes my spine fucking tingle. Just keep imagining a crack splitting on a wall. Trying to outrun it only to hit a closed bulkhead door. Yeesh.*"

There was a sound over the line, Fontaine dramatically shuddering. Ben swallowed, taking his hand off the wall, chuckling at his own spasm of fear.

"You've really got a gift for making me feel at home, know that?"

"*Bedside manners were never my forte.*"

Ben let Fontaine chat a while longer to soak up the miles, giving him a last rundown on scrapping techniques before he reached the dolly at Mile 90—said with the same veteran's contempt for the wet-nosed novice, interspersed with "college boy" and "superhero." After a while Ben bid the Ear goodnight and signed off.

He walked another half mile, glancing to the Atlantic above and around, imagining it pressing down on him.

Walking under all that water just makes my spine fucking tingle.

Ben tried to distract his mind before that phrase had a chance to stick. Maybe tonight he'd string his sleeping bag up between bulkheads like a hammock, keep himself off that cold grating. Or maybe he'd find another scribbled message from Holden or the previous scrappers.

He picked up his pace, heading for the blue-silver eye of a bulkhead ahead. Idly wondering about the last techs, and what made them think this place was haunted. Where was their breaking point?

What made their *spines tingle? When was too much?*

He wasn't singing anymore.

| BULKHEAD 83/84, BLACK |

Ben woke in darkness and knew something was wrong.

It was colder than it should have been and none of the lights were on—not even the lock's pinprick glow. On his fifth night in the bulkheads, each with the same droning sameness as the last, even the slightest change was enough to put his hackles up.

The night before he'd left his pack in the back tunnel for more space, then strung his sleeping bag between the two bulkhead doors. Laying in the makeshift hammock, the tunnel's near-imperceptible sway was heightened, rocking him to a peaceful sleep. He'd dreamed of that houseboat again. And of Ellie. And of the need to stop dragging his feet and get on with his work already.

Now something was off. Ben clicked on his headlamp and peered round. With no lights, the bulkhead had a distinct *dead* feeling, like a ship lying at the bottom of the ocean waiting to be found and plundered. Carefully, he swung down to the floor, shivering from the oppressive cold, and tapped the LCD screen in the corner. But it wouldn't turn on. He tapped it again, slapped it with a full palm, smacked the side like it was a faulty appliance. Nothing. The face stayed black and quiet, unwilling to wake.

"Huh."

He shrugged and stretched, now awake. Better to move on than worry about a bad screen. He broke down his hammock by headlamp and dumped his collection sacks into the recycling chute. He'd reach Mile 90 by midmorning, if he calculated right. Job start. His mind whirred, thinking about dollies, copper piping, and *ripping* things apart. Fontaine's phrasing felt destructive. And cruel. Not "deconstructing" or "dismantling." "Ripping." No respect.

Ben shouldered his sleeping bag, wishing he had coffee. He'd suggest that to Fontaine next time he got that bastard on the comm. If he wanted scrappers moving faster, caffeine was a surefire way. Ben would be happy just with the smell, daydreaming as he primed the lock back to 83 to retrieve his pack.

Except, the door wouldn't prime. The lock was quiet. Cold as the air.

Ben pressed it again, this time with a little force. Still nothing. He yanked his hand back, thinking all the time that an old structure like this probably has some bad kinks. A slow start-up time like a bloated computer. Like the LCD screen.

Which hadn't woken up either, had it? A tingle ran along Ben's tailbone, nerves firing from spine to fingertips. He turned around and tried the handle to Mile 84, the way forward.

"C'mon." He thumbed. No luck. "C'mon, c'mon." Gripped with both hands, yanking backward. Nothing. Both mechanisms refused to budge or stir in the slightest.

Locked.

He kicked at the door. Once, twice, earning a sore sole and little else. His eyes traveled up the length of the door to the oceanlight above, shifting blue dancing across his faceplate.

He clicked his relay. "Fontaine."

Hissing static.

"Fontaine. Come in, Fontaine. I"—He didn't want to say it. Didn't want to give life to it—make the situation real—"I'm having electrical issues. Might need assistance."

No response. It was still early, Fontaine probably wasn't at his post, just lazying his way across the wide, empty terminal. No care in the world about the college boy eighty-three miles from shore, all alone, trapped in a bulkhead.

There. He'd thought it. *Trapped.* Sandwiched between two massive steel doors, in a defunct tunnel, eighty-three miles from shore and a hundred fifty feet below sea level.

all that water just makes my spine fucking tingle.

"HELLO!" Ben screamed, kicking the door again. Not caring how much it hurt his foot or that there was no way anyone could hear him. He had to do something, couldn't just sit here and, what? Drown?

"Nope. *Nonono.* Don't even think about going down that road. No one is drowning down here." He'd suffocate before that happened.

So he kicked. And again. Tugged at both locking mechanisms that felt more and more like unmovable stone. Not an inch of give. Why hadn't they given him a goddamn welding torch, or tools to short-circuit the electricity? Something, anything. What was he supposed to do?

Ben slumped. Sliding to the floor, back to the unmovable barrier.

"Trapped. Fu—*fucking* hell."

He put a hand to his forehead, slapped the plate again. Trapped in the suit too. A Russian nesting doll. Stuck in a tunnel, stuck in a bulkhead, stuck in a suit. Claustrophobic. He'd never been, but now he understood. That worry about the walls closing in, the shortness of breath. His O2 meter clicked down a notch. Those finite resources.

That hurled him back to his feet. Pounding on the door.

"PLEASE! HELLO! ANYONE?"

The tunnel groaned. Shifted in an ugly current. Shadows passed over the oceanlight above, then were gone. Ben's lips were trembling. A coffin. He was sitting in his own coffin, just like his dreams. The walls—were they . . . were they getting smaller already? He wrung his hands. *Thinkthinkthink.* What could he do?

Ben clicked the relay again. "FONTAINE. HELLO?" He was aware of the wheedling in his voice. The edge of crying. Of despair. What would happen if Fontaine just disappeared? Never came back? Never told anyone about the scrapper too stupid to keep his supplies with him, slowly suffocating deep beneath—

"*Up with the birds today, superhero. Gunning for that little bonus I mentioned, eh?*"

Relief cooled him, spiking unevenly through his body. "Fontaine. I can't open the bulkhead doors. I think I'm trapped."

A long sigh. "*It's a bit early to be gettin' squirrely on me. You know, I'm not paying you for travel time to the jobsite. You bow out early you forfeit your pay.*"

"The doors won't open! Nothing's responding. I. Am. TRAPPED."

A dramatic groan. The squeal of Fontaine's chair. "*What 'head you at?*"

"Between 83 and 84." *You bastard. Come on. Let me out.*

Through the open channel, Ben could hear the lazy *click-clack* of computer keys. Underbreath muttering. "*First thing in the goddamn morning . . .*" The tapping stopped. Paused. A double tap. "*Huh.*"

"Huh, what?"

"*Just hold on, wouldya?*" Faster keystrokes. A ruffling of papers. "*Sit tight, Breck. Need to check something.*"

"Okay . . . okay, well hurry, if you can." But there was no response. "Fontaine? *Hello?*"

Fontaine was gone and Ben was alone again. He started pacing back and forth. Eyeballed the two doors like they were two giants who might enact a cruel punishment if he looked at them the wrong way. Close in, crush him in a slow, inevitable vice. Smash him down into a cube of pulpy pink flesh, rut with burst veins and teeth.

That shadow passed overhead again. A shape. Ben's head cocked up, trying to get a better look. Nothing there. Relax. He had to relax. It was going to be okay. This was a company after all, they couldn't have the bad press of a worker trapped undersea. Then again . . . how would anyone know? Who had he told he was coming here? No one who would go looking. No one who cared.

"*Breckenridge.*" A medley of tones in the Ear's voice. Authoritative fury, bewilderment, and maybe a little fear. "*Did you touch something last night? Fiddle with the screen or anything? Don't lie now.*"

"No. No, nothing." Ben was sure he could forgive Fontaine's prick nature if he'd just open the door. "You messing with me Fontaine? This some kind of hazing ritual for the new guy?"

"*I'm an asshole but not* that *asshole.*"

"Well . . . can't you just open the door from the command center? Got the whole thing at your fingertips, right? Flip a switch."

"*That's the problem. It's not responding. As in, not at all. The, uh,*" Fontaine paused. Ben could imagine him shaking his head too, rubbing his beard. "*You saw the display. Bulkheads get blue for closed and operational, green for open, yellow for warning, and red if there's a malfunction. That's it. Bulkhead 83/84, well. They're black.*"

Ben's mouth formed an "O." Froze there. Black for broken. Black for death. He'd been right: this was a coffin.

"What." Ben licked his lips. "What does that mean?"

"*You tell me, fucking PhD. I don't know. Never seen it before.*" More ruffled papers, then the crunch of something plastic. The faint hum of a dial tone. "*Let me call—*"

"No, Fontaine! Don't you fucking leave again!"

Gone. Rage roiled in Ben's gullet. He was far from angry most times, but the tunnel was changing that. The isolation. Now *this*. This trap. This tomb. He would die down here. He had enough food, water, and air for two weeks, but would he be able to get out in time? Or was that just the slow prolonging of his death? Would he be listening to Fontaine bumble about trying to figure out what *black* meant while Ben slowly succumbed to the deep?

Wait . . . no. He'd *had* enough supplies for two weeks, but most were in his bag, on the other side of the door. Stuck there, all because he'd wanted to sleep more comfortably. He had supplies for five days. *Maybe.*

Panic combined with a righteous fury. He roared. Slapped at the doors with his palms, only managing that dreamlike, lack-of-strength way. Ineffectual, unable to land a solid hit. Nothing that would see him through to the other side.

That roar turned to a screech, then a wail. The force of his rage disintegrating into a whimpering, broken cry. The same words tumbling over and over in his mind, his mouth.

Trapped. Black. Tomb. TrappedBlackTomb. trappedblacktomb. trappedblacktomb.

Choking him. Beating and breaking him down. Reducing him to inconsequence. Forgotten. A fly stuck between screen doors, waiting for someone to slide him open to freedom or swat his guts into oblivion. The words would kill him.

Trappedblacktombtrappedblacktombtrappedblackto—

The LCD screen sprang to life. The suddenness shocking him to silence. Broken pixels splintered across the screen like a fuzzy VHS. Letters and incoherent words cascading, building. Ben gaped, mesmerized, dumb. Waiting as it built to its crescendo. But to what? An explosion. An opening of the oceanlight. Here was that fly swatter, here was the end, and Ben could only stand. Wait. Wait for the deluge, wait for—

The door to Mile 84 hissed open.

MILE 84 | FORWARD

Ben hurled himself over the lip of the door before it had a chance to close again, moving so quickly he tripped and fell to his ass but kept crawling backward anyway.

The blue wash of the tunnel was comforting, and for a moment the freedom of being out of his coffin almost made him think he was outside, under the sun. Staring back at the bulkhead, its deep shadow and copper pipes made him think again of a maw. Scrambling out a monster's jaws before the teeth could come down to rend and chew.

"*Breck? Hey, Breck?*"

Ben fumbled the relay. "You did it!" His breath was coming out in strained, heavy bursts. He swallowed, stood. "Jesus, Fontaine. I never should have doubted. I'm out. I'm out into 84."

"*How?*"

"What do you mean 'how'? The door opened."

"*I mean what did you do?*"

"Nothing! I-I-I mean I kicked the door a couple times, but didn't break anything. It just . . . just kind of opened." Ben licked his lips. "You didn't open it?"

"*I mean, I didn't have time. Must've just . . . opened on its own.*" Fontaine chuckled, wary. "*Good. Alright . . .*" Then, clearly relieved, "*Alright, yeah, good. Wooh! This is why I need one of them suits, practically pissed myself.*"

"Yeah . . . yeah, no kidding." Ben stared at the open bulkhead. It seemed so inconsequential from the other side.

"*Right. So. Mile 84, yeah? Think you can make it to job start today at 90?*"

Ben cleared his head. Back to the task at hand. The work. "Uh, yeah. Think so. Wait. My supply bag. It's back in 83."

The Ear swore. "*Well why the fuck did you leave it there?*" Keystrokes again on the far side.

"Just open the other door, I'll grab it and get moving. Keep both doors open though, I'm not going back in there until I know I can get back out." Ben warily reached in and snatched the meager supplies he'd kept with him overnight from off the bulkhead floor before scrambling back again.

"*Have you not been paying attention? I didn't open the door. It's still black on my end. Go back and kick that one, see if it triggers.*"

"No. Absolutely not." The spine-tingling feeling came again. This time worse than the last: a cold shock physically jerked his body. "Fontaine . . . what happens if you can't get that door open?"

"*We'll cross that bridge when we get there.*" Sounds of rustling paper and furious keystrokes. "*Sit tight and relax, college boy. Let me see what I can do.*"

"Fontaine . . . you're telling me, I might be stuck in the tunnel?"

"*I said relax!*" But it was Fontaine who was riled now. "*Hang out a bit. If one door opened, the other's bound to follow any second now.*"

An hour later, the doors moved all right, but it was Mile 84 sliding closed again, not 83. Locking out. The mechanism in the center was dead, lifeless, and nothing Fontaine or Ben could do would bring it back to life again. Locked.

"*I swear to fucking God, Breckenridge, if you did something and I find out, I'm going to fix you good.*"

Ben heard him, but his thoughts were detached. The phrase "fix you good" tickling his brain, sounding like an old-timey threat you'd hear in a bad Western. But he wasn't in a Western, he was in the Atlantic, eighty-four miles from shore. Possibly trapped in a deteriorating tube whose electricity was firing off like the synapses of an Alzheimer's patient.

"Fontaine . . . do you think you might need to pull me out?"

"*How'd you like me to do that? Huh?*"

"I don't know! Cut through the door! Or send a boat!"

"You think I've got the money for fucking sub crews or industrial drill bits? No. Right now it's you and me, and it's going to stay that way. This situation . . . it's gonna be fine. Gonna be sorted out in no time."

Ben's fury was building again, along with a dawning horror. "If you can't get this door open, you need to call SGO. Or the police. The-the fucking Coast Guard. Alert the media—*someone*. You gotta get me out of here!"

"*I can't.*"

"What do you mean? Just pick up your phone—"

"*I mean, I can't. This operation isn't exactly . . .*" A grunt. "*Above board.*"

"What? The hell does that mean?"

"*It's not sanctioned by SGO. I'm just . . . here to babysit the station. There's not supposed be anyone in the tunnel.*"

Ben closed his eyes. There it was.

"All that talk about having the only salvage contract? You been lying to me this entire time?"

"*You wanted to get fucking paid, so I was getting you paid. It's just business.*"

It's just business. Ben wanted to spit so badly, but he couldn't. That's why Fontaine couldn't hold on to workers, that's why everything from the very start had seemed half-assed. Not a soul outside knew Ben was down here. He should scream, but that wouldn't accomplish anything.

"What about that contract I signed?"

"*NDA. So you can't talk about what you did, heard, or saw.*"

Hear no evil . . . speak no evil . . .

"You're a real asshole, you know that? A fucking parasite desk jockey getting fat off the backs of better men. You hear me? I said, do you hear me, Fontaine?"

Fontaine was silent for a long time. Coming back, his voice was cold. "*Hell, superhero. What you want me to say?*"

"What happens now? How are *you* going to fix this, Fontaine?"

Fontaine's long sigh. The squeal of his chair. "*Alright. Listen. There are Way Stations set at 130-mile intervals all through the tunnel. Maintenance quarters set up for repair crews and cleaners. Got air, dehydrated food packs, beds, and showers, even little TVs. Start heading for the first one. Mile 130. I'll . . . I'll make a couple calls, get support, get a better read on the situation by then.*"

"You want me to go deeper into this deathtrap?"

"*Unless that door opens in the next ten minutes, it's your only choice for more supplies.*"

"And if I get locked in another bulkhead again?"

Pregnant silence. "*Look. I'm trying. This is more than I've ever had to deal with. I'm . . . give me some time. I'll pull you out of there.*"

Ben felt himself nodding, that fury receding. Mile 130 might not be too bad. He could get there. They'd figure out a solution by then. Fine.

"*Breck? Alright?*"

"Yeah . . . yeah. Mile 130, got it." He tried wiping at the sweat on his forehead and popped himself in the helmet again. "Sorry. I didn't mean to bite your head off there. Getting stuck in there got to me more than I thought it would. Bit squirrelly."

"*Nah . . . nah, superhero. I should've been a bit more upfront from the start.*" An incredulous laugh. "*This hasn't happened before. But I'll find a way. Leave it to me.*"

Ben heard the remorse in his voice and regretted being hard. He could understand trying to make a buck in hard times. No matter what, they'd need a little kinship now. But Fontaine had to go and ruin it.

"*Don't think you're getting any extra hazard pay for this though.*"

MILE 90 | JOBSITE

He meant to pass the jobsite without breaking stride, beelining on to the Way Station, but as the dolly came into sight, he had the sense to stop and check it for supplies.

It sat abandoned three-quarters of the way through Mile 90, as if the last tech had said *fuck it*, and up and quit. A thin, rusting thing that Ben imagined would be hell trying to squeeze into a bulkhead just to push it on to the next mile. The bed was half-loaded with bits of copper mesh and tubing, everything jagged and ugly from where it had been ripped unceremoniously from the bulkhead walls and floors. Aside from a hammer stuck beneath one of the dolly's wheels, there was no sign of the tools Fontaine had promised, and even then, the hammer's wooden handle was so split and warped it would be more liability than asset. After a thorough search, he walked away empty-handed.

When he reached the mile's end, Ben saw his first bulkhead unmarred by scavenging hands. The inner guts below hidden behind sleek metal paneling, the walls covered with siding and paint to create a fluid stream from tunnel to bulkhead and back out. Untarnished, the space was almost beautiful. Inviting. Lending itself to a seamless whole.

He ran his fingers along the nearly invisible seams, searching for where a scavenger—*he*—would have to ram that claw end of the hammer. Not a simple task. He would have to strike in deep and *rip*, gouge the panels with holes and chisel the paint free. And that was only for the panels, not to mention the wires, the insulation, the floor. Everything it took to defile the space.

Ben marched the fifteen minutes back to the dolly cart, flipped it over, and tore the wheels clean off.

THE TUNNEL

The Transatlantic Tunnel was meant to be a monument to human ingenuity and progress. The first Wonder of the twenty-first century.

After long years of rising nationalism, water scarcity, and climate catastrophes pulled humanity to the edge of extinction, mankind needed a collective win. Governments and world leaders sought that infectious feeling that followed the first moon landing—a great unifying event that would see mankind banding together for a mutual cause once believed outside human capacity.

Their goal was simple: to set an example for a better world.

At first, scientists looked toward space. After all, what could unite humanity more than glancing at the Pale Blue Dot, knowing we all exist as one on Earth. Proposals filtered through the public eye: colonizing the moon, establishing a manned Mars base, making affordable public tours to the International Space Station, and more. Each expensive, dangerous, and easily refuted.

An American doctoral student named Nicholas Moore saw a different solution much closer to home. He said, "Why look beyond our atmosphere when we have the greatest unconquered frontier right at our feet? Imagine the possibilities we could forge on that horizon: the ocean."

Moore and his business partner, Dr. Reed, were determined to find a simple, tangible project that the world could connect with and rally behind—a metaphor for bridging the divide of nations and uniting mankind. The idea came like a lightning bolt, and Moore and Reed just needed to figure out how to make it.

And so was born the Transatlantic Tunnel.

There was only so much attention a mere student could garner—so Moore "leaked" their proposal onto the internet, drawing attention with a flashy video and some damning statistics on the effects of climate change and mankind's heavy hand in destroying the oceanographic environment.

Moore's post went viral, hitting the zeitgeist like a hurricane, flooding social media, political talk shows, and presidential debates. His imagination was praised, but his idea was deemed overly ambitious and far-fetched, smacking too much like science fiction. An ocean-spanning tunnel had been a known sci-fi/fantasy trope for decades, but the figures for actual construction had always been too cost-prohibitive and time-consuming. With an expected budget in excess of $175 billion, the idea had been dismissed time and time again.

So, Moore and Reed brainstormed maximizing efficiency—from labor, materials, time, and cost. They consulted with NASA scientists, former oil riggers, and even a famous Hollywood director. Possibilities came and went, methods were analyzed and dissected. A floating tube would be decimated by Atlantic storms. An ocean floor construct would be impossible, given the seismic unpredictability, not to mention the air pressure at such depths or the loss of life that would surely occur during construction.

Moore and Reed concluded that a floating construct, held in place 150-feet below sea level, and operated via magnetic levitation—like the technology already used for the bullet trains in Japan and the Netherlands—was the simplest, best idea.

Yet, even after hammering an airtight proposal, the cost of such a structure was astronomical. Construction would require every steel mill in the world to operate at full capacity for almost a year to create the prefabricated, segmented sections.

Facing the possibility of defeat, Moore locked himself away and engineered countless alternatives and solutions. What he invented, refined, and patented would forever change the face of commercial construction: an experimental glass and steel hybrid, created using nanofiber filaments and commercial 3D printing. The first of its kind and exactly what the tunnel would need.

Risking everything, the partners poured their life savings into a prototype. Their one shot. Once finished, they held a massive press conference off the New York Harbor where Moore explained that not only could these prefabricated sections be built and completed within five years, but at a fraction of the expected original cost. Furthermore, they would "give riders the chance to look through transparent glass and see all the wonders of marine life." With bated breath, they dropped their prototype into the water, watching as the section bobbed, tilted precariously . . . and floated. Their test had been a success.

The media ate it up, plate and all. Touted as subway-meets-aquarium, the proposal was immediately bought and funded by all the contributing nations within the UN. "The Bridge connecting the continents, a new era for mankind." The world was singing. Moore and Reed would not only be rich men but would go down in history.

Construction quickly went under way. Stretching from a newly erected hub in New York and ending at London's King's Cross Station, the tunnel was built simultaneously from either side of the Atlantic, racing to meet in the middle. Progress was closely monitored by news and social media with uncanny fervor, each new section's connection seen as a triumph. Though a few deaths marred early outings—quickly sensationalized in the news—the project moved along at an even keel.

But advances in science didn't wait on the tunnel's pleasure. As the era of fossil fuels faded, planes switched to electric and nuclear power. The flight from New York to London dropped from seven hours to three. The need for the Transatlantic Tunnel was called into question—yet still Moore charged on, claiming that his maglev train could make the journey in less than an hour.

Investors weren't so easy to keep on the hook. Many saw the tunnel as a failed venture before construction was finished. Worse, the project was hemorrhaging cash, and Moore and Reed's fifteen minutes were about to expire.

A week before launch, Moore returned alone to the States to oversee final operations. Speculation ran rampant that the duo had had a falling out. Rumors of corners cut to appease nervous investors, laborers forced into unreasonably long hours to hit an impossible deadline. Helicopters could be seen flying off the coasts of New York and western England at all hours of the day and night, carrying prefab sections and defying regulations.

When the day of the unveiling came, expectations had reached a humming fever pitch. The first trip was to be a grand spectacle: a symbolic bridging of the Americas and Europe across the Atlantic. Moore himself was slated to be aboard the initial outing, set to reunite with his partner at King's Cross Station, followed by a lavish ribbon cutting ceremony. Yet when the time came for departure, Moore was nowhere to be found. Reports hinted of a nervous breakdown. Therefore, it was up to Reed to give his speech to the politicians, celebrities, influencers, and lucky few regular folk invited for the trip. The first train was named *The Odyssey* after Homer's epic, and its maiden voyage was an event for the ages.

"The time has come," Reed said via video feed from the finish line in London, "to show the world what cooperation and ingenuity can create for the human race." With flashbulbs pulsing like lightning, a cheer went up, the passengers took their seats, and the train door closed. The train rocketed from the station in New York.

And disaster struck.

MILE 102 | SCRAPINGS

The three-line scar smeared across half a mile of ceiling, starting from the bulkhead and extending out. A jagged groove jumping across the glass like a heartbeat monitor readout. The point where *The Odyssey* disaster began.

Ben imagined the atmosphere in the train. Celebrities and dignitaries glad-handing, social media influencers fumbling for cell service to live stream the whole event, the "regular folk" who'd earned their lottery ticket spots holding hands and staring out the windows. All charged and excited, expectant.

Then the mounting terror as the smooth ride turned to turbulence. Seats gamboling out of control, tossing back and forth as the train jittered out of alignment in its womb. Darting glances and nervous laughter, hands gripping seats tight. The ceiling ripping in three points, like a monster's claw. The air rushing out, suffocating. The knowing, then the fire.

He'd read the news reports, every single one. All stuck to the same sanitized story given to the press from SGO. That the train would've been going fast enough to vaporize everyone on board in milliseconds. No pain, no suffering. But now, seeing the marks begin at Mile 102 of *thousands*, Ben knew they wouldn't have had time to build up speed. No quick death.

That end would've been brutal.

Ben clicked on his mic. "Hey, Fontaine. You there?" His voice was thick and he had to clear his throat.

Hissing static. A click, a grunt. *"I'm working fast as I can. Patience, superhero. Got some so-called experts coming in tomorrow."*

Hackles raised, Ben wondered what kind of experts. What they might find and do. "Right."

"'Bout to take off. Getting to that point where I'm doin' more harm than good without a little shut-eye."

"Taking off early?"

"Late you mean. Fucking 11:30."

Ben glanced to the water outside. Sure enough, dark as a crypt. Night had come to the North Atlantic. It'd been daylight when he started. Early still. How long had he been staring at the cleft in the ceiling? Should've been twenty minutes at most, not—

"Five hours . . . ?"

"Repeat, Breck? All good on your end? Nearing the station?"

"Yeah . . . no, I'm good. Not near the station yet. Actually, wondering if you knew anything about *The Odyssey*?"

"Ahh, reached 102, didya? The 'incident point.'" Fontaine didn't unclick his mic, so Ben could hear the creak of a chair leaning backward. Fontaine groaning. *"Before my time, obviously. Asked about it when I first got hired, which the higher-ups didn't appreciate. No one talks straight, there's this secretive air. SGO's got everyone's lips locked with NDAs, constantly hiring and rehiring—makes a man wonder. If there's one thing you've gotta learn about ol' Fontaine: I'm too curious for my own good, always sniffing for rumors.*

"Turns out there used to be video of the disaster. Not any of those news crew clips or bits from passenger phones—but a feed from inside the train that survived. Official word is old Dr. Reed scrubbed it himself so it wouldn't leak onto the internet, but I heard the video was so brutal it's what made his partner lose his marbles."

A *CLANK* from up ahead in the tunnel. Like a dropped screwdriver. Metal on metal.

Ben whipped round. Switched his headlamp on, peered down the emptiness. Nothing there, just unbroken tunnel and the twinkling of the bulkhead eye a mile down. The word "haunted" tickled his mind, but he tamped that down.

"Breck?"

"Yeah, yeah. I'm here."

"*Anyway, the video's gone but the audio exists. It made the rounds for a little while and I managed to get my paws on it for a listen. Morbid curiosity, I guess. I know the reports say it was . . . what do you call it, an 'act of God,' but from what I heard, some construction worker just didn't turn a few screws in tight enough so a bulkhead had a ragged edge. Ripped the train clean open.*"

"Don't tell me you believe that. A couple loose screws didn't cause billions of dollars of damage."

"*You the one with the inside track? Sure, might not be the* only *thing, but I'm telling you, couple loose screws were the start. Negligence bankrupted the company and murdered a train full of people. What three hundred eighty deaths?*"

"Three hundred eighty-one." Ben's Adam's apple fell from throat to stomach, feeling that ache grow. His light scoured the bulkhead. Sure enough, he noticed a spot where the rivets had been peeled back. Three screws were shining silver while the rest were blackened from rust or old paint.

"*Three screws. Shred a hole in the outer hull right at that spot you're at now. Mile 102. Pulled the ceiling open like a goddamn can opener. Train's still picking up speed, but all the air is goin' out. Boy . . . that recording? You could hear everyone in there. Screaming at first. Then choking, gasping as the air goes bit by bit. A kind of banging through the whole thing. Just a* bangbangbang. *After that, just sorta calm. Like everyone was just hoping they'd make it to the other side before it was too late. Little did they fuckin know, right?*"

Ben hadn't realized he'd sat down, back to the bulkhead, staring at the pivot point. The damage done by three misaligned screws. Seen and unseen. Irreparable.

"They . . . they burned too." A whisper. "The buoyant foam underneath the train, in the tunnel floor."

"*Sure did, burned the whole mile through. That came later, after SGO finally pulled the emergency stop. Not sure how it started though. Maybe one of the passengers went looking for air masks, trying to save themselves. Light fixture got yanked open. A spark—boom. Fire ripping through a vacuum. Train became a crematorium. All the SGO boys recovered were shattered teeth and bones. If that train had pushed on to London, would've just been charred bits of people. Instead, they came to a stop near eight hundred miles in . . . no one topside close enough for rescue, no secondary trains to get on down there. Passengers just sat and burned."*

"Jesus Christ." He didn't say it into the mic. He didn't have to. Tears tugged at his eyes, collecting in the helmet.

"Worse ways to go, sure . . . but I don't know them."

MILE 130 | WAY STATION 01

Ben came to the Way Station like a desert traveler to an oasis.

He could smell himself, like his sweat had curdled and crusted over, clinging to his coveralls. His legs had grown used to the rigors of the walk, but he'd been pushing himself to reach the station, worried about the paltry supplies he carried wrapped up in his sleeping bag. Almost thirty miles today alone, and he was ready to rest.

Fontaine's talk of *The Odyssey* had left Ben skittish. He saw problems in the smallest things. O2 springing a leak, water mysteriously running dry, or a spontaneous spark would rip through his suit and slough off his skin. He'd had a daydream nightmare of a faceless technician—his successor—coming across his body splayed out a mile from the station. In the dream his face was both blue and black. Airless and burned.

Ben saw the bulkhead eye close ahead, and to the right, half hidden by water and distance, a shadow sticking from the tunnel like a tumor. Way Station 01. He ran. Time to break the endless trudging. Time to break free from the suit, to have a shower, to lie in a real bed. The tunnel's sway was starting to make him nauseous. *Prime, twist, pull.*

Mile 130's bulkhead slid open to reveal the same cramped bulkhead he'd seen 129 times prior. Only this time, the LCD was moved to the opposite wall. Where the screen usually sat to the right stood a steel-gray door labeled: **Station 01-130**. Ben shut the bulkhead, practically skipped to the door and pulled, half expecting a janitorial closet, crammed with mop, bucket, and stray chalk.

The door slid away to a glass airlock, and beyond, a room like a college dorm. A single space with a minifridge, a dual action flat screen monitor/TV and keyboard, a narrow vertical locker, a bathroom with an open-air shower, and a twin bed. The entire far wall was made up of the tunnel's steel glass, exposing a stretch of ocean that teemed with life.

Ben stepped into the airlock, leg jumping impatiently, staring at the bed and shower with uncontrolled glee. He needed to touch it before it would be real. The airlock hissed, the handle lights turned green, and he bulled into the room. For a moment, he stood, staring. It was real. A plethora of space compared to what he'd become used to.

He flung his sleeping bag to the floor, wrestled with his helmet but couldn't find the release toggle.

"C'mon, *c'mon!*"

Hiss, pop! The helmet came loose and he yanked it off. Breathed deep. The air tasted antiseptic and flat but moved through his body as a soul-cleansing tonic. He gulped in deep lungfuls, eyes closed, feeling free. He stripped the suit off in earnest, not caring for keeping it clean—he needed *out.*

Pulled free, he felt lighter than ever before in his life. He mumbled incoherently, tripping forward and flopping onto the bed.

And passed right out.

He woke in inky blackness. For a moment, he panicked, thinking he was back in Bulkhead 83/84, that he'd never left, that he was doomed to listen to Fontaine's voice as he drifted off to an eternal sleep. But there'd been no bed in the bulkhead, and while the mattress was cheap and poorly padded, the feel of it beneath his body shed the panicked thoughts of black locks and tombs.

He lay there, blanket tangled between his legs, watching the ocean outside the window-wall. The soft glow hypnotized. A school of bluefish swam close then darted away with sudden panic. Algae clung to the window's corner, overtaking the barnacles. Ben just lay, watching everything sway.

After a while, he stood, flicked the lights on, and picked his helmet up from where he'd left it the night before. Recoiling from the stench of sweat wafting from inside, he clicked the relay.

"Fontaine? You there? I've reached Way Station 01." The Ear didn't answer. Too far outside business hours, he supposed. "You'd think after stranding a worker, he'd be more inclined to be readily available."

He stood at the room's center, unmoored. What now? It felt odd to be out of the suit, comfortable but restless. Like he should be doing something. He sniffed, could smell himself still, having sweat more while he slept. Feeling slick and ill-used, that scummy feeling he associated with sitting in an airplane cabin for hours, only worse. He decided to start there, stripping off everything except his wedding ring.

The shower was set too low, its nozzle only reaching midway to his chest. Water warm rather than hot, with feeble pressure, but it was still the best shower he'd ever taken. It made him feel human again, not like some mindless animal trudging ever on. Reinvigorating his mind, worries sloughing away like old skin to circle the drain.

After, he scoured the nearby storage bins, finding a toiletry kit in one, complete with an electric dry shaver and toothbrush, but no toothpaste. The shaver helped to grind away the nearly two weeks of beard growth, while the toothbrush cleared the fuzzy grime from his teeth without making them exactly minty fresh. In another bin he found an extra pair of coveralls that were too large but were stain-free and smelled clean. He whistled as he slipped them on and fell back on the bed, amazed at how a shower and fresh clothes could restore. Feeling close to whole for the first time in weeks.

Lazily, his eyes roved the room, taking in the studio-style space. It was a strange place, cold yet comforting. He checked the vertical locker first, pleased to find an extra backpack within to replace the one he'd lost. Otherwise, the locker was nearly empty aside from plastic buckets where cleaning supplies had once been housed, conspicuous by the bleach stains on the bottom and the single scrubbing brush with bristles worn by use and smelling of sea salt. Ben wondered what sort of cleaning these maintenance workers were tasked with—whether they meant to go up the ladders and out the mid-mile hatches to scrape off barnacles and coral, or simply to sweep the interior of dust and detritus. If the former, he imagined there should be diving suits in here and more O2, but everything was spare and bare.

He noticed a snaking tube just beside the airlock. It began as two shafts, one overhead stretching along the tunnel from end to end, while the second wound into the station, presenting as an open mailbox. A yellow light was mounted on its top, pulsing dully. Closer, it reminded Ben of the drive-thru systems outside banks and pharmacies that he had seen on Saturday morning car rides with his mom to drop off her paychecks when Ben was a boy. *Pneumatic tubes,* his mom had explained, powered by air to deliver capsules across distances. A piece of technology that felt somehow both ancient and futuristic at the same time.

The Way Station's pneumatic tube was dust-covered, hinges stiff from lack of use. It took the better part of five minutes to seal off the contents from the vacuum and open the swing door. The capsule was the size of his forearm, and he cracked it open like an egg, the contents spilling onto the floor.

Three parcels bound together with a rubber band: a letter envelope, a yellow document packet, and a bubble mailer. He opened the bubble mailer first, finding it crammed with a month's worth of ration tubes along with bland, military-style dehydrated meal kits and bars, and spare O2 canisters. He eyeballed a meal kit and its block text instructions on adding water then warming the mush to an edible state on the station's hot plate. His stomach groaned, reminding him that his last "meal" had been almost fifty miles and two days back, so he opted for a ready-to-eat ration bar instead. Biting in, Ben relished the sensation of eating solid food for the first time since entering the tunnel, attempting to ignore the taste and texture but failing. He swallowed as much as he could, then spit the rest out onto the floor in greasy, crumbling globs.

"Hey Fontaine . . . pretty sure Geneva Convention outlawed cruel and unusual punishment," Ben said, grimacing, then tossed the supplies back onto the bed.

The document packet was marked **URGENT** in a red-letter stamp, along with a handwritten note. *Simon—All techs need to fill them out. You're no exception, read that as mandatory. Has to be finished and returned before moving on to Way Station 02 —H.* For a moment, he considered not opening the packet, realizing now that this pneumatic capsule hadn't been meant for him, but a technician named Simon. But Simon was long gone, and that red **URGENT** stamp tickled that *taboo* section of his mind.

"I'm in international waters, aren't I? Pirate's law. Booty is mine."

Inside were two single sheets of paper and a pencil. A slug on the top of the first page read, **PSYCHIATRIC FITNESS EXAM— ISOLATION PROTOCOL.** Ben frowned, unsure what he'd expected to find—internal gossip or bizarre regulations from SGO—but a psych test certainly wasn't it. He threw the packet onto the bed.

The letter too was addressed to Simon, the tech's name scrawled on top in spidery cursive. Inside was a thumb-sized figurine of Yoda from *Star Wars*, whose head pulled off to reveal a USB flash drive. Alongside was a full-color picture: two women sitting in the New York command center. Both wore headsets and SGO branded polo shirts, posing for the camera with teasing grins. One, with dirty blonde hair and a constellation of freckles was blowing a kiss; the other, with a sharp chin, a sandy complexion, and picked-over skin, was winking and biting her lips. Both playfully suggestive. On their desks were two greasy hamburgers and fries, the photo captioned, "Enjoy those rations!"

"Assholes," Ben said, grinning.

He pulled himself over to the monitor—an old PC with the hard drive built into the screen, but only a single USB port. He ignored the growl in his stomach as the welcome screen chimed to life. Pushed the USB in.

The drive was filled with a few movies—mostly superhero and B-sci-fi fare, a few comedies, and—cheekily, Ben assumed—three seasons of *SpongeBob SquarePants*. He hovered the mouse to throw a movie on in the background, when he noticed a folder buried within the Sponge-Bob files. Innocuous and easily missed, full of video files with flesh-ridden thumbnails. Pornography. One file had its name changed to, "prob_get_lonely_;)"

Ben's laughter filled the Way Station, the first bout to breach his lungs in a long while. It brought a single tear to his eye. He considered diving deeper into the folder, maybe unzipping those new coveralls and delivering a quick dopamine shot to the brain, but he opted to shut the computer down instead.

He eyed the picture sitting atop the questionnaire packet again. The two women and their feast. His gaze fixed on the brunette girl. Her wink and smile. A familiarity to her. Something that made him sad . . .

Ben flipped the picture face down, the laughter that had boomed only moments ago now feeling wrong. There was no happiness down here. He was trapped, alone, waiting for a call that hadn't come. He needed a distraction, picked up the psych test, and bundled it free of the packet.

Six questions on two pages, multiple-choice with space beneath for explanation.

1. I believe others control what I think and feel.

Ben frowned.

2. I hear or see things that others do not hear or see.

Was it a test for schizophrenia?

3. I believe in more than one thing about reality and the world around me that nobody else seems to believe.

Why would they issue this to technicians in the tunnel?

4. I can't trust what I'm thinking because I don't know if it's real or not.
5. Others are plotting to get me.
6. What is the state of my mind?

"The 'college boys' were waiting for their techs to crack," he said to no one in particular. Paused. "Talking to yourself is the first sign."

Ben put the packet down over the picture and quickly stepped away. He grabbed the iPod from its suit storage pocket and plugged it into the monitor, fumbling through the computer's menus until music coughed out the screen's cheap speakers. He adjusted the volume so it filled the room, then settled back on the bunk and closed his eyes.

He tried not to wonder what he'd do if Fontaine never raised him on comms. He was supplied now to run a normal life for a time. Better than normal—*lazy*. He could sit and grow fat on rations, SpongeBob, and pornos. Then what?

He shifted as something firm stuck his back, hidden in the twisted-up sheets. His hands explored, probed. Found a steel box decorated like an antique cigarette case. Sure enough, inside he found three paper-rolled cigarettes, though oddly colored. He sniffed. Not tobacco.

Another smile pulled at his lips, almost another laugh. He plucked one free, feeling guilty for raiding someone's personal stash, hidden for the next time they returned. But no one was coming this way again. Not after him.

"Pirate code, Benny," Ben whispered, twisting the joint between his fingers, listening to the paper crinkle with age. It was still firm, well-rolled. "Give the boys grog to keep them happy . . . why not?"

Ben carefully lit the joint on the hot plate, turned off all the lights, and stared out the window-wall as the smoke drifted. Daylight was still coming on and the water was getting lighter by degrees. The shadows of fish exploring the deep far off, but for the most part—emptiness. Silence.

He coughed on the first pull, eased into the second. Had never been a big smoker, not liking how anxious it made him. How *aware* of everyone he became. Thankfully, this particular strain was calming and pleasant. Smooth.

Ben leaned back and let the THC slide in and relax his body. Feeling light all through his chest. Loopy and at ease.

The music from the tinny speakers and the cannabis melted together. Not exactly making him forget where he was, or why, but pulling him further and further away. He sank. Down, down. Into pure, perfect light.

EVERLAST

The earth shook as the festival crowd seethed and churned, driven by the music on stage. Ben fidgeted where he sat on the grass, anchoring himself on the slope just above the overwhelming wash of people below. He was happy Teddy had found a spot farther away from the crush, away from accidental elbow jabs and the press of sweat-stained bodies. Crowds made him long for the close confines of their office, away from the prickling summer heat and heavy humidity.

This was Teddy's idea of celebration, not Ben's. Ben no longer sought out the nightlife or bar scene—didn't see the point. Not when there was work to be done. But what was a partnership if not to go along for the ride once in a while, to challenge his comfort levels. Besides, he needed distraction.

Only two hours earlier, Ben and Teddy had sent their first professional collaborative design proposal to Chicago's major architectural firms: an arcology tower. A bold reinvention of urban living, all green spaces and self-sufficiency, wrapped in simple, brutalist design. It was a gamble—their mentor had already complained their design was too simple and "boxy," with too few windows—but if they were chosen, it was potentially that first dramatic step toward the rest of their lives. After months spent staring down their deadline date, circled in red on their office's small calendar—August 5th—now that it had arrived, Ben couldn't help but feel an anticlimax. All that was left was waiting, and it took everything for him to not brood.

"Shut it down, partner. I see that mind of yours churning away. All work and no play makes the lad a nervous wreck." Teddy flashed a grin as he rolled a joint with maddening, careless ease. "Rest after victory, my friend. Today, we try and relax."

"That's a paradox," Ben said, laying back to stare at the cloud-strewn sky. "*Trying* to relax."

Teddy just smiled. Since the accident of fate that'd brought them together at Northwestern's Engelhart Hall in the final year of their graduate programs, the two had been inseparable. An architect and an engineer, burning the candle at both ends with dreams of setting the world on fire.

Now, after months of sleepless nights holed away in their tiny Michigan Avenue office, they were turtles coming up for air after a long journey beneath the waves. Wanting nothing more than to shout the news of discoveries made and distance traveled before a return to the drafting board.

But there'd be no triumphant shouting for Ben, not here at least. Saturated bass hammered his ears, teasing the start of a headache. It'd been three years since he'd last been to a concert and he would've been happy going another three before the next. But Teddy was persuasive and the weather was good. Besides, if all went well, it might be a long while before he had another chance to sit still. Relax.

"I can relax," Ben said aloud.

"Sure. Regular Dalai Lama. You fixate, you know. One thing doesn't go your way and you start to pick it apart. Let it get all sour inside you. Gotta learn to let things go." He offered the joint with a smile, white paper distinct against dark fingertips. Typical Teddy, always up for a bit of mischief.

Ben shook his head. "No thanks. I get anxious. All these people..."

"Says the man who wants to, what was it, 'carve his name into the history books?'" Teddy chuckled good-naturedly. "Suit yourself, brother."

Ben watched Teddy prop the joint in his mouth and fumble his lighter. One of those cheap Bic lighters with a safety coil on the screw head. Teddy was right, wasn't he? All Ben's talk of greatness and bettering the world, of needing to taking risks and chances, it had led them here. Wouldn't do to sit idle now. Ben reached for the lighter.

"Thank—"

Teddy stopped short as Ben grabbed the joint from him too. Lit, pulled, and leaned back. Ben could relax. He knew how. He could just let this kick in, watch some bands, soak in the day, and—

It hit hard. Too hard. He started coughing like a madman. His lungs and throat feeling like he'd inhaled pure jet fuel. Each racking fit building with that surety that he'd be incapacitated in no time.

"That's what happens when you *try* and relax." Teddy laughed.

Ben flopped backward as Teddy took the joint back, feeling the grass as individual fibers on the back of his neck. Worrying his eyes were squinting and turning bloodshot, if anyone could see. No, he was wearing sunglasses. Thank God he was wearing sunglasses.

The build crept in, turning his head light and vision staccato. The music grew and became all-encompassing. An assault on his senses. He opened his eyes and saw the sea of people. Exposed. He was exposed. A one-man island cast out among natives, adrift and surely mocked. He could feel their stares burning on his face, convinced they could hear the secret thoughts that lived rent-free in his head: all the terrors and crippling anxieties typically kept at bay now coming screaming to the surface.

He couldn't take it. He had to get out.

Ben didn't stop when Teddy called after him, just wound a zig-zag path down the slope and through the crowd, trying to remain cool. Didn't matter that he was certain everyone around him was stoned too, his anxious mind was in control now, steady and sure.

Somehow, he crossed a bike path, stumbling through a copse of trees. The main stage behind him, its chugging cacophony of hip-hop beats fading, the day getting darker. That meant something to him, that those trees were going to close in. Somehow, he'd be lost in the crown of Grant Park. He'd never find Teddy again, never get a ride back. He'd be pissed, their partnership would fall apart. All because he took a hit off Teddy's joint.

Ben saw a light through the darkness. Bright white, a star among the dark boles. A beacon, somehow calming. He headed for it.

Nearby, a guitar suddenly split through the sheen of crowd noise. A drum taking a steady rhythm alongside. Not assaulting but calming. A bouncing tempo, a voice picking up with a kind of strained male falsetto, singing an impassioned request, bright as the light ahead of him:

Asking for someone to be their "everlasting light." Their sun when all lights have gone.

A word formed on Ben's tongue but wouldn't come out. "Serendipity." The song, the beacon he was heading toward. It *must* be right.

He was floating over the grass, past hipsters in jean jackets despite the heat, through a fugue of cigarette smoke. Years after he'd remember the moment. Breaking through to find a side-stage, a crowd—

Her. Standing on the outskirts, facing away from the stage. He saw everything about her in an instant, a near-perfect mental snapshot forever fused with the waking song.

She was slight but standing with a natural self-assuredness, scrounging through a stenciled sling-bag. Crimson-painted lips in stark contrast to the rest of her ensemble: a pale sundress artfully hemmed and Vans sneakers that had some years on them. Auburn hair, olive, sun-kissed skin, and a mole on her throat.

It was her nose ring—reflecting the sunlight that pierced like a laser through the trees. Ben barked a laugh—something so small drawing him in like a lighthouse to a floundering ship toward the safety shore. She looked up, made eye contact, then back down.

On stage, the singer continued. Needing that light, a guide to carry him out of the darkness.

It felt like the frontman was singing to Ben about this very girl. He stumbled forward, knowing he had to talk to her. Now. Now or he'd always chalk it up to being so stoned. Or he'd regret it every time he looked in the face of a passing girl, comparing, and never passing muster. If he truly wanted to do "great things," he needed to take chances.

"Wh— who is this?" Ben said, not trusting his voice.

She looked up. "What?"

He leaned it a bit closer—conscious to not be invasive or creepy. "Who's playing?"

A look over her shoulders, a thumb toward the banner that hung over the band stating their name in bold black letters. ***The Black Keys***. She turned, went back to searching in her bag.

Ben nodded, feeling more and more like an idiot with each passing moment. He knew the Black Keys, knew their singles, could read their damn banner—but it wasn't the Black Keys he cared about in that moment. It was her. But he was falling. Falling back into the anxiety. Getting the cold shakes—too high, couldn't stop from spasming no matter what he did.

"Hey." It was her, looking from his hands, up to his sunglasses. Cautious concern in her eyes. "You okay?"

Ben nodded. "Yeah, I—" He was blowing it. "I don't normally smoke weed. I'm a little lost."

She nodded right on back. Calm. Cool. Compassionate. An old hand at acting with kindness. She put a hand on his arm. Smiled. "You'll be fine. Just breathe."

Ben felt the words fall into his body like honey. Sweet, oozing, and warm, spreading through his chest, stopping his shakes and settling his mind.

Just breathe. Two words. So simple . . . but it was all he needed.

She went searching back in her sling-bag. A cigarette carefully placed between two slender fingers on her free hand. Without thinking, he lifted his fist—Teddy's lighter somehow, inexplicably, still gripped tight—and offered it. The girl looked up at him, and he feigned casualness, pretending to be far more relaxed than he was. Trying to recover from his disastrous start.

She took it, grinned sheepishly. "I don't normally smoke either."

"What?" He leaned in again to hear her.

"Cigarettes. I don't normally smoke cigarettes," she said, cupping her hands and leaning closer so he'd hear. Ben could smell her then. A perfume he recognized from somewhere—an earthy, sweet mix that made his skin break out in goose bumps.

"Why?"

"My parents." A shrugged explanation. She lit the cigarette, was about to take a drag. Ben—never knowing why he did it—plucked the cigarette out of her lips and flicked it away. Lost to the crowd.

"Hey!" More surprise than accusation.

"Sorry. I like to get in good with the parents right off the bat," Ben said, turning a smile on her. Exuding as much confidence as he could muster, hoping she couldn't see through it.

Her incredulity shifted. Shocked frown slowly tilting to a smile. Mischievous. Her eyes glistened, bright. She laughed—an odd sound, that didn't seem to fit her voice. Deeper, rich. Ben was sure he melted right then.

Above, the sun broke through the clouds.

"Well, looks like you'll need to buy me a drink then."

WAY STATION 01-2 | CHOICES

"We can't open the door."

Ben leapt off the bed as though yanked by an invisible hand. He'd been pacing and fidgeting in the station for hours, weed and cabin fever infecting his bones with a nervous electricity. But now, standing clear in the room's center, holding the suit helmet in hand, his limbs turned to marble.

"What do you mean?" Ben licked his lips. "Can't you plug in an override and open it manually?"

"*That's just the thing. I can't open it* because *I've been locked out.*"

"But you have run of tunnel operations, don't you have some . . . skeleton key or something?"

"*Nope,*" Fontaine responded casually, like he was telling Ben they'd run out of Dr Pepper.

"Well, someone has to have one, right? If there's a lock, then *someone* has the key!"

"Stands to reason, sure, but I can't know for sure. If I'm talkin straight with you, this is way, way above my paygrade."

"Then get the person whose it *is*, for chrissake. It's time for you to call SGO and tell them what's going on! You've got a man *trapped* down here!"

"*Listen, buddy, I know you're pissed—*"

Ben almost choked. Fontaine's nonchalance was infuriating. The ingenuine "buddys" to calm him down, making him see the positive side of this. The Ear didn't get it. Didn't understand.

That terrible sinking feeling from when he was locked inside the bulkhead was coming back, but worse now. The once spacious station starting to feel close. Consuming.

"—*but I've got my best guys here coming up with solutions, trying to figure how to spring you from this little trap. Don't you worry.*"

"Fontaine . . ." Ben closed his eyes, deep breaths. In, out. He almost preferred Fontaine being condescending, rather than this mousy, negotiator-type talking about "best guys" and telling him not to worry. "Why don't you just cut through the door?"

"*Well, yeah, that's one option we're looking at, but that's far easier said than done. Those bulkheads are mighty thick. Need special tools. On top of that, we gotta get said tools all the way to the 80s, then we need to pump air through the tunnel so the welding torch will take. Can't cut through in a vacuum. Or, least that's what I've been told. All that's gonna take heaps of time. Can't rightly give you an estimate . . . but it's not gonna be tomorrow or even next week or the week after that. It's probably our best option, but it's gonna take the longest.*"

Ben wondered if you *could* light a fire or welding torch in a vacuum. He was fairly certain you could, but that was beyond his expertise. There was a reason he was here and wasn't a NASA engineer. "What are the other options?"

"*We've got three, so it's player's choice, but you ain't gonna like any of them.*" The sigh returned, and the chair squealed once again. "*You've seen those sewer-cap looking things in the mileage sections, yeah? Above the breakers? Those are mid-mile hatches. First option, you go out through one of those and swim to the surface. Now, a hundred fifty feet doesn't sound too bad, sure, but the pressure gets funny. If you don't regulate yourself proper and come up too quick, you're liable to get something called 'the bens.'*"

"Bends," Ben autocorrected, plopping to the bed. He knew of the bends. Decompression sickness. Air on the brain from a too-rapid ascent, leading to anything from a bad cough to hallucinations and death. A nasty way to go.

"Wha—" he licked dry lips. "Would the suit regulate that?"

"*It's built to withstand some intense pressures, but never been tested for something like that. Leastaways, that's what I can find out. I mean, it's not a diving suit, but . . . who knows.*" He laughed. "*I'm new to this too, superhero.*"

He stared into the face of the helmet, imagining the front plate cracking and caving in during an ascent. Imagined all the effort of a controlled rise to the surface to keep the bends at bay, only for the ocean to burst in. Flood the suit and weigh him down like cement shoes. *Feed him to the fishes.* Drowning. Drowning quick. Even if he didn't, trying to fight the drowning without air from the suit . . . he'd definitely get the bends. Unbidden, he imagined his skull popping like an overstuffed water balloon. Rising to the surface with a helmet full of burst brain matter. He shivered.

"No . . . I don't think I could do that," Ben said, his voice far away.

"*Right, thought so. Second choice. You could always hang out in the Way Station there. Odds seem decent enough the door will just open up on its own. The other one did, didn't it? In the meantime, we come on down with our drills and presto, open sesame. The schematics make that Way Station look pretty comfy . . . we can send you care packages through the tubes. Movies, food stuffs, you name it. Hell, you could even get out and get to work scrapping the nearest bulkheads, eh?*" Fontaine laughed, but it was forced. "*Bad joke, I know.*"

Ben couldn't stay. Not here. Only a few hours in and he'd started to itch, like when he'd been trapped in Bulkhead 83/84. It would be his own solitary confinement. A prison cell that would get smaller by degrees until he finally snapped. Maybe if he hadn't seen that psychiatric test, the thoughts may not have wormed in and bit at the apple core of his mind. But he had, and it did.

What is the state of my mind?

"I can't stay here," Ben said.

"*C'mon Breck, why not? I'll level with you. Staying there, that's your safest bet. Think of it as a little vacation—I'll still make sure you get paid, even if you don't do the work. Good ol' Fontaine's got your back, yeah? How 'bout that?*"

It wasn't just the space that bothered Ben. Something else, something inexplicable. He turned toward the water. The empty, vast blue. All its possibilities there. All the horrors. A feeling . . . of *being watched*. He knew, if he stayed here long enough, the nightmares would catch up.

They would catch up.

"I can't, Fontaine . . . I just can't."

"*Fucking, college boy.*" Fontaine's voice didn't have malice, but resignation. "*Alright alright, last option, but it's . . . tough. Classic Hail Mary pass.*"

"You gonna tell me to walk all the way to London?"

A short, barked laugh. "*Not quite. Remember that blue spot at the center of the blueprint?*"

"The Belly."

"*That's right. There was a crew touching down there from the surface for a handful of months. Had a fleet of submersibles they used to travel up and down from topside to tunnel constantly, a salvage crew of a different color. I've an inkling that maybe—and hear my goddamn* maybe *before you go off half cock on this plan. But* maybe *there's still a submersible attached to the Way Station there.*"

"Left behind from eight years ago?"

"*Like I said, big 'maybe.'*"

"Why can't you just get those salvage guys back? Tell them what's going on?"

"*They're unavailable.*"

You mean, you didn't call them, prick. Fontaine's ass was on the line. Firing would be the least concern. A hefty lawsuit, more like. Government sanctions. "What marker would I be walking to?"

"*781.*"

Seven hundred and eighty-one miles. "That's . . . you're talking months. I'd be walking for months."

"*Just shy of two. Maybe. Depends on how quick you go.*"

"You expect me to walk six hundred and fifty more miles?"

"*Boy, I'm giving you choices. That's it. I've told you I think you should stay there, fucking relax, and get a paycheck. You're the one saying you can't.*" Fontaine's voice got low, almost a growl. "*I'm half liable to write you off, college boy. Let the sea swallow you up. Wouldn't be the first time someone went missing in them tunnels. Now you got your options. You plan to walk, I'll send along rations to each Way Station every hundred thirty miles, no problem, but let's not forget* you *are fucking up my operation here, Breckenridge. Now, make your goddamn decision. I ain't your mother.*"

Ben stared at the helmet in his hands. That'd been a threat. A writing off. Choice. He'd make a choice and pray for the best. Wait, swim, or walk.

Outside, the shadows shifted. The Way Station rocked back and forth. He breathed. In, out, in.

He clicked the relay. "What's at Mile 781? Why was there a salvage crew?"

"*Man, didn't you hear a thing I told you during the briefing? Crazy or stupid. Or both. I already told you. That's where the crash was. The Odyssey disaster.*"

And there it was, his decision made. Ben would walk.

| BULKHEAD 161/162, TAPS |

Ben pulled himself awake in the bulkhead, shocked how cold it'd become. He'd been too exhausted to set up his hammock and just fell asleep on the ground, using a new rucksack pilfered from Way Station 01 as a pillow. Otherwise, nothing was between him and the frigid freezer burn of the floor, the grating pressed into the fleshy material of the suit's arm. Ben shifted back onto the mat, cursing and shivering. He needed to make peace with the cold. If Fontaine was right, he was going to be freezing for the better part of two months.

Only a single day out of Way Station 01, he'd logged thirty-one miles. A new personal best. He hoped to beat it tomorrow, but the ache already working into his legs was telling him otherwise. No matter, he'd push. Get to the Belly as soon as possible and do what needed to be done.

Ben had kept his relay off the entire day to avoid Fontaine and simply listened to music instead, distracting himself by timing footfalls to drumbeats. He knew he was acting like a petulant child but didn't care. Let the Ear think he was pissed—he *was* after all. Ben decided on the walk, but angrily told Fontaine he should still cut through the door. If the drill got through first, they could send someone down for pickup. Send anything—a car, snowmobile, motorcycle with a goddamn sidecar. Anything. Just get him out.

"Amateur operation," He shifted further. Yawned. "If I were you Fontaine, I'd better believe a lawsuit is coming. Take that hazard pay right out your paycheck." Ben lay helmet and head back to the mat, trying to find the sweet spot.

And heard it again.

It wasn't the cold that had woken him up, but a sound. He realized that now. A faint tapping. Heard only if he pressed his helmet plate back to the grate, reverberating through the floor. The ghost of a rhythm, beat out and traveling along the tunnel's bones.

Taptaptap. Tap tap tap. Taptaptap.

What could that be? A fish bumping against the glass? Or some undersea woodpecker with its mating call? It was too regular. Deliberate. Ben put his fist to the floor, knuckled a response. Repeating the same pattern, communicating.

Taptaptap. Tap tap tap. Taptaptap.

The tapping didn't repeat or return.

Ben settled himself back in to get some sleep. Grunted. Grinned. "A new mystery."

MILE 192 | PREDATOR

"Fontaine?"

No answer. Seemed the Ear was giving the silent treatment right back. Ben had turned his relay back on the second day from the station, but Fontaine was absent. Just the crackle and hum of static sounding more distant with each passing mile. Ben convinced himself he was catching Fontaine at the wrong times. Piss breaks, out of business hours. But this morning he'd called in right as the sun came up. Punch-in time. Even then, all he got was empty airwaves.

The Ear's absence drove loneliness back through Ben like a railroad spike. Suddenly more untethered from the world above than since he'd started, now almost two hundred miles from the nearest shore. The thought made his skin crawl.

He shouldn't have so been flippant with him. Clicking the relay on and off as he pleased. Safe in the assumption that Fontaine would always be there when called. He hadn't realized how much he relied on the surety of the Ear's voice. A calming voice. A voice of reason. He needed him now.

A shadow was following.

Ben had first noticed it just after the Way Station, stalking just beyond line of sight. Too spindly to be a whale, too agile. Too large to be anything lesser. He hadn't seen it head-on yet, not even a good look. Finned or tentacled, he didn't know. Each time he tried to look, it disappeared only to return moments later. Just in his peripherals, coasting after him. Just out of sight and keeping pace.

Can't let fear get the better of me, he thought. Shaking and stretching his hands, occupying his limbs. Help him relax. *Face it. Just need to face it.*

Ben paused. Waited. Whipped round, trying to see it again. Nothing.

"Fontaine." Ben could hear a tinge of hysteria creeping into his voice. A dawning desperation. "Can you—"

The shadow blurred past the tunnel wall. Obscured by the near darkness of the ocean. Big enough to shake the tethers, sending a *thrum* like a struck guitar string, throwing the tunnel off-balance with its wake.

Ben ran. Didn't think, just acted. It wasn't enough to know there was three feet of steel-strong glass between him and this UFO. Fear of what could be *that* large spurred him on. Faster. Breath fogging his helmet. Sprinting now to—

A light junction. He fumbled at the plastic casing. Popped it open and punched the button with a shaking hand. Two dozen flares exploded from the tunnel's moorings, illuminating the sea around. Fish blinked, startled, and careened away. Blooms of plankton drifted like snow. Odd clumps of bubbles filtered upward.

Nothing else. No creature, no monster. Maybe it hadn't been there in the first place?

"No . . . I saw it. I know I did."

Unbidden, the questionnaire popped in his head. That one leading question, always close at hand to taunt. To set his heart pumping. Turn him panicky. *What is the state of my mind?*

"No. No, stop. Don't give into that." He closed his eyes. Inhaled deeply. He couldn't panic. Not down here. Not so soon. He had to be positive, *think* positive.

He scoured for a happy memory. Something simple to keep the paranoia from settling. Memories rose but slipped through his fingers, slippery as eels. Unable to focus on just *one*. The trips he'd taken. Books read, movies seen. Something, anything.

Ellie. The sun kissing the naked curve of her hips from the too bright window in their Chicago apartment, back when things were fresh and new and limitless. The way her eyes would shift from green to hazel, despite her smiling insistence they were brown. The way her left canine tooth— *"my snaggletooth"*—would catch her lower lip when she was deep in thought. Her voice. Light. Easy. Sure.

"Just breathe."

Ben did. Breathed. Let his blood, heart, and mind slow. *Slooww.* The anxiety receding, replacing tremors with a profound ache. A longing. *Why did she go?* Why—

He closed that pathway in his mind, not letting himself think of the times toward the end. Their favorite bench as the sun was going down. Her cool, emotionless tone. His despair.

Ben shook it away, noticing he'd wound up on the floor beneath the light breaker. He stood and took stock, making sure he hadn't lost anything in his terrified flight. Feeling foolish. A *shadow* had sent him running. A shadow *outside*. He closed the breaker box, then knocked on the tunnel glass. Tough as stone.

He reshouldered his pack. Willed himself not to look out toward the water, but down the long road instead. There was no predator. Not one that could reach him. He was safe. Safe.

MILE 234 | CHATS

"Y*ou know what a boondoggle is?"*
"Bet you're gonna tell me."
"I wrote it down. Ready? 'A work or activity that is wasteful or pointless but gives the appearance of having value.' You, my friend, were doin' a boondoggle even before this bulkhead fiasco."

Ben's helmet rang with Fontaine's good-natured laughter, mixing with the huff of his own breathing. It felt odd to hear a full-throated laugh—Ben wasn't used to the sound anymore. Something fading from memory. It wasn't unpleasant, just different. Odd.

He was on a good pace today, could smell the sweat along with the usual ration-baked stench of his breath. He was due for a shower, that was for damn sure. His greasy hair kept falling in front of his eyes and the constant jerking of his head to clear them kept leaving rainbow smudges on the visor-plate. But he was feeling good. On track. Purposeful.

Not a boondoggle to me.

Fontaine had reappeared the day before, waving away Ben's concerns with easy explanations, along with promises that it "wouldn't happen again." Turned out he'd been at his station the whole time, but they'd had a one-off malfunction with the communications. Even better, the drill operation was coming together—they had a driver and military-grade drill-bit on its way to the New York terminal now. Rescue was progressing.

But Ben was just thankful to have the Ear back. He noticed the loneliness always creeping close by, always ready to smother, blocking out all sounds. Having Fontaine's voice nearby kept the emotions in check.

It might have been his imagination, but days with Fontaine in his ear always proved the best outside the tunnel walls too. Today, the glass was hemmed in by a kelp forest—an undulating green curtain gripping and blanketing the glass on either side. It made the tunnel darker than usual but comforting too. Fish of every variety made the kelp their home—none he knew by name but he was coming to recognize by their colors: the two yellow-blacks racing around the tube in eye-blink swirls, the iridescent purple-blue nibbling and hoarding swaths of seaweed, the million-strong school of see-through tinies floating obliviously along, waiting to be eaten. Everything quiet and calm and beautiful. Part of him just wanted to sit and watch the ocean at play for hours on end.

He didn't think it was important to tell Fontaine about the shadow. After all, it was probably just paranoia and an overactive imagination. Anxiety. No monsters here.

"Shouldn't you be giving me support? Telling me the work I was doing was . . . I dunno, for the greater good or something? Clean up the oceans and all that." Ben enjoyed this black comedy routine, a seesawing of friendship and animosity.

"*Hah!*" Another small explosion of laughter. The sound of chips *tick-tack*ing as they hit the floor. The roller chair groan. "*'Greater good.' That's funny. Nah, your job was to help line my pockets—something you're preventing from happening right now.*"

He grinned. "I'm nothing if not accommodating. You know, you might find—*ah shitshit!*"

Pain seared across the bottom of Ben's foot. Before he could stop, he'd fallen to a knee, clutching his right foot in a clattering of tubes on glass.

"*Breck? Breck, you there? You alright?*"

Ben hissed through his teeth. Kneaded the foot as best he could. "Yeah. *Fuck.* Yeah, yeah. I've had a blister growing on my foot for a few miles. A bad one. I started off with only one out the gate, but it disappeared. Was hoping that since I've gotten this far without one, I'd skip the blister part and go straight to callus."

"*College boy with his soft hands and feet. Never worked a real day in your life, I bet. How bad is it?*"

"Not good. Probably popped it. Need a good cleaning and wrapping." Ben glanced at his HUD, forcing away thoughts of pus filling his socks. **MILE 234.** "Still twenty-six from the next Way Station too."

"Gonna be a tough slog. I'll drop a blister pack and some first aid in your next care package. You gonna be able to hack it?"

"Gonna have to, aren't I? Yeah . . . yeah, I should be fine." He glanced at the lock-eye down the path. "What would happen if I took off my suit in the bulkhead to check it out?"

"In vacuum? Shit, nothing good. Someone told me once your blood would boil right out through your pores, but who knows if that's true. Granted, you're not in a true vacuum, might be able to get away with it . . . but all the same, wouldn't catch me trying it."

Ben paused, caught his breath. His imagination switched from squelching, pus-filled shoes to boiling blood. Pores unleashing noxious fumes or eyes popping their sockets like burst, rotten eggs. Push it out, he couldn't think like that. He'd fixate.

all that water just makes my spine fucking tingle.

He kicked his foot against the glass wall, more to distract than to deaden the blister's itch. The kelp twitched as fish fled farther out. Sharp pain lanced up to his knee, a hiss streamed through his teeth. Wrong move. He sat back, staring out, trying to shift focus from the pain.

"Breck? Freak you out a bit there?"

"Nope, just in awe of your horrible bedside manner again. You're shit for morale."

Another laugh. *"Morale? Hell, all I need to do, Benny boy, is keep an eye on you. Nothing said about keeping things all sunshine and rainbows. Just make sure you're not sabotaging anything because you're pissed or thinking about dipping into the ocean without your helmet."*

"Wouldn't dream of it. Helmet's my life or death, right?"

"More like your wife. Can't just shed her off and leave her. You're stuck with her. Wait." The chair squealed, Fontaine's tone suddenly alert. *"Christ, Breckenridge. I didn't even think about your wife. All this time—jeeesus."*

Ben swallowed, mouth suddenly dry. He chuckled, mirthless. "Maybe you have a heart after all, Fontaine."

"You want, uh . . . I should give her a call, yeah? Tell her you're doin' alright?" Papers rustled on the far side.

"No, it's fine."

"C'mon, superhero. I'll call. Let me—"

"No!" Ben stopped, everything else forgotten. His cheeks flushed and hot. "It's . . . it's fine, Fontaine. Really. You don't need to. Things with Ellie are . . . they're complicated."

"Right . . . sure. Whatever you say." Ben could feel Fontaine wanting to press. Holding back. "She won't call SGO looking for you, will she?"

"No. No, she won't." Ben licked his lips. Insides a maelstrom. Move along now. Walk. Back on track. He forced a chuckle, trying to ease the tension, but the waving forest outside seemed to take on a constricting quality now. Like it might overtake the tunnel. *Claim it*, and Ben with it. "This blister is a real bastard. Feels bigger than my toes."

"You're the one who chose the hard way, superhero."

"If I'm going to fix this, it's the only way," Ben said. "Besides. A little blister won't stop the mighty Ben Breckenridge."

"Sure. Of course not." There was an awkwardness between them now. A wary air. "So . . . how 'bout that view. See anything good?"

Thought I saw something following me a few miles back. Hunting me. Ben didn't know why he thought the word "hunting." Just seemed to fit. He wondered if he ought to tell the Ear.

"Nothing worth writing home about yet. Hoping for something special."

Fontaine's low chuckle. The levity was coming back. "*Great white or something? You're bound to see a few things, but you're too high up. The real terrors are way down in the deep. Squid as big as houses, sharks a mile long.*"

"What? That's not real."

"*On my honor, saw a doc on it once. Big thing. Prehistoric. Had a funny name.*"

Ben forced himself to pick up pace, limping along. One of the yellow-black fish was keeping pace now with him now, skimming the glass with one tissue-paper fin. "Probably wrong, but seeing all these adorable little fish kicking about . . . just makes me want sushi."

"*Don't really eat sushi myself. Watched a documentary on that too. Fishing industry's a bitch. Turned me off from the whole gig.*"

"Didn't expect the moral high ground from good ol' Fontaine."

"*Fish are clever, boy. You know, octopus are smarter than dogs, though they'd probably make shit pets. Sperm whale's got the biggest brain on the planet. And dolphins—well, dolphins are almost as smart as humans apparently. I—*"

A squealing hinge over the comm cut him short. Soft whispers and a harsh, hurried conversation. An unfamiliar voice in the far background.

"Fontaine? That the rescue crew you're talking to?"

Just whispering. The unmistakable tone of panic. Plastic crunching and papers rustling. The door opening and closing.

"Fontaine?" That panic was infecting him too. He cleared his throat. *Easy.* "Come in, Fontaine."

The Ear came back, breathless. A forced brevity in his tone. "*Sorry, sorry. What's up, buddy?*"

"I, uh," Ben shook his head. "Everything all right up there?"

"*Ahh, stuff and nonsense. Unwelcome visitors stopping by. What were we talking about before?*"

"Um. Fish. Views."

"*Right, right. You're bound to see some good stuff eventually. Wild West kind of action. Life on land only happened because the weak were pushed out of competition from the ocean. That's us. The real killers in the world are all down near that tunnel with you.*"

Ben's scalp suddenly itched like crazy. Flashes burst across his mind. The shadow. The real killer. Hunting. He sped up again, his foot screaming, the bulkhead not too far. The kelp coating the tunnel like scales, overlapping end over end.

"That's . . . pretty dark, Fontaine. You're oh for three on morale."

Fontaine wasn't listening again. There was a flurry of activity on his end. The door opening again, rushed voices. Conversations too far to be intelligible, but with the unmistakable panicked tone.

"*Listen, Breck. I gotta sign off. See about something. How you feeling down there? You good?*"

Ben scrambled, thrown with such an abrupt end. "I'm, yeah, well, I mean. I'm feel—"

"*Great, I'll catch you tomorrow, buddy. Keep well, keep dry.*"

And Fontaine was gone. Ben hadn't realized he'd come to a stop in the middle of the tunnel. Feeling terribly small. Scared. Panicked himself. Unwanted visitors at the station. What did that mean for him . . . for rescue? He wanted answers, a comforting voice. The loneliness and desperation was creeping back in.

He glanced skyward, where he knew the sun should be, hidden from view by swaying seagrass. The tons and tons of water. The ceiling seemed to shrink down. How *did* he feel? Really?

"Like I'm being buried alive."

MILE 259 | WALLED

The last mile before the Way Station stretched on. Ben had never craved substance—booze, weed, pills—but with relief so close, he was itching for another stolen joint. Going mad with the need for something new aside from the same views, the same music, the same tunnel. He needed something to disrupt the tedium. Or at least something to occupy his mind.

That crawling sensation kept washing over his scalp. Ebbing cold. His limping steps dogged by worried backward glances. Constantly looking for the shadow he thought—he *knew*—stalked just out of sight. Convinced *it* was tugging on the tethering cables, causing the whole structure to dip and seesaw. Keeping him off-balance.

"Just your imagination. Relax."

Fontaine was missing again. Two days gone since their last conversation. Since the odd tone and the flurry of activity. He tried not to think that Fontaine may have disappeared. His threat from back in the first Way Station turning real.

I'm half liable to write you off. Let the sea swallow you up. Wouldn't be the first time someone went missing in them tunnels.

Way Station 02. Sanctuary. He needed to relax. Time to settle his mind before the tunnel took its toll. Two hundred fifty-nine miles, some seventeen days and change, and the straight shot road was seared into his retinas like a phantom blur on a TV screen.

He could see it on his eyelids when he tried to sleep. There the tunnel went on forever. No shining eye for the next bulkhead, no junction boxes to spray light outside and break the uniformity. Just the endless walk.

Worse, he felt the tunnel was shrinking. Getting closer, walling him in. The walls seeming to breathe, expanding and retracting. The tube was a vein, constricting as it ran out of oxygen. Getting tighter. Tighter. And tighter still.

"Five hundred miles to go," he said aloud, seeking reassurance in the sound. Understanding just how easily the madness could bloom. "That's it. Then it's over. All over."

The bulkhead to Mile 260—and the Way Station—loomed ahead. The blue-silver eye winking, his guiding star. Ben picked up speed. He wouldn't be beaten by this tunnel. Not now. He was stronger than that. Grown stronger over the miles. He'd grow stronger still.

So, he imagined he was being followed. Fine. It was just that: imagination. Irrationality spawning things in the dark. There was nothing there. Even if there was, the tunnel's glass was nearly as thick as a man is tall. The tethering cables triple reinforced. He was Ben fucking Breckenridge. A tunnel wouldn't beat him.

The walls seemed to retract. The weight of his rucksack lightened. The pinching pain in his feet lessened. He could breathe. The Way Station was just there. Waiting. For him.

Ben closed the last dozen yards at a jog. *Prime, twist, pull.* Strong and practiced, easy familiarity. To the right, the door. **Station 02-260**. He tore open the hatch, cycled the airlock, and fumbled into the station. A perfect replica of the first.

He ripped off his helmet. Inhaled. *There. Good.* The antiseptic smell and feel, the security. That's what he needed. The unease was receding like a wave. Crashing further off, leaving only an echoing hint. He was safe. He turned to hang up his suit and helmet.

And saw the writing on the door. Unmissable. Huge. The same handwriting from before. The tech. Holden's. The words bursting his eardrums with klaxon calls.

YOU BEING FOLLOWED YET?

WAY STATION 02 | WORRY

Ben paced, erratic. At first blush, Way Station 02 was identical to the first, but Ben was certain it was smaller. Were the bed and window wall closer to the airlock? Maybe a foot or two, nothing more. It was enough.

That wasn't what had him itching and hyperaware. SGO was back, the *real* SGO. And for a reason he couldn't explain, that made him even more nervous.

"*Fuckers practically stormed the offices,*" Fontaine was saying. "*Threw me in their goddamn . . . transit authority jail for a spell while they figured the hell was going on. Didn't ask me nothin', could've saved a few hours and phone calls. Surprised they didn't call you.*"

"They did . . . eventually. The comms were out." Ben counted the length from airlock to the window-wall in steps. Fifteen. Felt like fewer. "They told me there was a system-wide power failure."

After arriving at the Way Station, Ben had stared at the graffitied door leading back out in a trance. Time seeming to slip away from him as he gaped, rationalized, and panicked, waiting for a sign that could make sense of it.

Then he'd heard a tinny voice crackle to life inside his helmet. For a split second, Ben thought the moment of madness had finally come—the graffiti acting as the tipping point, hallucinations not coming as visual sensations, but auditory. His helmet speaking to him, calling his name. When he'd answered, he'd done so quivering, not knowing who or what to expect . . . but an official SGO comms man hadn't been it. A crisp, professional voice that felt too convenient to be legitimate. He'd asked for Fontaine instead, and when the comms man had said the Ear had been "temporarily removed," Ben had refused to talk to speak until Fontaine had been brought back.

Now, as Ben paced the Way Station's confines, helmet in hand and eyes bouncing from the bed to the airlock door, he was seeing the bigger picture: SGO had gotten wind of Fontaine's unauthorized salvage operation and Ben's dilemma. All hell was breaking loose in New York.

"Yeah . . . one problem then the next. Power, comms, hell, SGO fired my drill operator for having the wrong license. Lost a day there, maybe more. Almost tossed the kid in that cell with me. Never expected them to pull me out quick as they did."

"I told them I wouldn't talk to anyone but you."

"Really? The guy that got you in this mess in the first place?"

"Got myself in this mess. Not your fault."

Fontaine blew a hard breath. "*Might've saved my skin, superhero. I don't know what to say.*"

"Tell me some good news. What's happening up there?"

"Well . . . lots of red tape getting cut through, more people arriving by the day. That said, there's not much of an infrastructure to SGO anymore. Hasn't been for years, company's basically dissolved at this point, so they're scrambling to find someone to lay responsibility on. The 'ranking officer' here is a goddamn psychiatrist. Prissy bastard."

Ben scratched at his patchy growth of beard, noticing how long his nails had gotten in so short a time, how grimy beneath the nailbeds. He didn't bother looking for clippers or a file, instead began worrying them with his teeth.

"Beyond that . . . there's a hell of a storm brewin' off the coast. I told them it explains the power and comm troubles, but does anyone listen to good ol' Fontaine? No sir. Hell, you'd think there would be an emergency backup system for this sort of thing . . ."

There is always a backup system for an operation this large.

Fontaine's voice echoed from the helmet's hollow, held to Ben's ear like a shell. Not listening for the ocean, but across it. He refused to put the helmet back on to talk. Not yet, but held it close, feeling that need for human contact. The Ear's long absence had felt like abandonment, or punishment. His return, a salve to an open wound.

He hadn't mentioned Holden's graffiti to anyone.

"Breck? Breckenridge? You there?"

"Yeah . . . yeah, I'm here. Spacing out. Thinking."

"*Don't scare me like that, kid. Thought we'd lost the connection again.*"

I'm the one who ought to be scared of a lost connection. Lost, stuck, and voiceless. Scared doesn't measure half it. Terrified is a better word.

"Fontaine, listen. I'm trying to . . . be good about everything down here. I really am. But nothing—absolutely *nothing*—is making this any easier. First the stuck bulkhead, then the walk, and now—now we're having comms issues after less than three hundred miles? Are you kidding me? I keep thinking about what'll happen if you drop off. How am I going to get my food? What if I get to 781 and there's no submersible?"

"*Hey now, Breck. Relax. I get it, buddy—*"

"No, you don't! You don't get what it's like to be down here alone!" *Stop fucking calling me 'buddy.'*

"*It's a tough gig. None tougher, y'ask me. We've never had a situation before so . . . unique problems crop up. But now . . . well, the cavalry is here. These college egghead types always bump the wrong switch and the system hiccups.*"

"That supposed to be directed at me?" *Like 83/84? Are you blaming me?*

"*No, no, no. Little joke. Trying to inject a little humor here. For all our sake.*" A forced chuckle. A Fontaine sigh. "*Now, that little comms fuckwit you told off is telling me we'll have no more troubles here on out. Smooth sailing. You can chew me out as much as you want. Hell, you're gonna be begging to get rid of me. Alright?*"

"Sure."

"*Good. Good . . .*"

"What's SGO's plan? They calling the coast guard to get me out?"

"*Like I said, the first guy SGO managed to get on deck is a psychiatrist. Not exactly a search and rescue expert. He's been on the phone nonstop, but they're not telling me anything.*" Fontaine dropped his voice to a whisper. "*'Tween you and me, I wouldn't count on the coast guard or police just yet. Not with the storm, and not with SGO. This is a PR nightmare to an already bankrupt company. My advice—keep with the original plan and truck forward. This many eyes, rescue is a waiting game rather than a question.*"

"You telling me it was a question before?"

Fontaine chuckled. "*Well, it wasn't a certainty.*"

Despite himself, Ben chuckled. "You're a real bastard."

"*I try. Ah shit, wait a tick, Breck.*"

Lilting voices piqued in the background. When Fontaine returned, his tone was formal. Forced.

"*Now, Ben. I've got SGO's on-call psychiatrist here, wants a word with you. Ask a couple questions, see how you're doing.*"

Ben felt his stomach heave. "I don't want to talk to him."

"*Not really a request, buddy. Hands are tied. So, uh, yeah. I'm passing you off.*"

A shuffling on the headset. Ben felt his eyes go wide and dropped the helmet. His pacing quickened. What would he do now? He could turn the relay off or just not respond. They would hear strain in his voice and they'd know.

No. Normal. He would sound completely fine. Not mad. Normal as could be.

"*Hello?*"

Ben hesitated. Picked up the helmet. Cleared his throat.

"*Mr. Breckenridge? Are you there?*" A slightly effeminate male voice. A refined, Indian accent.

"Yes. Yes, I'm here." Ben could hear the change in his voice. Sounding fake, put on.

"*Ah, a pleasure to meet you, Mr. Breckenridge. My name is Ashvin Singh. As you may have heard, I'm a psychiatrist and have had the pleasure of consulting with Steel Glass Ocean for many years. I've been informed of your . . . predicament, and I would like to personally ensure you the company is doing everything in their power to guarantee your safe return to shore. Rest assured you are in excellent hands.*"

"Okay."

"*Excellent. Now, Mr. Breckenridge, as a psychiatrist it's been my duty in the past to look after Steel Glass Ocean's divers and maintenance technicians whenever they descend into the tunnel for extended periods. Ensure they're well cared for during the rigors of tunnel travel. I would like to offer my services now to keep you happy and healthy.*"

Making sure they—you—*don't go insane.*

"*Is it alright if I call you Ben?*"

"Sure."

"*Good. Your intake form filled out by* Mister *Fontaine was quite sparse.*" Ashvin's voice had a clear tenor of distaste for Fontaine, which warmed Ben up some. "*So, I have a few preliminaries to start. Again, just a little more information so we can properly see to your safety.*"

"Mhm."

"*How are you feeling?*"

Like I could be liable to go crazy anytime soon. Like I might be being followed by a shadow. Like I'm going to be left to rot down here.

"Okay. Considering."

"*An understatement, I'm sure.*" Ashvin grunted a small laugh. "*Is there a history of mental illness in your family?*"

"No," Ben said, startled at the abrupt turn in questioning.

"*No schizophrenia, bipolar disorder? Nothing of the like?*"

"No."

"*Do you suffer from anxiety, Ben?*"

Ben coughed. "Doesn't everyone?"

"*Yes, I suppose so.*" Ben could almost see Ashvin's tight-lipped smile. There was a click of a pen, quick scratches. "*My apologies to be so blunt, but are you normally so . . . monosyllabic, Ben? So brief, that is.*"

Ben felt his cheeks burn. "I know what monosyllabic means." Cleared his voice again, pitching lower. "Not normally, no. Just feeling a bit off. Overwhelmed."

"*Again, I'm sure that's an understatement.*" A pause, a calculating of approach. "*Ben, Mr. Fontaine has told us you plan to walk over seven hundred miles in search of salvation. Forgive me, but it seems rather unusual to hike rather than wait, given the alternatives.*"

"Is that a question?"

"*An observation, I suppose. It's an impressive feat, to be certain but . . . well, do you think you can handle the rigors of such a journey? Physically, as well as mentally?*"

"You make it sound dire," Ben said.

"*In many ways, it can become dire, yes. I'm sure you've already begun to feel the monotony. The unending routine. The same long, single shaped tunnel. Cycling the same bulkheads. Eating the same food, sleeping in the same atmosphere—all repeated ad nauseam. It can be . . . wearing.*"

"Just makes things easy, doctor. Simple."

"*Please, call me Ashvin.*"

"Hard to make a mistake if I know what to expect every time, Ashvin."

A long pause. Ben cursed inwardly. He'd sounded too flippant. Too easy.

"*Are you familiar with the effects of solitary confinement, Mr. Breckenridge? In prison, it's used as a method to rehabilitate the very worst offenders.*

They're placed in isolation for twenty-three hours a day without human contact, despite no evidence that it makes the prisoners less dangerous—the opposite, actually. They become irritational. Angry. Prone to mood swings and violence. It is said that all prisoners in solitary break . . . it's simply a matter of when." The doctor paused as if to gauge Ben's reaction. Hammered on. "The tunnel is similar. The isolation, lack of physical contact, the tedium. It's my hope you'll benefit from purpose and forward motion. Surrounding marine life. But . . . the worry is still there."

"I'm sure I'll be okay."

Ashvin's voice became deadly serious. "Sir, if you don't have a strong mind, that tunnel will *break you.*"

Simply a matter of when.

"Doctor, you just make sure SGO is working to get me out. I'll watch my own back."

A heavy, no-nonsense sigh. "*Fine. Good. In the meantime, I've had Mr. Fontaine add a short questionnaire to your Way Station packages. I would very much appreciate you filling it out and sending it back to me. We would like to monitor your health as you progress.*"

The psych packet. The one he'd seen at the first Way Station. The leading questions about madness and mania. "Sure, doc. Whatever you say."

What is the state . . .

"*Stay strong, Ben. We'll come for you.*"

The microphone fumbled away from Ashvin, and Ben was able to breathe again. He was glad that his voice didn't give anything away. Half hoping it might've.

"*College boy. Doc treat you alright?*"

"You guys are really that worried I might lose it down here, huh?" Ben said.

"*Just gotta please the eggheads. Precautionary stuff. Just give them what they wanna hear and they'll leave enough alone.*"

"Yeah . . . great."

"*Meantime, I'll be singing your praises, superhero. Lotta guys would be crawling up the wall, they were in your shoes. Not you. Told Ashvin there, he oughtta give you a medal when you're out for all the shit you've been through already. Weight of the ocean settled on your shoulders and all.*"

Ben looked up toward the ceiling. The weight of all that water, pressing down. Why did Fontaine need to phrase it like that?

"They can keep their medal. Now that SGO's involved, I'm expecting that fat hazard pay at the end of this odyssey." The word "odyssey" dropping between tech and Ear like a dislodged, ugly stone.

If Fontaine noticed, he didn't skip a beat. "*Sure, sure. Better believe it ain't coming from my paycheck. If I get one . . .*" Fontaine sighed. "*I really stepped in it, huh?*"

Ben couldn't help but feel for the guy, despite what he'd done.

"*You seeing your big fish yet? Anything interesting?*"

Sure, plenty. A stalking undersea monster. Secret missives from the past mad.

He turned to the graffiti. Debated telling Fontaine. Should've told Ashvin. They were all on his side after all, just trying to help. Now was the time.

"Schools of fish," Ben said, feigning indifference. "Big long tunnel. Usual stuff."

"*Don't get too excited, you'll run out of air.*" Fontaine chuckled. Far back in the miles, his chair squeaked. "*Alright, superhero . . . your care package is there. Dropped a little something special in there for you. Keep those spirits up.*"

"Yeah."

"*Sure you're good, Breck? Sound awfully quiet. Not getting soft in the head yet, are you?*"

Ben eyeballed the graffiti for a third time. Blazed across the steel capsule—so he wouldn't miss it. More than the ocean above, he felt its weight. What it meant, that *something* was out there. That something *was* following. But it also meant that Holden—that same Holden from before—had seen it first, and that brought damning implications.

"I'm fine, Fontaine. A little tired. Nothing to worry about."

He couldn't sleep. Every corner of the station demanded his attention, pulling him to look, handle, or overthink. The window wall's unseen terrors. Holden's message blazing like a scarlet letter. The questionnaire in the pneumatic. He rose, sat on the edge of the bed, and rubbed his eyes. Everything in its own time. But not yet. He sighed out of bed, deciding on another shower.

This shower was more invigorating than the last, the water hot, almost scalding. He could practically see the steam emptying his pores, purging the toxins from his skin. For a moment, Ben was able to push all the worry and tension from his head, scrubbing his brain clean.

"Appreciate this moment. This situation again." He said aloud, cementing it into the air. "A second chance. So, few people get that. Earn it."

His fingers traced the long scar across his stomach, not wanting to reach and pull the shower's shut-off valve. He wanted to sit in the blissful warm for a little while longer, to keep forgetting. But eventually he reached, pulled, and the cold air came rushing in. Still, for a moment he felt human again and held on to that.

Despite the shower, his hair still felt greasy when he ran his hand through. Ben stood in front of the mirror, pulling the black strands down as far as they'd go, reaching the tip of his nose for the first time in years, and feeling the slick touch beneath his fingers. He remembered how they'd streaked his visor, the ache developing in his neck from trying to whip the strands away from his vision. He fumbled out the station's dry shaver from its dock and instead of putting it to his cheeks, ran it across his head. Tufts of dandruff-flecked hair fell to the floor, the single mirror not enough to get a full, well-rounded buzz. Yet somehow, after the shoddy job was done, his scalp patchy and uneven, Ben recognized that man in the mirror better than who he'd looked at previously. The once-tawny skin gone pale from too much time out of the sun. Hollow eyes stark, yet familiar. He docked the shaver, rubbed his knuckles through his growing coal-black beard, and nodded.

He found Fontaine's gift at the bottom of the pneumatic packet, the sight bringing a smile to Ben's face, the first in a long time. It tumbled out of the padded envelope directly onto Ben's lap, seeming foreign and out of place: a Snickers candy bar. Only seconds passed before Ben was ripping the wrapper off and stuffing the candy in his mouth.

"Usually a Reese's man, Fontaine but *goddamn!*"

Saliva flooded his mouth, giving way to a groan two octaves above an orgasm. He closed his eyes as he chewed, savoring each morsel. Nodding, making a mental note that if he ever saw Fontaine again, he'd kiss that man right on the mouth.

There was a USB in this package too, just like the last one. As he reached, for it, Ashvin's psych test spilled out onto the floor, hitting with a weighted *thud*. It gave him pause. Ben turned away from it, like the other problems he faced in this room. Sidestepping like it could burn him.

"One thing at a time."

USB out and pushed into the port. Ben pretended he could feel warmth coming from the monitor as it woke with static glow. He purposefully kept his eyes fixed on the Windows logo as the computer labored out of hibernation. The number of things demanding his attention—the wall, the message, the questionnaire—were growing by the minute.

You say you're ignoring it, but you're really fixating. Ellie's voice in his head. Accusatory, but undeniably true. It was like *trying* to relax. The paradox. Another thing pushed aside.

He quickly guided to the video folder, hoping for suitable distraction. A ghostly grin was coming back, wondering what Fontaine might've—

The Snickers bar fell to the floor. There was a single video folder packed with thumbnails, all blue-washed and filled with teeth: *Jaws, The Beast from 20,000 Fathoms, The Meg, Leviathan, It Came from Beneath the Sea.*

Sea-monster movies. Every single one of them. Another one of the Ear's jokes, had to be. But Ben wasn't laughing now.

The station rocked under unseen currents. A wake large enough to shift his chair in place. Ben wouldn't look. If he did, he knew the shadow would be there. The monster, just out of sight. Waiting.

He instead looked at that message.

YOU BEING FOLLOWED YET?

"Yes," he whispered. Knowing it should be read differently. Knowing it should say—"you being *hunted* yet?"

Ben fired up *Jaws*, needing the illusion of company, voices in the background. Mumbling as he clicked the file open. "It's a goddamn classic. Only reason he sent it. That's it. I never told him about the shad—" He stopped there.

He hopped from one task to the next, never resting. Repacking his supplies, cleaning out his gear, dumping filled waste containers and grabbing empties. In the station less than a few hours, but already a resolve to get the fuck on out of there was rearing.

He examined the bottom of his right foot, finding a single, massive blister that had popped when prodded, oozing pus and blood. New pink, sensitive skin already forming underneath. He knew he should take time, rest, let the foot heal, but no. No waiting. He sprayed antiseptic across the raw wound, biting back a howling scream, then wrapped everything with blister bandages.

"Get it all done. Now," he said aloud, ripping off gauze with his teeth and wrapping it round the wound. "Then back on the road." He paced, getting used to the extra bulk on his foot. Like wearing a boot, all padding. It would do.

Ben paused, standing over the psychiatric packet. Wary of its contents, knowing it had to be done. It was all the same questions, but now they rang with new meaning. More sick jokes played out in a dead-pan, medical humor.

1. I believe others control what I think and feel.
2. I hear or see things that others do not hear or see.
3. I believe in more than one thing about reality and the world around me that nobody else seems to believe in.
4. I can't trust what I'm thinking because I don't know if it's real or not.
5. Others are plotting to get me.
6. What is the state of my mind?

The questions mocked him as the Way Station continued to list. As *Jaws*'s score swelled and the actors screamed from a sun-strewn beach. As Ben turned his head toward Holden's message scrawled across the door.

You being followed yet?
What is the state of my mind?

Ben penciled the answers SGO would want to see. Fine. Everything was fine. His mind was as it had been before he left the mainland, after he left the first Way Station, and even when he entered this one. His. His own.

He stuffed the envelope and sent it screaming back up the tube, along with a note to Fontaine about throwing something landbound for his next media drip in Way Station 03. *Mad Max* over *Waterworld*. A western maybe, or a movie about a drought. He made it cheeky enough to not raise concern.

The questionnaire safely away, Ben picked up the half-finished Snickers and sat back on the bed—back to the window—and let the movie distract. Relax him. Quint was giving his drunken speech to his shipmates about the shark. The unknown, haunting terror.

"He's got lifeless eyes. Black eyes . . . like a doll's eyes."

Ben took a bite of the candy bar. Swallowed hard. Dry, the taste seemed to have leeched out onto the floor. He hurled it against the door. Against Holden's graffiti. And stared forward. Not really watching.

What is the state of my mind?

MILE 261 | FOCUS

He breathed easier as the bulkhead slammed shut behind him. The silence of the tunnel closed in and the blue bathed over him again. He couldn't shake the feeling of being watched in the Way Station, whether from the window or . . . something *in* the station, he couldn't tell. It didn't make sense that it might change out here, surrounded wholly by glass, but there was a calm here. The snaking tube a comfort, reliable in its simplicity.

Yet looking down that long road, the task at hand was daunting again. More than five hundred miles to go. More open windows, more questionnaires. More shadows.

The goal. It was all for that singular goal. More than ever before, this could be where Ben proved himself.

He leaned against the wall, searching the water for signs of life, but it was empty today. Light-filled but barren. He traced the flow against the glass. Not wanting to go forward, understanding why. He was scared. Didn't make him less of a man to admit that.

"Sometimes you need to do the things that scare you." Ellie's words, crossing the chasm of time.

She'd taken him canoeing on their first date. After their fumbling first meeting, Ben had been looking for an excuse to call her, but any semblance of confidence came up short whenever he reached for the phone. He threw himself hard into work, letting Teddy rib him about "that girl he was too afraid to DM." The work was too important, he reasoned, couldn't let distractions blur.

But she'd called and his stomach went sideways. No text, but an honest-to-God call. "Wondering when I might hear from you," she'd said. "Either you're playing it cool, or you forgot about me, and I like to be memorable."

He'd stammered. Trying to think of something witty, to grab that easy confidence he'd fostered in high school when girls in drama class whispered and giggled as he passed by, but years among grad school engineers and long nights at the drafting table had left Ben with nothing but stutters and awkward laughs now. In the end, she saved him.

"I've been cooped up inside too much lately, how'd you like to get adventurous with me today?"

Her house was a peeling two-story in Little Italy. A rush of flags and old men lined the streets, watching Ben as he idled his car to a stop in front of her stoop. Ellie bounced into his passenger seat before he even had a chance for the gentlemanly move to open her door, or even for a quick hug hello outside the car. She was just *there*, a brightly colored bird flown through the open window. The afternoon sun haloed her auburn hair, her eyes lit with a smile that hadn't quite made it to her lips.

"Ready to become a captain?" She said.

Ellie pointed the way and Ben drove them through cobbled streets still reeling from summer tourism. He supposed he ought to strike up conversation, worrying the silence might grow awkward, but was surprised when it didn't. The air had the contented glow of longtime friends enjoying each other's company.

They stopped in a heat-hazed parking lot beside a river. Ellie hopped out to rent a canoe from a kid with a trailer hitch, while Ben pulled a cooler filled with beer and snacks from the trunk—requested by Ellie over the phone. Hauling the cooler into the bow, he could see nervousness plain on her face. An anxious lip biting. She noticed him noticing.

"I've never done this before." A shy smile. "I had . . . an incident when I was a kid. Caught in a riptide, you know the cliché. I, uh . . . I have a bit of a fear of water."

Her unease made Ben relax some, evening the playing field. "We can do something else, if you want. Catch a movie, play darts, or something. Whatever works for you, I'm easy."

She shook her head, smile gaining. "This was my idea! My friend told me about a spot we should check out. Canoe's been rented and beer's been stored. Besides," she hopped in the canoe, feet momentarily unsteady but quickly settled. "Sometimes you need to do the things that scare you."

Ben felt the mirror of Ellie's smile growing onto his own face. "Aye, aye, captain." He pushed them off the bank and hopped into the back, taking up the oar and setting to.

If Ellie hadn't told him she was afraid of the water, he would never have known. Her poise was an anchor, like her feet were always firmly on solid ground. He watched as she paddled, mesmerized by the curve of her lean arms as she stroked, the way the sun turned her skin to gold, the charmingly sloppy way she tied her hair back.

She pointed out names on the small boats they passed, laughing at the best puns. After a while, Ben started pointing out his favorites too, giving them twists of bad accents. Before too long they were laughing together, floating along.

They came to a few forks in the river, and by silent mutual agreement let themselves get lost. The usual first date questions came and went. Ben pulled out a bag of Good & Plenty and Ellie teased him for liking black licorice "grandma candy," while Ben teased Ellie back for still using an out-of-date iPod that she plugged into a portable speaker. They took turns playing favorite songs—sometimes singing along, sometimes just listening—that contented glow he'd felt in the car evolving to a charged air.

Ellie told him about growing up as one of four kids in a crowded Italian household. Always vying for clever ways to gain her parents' attention and making sure to eat quicker than her brothers or risk not eating at all. She confided in him about her tomboy years, navigating public school in an underprivileged part of town, and surviving as the daughter of an Internal Affairs detective in a neighborhood teeming with police brats. Despite her father wanting her to follow into law enforcement, Ellie was studying to become an immigration lawyer, dreaming she might be able to help other families from facing the same rigors her parents faced in pursuit of a good life.

Ben had never been a good listener, a fact his mother and teachers loved to point out. Always waiting for his turn to talk. But floating down that river, he could've listened to Ellie's voice until the sun went down and the night birds stole the sky. Nothing had ever sounded more perfect, and he wondered what it'd be like for her voice to be the soundtrack of his days.

But she turned the tables, asking about his work, family, and ambitions. Try as he might, once he got started, Ben couldn't keep from rambling. Talking about Teddy, the grant they'd just won with a major Chicago architecture firm, the early praise and plaudits that Teddy whispered were indicative of grand things to come.

"Teddy likes to rib me a lot, keep me grounded, but then he's always the first to say we're only gaining momentum because of my work ethic and ideas," Ben said, feeling a flush run up his neck. He wanted so badly to impress her. "But, I don't know. It's hard not to feel like an imposter."

"Everyone feels that, I think. I always took it as a sign you're on the right path. The real imposters are the ones who think they've got it all figured out. I'm sure your parents are pretty proud."

He laughed. "My mom's just happy I like to work. She always says, 'there's no use in wasted days.' My dad's an artist. A painter. He's always had this thing with 'the greats,' not their paintings but the adoration they always got. Spends more time looking for compliments instead of actually painting. I'm pretty sure he wants nothing more than the world to see him as a great too, but it's an obsession for him. Problem is, he's so preoccupied trying to *look* like a great man he forgets how to be one." Ben realized he'd been fiddling with a snapped off beer can tab, so he tossed it in the bag they were using for trash.

"What about you? What do you want to be?"

"Can't say I want to *be* anything. But . . . I want to make something. Teddy too, it's what drew us together at school. He wants us to design the biggest skyscraper the world has ever seen."

"But you don't."

"I'm not sure." And then, maybe because of that electricity in the air, or that undeniable comfort he was feeling or because once he'd started it was difficult to stop, Ben gave breath to his whispered dreams. "Whatever it is, I want to create something different. Something that'll do some *good* in the world, you know? Dig deeper wells rather than build walls or fences. Something that will stand the test of time."

He could hear the tinge of awe in his own words, and that flush on his neck spread to ears, cheeks, and beyond.

Ellie looked back at him, squinting from the sun. "Those are pretty lofty goals, sir. But I bet you'll manage. You've got that look."

"Oh yeah, what look is that?"

She spread her hands wide like writing across the air, lilting her voice to a magician's dramatics. "*Visionary.*"

And her smile made him believe he could be just that. Ben's heart galloped in his chest, the world suddenly brighter than he could ever remember. Ellie eased forward again and the shimmering water danced on her cheeks. "Just make sure you don't forget about us little people when you hit it big."

"Wouldn't dream of it."

They were drifting closer to one another in the boat. His legs touching her side. Her hair ticking the back of his forearm when she looked one way or the other. All of it mutual, and sweet, and *right*.

"There! That's it!" Ellie pointed as their canoe entered a secluded grove of trees along the riverway. The air was cool in the shade, smelling like clay and teeming with the call of crickets. A muddy bank rose nearby with a weathered rope swing attached to a tree far above. "My friend set this up ten years ago. It's been here ever since apparently. He said people come here all the time and swing off."

Ben pushed his oar into the water, testing the depth, feeling the wood hit mud just a few feet down. Seeing this, Ellie leapt from the canoe without a hesitation—her fear evaporated. They pulled the boat close to the bank, Ellie tripping through knee-high mud, smearing her ass and elbows.

"Don't laugh!" She snorted.

Ben followed, the claylike mud suctioning his ankles. He nearly fell too, but Ellie grabbed and steadied him, smearing handprints on his bare back and arms.

"C'mon." A mischievous grin and she grabbed the rope, ascending the slippery bank without waiting to see if he followed.

He did, the more cautious side worrying about stray sharp sticks and rocks embedded in the mud. Panting by the time he made it up, the warmth of the sun was gone, replaced with cold sweat. Ellie stood defiant on the ridge top. She'd marked her face with the mud like an Amazonian warrior, smiling as she held onto the rope.

"You ready, Tarzan?" Ellie said.

"We just swing off?"

Ben eyed the river water. It couldn't be too deep—deep *enough*, sure. But what if it wasn't? He might not be scared of drowning, but the unknown, the unseen, was different altogether. From the hilltop, the muddy depths spoke of hidden horrors beneath. He imagined the mud sucking him down with quicksand, fatal slowness. Ben swallowed, suddenly unsure. Wanting to retreat to the safety of the boat.

"Hey," Ellie said.

He turned to her, and for the first time since they'd stood listening to the Black Keys, and she talked him down from his high, they locked eyes. No furtive looks, no shy glances.

Just him and her.

Will you be my everlasting light?

Ben smiled, and Ellie smiled back. She handed him the rope and their hands touched—slick fingers radiant with electricity.

"You can do this." A tree swayed. Light dappled her face. "*Just breathe.*"

He swung free of the ledge without a second thought.

Ben stepped away from the tunnel wall. He could feel the cold around him like a physical force, but he could beat it back. He could do this, all he had to do was—

"Just breathe."

In. Out. In. He stepped out onto the tunnel way, feeling stronger with each step. He counted them as he went, humming to himself, watching the eye of the bulkhead coming closer. Closer.

He wished he hadn't let his fears get the better of him, that he'd stayed longer in Way Station 02. Already itching for another one of those joints. His bandaged foot was aching, the blisters reforming just to burst. But no matter. He was back on the road. Back to his purpose.

He endured. He walked. He focused on the miles.

"Just breathe."

| BULKHEAD 290/291, NEEDLES |

Ben swayed in his improvised hammock, listening to soft guitar coming through the helmet speaker. A voice crooned over the fingerpicking, soft and light, lulling him toward sleep.

"... 'cause I know nothing ... no nothing ... about love."

Music had become his solace. Comms with New York had become staticky from the "storm" as the 300-mile mark approached and the days became shorter, but he'd found a bastion in the swinging iPod. The constant, reliable companion. It'd helped him find a groove again—longer mile stretches and little exhaustion at night. At this rate, he'd make the Belly in no time.

Ben shifted, trying to get comfortable in the bulky suit, hammock swaying violently with each twist and settle. He stared up through the oceanlight, one arm tucked behind his head. There was a ribbon of light high in the darkness. An undulating, shimmering serpent of a fish that kept dancing close to the tunnel, drawn by the interior lights, daring a closer look before peeling away again. It never came close enough for Ben to get a good look, yet just enough for him to question and marvel, letting his imagination give it a fantastical bent—maybe it was an electric eel looking for a recharge or, better yet, an undiscovered variety of sea snake seeking a mate in the long dark but finding this explorer instead. Ben smiled, imagining how he looked: a spacesuit strung up in a hammock, 150-feet below the surface.

"Like my own little cocoon," Ben whispered over the acoustic and baritone. "And when the journey's done, I'll be a butterfly. Maybe not a *beautiful* butterfly but changed noneth—"

Ben paused. The music had changed. Jumping over one set of words then the next.

"*I know nothing— nothing, about love.*"

He'd listened to the song enough to notice the change. He'd cycled through every discography in his collection three times. Each guitar strum, snare beat, and bass warble committed to memory at this point. Ben reset the screen and started the song over. No matter. He had all the time in the world to listen again and aga—

It happened again. Worse.

"*I know— no— out love*"

Probably a simple problem, easy to solve. Not the battery, that was fine, connected straight to the suit's power source and the helmet HUD was giving him green. The iPod might be old and look like shit, but it couldn't corrupt the audio file enough to blur over song sections like a scratched-up vinyl record.

"Odd . . ."

He clicked onto the next song. An instrumental. From his "Quiet Ride" playlist curated for plane and train travel to lull him to sleep. Perfect. If there was a problem with the player, he'd take a look tomorrow. Sleep now, that's all he needed.

Ben twisted again, still uncomfortable. The suit made it impossible to sleep on his right side, how he liked. The cocoon comparison slipped away. More like a net. Wrapping him up, not giving way no matter how much he slipped and squirmed. The netting would only tighten and tighten and tight—

Another skip, now in this new song. It was a second, no more, but it was enough. Aggravated he clicked to the next song. Too quick a tempo. *Click*. There. Better.

But he was agitated. Annoyed. First the music, now the hammock. He bucked. Grunted. His O2 meter dropped a percentage.

"Relax. You gotta relax," Ben said. He barked a quick laugh, as much to inject a little humor than actually feeling it. "Getting caught up in your hammock isn't the worst thing in the world."

No, not the worst thing. But now he *was* thinking of what could happen. Sudden flashes of *the worst thing* spawning inside his imagination. Nightmares given space on the movie screen of his mind.

A tunnel section splintering at the ends and plummeting down to the ocean depths below. A mile-long coffin sitting on the ocean floor. Or the glass above shattering and flooding the bulkhead, slowly drowning him while he slept.

The song changed again—this time skipping like a record might, stuck on an infinite loop of repetition. Ben's hackles rose with each repeated line over and over:

"— *rest for your soul*— *rest for your soul*— *rest for your soul*—"

Click.

Or that shadow he's been seeing. Maybe it wasn't a fish, but a boat casting its silhouette down in the water, and its rudders would somehow churn up a tether and hurl the tunnel out into the sea.

More skipping. *Click.*

Or a submarine out in the Atlantic fog. Blind. Coming straight for me, unable to stop, ripping into the tunnel, tearing away glass like it was aluminum foil. Its—

SKIP. Click. SKIP.

—payloads erupting and spreading not only water down the tubes, but unholy chemical fire.

SKIP. SKIP. SKIP. SKIP.

Ben ripped the iPod from its housing, hurled it away screaming. Heard it smash into the bulkhead with the fragile crunch of punctured plastic.

He seethed. Chest heaving, falling. Slowed. Rage evaporating to a certain, undeniable foolishness. Regret and fury causing his teeth to clench.

It took him a moment to climb down from the hammock, another to find the iPod, another to see a screen so shattered he could see the circuit board beneath it.

"No . . . *nonono.*" Ben tried to plug it back into the suit, punching the tactile buttons on the face and sides, but no response. Not even a spark. "Fuck!"

He clutched the iPod, holding it to his head, rage mingling now with profound regret. Ellie's iPod—survived so many countless years and memories only for him to smash it in a momentary fit. Typical. He exhaled, whispered again. "Fuck."

Without music, his whisper sounded both loud and yet somehow weak. Insubstantial. *Damning.* The weight of it coming home. Walking without music. It was going to make things harder.

He climbed back up into his hammock and tried settling in to sleep. Furious with himself, fiddling with the iPod until he couldn't look at it anymore. Not surprised to feel legitimate grief for a piece of metal and plastic. It'd been so much more than that.

He stared up through the oceanlight, hoping the ribbon-dancing fish could help settle him but that too was long gone, leaving behind an impenetrable wall of black.

Ben twisted to his side, pressing the iPod to his body and hoping for reprieve in sleep, unable to stop his eyes from leaping open with every creak and groan of the tunnel. Everything now infinitely louder, clearer. Each sound, a new, undiscovered terror.

Ben wasn't certain, but he thought he heard that same tapping from way back in Bulkhead 161/162. A steady, deliberate rhythm. Beat out just for him.

Taptaptap. Tap tap tap. Taptaptap.

MILE 346 | CLEAR SKIES

The oil rig loomed out of the clouded depths, a ruin of corroded iron and steel.

It must have been abandoned for a decade or more. Time enough for the struts to become overrun with algae and barnacles, for the ocean to claim as its own. Its siphon was mottled and bent, thrust down to the floor below where a pocket of oil would've been black gold decades past.

Ben wasn't certain why, but it fascinated him. Looking like a brain flipped upside down, disintegrating with age. Veins leaking crude, black sludge into the calm blue, its insides crusted and corrupt.

More than anything, it made him furious.

Derricks like these that had lain the bedrock for SGO's incarnation. The answer to a worldwide crisis brought on by pollutants pumped up by Big Coal and Oil. Greed sunk so deep it was thrust into the earth's mantle like a straw, 350 miles off the nearest coast. The decimation of 90 percent of marine life before anyone had the strength to stand up and shout, "No more!"

Years later, humanity was learning from its horrific mistakes. The Earth was slowly recovering but it would take generations to return to a state of normalcy. Back to a time before the mass flooding, deadly heat, gas masks, and smog choking the skies. Natural life would never return. Extinction was exacting.

Ben imagined crawling through a hatch and swimming out to the rig. Climbing the rusty rings like a pirate scaling a mast and setting fire to the structure. Watching as it burned in a reversed candlestick inferno, setting fire to the old world. That would show them, that—

He collided with the bulkhead at 347's end. Rebounding to a dead stop. The handle-eye of the lock gleamed with its watchful stare. Just above it: a black marker splash, dripping with condensation. Nearly rubbed free.

A message from Holden. Another. Scrawled in pointedly sharp block letters as if to convey the fury in his words. An arrow beside it, pointing to the rig.

BURN THEM ALL DOWN

Ben wasn't surprised to see it. He'd been seeing small signs of Holden more frequently. A bootprint here, a discarded ration tube there. Ben was following breadcrumbs through a dark forest, like Holden was getting sloppy. Or was leaving a trail to follow.

He'd decided Holden wasn't a scrapper like him, but one of the lowly maintenance workers or techs from years back. None of Fontaine's scrappers had gotten past Mile 90, or so the Ear had said. Even still, he felt a kinship with this wayward soul. All alone. Trudging forward and jumping at shadows. Longing for companionship of any kind. Ben could relate. Fontaine and SGO had been missing for four days now. Even when he did get the Ear, Ben couldn't keep the needy wheedling from his voice. That same tenor that seemed to coat Ben's voice from earliest memory: the kid vying for the attention of too-busy parents. SGO was working to help him, sure, but it didn't matter. Ben couldn't help it. He needed the Ear. Needed *anyone*.

Here was Holden. A comrade in misery, echoing Ben's own thoughts. Their connection boldened by a shared disdain at whoever left this rig to fester in the middle of the Atlantic Ocean. Ben wished he could speak to the tech somehow, over the years and miles. They'd have a lot to talk about.

Maybe Ben could do something about the derrick. Convince Fontaine to . . . what? Get it ripped down? He imagined talking to the media, the conquering hero:

"Oh yeah, I saw that derrick at Mile 346," Ben would say, daydreaming. "Called my Ear and said it looked like it might've been leaking . . . contaminating the water. Would catch hell from the EPA if they didn't do something about it. Better send someone to rip it down and recycle the parts."

He chuckled, a small, mad sound. What could it hurt? The greed of the old world didn't deserve a monument out here. But Fontaine hadn't been around for miles and miles. If he got ahold of the Ear, an oil derrick was the least of his concerns.

Ben thumbed the relay. "Hey Fontaine, I—"

The tunnel lurched *hard*.

Ben was thrown face down to the floor. The runner lights wavered and blinked. There was a soft *crunch*, like when the iPod had broken. More solid this time, glass instead of plastic.

Glass. He rocked sideways, looking for a splintering in the glass. Praying there was none, keeping the *worst things* out of his head. *There*. A crack. But it shifted, twitched in his vision. Moved when he did.

It was the helmet faceplate that had cracked, not the tunnel. A spiderweb fracture where the front had smacked the ground.

"Oh, fuck . . . *fuck!*"

He froze. Waiting for the crack to spread. Knowing that if it did, he had minutes before the tunnel's vacuum rushed in, the air sucking out. Before his lips turned blue, his eyes rolled over, and his blood boiled out his pores. He waited . . . *waited*.

"*Breckenridge! Where have you been? Singh's crawling all over my back, screaming for me to find you.*" Fontaine's voice hissed into life. Faint and far off.

Ben stared at the faceplate. Slowly . . . *slowly* put his hands to the floor. The runner lights had stopped blinking, shining steady and sure again. Their glow danced across the crack, the small fracture glittering like a prism. The helmet plate held.

Past his hands, Ben could just see the point where the left-hand tether parted from the tunnel wall and arrowed down toward the ocean depths. The cable was swaying as if from a blow, absorbing the impact like shocks. Straining and stretching. Went still. Ben breathed. Stood up on wobbly legs. Uncertain and dazed . . .

. . . and saw a shape slither past the glass. Black as the depths, studded with circular cups. A gigantic tentacle.

"*Breck?*"

Ben followed the tentacle. Saw another in the inky darkness. Another. All coming to join with a shadow in the depths. *The* shadow.

Colossal. As immense as the derrick, maybe bigger. Just beyond reach. Face unseen yet exuding a malevolence colder than the Atlantic at night. He knew beyond a doubt, it was what had been hunting him. His predator.

"An octopus . . . it's a fucking octopus." *Fucking kraken, more like.*

"Breck? Are. You. There?"

The octopus slipped away. Out of sight, its damage—*its threat?*—done.

Ben thumbed the relay. "Yeah, Fontaine . . . I'm here."

"Where've you been? SGO's been trying to hail you for days. You shut your relay off? Boy, you can't be doing that."

"What, uh," Ben stammered. Shook his head. "No. It's been turned on the whole time. I've been trying to get you too, but heard nothing but static."

"Shit, superhero . . . How you doing? What mile are you at?"

Ben stared out, trying, not hoping, to see the octopus again. He'd never seen anything so huge. It couldn't be real. Monsters didn't exist.

He stepped away from the glass. Shook his head again. *Clear it. CLEAR.* Too much was happening all around. *Focus.* Fontaine. Fontaine was talking.

"346," Ben said. "I'm at Mile 346."

"*Cracked 300, eh? Got some legs on you. Might explain why we're talking now, eggheads tellin me there's different relay systems every hundred miles. There must be a shortage in the 2s, but the connection sounds strong now.*" Fontaine sounded nonplussed, even professional. Ben wondered who else was around, or if they'd been giving him negotiator training. Be the calm in the storm. "*We should be connected for miles to go now, hopefully you're just past the problem. Make the tech wizards patch everything up.*"

"The eggheads," Ben said, absentmindedly. By Fontaine's logic, they should've been connected for forty-six miles.

"*Exactly. Damn eggheads. You holdin' up fine?*"

Holdin'? *Holden? Did he say that on purpose?* Ben shook his head again. *Easy now.*

"I . . . I think so." His eyes homed in on the crack in his helmet. Froze. "Actually, no. No, I might need a new helmet. My visor has a crack."

"*You fucking what? You've seen those tubes, think we're gonna fit a whole helmet in there? Goddammit, what'd you do?*"

I'm being hunted by an octopus the size of a 747. He had to tell him. Right? Fontaine could be trusted. This was his Ear he was talking about. If he was in danger, Fontaine needed to know.

"I tripped."

Not a hint of a lie.

"Hell, you're not leaking, are you?"

"No, my levels are fine." He put his hand in front of his helmet, thinking he could try and feel air escaping. Possible or not, he felt nothing. "Seems . . . seems okay."

"Small miracles, I guess. Takes a lot to bust through those things. Lot like windshield glass—might splinter a good bit, but it'll take a lot to get through. Not that that's not possible."

"Yeah, great." Ben was feeling a bit better. Spooked. But the Ear was calming him down.

"Next Way Station, we can get you some sealant, patch it right up. Meantime, slap some duct tape . . . bad boy."

"Done. How's the drilling coming along—any news?"

"About as good . . . Su . . . plugging t . . . aster co . . ."

"What's that? You're starting to break up again."

Ben tapped the side of his helmet like they did in the movies, trying to jolt the interference out. But the Ear was fading. He should tell him about the octopus. Now. And the oil derrick. Holden's messages.

"Fontaine? Fontaine, listen—"

"M . . . uck . . . stay safe and . . . clear. Anything else?"

He wondered if this was it. The octopus an omen that he should pack it in. Head back. He gave it the ol' college—*boy*—try. Back to Way Station 02, then 01. He could connect with Fontaine there. Hole up and wait for the cavalry. Now. Now was the time to tell Fontaine. *It's starting to get weird down here. I'm heading back. Giving up.*

Ben clicked his relay. The words forming as they fell out.

"Send something special for me up ahead, Fontaine . . . liquid courage. I could use it."

MILE 388 | SLEEP

The octopus was everywhere. Every swing of the tunnel, every shadow, every sound. Ben knew—*knew*—with his rational mind, that it couldn't be possible. That nightmares didn't exist. He was just getting loopy under the sea, needed to force himself to be calm. He would ease up, let his defenses fall.

And the octopus would strike.

The second attack rocked the tunnel so hard, Ben was certain the tethers had snapped. He'd lain beneath the junction box at Mile 363, staring out the glass. Rationalizing.

If the tethers snapped, it would be fine. The next in line would take the brunt of the work. They'd stay on course. It'd be fine. But what if those broke?

Then he'd become an astronaut, flung into space. Adrift in the current, the tube undulating across the Atlantic like a hissing live wire. But no, he wouldn't be an astronaut. Astronauts had room to breathe, to float. A whole solar system to die in. He'd be trapped with nowhere to go. Unable to stop the tunnel from plummeting to the ocean floor. Trapped in that watery grave.

The third attack came when Ben had just fallen to a fitful sleep inside a bulkhead, strung up in his hammock rig. When the octopus came, it wasn't just a single hit, but many. Tentacles gripping the tunnel and wrenching it. Once. Twice. Three times.

"It's trying to keep me awake. It doesn't want me to sleep. It wants me to look up to the window and make eye contact. To acknowledge it. I won't. I WON'T!"

Ben squeezed his eyes shut. Curled tighter into a ball. Way Station 03 was close. Tantalizingly close. Two miles, just *two* miles. He needed to reach it.

It wasn't purpose fueling him anymore but fear. Fear of the octopus. Of the tunnel. And now, on top of those, fear that the duct tape would betray him. That the helmet would collapse in on itself and he'd suffocate mere feet away from safety. He'd overdone it with the tape, covering almost a third of his visor before sheepishly peeling some back so that he could see.

All while his eyes darted back and forth, combing the depths. He was still being hunted. No doubt now.

"Can't sleep. Won't sleep."

He swung down from his hammock. Pulled it free and packed it up. Out the door and back on the road in less than five minutes. *Primetwistpull.*

Outside, the tunnel was pitch-black. It wasn't just the night sea, but something else. It'd become harder to see outside the tunnel. *Since Him.*

"No. Nonono. I'm further from New York, the light can't penetrate the gloom. That's all."

It's because you're sinking lower . . . deeper down. Inching closer to the Belly.

It shouldn't be getting this dark. Another dozen feet or so shouldn't have this much of an impact.

Ben crept down the corridor like a rat. Tiptoeing along. The silence was absolute. No footfalls, no creaking tunnel. Surrounded by a curtain of night-blank darkness. The marine life was nowhere to be found. Companions for so long, now missing. Just like Fontaine. Only the tunnel and the bulkhead blue-star ahead to guide him.

Cold. And alone. Alone for so long. Aching like a physical wound. He wanted a voice. A friend.

"Remember why you're here. Remember your light. *Just breathe.* Trudge on. And on."

Just him and the dark.

WAY STATION 03 | SEVER

"Fontaine. Come in, Fontaine."
Ben pushed the relay button so hard his thumb went white. Blood running and hiding. He stood on the bed, thrusting the helmet up to the corner like a cellphone with a bad signal.
There'd been no message from Holden in Way Station 03, but also nothing out of the ordinary. Same bed, same window, same welcome packet. Notably, no sealant for his helmet. And no Fontaine.
"Fontaine... fucking Fontaine—I need this communication established again. Please. *Please* find a way to make it work." Tears in his eyes, in his *voice*. "I need you. Please. I need someone." Then, in a smaller voice. "I'm scared."
Static. A hissing crackle. Something—
"... *ridg... Wh... uck ha... een?*"
Ben hopped off the bed. Shoved the helmet on, thumbing the relay, nearly tripping over the suit discarded on the ground. Something sparking to life in his chest. Something he hadn't felt in a long while, so foreign now he almost forgot the word. Hope.
"Fontaine, I'm here! Can you hear me?"
"... *mile... eyond. Didn't... questionnaire pa... ork...*"
"Questionnaire? Jesus, Fontaine. Listen—I *need* you to listen. I'm at Way Station 03. We need to reestablish connection. Now. It's getting worse."
The hissing pop. Static warbling in and out like a bad FM radio reception. His hope flickered.

"Fontaine, there is something *HUNTING* me. Alright? A giant octopus, o-o-or maybe a squid? I'm not safe. The tunnel might not be safe!"

"... *need a ... tion ... progress repor ... olden now.*"

"Progress, yeah. Y-yeah, I'll give you a report, sure, but, I-I-I," Ben squeezed his eyes shut. This was it, but it had to be done. He couldn't do it. Couldn't see it to the end. "Fontaine. I need out. I need you to hurry up with the cutting. It's not safe anymore. My head . . . I'm really—" Coughed, shook. Tears were stinging his eyes. "I can't do this. I thought I could . . . b-but I can't."

". . . . ."

"Fontaine? *HELLO?*"

". . . . ."

"FONTAINE?"

He slammed a fist against his helmet. Willing the connection to reestablish. Cycle on and off like a jolt to the electronic brain. *Restart.* But it was just prolonging the inevitable.

"Please . . . please just answer . . . *speak.*"

Nothing. Not the familiar empty static of a distant connection. No hissing. Nothing at all. A dead line. That sliver of hope guttered out as quickly as it had come. Ben knew. Knew it with acceptance and clarity. The connection with New York had been severed.

Comms were officially gone.

Ben didn't leave the Way Station for three days, and only then because the shadow of tentacles was closing in. Closer every day. He kept dreaming about the octopus grabbing the Way Station box, wrenching it back and forth until it splintered off, then carrying it down. Deep, deep into the abyss.

His latest care package had been stuffed with tiny airline bottles of vodka and gin. A few movies: *Little Mermaid, Deep Impact,* and *Pacific Rim.* More. All water based. It made Ben want to laugh, but he found he couldn't. His face was stuck in a rictus of smiling with no mirth to it. He popped a movie on at random, unscrewed a vodka bottle, and chugged.

Each day, he sat with helmet in hands. Staring. Speaking to it. Waiting for Fontaine to speak back, knowing he wouldn't. When Ben wasn't waiting, staring at the helmet, he'd sit in the shower until the water went icy and his body spasmed out of control. When he didn't shower, he drank.

"Did he hear me? Are they . . . hurrying for rescue?"

Is that what I want?

He clinked two empty bottles together. Wondering how much effort it would take to *break glass*.

"I'm changing. *Unsound mind*, they'll say. What else is new." He choked on the words. Gulped. *Clink. Click.* "But they can't understand what it's like to live down here. Under the sea. Miles away from anyone and anything. Afraid. Always afraid."

He stared at the window wall. Dark. All shadows. The octopus could be *right. There.* He'd never know.

Ben considered turning around, walking the opposite way. He should. It was past time. The die was cast—he needed out. But . . . but there wouldn't be supplies at Way Station 02. No guarantee he could reestablish connection with New York to have more sent. He could reach the station and still starve. But supplies would be at Way Station 04, that much he knew.

He hurled a bottle at the window, but it didn't shatter. Just *clinked* off ineffectually, clattering to a far corner. He buried face to hand. Wanted to weep, but he'd done enough of that already.

781 . . . 781 . . . 781.

It was time to go forward.

When he finally cycled the airlock after the third day, he left empty bottles strewn across the floor, joint roaches stuck between keyboard keys, and questionnaire papers tacked to the walls. He'd sent an emergency letter to Fontaine and SGO through the pneumatics. "*Heading to WS4. I NEED OUT. HURRY.*" Then wrote his own message on the airlock door, so it would be the first thing whoever followed behind saw when they walked in.

What is the state of my mind?

PART TWO
ALONE

MILE 422 | THINGS SLOW

Ben was sleeping too much.

Most days he didn't wait to reach the bulkhead, just collapsed wherever he was in the tunnel. His sleeping fitful, staccato bursts only extended his exhaustion rather than cure it. A draining fatigue like unquenched hunger. There was no true rest, not anymore.

His progress slowed, unconsciously at first, then deliberately. Ben wandered down the tunnel in a dream. Stumbling and weaving as if he'd been able to extend his drunken high from Way Station 03 to last weeks rather than a few hours. Sometimes he didn't make five miles a day. Once, he only made two. Each day in the single digits, he would tally the progress in his head, first chuckling at the absurdity, then swallowing the hopelessness that would inevitably rise. He'd walk the wrong way for hours, sing-mumbling while zigzagging from end to end, before eventually righting back on course. Or just sitting. Winding down the dog hours of day without twitching a muscle, just gaping out at the water. Hoping to see something, *any* living thing that he could call a companion. But the sea remained empty, impenetrable, and endless.

Ben knew why he slept and dawdled. Knew it as intimately as a lover or old familiar friend: despair, curling its way around his brain stem. But naming the feeling couldn't blunt its horrible, blanketing fog. The all-consuming loneliness and helplessness. He could only endure, letting pervasive dark run its course through his body, his brain, and hope to see the other side. That and sleep. Sleep seemed to be his only respite, and he was too glad to indulge.

By Mile 422, he was convinced he was nearing his end. Had known he'd been approaching it, almost welcomed it. Could feel his legs weighed down further and further. He plodded to the mid-mile mark and collapsed beneath the light junction box, watching his HUD and the slow tick of his O2 gauge, blinking lower and lower.

"How long until zero?" There was a croak in his voice that hadn't been there before as he split into song. "Ninety-nine bottles of O2 to go. Ninety-nine bottles of O2."

The gauge clicked down and he laughed. Half-heartedly pumping a fist in the air.

He tried getting comfortable, splayed against the wall, but the tunnel sloped just enough to make sitting easily impossible. He hunched, lazily pointing out the glass at the distant shapes of fish, feeling like a madman or toddler. His finger roving like a pointer stick outside and inside the tunnel. Finally landing on—

The mid-mile hatch. It gave him pause. The hatches had been embedded in the ceilings from the very start, hadn't they? Since Mile 1. Yet it felt like he was noticing it for the first time. A circular cap set at the section's halfway point, including wheel lock and digital keypad stenciled white with **MILE 422**, and the half-ladder hugging the tunnel curve to reach it. An emergency escape, in case of dire circumstance.

"Times have gotten dire indeed," he said, smacking his lips.

Ben stood and stretched for the submarine-style wheel lock, failing to reach across the thirteen feet. Could he jump and grab it? He shrugged his pack off and leapt, cumbersome in his suit. Nowhere close. He set his sights lower, the ladder. Standing straight, his fingertips just brushed the first rung. Ben could grab that no problem, but would he have the energy to pull himself up, rung after painful rung? No. Even thirteen feet was much too far for him in his current state. He sat back down.

"Not that it would matter. What was I planning to do . . . take a dip?" He sprawled across the floor, feeling the tunnel sway. "If I died down here . . . who would come to find my body? Would I have skin by the time they found me, or would I rot away . . . just bones in a suit?"

He felt a laugh gurgling in his throat. Clicked on his relay. It'd been almost a hundred miles since last contact with SGO, but the humming line was oddly reassuring. The possibility that Fontaine might be reachable. Still listening, even now.

"How about a math problem, Fontaine? A train leaves SGO station in New York, gaining speed in a vacuum. How long would it take to reach an object at Mile 422? Bonus question: What would happen if it hit head on?"

Always the familiar *hiss* replied back. Static.

"Would the object just explode? *Poof?* Or-or." Now he did laugh, and the sound of it was odd. Worrying. Devolving to a sob. ". . . or would the train . . ."

He was changing all right, falling into a personal black hole. That despair winning. Sitting on him like a weighted blanket that offered only suffocation and no comfort. He was coming to a pivotal fork: break and be consumed, or fight on.

"*All prisoners in solitary break*," Ashvin had said. "*Simply a matter of when.*"

But he didn't dare face that question now. Instead, he lay. Staring. Disengaging.

Drifted up . . . up and out of his body. Able to see himself from a long way off as if he were outside the tunnel and looking down. Free floating in the ocean. He was unafraid here in the vast blue, staring at the serpentine tube down below. It looked like a river.

Ben imagined the rope in his hand and Ellie just beside him. The mud she'd slathered on her face like war paint, drifting off in small globules and absorbed by the sea. The rope extended high, high above, breaking through the ocean. It was gold, made from pure sunlight, maybe connected to the sun itself. The cords were burning his hand, leaving bright slashes across his palms. Comforting.

"*Hey. You can do this. Just breathe*," Ellie said through a mouth full of shattered teeth. Her eyes pure white fire. Morphing, molding, condensing to a gelatinous black ooze. The comfort of the sun melting, light turning rotten.

No . . . this was wrong. Get away, he had to get away before it consumed him too.

Ben gripped the rope and swung, hurtling toward his slack body in the tunnel below. He had to get back before everything else spoiled. His body, his mind, his plans. Plunging down. Undershooting. He grabbed at the tunnel as he passed, his fingers slick, struggling to find purchase. He wanted to crawl to the hatch, twist it open and drop in, but the glass was too slippery. He fell.

Back and down. Into the void. An abyss the color of absent light.

It was waiting for him. The octopus. The tentacles whipping out. Reaching, suctioning, gripping, squeezing. Pulling him farther down, the blackness enveloping. Somewhere, someone, something was *screaming*. Down, down, down, into the—

Ben bolted awake on the tunnel floor. Tinny alarms were blaring in his helmet—he'd been hyperventilating, burning through O2. His throat was raw and ears were ringing, must have been screaming too.

He scrambled off the ground and swayed over to the wall. Put a steadying hand on the glass and scanned the upper seas. Of course Ellie wasn't out there. What could he have done if she was? Nothing. He backed away without looking *down*. Ellie might not be there, but the Other could be.

Ben hit the helmet. Once. Twice.

"Fucking get yourself together."

Again.

"Get. Your. Shit. Together. You're not dead. Adrift, but not dead."

All break . . . simply a matter of when.

"*NO!*"

He put both hands on the wall and stared at his reflection. Past the growing fuzz on his scalp, the wild beard, the gaunt cheeks and puffy eyelids to the eyes themselves. Stared. Seeing the terror there, the uncertainty.

"You are not going to break. You won't. You're made of sterner stuff now. You're going to see this through. Ben Breckenridge is going to see it done. 781. *781.* Get there. Get it done . . ."

Then, whispered.

"You. Will. Not. Break."

It was all down to how he coped. Be overwhelmed or overcome. He would do what needed to be done, walk the miles and endure. Not think about what might be waiting for him ahead, in the dark, in the Belly.

Just breathe, walk, and try not to go mad.

MILE 451 | UNBROKEN

The miles marched on. Straight shod and relentless. Unbroken.

It was a catwalk, or tightrope. But if he fell off this particular tightrope, he wouldn't plummet to a brutal maiming or death. He'd still be here. Still walking the same path. Clocking the same miles. The days blurring together.

"You warned me, Ashvin, but I didn't listen." He shook his head. "Wouldn't have mattered anyway."

The sections felt longer, three thousand steps instead of two. Maybe even four. An eternity between bulkheads, the lock light seeming to push farther and farther away. He argued with himself, certain of the extra length, but knowing it couldn't possibly be true. Each section had been prefabricated, cut from a mold to fit a perfect mile every time. It was just his hyperactive mind morphing and elongating the distance. Still he walked, fingers itching for a bulkhead lock.

Prime twist pull. Prime Twist Pull. PrimeTwistPull. primetwistpullprimetwistpull.

Ben longed for air. Fresh air. A cool, rejuvenating breeze to ruffle his hair. Stir his senses and let him relive old memories through smell. Newly cut grass or damp earth, fresh bread or old books. Anything. He'd take anything. All he smelled was himself: putrid breath and sweat-drenched skin. All he breathed was canned recycled air.

"No one likes canned food. You peel back the lid of a canned tin, everything's congealed. Swimming in its own filth. All . . . soggy. Like me." He scraped his tongue across his front teeth, grimacing. Wanting to spit. "Everyone needs the stuff that's been touched by the sun. Nourished."

Air and sun. Vitamin D. Warmth on his cheeks. He'd give an arm for a sunburned patch of skin, to feel the ache of crab-red scorch marks on his shoulders or legs. Just to sit and watch it blister, dry, peel, all to be grown anew. If only SGO had installed sunlamps in the Way Stations for technicians. That'd be inspired. Or the bulkheads. A UV lamp. A goddamn tanning bed.

"I'll be pale as a ghost before I reach the end. A vampire." Ben grunted, trudging along. "Vampires don't get any sun either. No sun for them. No sun for me. No sun today."

The monotony gave room for his mind to wander. Unbidden, memories rose to his subconscious from across the spectrum of years. Innocuous things, random but never positive. A flood of disgraceful, vivid snapshots from throughout his life, dredging up those feelings of shame, of regret. Delving deeper and deeper, until the worst. Until—

Ellie.

"No . . . no. Let hers sit. Please. A little while longer. Just a little. We'll get there."

The weather didn't change. The water still and so dark as to seem bereft of life. But there were things out there. Watching. Always watching.

He hadn't seen the octopus for days except in his dreams, but he knew it was trailing. He could *feel* its presence like it was a part of him now. His deprived senses were heightened. Imaginative. Thinking of the predator: the taste of ink like ammonia, the undulating softness of its flesh, the tentacles. Coiling around Ben's spine, tracing up to his crown. Suckers gripping his skin, pinching his hair while dripping mucous thick tendrils of octo-snot.

"Stop!" He came to a halt in the tunnel. "Just . . . fucking stop thinking about it. Nothing can get in here and I'm . . . I'm not going out. Push it aside."

He walked on, shaking his head. No shadows were following him. No octopus would find its way in and hug him to death. Besides . . . it wouldn't *hug* him. Those tentacles were too big.

"They'd suffocate me. Like an anaconda. Vise grip."

But wasn't he already being suffocated? By the tunnel. He needed out. Not the reprieve of a Way Station, but actually out. *Need* was a physical thing. He needed human contact. He needed the reprieve of distraction. He needed Fontaine to coax him down off the ledge. He needed air and sun.

"The Way Station. Just get there. *Get there.* Keep the bulkhead in view. Walk." So he did.

The miles marched on. Straight shod and relentless. Unbroken.

MILE 519 | BASEMENT

Ben couldn't make the last mile to the Way Station. The misery had become too much, the mile too long. Barely past the mid-mile hatch, he was convinced this section would stretch on until he finally let go. Gave up the ghost.

He was too weak and too tired. The fear that his splintering mind would finally dissolve was always there, but at this point he'd welcome it. No longer caring to jump at the shadows.

"Let him come. Let the octo in. I'm here . . . not going anywhere."

Ben ran his hands along the glass, feeling cold smoothness against his glove and staring at empty darkness beyond. He longed for the marine life of the early miles, the anticipation of seeing the awesome secrets of the far-flung ocean. Schools of fish bucking and weaving like flocks of starlings. Dolphins using the tube as a playpen. Tiger sharks, starfish, seahorses—something, anything.

The absence of life was disquieting. Disquiet was quick to grow to fear. Fear made the shadows loom.

His knees buckled, first one, then the other. Flopped to sitting without the will or energy to stand again. His helmet drooped against the wall, and he closed his eyes. He tried to spit, but he didn't have any saliva. Maybe if he drank some water . . . but what was the point of that?

"Delaying . . . the inevitable."

Here was as good a spot as any to die. Five hundred and nineteen miles in, some forty odd days.

"Sorry, Ellie . . . I'm . . ."

Drifting . . . drifting away.

His eyelids flushed red with spots of light. Here now, then gone. He brushed it aside as a trick of the eye or a dying synapse firing. But another flash came and went. Another. A steady stream of light dawning. He creaked his eyelids open.

The ocean had become a light show. Clumps of fairy fire set against the dark. Jellyfish. A whole bobbing swarm, trailing cords of neon. All alien and iridescent, turning the sea into a kaleidoscope of color. Stark violets, blues, and reds. A pulsing, fireworks display.

Ben gasped, falling backward. Laughed. These were new stars of a foreign night sky, playing just for him. Twisting and dipping in a complete stillness. No threats, no messages, just him and the sky.

He traced the path of one, then another, his finger lazy in the air like a conductor's wand. Understanding, somehow, that these jellyfish were for him. A reminder to not let his will soften without a fight. That when things got hard, he just needed to stop and enjoy the journey once in a while.

"Relax..." Ben whispered. "Need to try and relax."

Who had said that to him, from which past life? Teddy. In Grant Park, that first day. First day of work, first day he'd met her. First day of the rest of his life, marching toward this inevitability here—

Laughter echoed down the corridor. A man's, familiar but distorted. Wrong.

Ben turned toward the sound. It seemed to come from behind, back west. But of course, there was no one there. Had that been... was that his own laugh? Must've been, even though he hadn't felt it. There was no one else down here. He was alone. Alone for miles and miles. Hundreds at least. Still, he felt unnerved.

Reaching deep into that last reservoir of strength, Ben got to his feet. Outside the jellyfish continued to dance, but his attention had shifted. The magic of their presence spoiled, colors muted. He knew, without his watching, they would blink away into nothingness again. Maybe they'd simply been fragments of his imagination.

He stumbled back onto the path. Less than half a mile to go. He could clear that, then sleep. Rest and recover his mind. Maybe there'd be a message from Fontaine. Or Holden.

"aaaaaaa *hah*!"

The laugh. A barking, shocked thing. Unmistakably originating behind him.

"Hel . . . hello?" He shouted toward the bulkhead without turning around. He wouldn't look, that would be a mistake. If he looked, he might *see*. Might give the monsters flesh.

No response. Just quiet. Quiet . . . then the *laugh*. Ben ran.

When he'd been a kid, it'd been up to him to turn off the lights at night. His mother would be fast asleep for her early shift, his father locked away in his studio chasing a dream of greatness that he couldn't admit had long left him behind. So, it was left to Ben to maintain the sheen of normalcy, shutting off the lights a single aspect of a tattered and fragmented whole. It frightened Ben to do it, but it would be worse come the morning, being blamed for burning through the electricity bill. He would walk the house from front to back, flicking switches then hightailing out of the room, outrunning the darkness. He knew darkness gave monsters powers. Free reign to slink across the room. To trip Ben up, catch him, and probe his skin with knife-thin nails. To turn Ben into their living doll to poke, prod, and turn inside out. Ben couldn't breathe until he was safe beneath the covers, never looking back. If he looked, if he saw, that'd make the monsters real.

Now, the monsters were stalking him again. Behind him, laughing in staccato bursts.

"aaaaaaa *hah*!"

Footsteps now too, like sparks popping from a fire. Not one set of feet. *Two*. Dogging his own. *Catching up.*

Or . . . or was that the tapping he'd heard miles and miles back? That steady rhythm. *Taptaptap. Tap tap tap. Taptaptap.* Coming from all sides—behind and running ahead, or vice versa.

Too many sounds, too much distraction. The laughter, the footsteps, *his* footsteps too, his breathing. A sonic assault.

Behind. Something definitely behind.

What could it be? A nameless sound . . . or a nameless *terror*? He had to look. He was an adult. A fucking adult. He had to look, had to be certain. Otherwise he'd sweat and hyperventilate and let his imagination continue to make beasts of the darkness. That couldn't happen. Not when he was by himself with miles to go. The bulkhead to 520 was just ahead. The shadow of the Way Station. Now. Now he would look.

Ben stopped, planting his aching, tired feet on the ground. The other footsteps stopped too, not matching his own but a moment later like an ill-timed echo.

"Who's there? Answer me!"

No response again, not even the laugh. Ben steeled himself. Turn around. He'd have to turn around or keep running to keep the darkness from swallowing him. Two deep breaths, licked cracked lips. Slowly . . . slowly twisted his head around, facing the long way back. Everything lit and watery-bright from the floor runners. Good. Light always triumphed over evil.

But the runners flickered. Sizzling with failing electricity. Switched off. Back on. Strobing. Enough that—

There. Were those . . . *shapes* in the near darkness? Like people. It couldn't be. No one could be here, not this far, not now. The sounds had been tricks of his imagination, now his eyes were playing along too.

No, there. Right there. Someone, *something* three-quarters of the way back. A figure slinking along the curved walls. *Inside* the tunnel. Bouncing in an ephemeral, gravity-less jaunt. Holding hands with a second figure. Smaller. Both bloated in a crude imitation of human form. Skin blackened, sloughing off their frames to the floor in wet-sick *plops.*

Horrors. Coming toward him.

Ben ran. Tearing down the way toward the bulkhead. Equipment slowing him down, the suit cumbersome, working against him. He couldn't let it. He wouldn't be pulled back. Wouldn't become a plaything for the monsters to turn inside out and gawk at his precious insides. Monsters that *were there.* There's always a bigger fish, and now that bigger fish was coming for him. A scream was building in his chest but wouldn't come out. It was trapped, like him. He felt out of air. Suit screaming to slow down. Chest burning.

Don't look back again. Don't look. Not now not *now not nownotnownownow.*

He couldn't slow his momentum, slammed into the bulkhead. Bounced backward. Regained his footing, ignoring the pain and fatigue. Fumbled his hands into the locking mechanism.

"aaaaaaa *hah*!"

The laugh. Closer. Distorted. Building from a bark to a terrible banshee wail to something else. Something dreadful.

Prime twist p— . The mechanism stuck. Wouldn't open.

"COME ON!"

He punched it. Kicked. Pain flaring, snot dribbling from his nose. *Pull.*

The blue light switched to green. The doors hissed and parted. Too slow. Ben hurled himself over the lip when it was only halfway down. Gripped the opposite mechanism and rammed it closed. Reversing, open to closed. Still too slow. He grabbed the door and tried pulling it down. Faster. It needed to close faster. *He* needed it closed.

He could see them in his periphery. Getting closer. People. An adult and child. Not humans, but demons. Laughing, laughing, and laugh—

Ben heaved his weight onto the door and it crashed shut, hissing out steam. His hands twitched and shook as he primed the mechanism.

"Not there. Not safe. Not yet. Not. There. *Yet!*"

Locked.

He stepped back, lungs heaving. Staring at the door. Was that it? Was that –

"aaaaaaa *ha!*"

He fell backward, bumping into the door to Mile 520. Twisted his ankle, fumbling toward the Way Station door. Another lock. Another shaking hand. Laughter filling his head. He could just—

WAY STATION 04 | TIGHT ROPE

O*pen it!*
Ben fell into the station. Closed the door but unlike the others, there was no lock above the handle.

"Lock! Where's the fucking lock!"

There, on the floor against the airlock's far wall, blown out of its housing. Irreparable. Fine. Fine, the bulkhead would be enough to keep them out. *Had* to be enough.

He pushed the air recycler through its machinations, huffing with exertion—but air kept whistling through the lock's hole. Quickly, he pulled his duct tape out, slapping three strips over the hole, then a fourth for good measure before punching the recycler again. The air hissed and heaved against the strip seeming like it might rip free, puffing outward, outward. Holding. Green light. Ben's hands were already on his helmet as he pushed into the Way Station and slammed the door behind, obscuring vision as he groped at the clasps, his breath coming in short, jagged bursts.

Something in the tunnel. Things. Plural. *Not just a figment. Something REAL. Had to be.*

Tears began to stream from his eyes as the helmet's strap stuck. He'd been warned this would happen—hallucinations. Now, they were coming. He needed out. Out of the helmet. Out of the suit. *Out out out.* He was roving around the Way Station like a drunk. Rocking back and forth, wrenching at the helmet.

"I'm already losing my mind. I'm . . . I'm fucking," the clasp *clicked*, unlocking. "*LOSING IT.*" He ripped the helmet off his face with a roar.

And saw the ransacked Way Station.

The bedding had been torn apart and flung across the room in an array of puffy white-cloud innards. The computer monitor was smashed in, its circuitry ripped out and dangling from its fragmented screen like bright intestines. The pneumatics looked marred from an unsuccessful attempt to rip it from its bearings.

The walls were wet. Soaked. Black-red liquid splashed and streaked. Lots of it, too much. Dripping from the ceiling and corners, spattered across the window-wall then used to write a series of indecipherable words.

Ben gaped, uncomprehending. Tasting the iron tang in the air. Blood, had to be. Mingling with the stench of his own fear—a noxious, heady fume.

Careful now. This is the tight rope. Is this real, or only your mind? Step carefully or this is the moment you crack.

"I . . . I . . . I c-c-can't break. I. Will. Not."

Only a matter of time.

Ben walked to the window. Reached a shaking bare hand to the glass. Feeling the cold emanating. Touched, smeared the writing there. Looked at his hands. Real. Real as could be.

He jumped back as if electrocuted. Wiping his hands, frantic, against his jumpsuit. Smearing it there too, down to the knee. Spreading it. It wouldn't get out now. Now he was marked.

He wanted to pace, to move. Somehow locomotion felt like progress, but he could only stand. Stare. Shadows outside, horrors in the tunnel, blood in the station. Surrounded. Watched. Always watched.

Ben snatched his helmet. He needed them now. Out. It was time to leave. Evac. *OUT.* He punched the relay.

"Fontaine . . . *FONTAINE.* I need you!"

The empty drone.

"Fucking, *Fontaine.* I need *out.* Now. I'm in DANGER!"

He let go of the relay. Gripped the helmet in both hands. Banged it against his forehead. The duct tape leaving a sticky scum across his skin. He punched at the wall—not knowing what else to do—over and over. Tears dribbled down his nose. It was useless.

A matter of time A matter of time A matter—

He backed up. Needed to run. There was nowhere to go, but nothing else he could do. Not even put on his helmet, just rush out into the miles and miles of tunnel until air failed him. Until his blood boiled. His breaths came too hot, too quickly, his vision blurring at the edges.

It was mad. *He was mad.* It was a fact now. It was the only explanation. He stumbled to the door, slipping on the blood. Reaching for the air cycler handle.

And felt a caress on his face. No, not his face. His head. His frontal lobe. A gentle warmth welling and spreading from within. His eyes clouded, the world went dark. Momentum threw him to the floor.

VISIONARY

She stands in front of him, dressed all in white. Cheeks dimpled with a smile. Surrounded by people.

Not people as they should be, but splices of time molded to human shapes. Component parts torn from a vast fabric, stitched and sewn haphazardly. Light and dark, yin and yang, summer and storm.

Summer. Ben and Ellie moving into their Chicago apartment together. A joking fight about an ugly clock taking prominence on the mantle. Comparing rug burns from sex on the carpeted landing. The sunlight coming through the too-bright bedroom window, waking them both. Whispering potential names for future children over a bottle of wine.

Storm. Teddy and Ben receiving a life-changing grant. Popped champagne bottles, press conferences, and television interviews. Red-penned calendars and deadlines. Late nights and missed dates. The need to move halfway across the world to London to be closer to investors and contractors. The shouting matches with Ellie, the breakup and mend.

Summer. Jet-setting across to England together, leaving everything and starting fresh. Tea along a canal near their flat. A glue fight while wallpapering a shoddy room. Nights out at an art class, drinking wine and painting. A spontaneous trip to Amsterdam. Ice-skating and walking through fresh fallen snow. A whirlwind proposal. A yes.

Now the wedding. Ben coming forward, knowing there are people all around, but seeing only her. Emerald eyes and auburn hair. A hitching hyperventilation, but not fear. Only a sense of being *right*.

Just breathe.
Lifting her veil. Fire in her eyes. Her hair.
Camera shutters like pattering rain. Flashbulb lightning. Rolling thunder.
Ben turns away. A moment, only a moment. The control room, a desk with a single piece of paper beneath a lamp. A pen. Waiting for him. Stepping closer, the cameras *click-clicking*. Another moment. His moment.
"*You want to be a visionary, it starts here.*"
Just breathe just breathe.
The pen in his hand. Signing. Feeling wrong. Wrong name? Wrong time? Blue ink flowing out, turning black, becoming fire. Burning across the page, traveling to his hand. Engulfing. Red. Red flame. Hyperventilating harder now.
"Ben."
The veil is back across her face, but she's not smiling. Isn't wearing white anymore, but gray-black, like ash. The people around not dancing but jittering, as if living in extreme rewind. Jostling. The whole ceiling on fire now, water up to their ankles.
Ellie's face framed perfectly. Just *there*.
He reaches forward and his red-flame hand touches hers. Travels up her arm, engulfing. He can't feel it, but she can. It hurts her. No. No, not now. Not on their wedding day. He moves closer, but the water holds him back. And the cameras. The people calling his name. Not people. Bodies. An unholy chorus melding with the cacophony of a storm.
Justbreathejustbreathejustbreathe
Ellie screams.

WAY STATION 04-2 | SIGNAL

He woke still feeling Ellie's fingers interlaced in his own, but when he tried holding tighter, they were no longer there. Like a phantom limb, a part of him once, now cut away. The wedding ring caught the gleam of the fluorescent light, the gold band reflecting white against his tawny skin. He'd almost forgot it was there, then felt guilty at the thought.

Ben sat up and rubbed at his jaw through the mat of his beard, chin sore from where it had smacked off the floor. Momentarily confused—and terrified—to find he wasn't wearing his helmet or suit, not knowing where he was or how he'd gotten there. Then he saw the clear plastic cube of the airlock and his disorientation receded to cool clarity. The Way Station. The tight spaces and undulating blue aura of ocean. He wondered if being down here could permanently impair vision, like opening your eyes after sunbathing and the world takes on a single-shade hue.

Dawn was breaking in the world above, the ocean around growing lighter by degrees with each passing moment. He struggled to remember why he was in the airlock without helmet or suit. Or why his knuckles were sore, throat scraped raw.

For the moment, it didn't matter. He could still smell Ellie's perfume. Could almost feel her body next to his on the uneven double bed back in their old apartment. Before the move. Before things went wrong. That's why he was *here*, in the tunnel.

His hand brushed shattered plastic on the floor. Pieces of the computer monitor lay pulverized nearby and there were white-line scrapes on the window glass. Ben twisted where he sat, events coming together in a flooding, seamless stream. The jellyfish. The horrors. His building panic. The blood.

But everything was . . . different. The monitor was still broken and the station ransacked, but also looking as if there'd been a shoddy attempt at cleanup. The detritus brushed off to the room's perimeter to leave an open space in the center. And the blood. There was no blood. Not on the floor, walls, or window. Nothing.

Only a matter of—

"Fucking stop it! Enough. There's . . . there's an explanation for all of this . . . Has to be?"

He groaned as he found his feet and stepped back into the Way Station proper. He could almost see the path he took before he'd passed out: his discarded suit and helmet, a greasy handprint on the wall. He went closer.

There was a discoloration on the glass. A faint smell of bleach and ammonia, evidence of circular wiping on the wall.

"Was . . . someone in here?" The thought should've alarmed him, but it seemed impossible.

He noticed a spot on the wall—missed during clean up. A flake of rust-brown, not red. *Dried* blood. Old. Old enough for the moist air to cool and stick it into the glass. Far older than how long he'd been there.

There'd been blood here before . . . but no longer. Cleaned up. So how had he seen it? *Touched* it?

"Is this it? Have I . . ." Swallowed. *Mad.* He could say it. "It's delusions. This is what Ashvin warned me about. Solitary, the-the fucking . . . isolation. This is what happens. Only a matter of time."

Shadows shifted and Ben shrank backward, raising his hands. Afraid, breath hitching.

"Stop. *FUCK*. Jumping at shadows."

But what if it's the octopus? What if the demons are outside, watching you now? Waiting for you to leave?

The calm was slipping away. Quickly. Realization spiking his blood, forcing him to stare at the glass again. At himself.

"Oh fuck . . . you're losing it, aren't you? You're losing your mind. Coasting right on that edge."

Saying it aloud made it real. Made his chest hitch and tears rise. Did he know what was real anymore?

"How do you plan on fixing things if you can't fix yourself, huh? Can't go forward if you lose your mind. What are you going to do?

Now, while you have your wits, it's time to figure it out." A shuddering breath. "While you still can."

Turning around would be retreat. Giving up. But could he outlast his crumbling mind for another two hundred miles with nothing to stem the flood of anxious thoughts? And what about the monsters—

did you really see them?

—waiting for him behind the bulkhead door? At least he'd seen them and knew what to expect. The way forward was entirely unknown to him. It could be better . . . or infinitely worse.

"But I promised myself I could do this. For her."

But that'd been before. Before the terrible shadows, the loneliness, the crushing solitude. Could he face it again, could he handle it? His lower lip trembled, knowing the truth.

"I was a fool . . . I was a fool to think I could do this."

What about Ellie?

"There has to be another way. They haven't dismantled it yet, right? Where there's a will, there's a way."

He smiled but didn't *feel* it. His journey was coming to an end. He could sense it, resigned but somewhat glad.

He would turn around.

Ben started gathering his things. As he pulled the packet from the pneumatic tube, he noticed how loose the coveralls sat on his body, wondering whether his all-paste diet wasn't nourishing but withering him to skin and bones. He checked his rations and air in his bag, calculating how much he'd need to reach a radio signal. But even as he put his mind to the practical future, self-revulsion tugged the corners of his fake smile down.

"I didn't fail. I'm not. This is the way it has to be. I *have* to turn back. No choice." He breathed deep, forcing the self-deprecation toward anger. "I didn't fail. I didn't!" He picked up his helmet, screamed into the mouthpiece. "You hear me, Fontaine? I didn't fail!"

He screamed it out, wanting to give life to the words. Make them real for himself to hear. For the octopus or fucking demons dancing in the tunnel. Fontaine would never hear his defiance, the connection to New York was long severed.

Which made it all the stranger when a tinny voice came from the helmet. Pitched low, quiet. A whisper.

"*. . . further. Just a l . . . further.*"

Then.

"He's tryi . . . o stop yo . . . please."

A voice. There'd been a voice. Was . . . was this another delusion? No—maybe he *was* going mad, but there had been someone on the other end of the line. Not Fontaine. A woman.

"Hello?"

Nothing.

"Who's there?"

Could it have been SGO? Outside the ocean swelled and dimmed with light. Like a passing cloud.

"Hello? ANSWER ME!"

Nothing returned. No words, no response. But there was something there. The hiss of an open line. Ripe with possibilities. Ben felt his bowels twitch and heave. His body unsure how to handle. Overloaded stimulus.

The devil. The blood. The darkness. The station.

Whispers. Whispers down here in the ocean depths. Speaking. Speaking to him.

"Please . . . are you still there?"

Taptaptap. Tap tap tap. Taptaptap.

The pattern he'd been hearing. Those distant echoes, but over the relay—not in the tunnel at all. Beaten out. Clear and deliberate. *Taptaptap. Tap tap*

"Ellie?"

The line went dead.

Ben thumbed the relay, but knew it was useless. Understanding now that someone was signaling to him. Whoever had spoken to him just now—

Ellie? Absolutely not. Couldn't be Ellie. The London station ahead? Rescue party? Communications from a boat way above water?

—had been signaling down the tunnel, had been doing it for him to hear. Had been trying for a while. The same sequence over and over. Somehow familiar to him but he couldn't quite place it.

But then he did, becoming clear in his mind. As clear as the pattern had been over the line moments ago. Of course Ben knew that sequence, just as any fisherman, sailor, or Boy Scout did. Three quick punches, three elongated, then three quick again. Morse Code.

SOS.

WAY STATION 04-3 | SCRIBBLE

~~S~~*~~omething seriously disturbed down here.~~ Not alone(?). Marine life attacking the tubing. ~~It's all gone fucking haywire.~~ This is wrong. Please report.*

Ben scribbled furiously on the backside of the psychiatric test with a pencil. Why hadn't he thought to send a message this way back in Way Station 03?

Idiot. Goddamn—

The pencil tip snapped. He switched to a pen, cursing all the while. Writing, crossing out—his handwriting manic and jumpy. That wouldn't do, he needed to slow down.

"Can't *look* like I'm losing my mind."

Ben balled up the paper. Deep breaths. Calm. *Calm*. He pulled a fresh sheet of paper.

Have arrived at Way Station 04, Mile 520. Radio communication has been severed.

Did he mention the demons? No, he wasn't sure they were real himself, was he? What about the ransacked Way Station? Something wrong had definitely happened in here, but what could he put? Chaos inside the station, possible years-old blood staining the walls? That wouldn't go over well either, better keep that to himself too.

Marine life potentially compromising tunnel integrity. Have begun receiving SOS signal.

He looked it over. Good. The writing was lucid and clear.

WHAT IS STATUS OF DRILL? Mission has become hazardous. Send resupply to

Only moments ago he'd resolved to stop and turn around. But that'd been before the woman called over the line. Did he go forward—toward 781, the Belly, the unknown, farther from comms—or did he turn back—*face the possibility of no rations, water, or O2, not to mention devils, octopi, and other monsters.* Which way would he go? Had to commit.

Way Station 05

Forward. Someone—a woman—was asking him to go further, and he'd go.

"If she was talking to me . . . if she's real."

Delusions were his real problem now, no getting around it. The isolation and potential madness creeping in. The issue wasn't whether he was hallucinating—that point was well established—but determining which things he saw were fabrications and which were real.

Ben didn't fill out the psychiatric test on the opposite side, but carefully folded the paper, fit it in the pneumatic tube, and sent it off toward New York. He waited until he was certain it had passed another bulkhead and joined the general pneumatics system. Listening closely. That done, he faced the room.

What happened here that resulted in the complete teardown? That, at least, was not a fabrication. And the blood? If he had to guess, there'd been a struggle a long time back, someone had been hurt, followed by heavy cleanup.

"But I'd touched it . . . *slipped* in it. I even wiped it on my—" But when he looked down, there was nothing on his jumpsuit. No blood, no evidence there ever had been any. That was disconcerting. *Still*, something had definitely gone wrong here . . . something he felt he should know but couldn't quite place. Pieces to a puzzle he didn't know the shape of.

"Maybe this was the last scavenger's blood . . . maybe this is where he went mad."

No scavenger had made it this far, so Fontaine had said. But the Ear had also told Ben he wouldn't have been the first person to disappear down here . . . maybe another scavenger was still down here, creeping along the walls. What had the voice said?

He's tryi . . . o stop yo . . . please.

"He's trying to stop you."

Who . . . who was trying to stop him? And who was *HE*? For that matter, who was *SHE*?

"He. He . . ."

Could it be the octopus . . . ? Could whoever had spoken *know*?

You being followed yet?

Ben set about scavenging the room, feeling more in control with purposeful action. Faced with the impossible yet again, he was finding his footing. He'd read once that if depression or anxiety were threatening to overwhelm, one of the best things to do would be to clean your room. A small act to set the derailing train back on track.

"First and only bit of scrapping I've done all journey, Fontaine. Maybe tearing this room apart will keep my mind from snapping." He shook his head, ripping the sheets off the bed. "Cause I'm getting real sick of this crazy-sane-crazy routine."

He draped the bedding across the ocean-view window, pinning it with duct tape and blocking out the wide beyond. That was good—out of sight, out of mind. Nothing to watch him now.

Next, he tore the pneumatic tube off the wall. Smashed the PVC piping against the floor and picked through the splinters looking for a suitable piece. He had to break an especially long bit, cracking chunks off the side to fashion a jagged edge.

"Goddamn tunnel under the sea, trying to kill me." He looped tape around the shard's smooth bottom, making a makeshift handle. Leaving enough room for a six-inch length of jagged PVC. A knife. Really a prison-style shiv. "Well, I'd like to see them try."

He took a few practice slashes, getting used to the feel and listening to the whistle as it cut air. Ben didn't know what he expected the fragile plastic to hold up against, more likely to shatter than inflict damage. Besides, he wasn't a brawler, hadn't been in a fight all his life, but having the makeshift knife made him feel better. Less vulnerable.

Ben tore the care package open then pooled his resources together on the room's floor like a kid counting Halloween candy. Saved rations tubes plus the new supply gave him just enough to see him through two Way Stations. Water was well stocked, no issues there. O2 could potentially become a problem. He was good for one Way Station, but not two. He'd have to be careful, but all in all, he was doing well with supplies.

He tossed aside the USB drive from the care package—useless—and searched deeper, looking for anything he may have missed. He upended the bag on the floor, shifted through, found a small gray-white tube in a plastic bag. The sealant for his cracked helmet. He sat cross-legged on the floor and pulled the helmet close, face up. He peeled the strips of duct tape off with his overgrown fingernails, exposing the spiderweb cracks below now smeared with tape scum, uncapped the tube with his teeth and poised the nozzle over the first indentation.

Stopped. Not certain why. Compelled. Instead, he stared at the visor for a long while. Smelling his sour-sweat stench wafting out, sickened at how comforting he found it. There was a scratch just above the glass where his head had hit the floor, looking like a bullet ping.

He thumbed the relay.

"Can anyone hear me?"

Hollow static, like listening to a shell washed up on a digital shore.

"My name is Ben Breckenridge. I was hired as a scavenger for Steel Glass Ocean . . . I'm not sure what I am now. Currently located at Way Station Zero-Four at Mile 520, heading east."

His voice had an air of authority that was surprising. How quickly things changed in a matter of moments. Mad to lucid, glass to steel.

"If you're listening, I mean no harm."

Quiet. Empty and flat. He stared at his makeshift shiv. Nowhere near enough to battle whatever was out there.

"Please, whoever's listening . . . I'm . . . I'm just trying . . ."

Ben tossed the helmet onto the bed without applying the sealant. If things got hairy, he wasn't sure he wanted to stay alive very long anyway. A few punches to the glass and he could end it quick.

But then no Ellie. No sun.

Sleep. He needed to sleep. Ben curled into a ball on the cleared floor, trying to pretend he was somewhere else. Maybe, when he woke up in the morning, comms would be back. The station would be clean, how it should be. There'd be knocking . . . knocking on the door. Rescue. Calling him a fool for walking so far but pulling him out. Kicking and screaming.

"Sleep . . . just sleep."

The tunnel bucked in the current and he tried to slip away. Knowing he wouldn't.

MILE 520 | STEP

That first step back on the road was the hardest, like crossing an unpredictable frontier. His fevered eyes jumped from the immediate corners to down the path, then out to the water beyond looking for dangers. Saw nothing—no demons, no monsters. Just the empty tunnel and quiet seas. Shadowless and silent.

He drew a shuddering breath, fingers flexing on the makeshift knife.

"Come this far . . . now it's time to go forward. You got this. One foot, then the next."

A shudder, a swallow, a step. Out the bulkhead, into the mile. The door slid closed behind him, an ominous drop of tumblers cycling shut. He felt exposed, sandwiched between the suffused blue light, and tried to rediscover the awe he'd felt on the first mile. Seeing what so few people had experienced in their lives. The quiet. The peacefulness.

Now, it just made him feel cold and vulnerable. A cruel joke. He was alone. So utterly alone.

RECOGNITION

Ben was late more often than not.

He could blame London for that: a lack of familiarity with its winding streets, the ever-present rain constantly slowing traffic to a crawl at certain intersections, work swallowing up more and more of his time until "work/life balance" became more morbid joke than reality—but those were all excuses. Half excuses at best. The truth was he knew London all too well now, the rain did nothing but patter and stain his new expensive boots, and work... well, he did that to himself, and gladly.

His hands had seemed fused to electronics ever since the move overseas: either with a mouse or stylus at work—clicking, drafting, shaping—or his phone outside of it—emailing, checking, tapping in frustration. His world reduced to pixels and panic, so much so that he nearly passed by the cinema while checking his inbox for the eleventh time since leaving the office.

"Sorry, sorry sorry sorry." Ben shook off the rain as the Barbican Cinema doors hissed closed behind him and he beelined across the carpet.

Ellie sat at one of the café's tables, teacup steaming in front of her, a magazine on her lap. She looked up as he came in, her mouth set firm, gaze sharp but not yet hard.

"Sorrysorrysorry." He kept repeating, blending the words together and giving them a higher lilt, as if cutesiness could make up for transgressions. He leaned in, kissed her cheek, imparting a few raindrops from his hair to dot her knit sweater.

"It's fine. *Stop.*" A smile, a firm word.

"Better finish that tea quick, doubt you can bring it in the theater." Ben scanned the room, trying to clock anyone who might be around, might recognize him. The thought both annoyed and thrilled him . . . but the room was empty, only staff clearing tables and refilling coffee creamer jars. "Where is everyone? I thought you said this movie was supposed to be some big thing."

"Everyone's already inside."

"Well, we better get in there before it starts. Previews are—" Ben looked at his watch and froze. Forty-five minutes late.

"Long over." Ellie looked up at him, then motioned to the seat in front of her.

"*Shit.*" Ben slumped, the exhaustion coming through him now, the day's rigors finally catching up and pulling him into the chair as if it were magnetized. "I'm sorry, El. You were looking forward to this. You'd told me so many times!"

"It's okay." She crossed her arms, smirked. "I'm just going to have to start going to my movies without you is all."

He could hear the lightness in her tone, but knew the truth lay behind it. It was becoming a pattern of his: ten minutes late here, a forgotten text there, Ellie calm, measured, frustrated. Guilt twisted his guts to knots.

"I'm kidding. Really," Ellie said, sensing the air. "I know how busy you are."

She dropped the magazine on the table between them, and suddenly Ben was staring at himself, with Teddy just behind. Their faces splayed across the front page spread of *Architectural Digest*, stamped with a heading, "Visionaries?," the question mark artfully larger than the word.

"Seems I'm married to a celebrity now." Ellie grinned, her snaggletooth catching her lip. "You want to tell me I was right now, or . . . ?"

Ben chuckled, picked up the magazine and stared himself in the face. He thought his eyes looked funny. He was smiling in the picture— could remember smiling at the photoshoot—but it seemed his eyes said more than his face and mouth were putting on. Wanting to soak up the moment but uncomfortable in his skin. Like he didn't belong there.

"I bet Teddy is loving all the attention," Ellie was saying, but Ben was only half listening. "Using it in the pubs on all the unsuspecting London girls."

Teddy, that's right. Ben finally shifted focus, noticing him in the frame too. Teddy, carefree as ever. It'd always been easy for him, hadn't it? Even back in Chicago—*before then*, he was sure. Teddy stood assured behind Ben, hands in pockets, smirking and leaning, at ease even when he wasn't. *He* looked like he belonged.

Ben started rifling through the pages, looking for the article. It was all coming back now. The interviewer had homed in on Teddy like he was the brains behind everything. But Ben knew who was truly to thank—Teddy did too for that matter, though he'd never admit it. The attention should be on him, right? After all, it was Ben's drive to better the world that pushed them through all those long, thankless nights. That brought them *here*. He longed for the moment the spotlight would swivel his way and dreaded it in even measure. Could already hear that question: "Why now? Why *you*?" Where was the damn article? He—

"*Hey.*"

Ben's face shot up. Ellie was staring at him, steam no longer rising from her teacup. He thought he could hear the lingering echo of her voice but couldn't place the words. A whole conversation slipping by without him noticing.

"Are you okay?"

"Yeah." Ben shook his head, closed the magazine quickly like its contents might burn him. "Sorry, sorry. I got carried away there." He forced another chuckle, shook his head again trying to clear his thoughts. He reached his hands across the table, took her left in both of his. Pushed Teddy, work, everything out of his mind. Focused on her. "How was your day?"

She glanced at him, worry lines creasing her forehead, then looked down to their hands. She brought her free hand up, joined it to the others, and squeezed. "Good. No, it was just fine. No one speaks up in class so there's just long silences. Feels like a waste. And I haven't heard back on any of my applications. Just realizing how hard it is trying to work in immigration in a country that's not your own, blah, blah, blah." She grinned, looked out the window. "I think I'm just out of sorts. You know how I get with the rain, never can quite get on the right footing."

"You're like a little flower, need sunlight."

She turned back to him and raised an eyebrow, avoiding comment on the terrible line. "Just getting used to the city is all."

"I get that." He squeezed her hands back. "Well, seeing as I ruined our movie date, how about I take you to get an early dinner? Even I can't mess that up right?"

"Sure. Sure, I'd like that."

Behind her, Ben could see the sky beyond the window lighting some, the patter of the rain dropping to a whisper. "And would you look at that? Perfect timing." As he helped Ellie put on her coat, Ben found his gaze lingering on that magazine. His eyes. The overlarge question mark beside "Visionaries"—then he purposefully tuned it out.

Outside the air was crisp, the smells sharp and welcoming. They wandered south, hands clutched and pressed close, tripping over one another to avoid puddles, and Ben knew if he could stay like this with Ellie, just wander the rain-slick streets without worrying about work, and tomorrow, and magazines and interviews, he could consider himself full. Happy.

It wasn't until they'd wandered for two blocks that Ben felt his phone buzz with an alert. He tried to ignore it, waiting as long as he could until the weight in his pocket felt like a live wire, something writhing and dangerous that needed to be freed and dealt with before it hurt him, then finally pulling it free.

A text from Teddy. An email in the business account. Red exclamations and *Urgent* labels. Before he knew it, numbers were moving through his head again, a response being drafted, his hands no longer entwined in his wife's but fused to black plastic. Working on the move.

He thought Ellie might have said his name, but for a moment he pretended not to notice. *Just send this email, then you're done with it. Then it's just you and her.* Another email came in. Another.

The tapping of his thumb on the screen became faster, frantic, drumming to the sound of the rain returning.

|BULKHEAD 558/559, TORRENT|

The door to Mile 559 was leaking through its seams. Saltwater rushed over the locking mechanism like a pivot point in a dam, pulsing with a faint but steady yellow light. Ben had never seen a yellow lock before, all the rest had been red, green, or blue. Yellow was for warning, for caution.

"Don't panic yet . . . could be nothing. At least it's not black."

He tiltded his voice higher, trying to offer matter-of-fact encouragement to himself. Surprised at how quickly his mind set to the problem at hand like in Way Station 04. Strangely comforted by a physical problem, rather than something in his head.

Ben thumbed the relay out of habit.

"Hello? Is anyone there? Fontaine . . . ? Uh, lady . . . ?"

Still the empty, dead-air channel. He could count on *that* consistency at least.

Ben smeared water on the LCD screen as he punched it to life. SGO's logo appeared, the power-up bar began to fill. He tapped his foot, impatient, trying not to pay attention to the babble of water behind, wondering if he should be concerned about standing in a compromised bulkhead. Ready to retreat into the open tunnel to his right at a moment's notice.

The spartan menu appeared with its feed of status alerts. Ben scrolled past *MILE 558* and its flurry of green OK symbols: all systems normal. But the readout for *MILE 559* was the opposite: punctuated lists of angry red text. When Ben saw the single rectangle of blue surrounded by red, it confirmed what he'd already suspected:

Mile 559 had flooded.

Ben backed up, watching the water leak down to the floor grating. Staring, as if it were the scene of a horrible accident, one he couldn't look away from. This was exactly the sort of thing he couldn't handle. An insurmountable problem, numbing his limbs as he stared.

Water. So much water. If he opened the door it would rush in, fill the space. His suit would weigh him down. He'd become an immobile statue, stuck at the bottom of the ocean. Hyperventilating until he ran out of O2 or his suit sprung a leak. Turns out he'd been right all along: things were getting worse the deeper in he went. Without support, without resupply, he was marching toward his doom.

Drown. He'd drown.

"I c-c-an't. I can't do this."

Ben backed away from the door, away from the gushing water. How didn't it flood? He could hear a gurgling somewhere below, like a shower drain slurping water. The bulkhead's redundancies seemingly doing their job. He was curious to see it at work, but not curious enough to start ripping up the floor for a closer look. He should get out. Get out of there. Go back. Damn whatever might be backward. It didn't matter. Only survival mattered. He'd been right to want to turn around at Way Station 04, now he was just another forty miles deeper into his supplies.

Stupid. Dumbass. Idiot.

End of the road. Now there truly was nothing he could do. He'd tried. He really did. And he was sorry. Sorry for everything. He turned, ready to hightail.

"... need help ... anyone. My n ... cean. Please. An ... help."

Ben slowly closed his eyes. Damning himself. Knowing, but not moving. Staring at the backward facing open tunnel. So close. He flicked the relay.

"Hello? Can you hear me?" Nothing. Radio whine like a tuning receiver. "Hello? Who is this?"

"... lass Ocean. Send ... OS ... amn, help. Please."

The voice didn't change, like she hadn't heard him. Was only repeating, frustrated. Getting farther away and harder to hear.

"Hello?" Ben said. "*HELLO?*"

Ben wanted it to be wrong. Desperately wanted the voice to simply be a trick of relays or another delusion. Any reason to not go forward and face this problem. It didn't matter that she'd said the company name. What did matter was those two spoken words that cut straight to his heart.

Help. Please.

He looked down into 558, bit his lip hard enough to hurt, and whispered to himself. "You fucking idiot." And turned back into the bulkhead.

He reexamined the LCD screen. Nothing to indicate why the section had filled, whether by a breach or something else. Possibilities and explanations piled in his head, each worse than the last.

Maybe the mid-mile hatch had ripped off leaving a gaping wound. Or the pneumatic tubes had burst, breaching the tunnel—which might mean no care packages ahead. Worse still, maybe the whole tunnel had shred apart and become untethered, end of the line and open to the sea.

What about things inside the tunnel . . . electric eels lying in wait, or sharks, or worse yet—

"Enough! Don't let your mind run. Figure out the problem. Fix it. Help."

Breathe. Just breathe.

Ben paced, tapping on the side of the helmet. He could bypass this section completely if he truly wanted. Backtrack to the porthole hatch in 558, swim out, then pull himself along, hand over hand, until he reached 560 and dropped in. Then carry on.

"Oh, sure. Best option is the fucking *open sea*." He laughed. Gallows humor. "Besides, that'll fill 558 up . . . and 560. Three flooded sections instead of one." He shook his head. Shivered. *All that water.*

That left the second option. The only real option: open the bulkhead door, swim/walk *through* 559, find the problem, and drain the section.

"Easy."

Panic ebbed over his skull, mind racing with plans and problems. The runners might be out and he'd have to go through blind. Bogged down by his heavy pack: blind *and* slow. He could leave the bulk of his pack here so he could move quicker and freely, return when he'd cleared out the tunnel section?

But what if I can't drain the tunnel? What if I can't come back?

He'd have to go forward then, no getting past that. No retreating. No guarantee of rescue or retreat farther on. Split half the equipment and take all his O2, that seemed the best course. If there was one thing he didn't want to go without, it was air.

Ben put his hand on the bulkhead lock. The silver-blue light of the bulkhead to 558/557 a mile back glinted like a distant star, beckoning. He could just walk back the way he'd come. The original plan. Retreat. He didn't have to do this.

"I do. I do have to do this."

He shrugged off his pack, splitting the rations and water, leaving half of both on the tunnel floor just outside the door. Ben stared down at the pile, wondering if he wasn't making a terrible mistake and cutting himself off at the knees. No, he needed to move fast in there, this needed to be done. Besides he'd be back for it. He cycled 558's lock. As the doors whined, he stamped two more pieces of duct tape on the compromised side of his helmet, watching all the while as the bulkheads met and clanged shut, sealing him inside.

Ben turned with exaggerated slowness to 559's door. Breathing heavily, trying not to think. With the doors closed, the leak sounded like a torrent. Clearer, aggressive, and unstoppable.

All that crushing water.

He thumbed the mechanism forward. *Prime*. It flashed red for danger. He bypassed the warning. *Twist*. Flexed his hand on the opening trigger. Paused.

It was dark in the bulkhead, no sun-brightened wash from the window above. The only light came from the angry pulse of the lock. The only sound his own agitated breathing and the water cascading over his hand. He slowed his breathing. Cautious. Urging calm to wash his limbs.

"Easy now. Easy," he said to the lock. "Sometimes you need to do the things that scare you, right?"

Ben jerked the handle back. *Pull*. The lock released.

MILE 559 | DIVE

Water gushed in as the doors peeled away. First a tight spray, then a deluge, spreading over the lips and into the bulkhead. Ben was hurled backward against the door to 558 from the force of the surge, pressed hard.

Wait. Wait for it to fill up, don't try and fight it.

But it was fighting *him*. Pinning him to the wall, the ocean exerting its dominance against this interloper that dared to plunge its depths. Trying to drown him.

The water level built quickly. Cold. Cold like he couldn't believe. Ankle-deep. Knee. Past his waist, chest, then covering his head. Until finally, *finally*, quiet. Still.

Underwater. Truly, for the first time. Entering the submerged tunnel.

It was odd to see the tunnel section so different. Hundreds of miles without variation to face a world entirely distinct from what he'd seen. The runner lights flickered weakly in the gloom, warped with the gentle sway of the water. All else was black as the deep ocean, an ink-stained swirl. Pinned against the bulkhead, it almost seemed as if Ben was looking *down* an illuminated ladder into a vast void.

Ben thumbed his helmet's lamp on, cutting through the night with the thin, white light beam. The helmet's HUD registered he was underwater, its interior scheme shifting to a sudden swamp-green glow. Warnings pulsed in the corners. CAUTION: SUBMERGED.

Yeah, no shit.

"Alright . . . nothing to be alarmed about here. Keep your head. Get in, get out." He crossed into 559 and shut the door behind.

It was a new sensation, walking underwater rather than in the near vacuum. Water pressed in on his limbs, making each step feel leaden and slow. He'd joked that the suit made him an undersea astronaut—but in space there was a buoyancy to your steps. Here, weighted down with his pack, it was like he wore iron shoes, struggling to cut through the depths.

Ben pointed the headlamp at the tunnel walls, the floor. Side to side, up and down. Searching for a telltale rip or rupture, seeing nothing but the aquarium 559 had become. Clownfish explored near then darted away, sensing danger. A starfish puckered the glass to his right and a pod of seahorses pumped past in the speckled light. He reached out to touch them, smiling as they whirled around him then sped away.

"Not so bad, underwater." His voice sounded hollow, yet more intimate.

He stumbled, foot catching what looked to be milk-white coral. He shook his boot free, watching as the "coral" drifted up in the lance of light, then back down. Bones. The skull of a hammerhead shark.

Ben's hackles rose. Wary. Questions and explanations skittering over his mind. Maybe the hammerhead got in but was too big to get back out? Starved? Or . . . could there be a predator down here? Something powerful enough to kill a hammerhead *shark*? Could . . . could it be the octo—

"*Stop.* Don't think. Move. Just move."

Ben pushed against the rising fear. *Stay on target.* He counted each step. Each breath. Searching, searching. Time slowed with his movements. Nearly to the halfway mark. He was sweating in his helmet. He could taste the salt tang on his lips. Listening to the groan of the tunnel or its tethers. Feet slipping on the lichen that sway like grass on the floor. Ahead, the junction box, still there. And—

The hatch above was open. Its hinges swung away from the ceiling, rust just beginning to form at the pivot points. But the cover was there, not ripped away. Just an open porthole, a problem he could fix. Simple.

Ben jumped, hoping the water would give him the extra bounce to reach the hatch, but his heavy pack kept him down. He shrugged the straps off, immediately feeling closer to weightlessness. Freed. Crazily, he thought how nice it might be to swim a bit. To enjoy himself.

All work and no play—

"Nope. Cut that line right there. No *Shining*, no swimming. Get it done."

Ben kicked up to the hatch, gripping the wheel handle with one hand, the open lip with his other, feet firmly planted on the half-ladder stuck to the tunnel wall. He purposefully didn't think about the empty vastness beyond the circular hole and tried to swing the lock inward. The hatch held firm, stuck. Using both hands, he put his weight in and tried pulling it closed, pleased as the metal shifted slightly, groaning.

A shadow moved beyond the opening.

Ben froze. Stared out. His helmet light arced across the consuming dark. Nothing. *But there* had *been something there.* Something large, moving with a bizarrely fluid grace.

"If it's that big, it can't get in here. Focus."

Back to the hatch. He gripped. *Tugged.* Yanking as hard as his body would allow. His bruised knuckles roared with pain as he made a fist, but he carried on. Close the hatch, drain the tunnel, then he'd be safe.

The hatch shifted again. Whined. Caked-on rust shed particles like dirty snow in his helmet beam. *More, come on. Pull. PULL.*

Gears shuddered. Loosening. Already, Ben's body ached—his legs from the stress of walking in the water, his arms from the work now. But he was close, he—

A massive tentacle wrapped around the hatch's lip. Probing.

Ben screamed, startled, swinging away. Terrified as he watched the tentacle floating with the eerie purpose of sentience. Searching. For something. For him. Ben eased off, floating away from the appendage. Trying to shut out his mind, whispering:

You know what that is. You know what that belongs to.

Another tentacle slapped at the tunnel glass by Ben's head. Then another. Suctioning the glass with purple-white nightmare mouths. Folding around the manhole-sized opening. Thick, oily tentacles gripping any available surface with slimy muscles. Trying to get in.

An octopus can bend itself. Fold.

"It can get in."

Ben yanked at the porthole cover, screaming with the effort. Adrenaline both sapping and pushing his strength. The hatch was closing but not fast enough, mere inches at a time. A tentacle twitched in the water, feeling the movement. Slithered, snakelike. Lashed out. *Wrapped* around Ben's wrist and tugged.

He yelped, pulling back, fighting. Headlight arcing into the space beyond the hole in panicked jerks. Showing flashes of a face beyond the dark. Alien and menacing. Leathery skin, black hole eyes, and mandibles like writhing, putrefied intestines.

The octopus.

Warning bells pealed through Ben's head and helmet. More tentacles appeared. More than he could count. Engulfing the glass, the hatch hole. Groping for Ben's arm. Now his *head*. Suction cups wrapping around his visor glass, obscuring sight. Making the fragile glass creak and crack.

He groped at his belt, blind with panic. This was it. He'd be pulled out into the open ocean. Ripped apart by a fucking *kraken* from the deep. Devoured. Unless he fought. Unless he found what he needed. Unless he found—*there*.

Ben lashed out with his PVC shiv. Slicing at the tentacles on his arm, his face. Flailing. Striking as quickly as the water would allow. Screaming from sheer terror. Not caring what he hit. The octopus, the tunnel, his own arm.

The octopus made no sound. No crazed scream. No groan of pain. The face-sucking tentacle recoiled. Slackened, wary. Ben hacked at the one round his wrist until it eased its grip, trailing dark blue blood. Just enough for Ben to swim backward, back behind the hatch to use it as a shield.

He couldn't hear his own panicked breaths. Just the *ping*, *slide*, and *slurp* of skin-like tentacles groping the hatch again. Searching. Searching for him.

Ben dropped the shiv, taking the wheel lock in both hands. He twisted upside down so that he was staring down at the floor, fumbling for purchase with his feet on the ceiling. Slipping, sliding. Finally, sticking. Tensed. Gave the hatch a good *heave*. Felt it buck, shift. Groan. Squelching as it worked against the soft rigidity of the tentacle mass.

The octopus's appendages railed against the pincer press between hatch and lip. Flailing wildly now, spasming.

Ben was lightheaded from effort. Black spots filled his vision. Determined. A tentacle slapped against his face. Suctioning. Ben kicked against the glass with both feet. *Pushed. Screaming.*

The hatch snapped shut with a heavy, metallic *clank*.

Ben quickly spun the sub-style wheel lock hand over hand until it would go no more. Fast as he could. Breath hot and rapid, filling his helmet. A tentacle drifted near. He yelped, twisting away. But it had been severed from the main body. Floating limp, down to the floor.

He punched the locking sequence in the keypad. A digital trill screeched out. A light appeared on the hatch. Green. *LOCKED.* Safe.

Relief depleted the last of his strength. The danger over, the tension drained from Ben's body and he fell away from the ceiling, dropped slowly back to the bottom. Tired. So goddamn tired. But the threat was still there. He didn't want to look, but he had to. Had to see the octopus's vengeful face staring back. But there was nothing there. Just the darkness.

His back hit the floor just as a long *beep* filled the tunnel. Then a gurgling hum of a drainage pump kicking into gear somewhere below. Slowly but surely, the tunnel began to drain.

Ben had done it. Could finally breathe. He laughed, the whole of his body aching. It would take at least an hour for the section to drain completely, but that was fine. He'd lay right here and watch the level tick lower, until—

Craaaack.

Ben pushed to his feet. Ready. Expecting to see tentacles enveloping the glass in that python vise grip. But his light fell on . . . nothing. Nothing changed, just the water draining.

Crackcrack. Craaaaack.

He spun in place, couldn't tell where it was coming from. Where . . . where was it—then he saw it. The crack on his helmet visor. Spiderwebbing. Spreading. *Collapsing.*

"Nonono."

He started to run. Half walking and half swimming, moving quickly toward Mile 560.

The tunnel was draining too slowly and he wasn't moving fast enough. Visions flashed in his mind of the helmet flooding with water. He should've used the sealant when he had a chance. Why didn't he use it? Now, it might cost him his life.

The pressure was building. The cracks spreading. The glass buckling. How soon would be too much? If the visor broke, it wouldn't matter if he made it to the bulkhead—his suit would be useless.

Go. Go now. No time to waste. One foot in front of the other. Walk. WALK.

Water breached one of the cracks. Then another. *Another.*

Not rushing in like with the bulkhead doors but dribbling down the plate. Enough to signal the plate's integrity was failing. The visor would buckle. He could feel the cold of it brushing his chin, dripping along his neck and down into the suit below.

"Fuuuck. *Fuck!*"

There was true panic in his voice, images flashing through his mind of a sudden surge shattering the visor, spreading out across his nose, his eyes, his mouth. Water filling his suit, all the way to his feet. Weighing him down even more. Drowning him standing up.

"No. *Nonono*. It's still holding. I'm still alright."

Concentrate. Easy now. Don't panic. You panic, you die.

But the bulkhead seemed so far away. He thought he could see the door ahead, the lock light, but knew it could just be shadows on the wall. All while the water coming through the visor crack was gaining speed. He could hear it bubbling through, pulsing in tandem with the flickering, inconsistent runners. Everything around bathed in eerie silence. In shadows. As if the tunnel was holding its breath, waiting for the inevitable. Ben pushed forward, his body screaming alone. Move. Move or drown.

Crack. Craaack. Crack!

The visor seemed to dip toward his face. The water no longer dribbling but spraying inward. It shot into his face like a burst fire hydrant, slashing his right cheek with ocean water in a tight spray.

Cold. So cold it hurt. Paralyzing the right side of his face and seeming to sap the strength from his limbs as it coursed down into his suit. Made him want to stop, for his body to freeze up and collapse inward. He was running out of time.

Something struck his leg. He twisted, fell. Nearly screamed out. Kept his eyes on the door, just ahead, no time to dawdle. His imagination running with images of the octopus pulling at his legs, keeping him just a few steps away from the door.

He wouldn't let it win. Couldn't let the ocean get one up on him. This was his hurdle, and fuck if he wasn't going to get past it.

One foot . . . in front of . . . the other.

The spray was growing, pelting his eye now. His entire right side was coated in the invasive water, limbs so cold it felt like freezer burn. He was surprised they didn't ice over. Where was the door? *Where was the goddamn door?* Half-blind, pushing through by instinct alone.

He shrugged off the last of his equipment for speed. Heard O2 canisters hit the ground with a dull, metallic clang. A bell, calling the predators to dinner. Telling Ben to give up. Let the cold take him. His body growing numb. Becoming warm. Like a bed. Like Ellie's arms. Like—

The top of the helmet smacked off something heavy, hard. Stars blinked across his vision. He nearly passed out from the sudden pain. A new crack broke open, more water rushing in, cascading down the crown of his head. Filling Ben's mouth as he yelped. Choked. Spluttered. Looked up.

The bulkhead door. Toggles pulsing yellow. Still working. He fumbled with the lock. Hands thick, numb, refusing to act like they had five hundred times before.

The water was surging through the cracks. Visor bowing inward. The final, full tilt buckling only seconds away. Everything was wrong. He felt himself drifting. His bowels, his mind, unloading.

Let the water in . . . just let it take you . . . you've gone far en—

There was a long hiss. Ben was propelled forward. His legs cut from under him, folded over something. *Smacked* against another wall, the back of his head bouncing again. He collapsed to the ground, skull ringing. Pain blooming across his body. A waterfall deluging onto him. He could hear a sound. A warning klaxon. Gears grinding.

Ben could hear air whistling nearby, but there was no water coming in anymore. Nothing at all except the pulsing pain in his head. He groped for the visor, floundering.

And all went dark.

ABYSS

Avoid.
 He moved his hands but couldn't see them. Floated. Suspended in air. But no, not air. Water. Bottomless.
 Light came from above. A pinprick so far away he'd never make it. Not without help. Not without air. But he didn't need air. He could breathe in the ink. He started swimming.
 Stroke... stroke... stroke...
 The light was getting closer. He could almost feel its warmth. Sun on his cheeks. He wanted so badly to see the sun again. To smell his own skin being toasted by its rays.
 There was no sun, but a child. Standing, not floating. Bloated by water. Burning. Surrounded by a halo of flame. The child looked at him with terribly sad eyes. A familiar face.
 More figures joined the child. Walking across the open emptiness. Staring. Surrounding. Everywhere he turned, they were there. Pressing closer in. Flames hopscotching between them. Frames bloating, sagging. Teeth dropping out of skulls to *ping-ping-ping* on the floor. Too close. They were too close.
 A shadow flitted among them. The octopus. Treading the dark. Dancing. Staring with black, rectangular pupils. Coming close now, tentacles reaching.
 Stroke... stroke... stroke...
 He pulled harder. Away from the crowd. Away from the octopus. Trying to reach the child. The flames wavered. Guttered out. An all-encompassing wail filled his ears. A woman. A banshee.

The tentacles found him. Suction cups latching onto his skin. Pulling him down into the deeper dark. The midnight black. The unimaginable.

Stroke... stroke... stroke...

He fought. Wouldn't be beat. Couldn't. Hope burned in his chest. His wedding ring glowed in the darkness. A promise that he'd see daylight. He would reach the sun again. He'd follow this star to her, to his everlas—

The tentacles *squeezed*. Merciless. Pulled him toward the maw. A place he'd never seen but could only envision. Tantalizing, terrifying. He yelled. But it was no use. The light above and on his finger faded. He went slack, giving up. Let the octopus worry at him like a dog at a bone. Take him into the abyss.

The octopus shook. Squeezed the last bit of strength out of him. Crushed him. Tighter. Tighter. Air. He needed air.

Now, quick.

Please air.

He needed—

| BULKHEAD 559/560, ALIVE |

Ben gasped, spluttering vomit out. His lungs horribly tight and far away, straining for a full breath. His vision was obscured by—

The spiderweb of cracks across the right side of his vision. His nearly shattered visor *hissing*. Expelling air. Unable to keep his helmet filled with all the air being sucked out by the vacuum.

Somehow, somewhere, he found the duct tape, still wet from his foray but usable. Ripped a strip off. Patched over the front. Another. Two more. The hissing stopped. Air filled the small confines of the mask. He gulped to fill his chest, over and over until he'd had his fill.

He flopped backward, staring beyond the strips of tape and up through the bulkhead window to the ocean above. Kissed by a dawn sun, one hundred and fifty feet up. Ben could feel a small bit of water trapped in his suit sloshing around as he lay, but he didn't care. He was alive. He was alive when he shouldn't be.

Both bulkhead doors were closed, one yellow, one red. But no water bubbled through the seam for Mile 559. He wondered if it had been completely drained yet. If the octopus was in there waiting for him. If the severed piece of tentacle was groping at the door, trying to get in and claim vengeance.

He'd have to go back in. Double-check the hatch and walk the long mile back to his supplies. But not now. Not yet.

Ben fell back to exhausted sleep.

MILE 559, RUIN

He found the severed tentacle in a puddle beneath the mid-mile hatch. A four-foot tip and half a sucker, shriveled and impotent. He bent close, grimacing as his mind distractedly tried to do the math on just how big the full tentacle would be.

"Don't have to know . . . I saw it. Felt it." *Too big*, was the answer.

He brought his boot down on it, satisfied when it splattered.

The ceiling dripped as he walked through—little droplets of ocean falling like rain to tap his helmet. Fish flopped over his boot in their last spasms before death in the airless chamber. The algae he'd seen waving like long grass was limp and dead.

Everything drying and dying, 559 exposed like a river in drought, laying bare all the secret things that had burrowed in the deep comfort of the forever dark.

The abyss. His dream. He couldn't remember it fully, but afterimages strobed. The child. The octopus. He felt different. Changed, but uncertain *how* exactly. Maybe it was the near collapse of his helmet—his near *death*. Or being touched by the octopus. Whatever it was, it left him even more lightheaded than before. Jumpy. Each sound a threat.

Ben collected his things strewn across the mile as he walked, constantly touching at the tape on his visor to ensure it held. The spare O2 canisters near the bulkhead first, then the pack just beneath the hatch. Looking up, he could see the tension marks where the octopus had tried to rip the manhole wide. A streak of blue blood not quite washed away stuck to the rim.

He cleared debris as he walked the half mile back to collect the rest of his pack in 558. Most of what he found was small: the gasping fish, algae, and crab carapaces. The bones of the hammerhead he'd stumbled into were strewn in a wide arc of bleached portions. He considered grabbing some teeth to upgrade his shiv but decided against it. Too many opportunities to cut his suit.

"Fontaine, ol' buddy, ol' pal." Ben thumbed his relay on. The Ear couldn't hear, but Ben enjoyed the empty *hiss*. "You better fucking believe I'm getting that hazard pay when I get out."

Ahead, the steel of the bulkhead gleaned with its new wash, the locking mechanism like a dead eye in the middle of a massive face. Ben stopped. Wait. Not black or any other color, but simply *dead*. He ran the rest of the way. Tried priming the mechanism, but no light pulsed beneath his hand. He twisted at the lock, tugging and pulling. Nothing.

"Nonono!"

Ben threw himself against the door. Pried at the horizontal seams, trying to goose the gears. He kicked it. Once. Twice. Nothing. He banged, punched, *roared*. No use.

The door was locked. No going back.

Ben slumped against the metal. Put hand to head. He'd always had the option to retreat back to the previous Way Stations if things became too intense or unmanageable. No longer.

"That's fine . . . it's always been the problem right? Locked in, no going back. What's another barrier? One more roadblock."

But no matter what he told himself, he knew this one was different. The nail in the proverbial coffin.

"Nothing you can do now. You have to press on."

He pushed himself back up to his feet. Sniffed at the tears that welled but didn't fall. Paused as another realization hit him, causing him to turn slowly. Pressed a disbelieving hand to the door.

Half his supplies were on the other side of that bulkhead. Gone. One fell swoop and he was in survival mode.

"They're . . . right on the other side of the doors. Five feet away."

Ben scoffed. Swallowed. Stumbled away, weaving slightly. Not wanting to look at the door. He felt woozy yet hyper aware. Cognizant of a strangeness dawning in him. Neurons firing.

A flooded tunnel. An octopus. Now . . . *doomdoomdoom*. No, he couldn't dwell. Not now. If he dwelled on those thoughts, remained at that door and didn't move, it'd be disastrous for his health.

"The end. It'd be the end."

Time to get back to the hatch. The bulkhead. Mile 560 and beyond. Only two hundred miles and change to go. He had no choice.

But he couldn't seem to walk in a straight line. He remembered a game once when he was a kid. Putting his forehead on a baseball bat, running round it until you were dizzy, then trying to hit a pitched ball. Dizzy, yeah, that was the word. The world warping around him.

He was becoming aware of excess water sloshing around inside the right leg of his suit, settling just above his ankle. Five or six inches of it. No way to drain it until Way Station 05, so he'd have to live with it. But the station was a long way off—at least a week with a damp foot and no reprieve.

"What'd the guys in World War Two get? No, World War One. Gangrene? Trench foot? Wonder how long that takes to settle in."

He kicked out in the air, grinning as the water splashed up around his knee, coating the back of his leg. He imagined his foot was already turning pruney, like sitting in the bathtub for too long. Soon enough, it'd get spongey. The skin would slough away and he'd walk on bone.

"Like I'm wearing coveralls made into a waterbed. Things get much worse, I'm not gonna have a foot to walk with!"

He giggled to himself. A low, mad sound. Entirely new.

His helmet ticked lower: **Oxygen Reserve: 42%**. For now, it seemed a fair amount. That plus what little was left in his spare canister would have to last him until the next Way Station almost ninety miles away.

Quiet minutes later, he was back at the mid-mile hatch. Ben smiled upward as he passed it, his helmet light bouncing off its surface. The source of all his new woes. How could it have opened in the first place? That octopus couldn't have done it. Ben's tentacled friend would've had to rip the cover clear from its hinges to get in. No. The only way the hatch could've opened was manually. *From inside.*

"Maybe that's the route I should take. Early exit. Pop the hatch top and swim on up. Like coming out of a sewer manhole. Outta the sludge and shit, up to fresh air. Take my chances with bubbles on the brain. Then . . . the open sea."

"The blue desert."

Ben chuckled. "That's right. The blue desert." He started walking, thinking about that image. The endless stretching of wind and wave. How right it was, how clever for them—

He stumbled. That hadn't been a voice in his head. It had crackled over the radio. Ben licked his lips. Thumbed the relay.

"H-hello . . . ?"

"Hello?"

Tinny and far away, but yes. Yes, there was a voice there. Ben's knees wobbled, suddenly weak. It couldn't be. He didn't believe it.

"Can you hear me?"

"I . . ."

Realization made his spine quiver. Longing hitting him harder than three thousand tons of water. It couldn't be . . . but it had to be. He knew that voice anywhere. In memory, in dreams. And now, she was speaking over the radio. To him.

"Ellie?"

Long silence on the other side.

"Ellie, is that you . . . ? It's me."

It was the delusions coming back again, had to be. He'd just had a traumatic experience, in all likelihood his mind had finally had enough and fractured into a thousand tiny pieces. But this voice . . . this voice felt so real.

"I'm not Ellie," the voice said.

Now he heard it. It wasn't Ellie. This woman had a different cadence to hear voice. An accent—Brooklyn, maybe. Ben felt that hope turn to smoke, evaporating before he had a chance to hold it.

"My name is Amelia Holden," the voice went on. *"Jesus, you can really hear me, can't you? You're real."*

PART THREE
BREAK

MILE 559 | CONNECT

"Yeah . . . yeah, I'm real." Ben clasped his hands together to stop them from shaking. "You're Holden? *The* Holden. I've been seeing your messages my entire walk. You're the last scavenger. You're"—a pause, a frown—"You're not supposed to be in here. My Ear said the tunnel was empty. No one here but me."

Fontaine said you went mad.

"Sorry to disappoint. I'm a tech, not a . . . a scavenger." A grunt on the other side. A shifting of limbs. "*Wait, someone said the tunnel was empty? That's . . . aren't you here to rescue me?*"

"I . . . no. No, I'm not here to rescue you. I was hired to strip the tunnel."

"*You're . . . they forgot about me?*" Holden's voice cracked on the far end. She tried speaking again, but only a guttural coughing came, followed by a quiet snuffling. Holden was crying.

"I'm . . . I'm sorry."

"*Well, if you're scavenging, that means you're in contact with Steel Glass Ocean, right? You need to tell them I'm still down here. Tell them to send a rescue team. Call the navy—call anyone!*"

A ghost of a smile passed over Ben's lips. He remembered saying almost those exact words to Fontaine.

"Listen, Holden. I haven't been able to speak with SGO for hundreds of miles. I've been trapped down here since Mile 83. I'm heading to 781 in the Belly to try and find a way out of the mess I'm in."

Holden let fly with a dozen curses, making Ben recoil with surprise. He hadn't been expecting the next voice he heard to drip with such venom. But the string of colorful words was strangely heartening, like being impolite could act as a defiant talisman down here.

"Woooh. Okay, right. Easy come, easy go. Well, scavenger guy, you might not be my white knight, but I can't tell you how good it is to hear another voice. Even if you are just another stuck schlub like me." Holden scoffed, laughed in a pitiful, sardonic way. Coughed a string too. She didn't sound good. "We're comrades in misery now, I guess."

"Seems that way."

"How far are you?"

"Mile 559." He looked round, the cave-like drip still settling in puddles on the floor. Laughed. Funny how he could laugh now. "Toughest section I've hit so far. Nearly killed me. I had to swim through and drain it. The mid-mile hatch was open and the entire tunnel section was underwater."

"I know. I did it."

"You what? You flooded the tunnel? Why would you do that?"

Holden sighed over the comm, a tremor in her voice. "You never told me your name."

He told her.

"You haven't even cracked the 600s, Ben. The game's different in the Belly. We're not trying to fix things down here anymore. We're trying to lock things out."

MILE 560 | TRUST

Holden wanted Ben to pop Mile 559's hatch and reflood the tunnel, but he refused. He told her he was worried his cracked helmet might break all the way open, didn't want to risk it. Quietly, he didn't want to give the octopus a chance for retaliation.

"What did you mean we're trying to lock things out? What sort of things?" Ben said.

Back on the road, he was remembering how quickly the miles shed away with someone else to talk to. It took away fixating on the pain in his legs and feet, or the slow trod of distance. The miles felt like actual miles again. Holden's presence almost made the journey pleasant. He'd been so far gone without another voice, he wanted to fill the air with talk. Hers or his—it didn't matter.

"*This place, I—*" Holden sighed again. Ben was getting the impression half this woman's vocabulary was grunts and sighs. "*This'll sound ridiculous, but . . . there's . . . well. For a while I was seeing things down here. Strange stuff. Things that shouldn't have been there but were. Horrible things. And the Belly is . . . unexplainable. I should've reached 781 myself a long time ago but somehow things just . . . go wrong.*" Holden got quiet for a moment and Ben wondered whether he should butt back in, but then her relay clicked back on. "*This tunnel should've never been made.*"

Ben shivered involuntarily—a cold spasm that ripped through Ben's body, setting the hair on his arms standing on end like he'd been made of pure electricity, goose bumps rising. What was the phrase his father used to say?

"What's the matter, goose step over your grave?" He whispered.

The words seemed to echo throughout the tunnel. *Your grave.* Made him look up, past the glass, to the countless tons of water high above. The dirt above his grave. It was getting dark again.

"What? You still there?" Holden said.

"Yeah, yeah. I'm . . . I'm here." Ben cleared his throat. "What have you seen?"

"Nothing I . . . sorry, I just . . . I don't know you. I want to believe you're actually real but . . . don't blame me if I don't wanna spill my demons to you just yet."

Demons.

"Fair enough."

She didn't trust him. Good. That went both ways, despite how happy he might be to hear her voice. He wouldn't tell her about the horrors he'd seen either.

They sat in awkward silence for a moment. Only the click of Ben's boots. The water sloshing around his suit. He could smell it now. Ocean water and the sickly-sweet tang of body odor mixing into some noxious human stew.

"How far in are you?"

"Mile-wise? Can't tell. Readout on my helmet went dark after I hit the Belly. I've been in the same section piece for . . . a long time. I'm not sure how long. I crushed my foot trying to barricade a door—"

"From what?"

"— *ollowing me*," she hadn't heard, was still talking. Ben wished he'd just shut up and listened. "*I'm fine on water but my rations are low. My air reserves are almost gone. Worst thing is . . . having no lights.*"

Holden paused for a second, but her relay was still on. Ben heard a shuffling sound. A ripping. No, a *sniffling*. Holden was crying again.

"I was sure I was going to die down here. Still am. I've been beating SOS against the walls for what . . . weeks? months? Hoping some fishermen or-or researchers—anyone *might hear*. Carry it back to SGO or the navy . . . but we're in international waters, aren't we? You know what it's like to just sit in the dark? All by yourself. Listening to things . . . whispering in the dark around you. Doubting your senses, doubting yourself. Worrying . . . panicking. I've just been scared."

Ben didn't know what to say. He could only partly relate, but was certain that if anyone could understand, it was him. It made him want to comfort her, but what could he possibly say to truly reassure her? He could barely comfort himself.

"I . . . I heard your SOS. Way back now. Toward the start of my trip."

But that couldn't be possible, right? Hundreds of miles back. Sound traveled differently underwater, sure, but not near so well to travel almost five hundred miles. It was impossible . . . he wondered what that meant.

"*Does SGO know? Are they sending a team?*" There was hope in Holden's voice. Yearning. He thought about lying to her, but he didn't want to give her false confidence. She beat him to it. "*Course they haven't. We wouldn't be talking now, now would we?*"

"I haven't been able to connect with my Ear for a few hundred miles. I think the radio range has gone."

"*Figures. I wouldn't trust them to follow through anyway.*"

"SGO? Why not?"

"*Because Steel Glass Ocean is a company of con men.*" A new tone in her voice. Disdain. "*There was more to* The Odyssey *disaster than they let on.*"

"Like . . . like what?"

"*Like a cover-up. Like one person being responsible for the disaster.*"

Ben's head jerked. "That . . . would make that person a murderer."

"*Why do you think the creator was tossed in an insane asylum?*" Then, quietly. "*I'm starting to understand how that might happen.*"

"Who's the murderer? What else do you know about SGO?"

But Holden didn't say anything. Ben's mouth had gone dry, implications spinning like a broken wheel. Trust. He had to trust her a little, give her a reason to trust back.

"I've been feeling pretty skittish too. Was starting to think I was on the edge of cracking. Seeing . . . well, monsters."

Ben scoffed, trying to ease the tension. *Isn't that ridiculous? Monsters!* But Holden was still quiet. He leaned his head to the side, as if that might help him listen over the miles. Hear what she was doing. *Why won't she say anything?* He'd been truthful . . . she should say something. Tell him there are no monsters.

Because there are monsters. What did she say? "Unexplainable" things.

A *thump* and *slide* on the other end. Like Holden had slumped against a wall. "*It's not the range stopping the radios. It's something else. Blocking it.*"

"What could block radio interference this far out?"

Again, no direct answer. Ben wanted to ask if she thought it might be the octopus—or if she *knew* about it. He had so many questions he needed to ask: the ransacked Way Station, the *"you being followed yet?"* sign. He was convinced they all had to do with her. What was in the Belly? *What was happening?*

But Holden was still holding back. Not showing her cards. Maybe he shouldn't either. That was ridiculous though, wasn't it? Like she said, comrades in misery. They were the only two down here. They should help one another. Support.

"Listen, Ben. My batteries are low . . . I need to conserve. I'm going to sign off. I'll try and check in when I can."

Batteries? Ben's suit wasn't battery powered. Maybe techs were outfitted differently. Regardless, he nodded to himself. Realized she couldn't hear that, so clicked his relay back on.

"Okay. Listen, Hold— *Amelia.* I'm coming. I'm light on supplies but I'll be at a Way Station soon. I'll get to you, we'll get you feeling better, then push on together. Two heads work better than one, right? Maybe we can figure out how to get ourselves out of this place. Okay? Sound like a deal?"

A long silence. "*You get here, I'll show you everything I know about SGO.*"

Then she was gone, Ben's relay filling with the familiar empty hiss of static.

He hadn't planned to promise to reach her, but it was said and done. Reality was, he had no other choice but to go forward now. Might as well make the best of it.

Ben shouldered his pack, conscious of how much lighter it felt. That should have worried him, he'd been halved after all. But maybe, maybe it was lighter due to a renewed vigor coursing through his veins. A sense of purpose. Reach Holden. Get her and get out.

"A rescue mission," Ben said. Smiling. And plunged deeper toward the Belly.

MILE 572 | EXTINGUISH

Once the buoy of Holden's voice was gone, the tunnel pressed in again, closer and tighter than ever before. That night, Ben sat and watched the light fade out the oceanlight, clinging to the knowledge that she was near, somewhere down the long road ahead. A flickering hope to keep the shadows at bay until morning.

It was the last time Ben Breckenridge saw the sun.

GRINDING

"You're doing it again."

Teddy stood in the doorway to Ben's office. Had he been there for a long while and Ben was only just noticing? Leaning with that smug grin plastered on his face. It came off like disinterest to Ben, a blasé attitude that infuriated and reinforced the small whisperings that had started percolating in his head.

I'm the real architect of our success. I'm the true visionary here. Not you, me.

Staring at his partner, Ben saw laugh lines above Teddy's cheeks that he hadn't noticed before. A little less glimmer in the eyes where the mischief used to sit, back when they were still fresh-faced and young, dreaming big in a small Chicago office. The years and work were showing on Teddy's face, and Ben wondered just how much he'd changed too.

"What?" Ben said.

"Grinding your teeth. Christ, I can practically hear you from down the hall."

He wanted to tell Teddy to fuck off, to get back in his own office and help Ben chase the deadlines before the fickle investors came calling again. Before everything they'd worked for all these years came crumbling at their feet. It was their one shot to really do something that mattered—*his* one shot—and Teddy would squander it.

But . . . no, he was right. Ben could feel the pain in his neck and chin. His teeth. Unconsciously, his tongue ran along the bottom of his canines, feeling the shape, trying to tell if they'd gotten flatter since yesterday. He'd noticed a muscle on the side of his head gaining mass from the sheer exertion of clenching and unclenching his jaw. Ben hoped it didn't show up on camera. Wouldn't do for the visionary to look haggard.

"Sorry," he mumbled, pulling his tongue back with an effort.

"Man . . . I've been meaning to talk to you. I'm getting worried. The hours you're putting in, the demands on the staff. There's a rumor going around that you've been sleeping under your desk."

Ben looked down, not wanting Teddy to see the flush creeping onto his cheeks. Not embarrassment, but anger. Teddy didn't understand or was willfully ignoring the facts. Their deadlines. The pressure mounting by days, and hours, and seconds. Yet Teddy was worried. Smug, blasé, and *worried*.

"Partner. Buddy," Teddy stepped farther into the office. His voice calm. "It's all gonna work out. Really. You just gotta rel—"

"If you tell me to relax, Teddy, I will fucking scream," Ben's head snapped back up. "I'll relax when we've got transport showing up on time, when the material thickness handles the rigors and stops buckling, when I get one—fucking *one*—competent specialist who understands what we're trying to do and how fast we're trying to do it so we can hit deadline. Give me one, just one easy day, then I can relax! Until then, I'll be here. Doing our fucking job."

Teddy's grin was gone. He raised his hands and patted the air. *Easy.* "Okay . . . okay. Not here looking for a lecture. I'm just a messenger."

"What message? What message could possibly be important right now?"

He pointed. "To answer your phone. Ellie's been trying to get ahold of you for two hours."

Ben's anger turned to water. He scooped up his phone, Teddy utterly forgotten. Four missed calls, six texts. All Ellie. He noticed the date on his home screen and it came rushing in. August 5th. They had a date. An anniversary.

"Shit." His jaw clenched.

He was heaving huge, hot breaths through sore teeth by the time he reached the canal. Their favorite bench beside a small patch of green grass, overlooking a short bay. It wasn't the best spot, not even the best bench, but it was theirs. They'd scratched their initials in it months back, during a wine-fueled bout of rebellion. A view of the bridge, the canal, and a cute brown brick and glass office building across the way. The sun was lowering behind houses across the water, the joggers thinning out.

Ellie wasn't there.

His hands fell to his knees from exertion, then fumbled again for his phone. Expecting—*hoping*—for texts calling him an asshole or similar. But there was nothing. Just an empty inbox that spoke to her anger and hurt more than any voicemail or email could've. He'd get her some flowers on the way home, some chocolates, all the cliché things movies told you to get when mending a husband's fuck up. She'd be mad, of course she would be. But it'd clear. Eventually. Just like last time, and the time before that. Like it always did.

Ben's eyes drifted to the canal, the reflecting water. Peering at himself. Preening. Retucking in his shirt, adjusting his tie, and checking his complexion, remembering how he used to balk at the need to look good for investors and press. At first. Now, it was just another part of his job becoming *the visionary*. The great architect of a better future, the man he'd always wanted to be and was quickly becoming. His and Teddy's names were being splashed across magazine covers and trending on socials these days.

He saw the muscle in the side of his head sticking out. Could feel it with his fingers. Becoming a problem. He grimaced, trying to see his teeth. Bending ridiculously close to the water for a better view. Too close. He slipped.

But when he stood up, Ben wasn't on the path anymore. He was standing on the water in the center of the canal. *Walking* on the water. He laughed, taking an experimental hop.

The sun was already down but there was an inverted quality to the air. Colors heightened, screaming out. The benches lining either bank were suddenly filled when they hadn't been before. Two people to a bench, all staring forward. At Ben.

There was a businessman in a suit, sporting a briefcase and fresh haircut. A little boy holding his grandmother's hand in one pudgy fist, a Game Boy in the other. A woman in a blue-and-white attendant's uniform adjusting her makeup in a hand mirror. More. Their faces clear and bright. Watching him. Whispering his name.

And at the end, at *their* bench, a figure too far to be seen.

"Ellie?"

Ben started forward across the water, walking atop it at first. But the more he walked, the heavier he seemed to become. His feet slipped underneath, shoes filling. Weighing him down.

Ahead, their bench burst with light. A second sun burning in this strange world of inverted darkness. Urging him closer like a moth to flame. Faster. Get there faster. *Before it was too late.*

He slipped deeper in the water. To his knees now, thighs. On shore, the people's faces were swelling, bloating to cartoonish proportions. Blistering with a sudden burst of flame.

The water was rising around him. Becoming walls on either side, curving at the top to form a ceiling.

"ELLIE!"

The sun at the end of a funnel. Still beckoning. Faster. Get there faster.

The solidity fell away beneath his feet. He was in the water now, trying to swim, burdened by his clothes but struggling forward. The water wall narrowing, coming closer. Pressing in. Warm. Sickeningly warm.

He just needed to get to the sun, if only the walls weren't so close. The water—

Was full of bodies. Bloated corpses. A teeming mass, piled one on top of another, jittering against him. Pressing in with a gelatinous, oozing crush. Their heads bursting like overripe melons. Sizzling in the heat. Ben struggled against them, trying to pull away.

And watched as the corpses came together. Forming long, roping strings of flesh and bone, fused together by the heat. A dozen, writhing threads. Like tentacles.

Ben knew he should turn back or make a mad dash. But it was too late. The oozing, abomination was taking shape. Wrapping around him now. Legs, arms, chest. He tried to scream but it was too late. A tentacle was coiling around his throat. Probing. Filling his mouth.

Pulling him down. Down.

Drowning him.

MILE 597 | RAVAGED

*C*lick. Clickclick.
  Ben woke face down on the floor, shrugging away the nightmare and trying to orient himself. Not in the bulkhead, but the tunnel. Midway through a mile, beneath the junction box and a hatch marked 597. How'd he get here? He remembered being exhausted . . . too exhausted to make it the mile to the next bulkhead.
  No. Not a mile to the next bulkhead. Longer. Getting longer again by the day.
  Clickclickclick. Clickclick.
  He stiffened. Listening close. It wasn't Holden's tapping SOS. This was different. Echoing close enough to trickle through his helmet, enough to wake him. He punched his headlamp on and peered down the tunnel in either direction. Empty. Silence. Only the sway of the tunnel and the creaking of tethers. Maybe he'd imagined it.
  Ben guessed it was night on the surface, but there was no way to be certain. Not anymore when night and day blended together into a gray-black haze. His sore teeth told him he'd been grinding in his sleep. Too anxious, too stiff. He glanced to his HUD, a new thing to fixate on. **Oxygen Reserve: 29%.** Dropping much too fast.
  He'd hoped Holden's voice would've woken him up, but the tech had been quiet since their first talk after the flooded tunnel. Ben longed to hear her voice, convincing himself it was solely for the extra chatter to thin the miles. But that wasn't it . . . why else? Loneliness . . . reassurance . . .
  Or was it because she reminds you of Ellie?

"She doesn't remind me of Ellie. She's just a woman. Not every woman reminds me of Ellie." He flicked off his headlamp and settled back beneath the light box, getting comfortable this time. Yawning. Couldn't sleep. What had woken him up? Were Ashvin Singh's hallucinations returning? The isolation reasserting its dominance in the deepening dark. The effects changed how he saw the world: sensations dulled or heightened, agitation becoming commonplace. The mind wasn't metal—it was as pliable as driftwood. Ready to break at the suggestion of pressure.

Simply a matter of when.

Ben didn't want to open the door to the delusions again. They'd come once, but he hoped that would be it. Stop himself from taking those extra steps. Keep his m—

Click. Clickclick.

His eyes peeled open. Heard it clean and clear that time, like fingernails on ceramic. Coming from the top of the tunnel.

Ben wouldn't look. No good would come from adding to his menagerie of terrors. Nothing he could do about something outside the tube. Ben closed his eyes again, willing it to go away. That always worked when he was a little kid. Slip under the covers and *will* the monsters from his room. Out of sight, out of mind.

Clickclickclick. Clickclick.

"Go away . . . please, go away."

But the monster was taking shape in his imagination. A nightmare hybrid of man and squid: spindly, flesh-colored claws billowing beneath a ragged torso, chest sporting a gleaming purple, putrescent eye. Grinning. Pricking the glass. Convincing Ben to crawl out from his safe spot beneath the light box.

All he had to do was look and make it real. Watch as it peeled away the hatch and slithered into the tunnel. Squeeze those claws around him. Knife his chest, neck, and finally his eyes. Kill Ben, then *become* Ben. Ben the monster.

Click . . . click.

"GO AWAY!"

Ben jumped to his feet, punched the lights. Bright flares exploded outside, bathing the water in neon bursts. Eyes searching. *Show yourself. Show me you monster.* Saw—

A crab sat atop the tunnel. Not even full-grown, showing all the cool malevolence of a squirrel. It shrank back from the harsh glare of the lights. Slipped, shifting this way and that, trying to find purchase on the unfamiliar, slick surface.

Click. Clickclick.

Ben chuckled, wondering how it might've gotten there, relief ebbing in cooling waves. Fell back to his ass. He tried wiping at the gathering of sweat on his nose but popped himself in the helmet with a fist instead. Somehow still not used to it.

"Sorry there, bud," Ben spoke to the crab, waving an embarrassed hand. "Pretty sure I'm . . . getting a little funny in the head."

The crab clipped its pincers.

"Hope you don't mind me sleeping here?" Ben said. "Don't mean to intrude, if this is your spot. I'll be gone come morning."

The crab explored along the tunnel curve. Paused, forelegs twitching. Ben pushed back up, stretching on the tips of his toes, tapped at the glass ceiling a few feet below the crab. It skittered closer, slipping some on the tunnel's curve, following the sound, its sunburst-colored carapace glinting in the flare light. Ben tapped again a little lower. The crab followed again before retreating back toward the top.

Ben laughed, tickled. "Smart little guy, huh? We could have a little routine. Make some money. Stick with me, friend. Maybe we can travel this weird tunnel together. Keep each other company."

The crab clicked its mandibles, waiting for another touch from Ben. The flares dimmed, dying. Ben groaned as he sat back down. All this standing and sitting was making him sore. Getting to be an old man with aches and pains. The crab just watched.

Click. Clickclick.

"Do me a favor, buddy, and keep it down. I need to sleep for—"

A shadow tore the crab away. There one second, gone the next. A squelching *crunch.*

Ben was on his feet for a third time. Staring. Had he truly seen something? The crab was just there, or-or . . . *had it been?* Of course it had been. That was no delusion. Because he could *hear* something just above the tunnel. Out of sight. Carnage, hidden in the gloom. His fear was coming real—a monster was here.

The shadow twisted and writhed like smoke. Smashed the crab back down onto the tunnel. Bright blue blood puffed out on either side of the glass. An eyeball popped free.

Then the crab *spoke.*

"Help me, old boy, will yeh?"

Ben screamed. Fell backward, scrambling, trying to press deeper into the wall.

The crab's one attached eye drifted in place. Mandibles still twitching as it continued to speak.

"Old boy, old boy. Help me out. Please? Benny Benny Benny . . ."

The shadows shuddered. Yanked the crab away, leaving a smear of blue blood. Followed by a decisive *crunch*. An off-kilter scream. Then silence. The lights finished their dimming sequence, and the night pressed in again.

Motion electrified Ben's bones. He jammed the flare button again, but it only whirred, spent. Light. He wanted the light. *Needed* the light. He needed to see what was up there. If he saw it, he might be able to salvage his mind. His nightmares would be worse than the reality.

"C'mon. Cmoncmoncmon." This was what he was now. Begging to be shown violence. He stood on the tips of his toes again, willing his headlamp to pierce the gloom beyond.

But there was nothing. Just the telltale cloud of crustacean blood like a fine mist. White particles of crabmeat drifting down with winter snow lethargy. He gaped. Wondering what could have killed so quickly.

The curtain of shadow twitched. Loomed.

Ben's will broke. He threw himself back to the floor and shut his eyes. *No, no, no.* He didn't want to see it, not now. Didn't want *it* to see him.

The octopus. That had to be it. For a short while, he'd convinced himself the octopus wouldn't bother him anymore, that losing the tentacle had curbed its taste for violence. But Ben was wrong. The malevolent shadow was back, and it wanted vengeance.

Something huge hit the tunnel. *BOOM.* Not the octopus's wrenching, but something solid *striking.* It moved, creating a wake that buffeted the tunnel, set the tethers screeching with strain. Ben curled into a ball. Whimpering.

No monsters. There are no monsters.

The tunnel waved and ebbed, went still. Ben remained in his ball, pressing himself up against the side, feeling the cold comfort of the wall.

"Breathe . . . *just breathe* . . ."

Adrenaline pushed and pushed. He couldn't sleep. No. He'd be vulnerable in sleep. No sleep. But before too long, the exhaustion put him back down.

The crab leg floated in his headlight beam, one end stuck fast to the glass by a splotch of sticky blue.

Ben stared upward for a long time. Not bothering to stand, just staring. Questions boring deep rents in his mind. *What could move so fast? Why was it so huge? Was it the octopus, or something different?* He was certain there were rational answers there, somewhere, but that dread—ever present now—would not allow him to think on it further . . .

So, he stared at the crab leg. The simplicity of it. Once part of a whole, now isolated and abandoned. Dead.

"Maybe that's what happens . . . when you remove yourself from a mass. You become inconsequential. Just . . . cease to exist. Poof. Gone." He cocked his head. "Maybe that's what's going to happen to me?"

Isn't this how your trouble started? Yearning to be someone of consequence, screaming about saving a broken world, thinking you had that power all on your own. Wanting to be seen, terrified of being forgotten . . .

"Maybe . . . maybe it's better for people to forget."

But he didn't really feel the words. *Forgotten.* Somehow that was the most terrifying thing of all.

Ben clicked the relay on his helmet in a slow, dreamlike trance.

"Holden?" He could hear a hollowness in his voice. No answer. He needed answers now. Needed them like he needed more O2, water, and food. And sleep. Lots more sleep. "Maybe she forgot me too."

A scoff burst from his mouth. A mirthless chuckle, teeth flashing in the reflection above. He wondered if it was a trick of the glass or if he'd really become so *thin*. So ghoulish. He snarled and, in the warping mirror, his teeth and the crab leg fused into one. Became a twisted, unsettling visage—another monster haunting this long-shadowed corridor.

Ben winced, stepped back. "It's only a trick of the reflection. You're not a monster."

Are you sure? Are you absolutely sure?

And nearby, one hundred and fifty feet beneath the waves, Ben heard the peel of thunder.

MILE 605 | STORM

He rationalized for eight miles that he couldn't possibly hear the storm. It was his mind, slowly—
not slowly, quickly
—unraveling. Those sounds were in his head, his suit. What did he expect, a storm breaking out underneath the sea? Or so loud above that he could hear the squalls one hundred and fifty feet down? Impossible. So, he rationalized and walked.

Still, the ocean around was strange, cast in a sickly hue. Green instead of blue, and bizarrely empty. Of course, it had been empty for a while, but there was a pall wafting off the water like a poison cloud.

A peel of thunder rumbled like a bowling ball careening down the tunnel's roof.

"All in your head," he whispered, walking. "You're getting closer to the Belly, that's all. Fifty miles to the start now, it's bound to get strange." But even the threat of the Belly didn't seem so bad now. Not as static electricity teased the hair on his arms and legs. Worry like itchy spots on his brain.

He reached for Ellie. Think of Ellie. A memory. Walking hand in hand to their local pub, the sky flush with clouds. It brought a smile as he walked, and he clung to the image like a talisman. He focused on those clouds. Some puffy and white, others dark and pregnant with rain. The sun shining, tracing angelic outlines to the clouds as they lazed—
boooOOOOOOOMMMMMMMM. The roll and strike.

Shouldn't let yourself relax. Not here. Not so soon after the crab. The crab had been a warning, hadn't it? *Don't let your guard drop.*

Thunder. It was thunder. A storm. He could remember nothing but storms for the past eight years. Eight years of rain, hail, and cold. Why couldn't there be a storm down here? He wasn't in a rational part of the world. He was in the *sea*. Whatever lived—
ruled, whatever ruled down here
—was close at hand, exerting its dominance.

Flashes lit the water. Lightning like torpedoes bursting. The sea was restless. Too restless. Tossing, turning, *churning* in a maelstrom. Ben could hear thunder splitting apart the sky. Still trying to rationalize it away.

"It's not possible—not with the distance. Not with the glass's thickness."

But he *could* hear it. And the tunnel—the tunnel was being buffeted about. Jostling. Ben was thrown toward the left-hand wall. Braced himself. Hurled again to the opposite side. Nearly tripping, losing his feet.

"Fine. It's a storm. Only a storm. It can't reach you here."
That's what you said about the octopus.

Didn't matter. Keep calm. Ever calm. There have been storms all the time since he's been down here, Fontaine had said so, and he'd never known. When the ocean raged above it never registered to him down below, safe in his cocoon. Why now? Why was he feeling it now?

Because your mind has split down the middle and the nightmares are pouring out.

"*No!* I'm still okay. I'm still in control. I know the difference between delusion and fantasy. I know! I'm fine. *Fine!*" Ben stopped in the middle of the tunnel, looking to the ceiling. Raised a middle finger. "You hear me? Do you *fucking* hear me out there! I'm in control! Ben Breckenridge! No one else!"

And Ben was given sight of the surface.

A massive wave ripped across the tunnel. Smashing Ben into the side wall. He staggered. Dazed. Right side up and back on his feet. Panting. His shoulder pulsing with jolting pain where it had met the hard glass. He looked up back up, ready to hurl more obscenities.

And saw the sky for the first time in two months. Gray-black and furious. Lightning arced in static forks. Rain deluged on the walls obscuring his view, but Ben could see the roiling sea. The rising waves that seemed too high to be true. Tall as skyscrapers.

Dreaming. He was dreaming. He had to be. Everything a blur between waking and sleeping. He would close his eyes. Scream. And wake back up in the creeping, calm dark. The only terror being the wine-dark sea.

Another wave came, so large it pulled the water from beneath the tunnel. The tethers tightened and yanked the structure *down*, rubber-banding back to the water below. Ben was lifted off his feet, flung on his back against the floor as the tunnel crashed like a megaton fist. The back of his head *cracked* against the unforgiving surface.

Tinnitus seared through his skull like a grenade had gone off. Everything hurt. He staggered. Nearby, a giant was roaring. Thunder pealing. He knew he should stay down. Not get up. Let the storm blow itself out. But no. He had to move. Had to outrun the storm. Get to safety in a bulkhead.

Ben got to his feet. Tripping. Tumbling over himself. The tethers outside screeching with strain. His own breath hot and terrible. He ran. He would live. He would outrun this tempest.

"Forward. Just go *forward!*"

A shape loomed. He looked. The rain still obscured, but he could see the wave coming. Colossal. eight hundred feet at its peak. Plummeting toward the tunnel. Toward him. It would break and peel the glass like aluminum foil. Thrash him from stem to stern. He'd drown, but not before he was devoured. Devoured whole.

Ben screamed as it came. Pure, distilled fear. One last piece of him hurled into that black void. Dropping now. Cascading. A shape in the water. Eyes. Teeth.

It crashed. Yanking him off his feet again. Airborne. Falling down the tunnel. Falling for a long time. Miles, and miles, and miles.

Into the dark.

MILE 631 | IMPOSSIBILITY

A cough tore through his chest as bile rose in his throat, pulling him violently awake. Ben fought to swallow, to hold the threat of vomit down, but he'd always had a weak stomach. He could taste acid creeping up his throat, pushing forward in waves. The possibility of him being sick tipping dangerously from possibility to certainty. Growing closer . . . closer . . . finally receding.

He rolled onto his back and stared upward. Clear blue water shimmered across his vision like heat haze. The tunnel rocked softly, back and forth. Quiet. Quiet as could be.

Ben had expected carnage. Tethers torn free and drifting loose as limp spaghetti, the tunnel off-course and adrift, higher in the wide Atlantic. But there was nothing. All was as normal as could be. Nothing changed. Nothing lost. The sea calm and placid.

One palm down, then the next, Ben sat up. His head rang. He didn't question whether the storm had been real. It was too clear, too vivid. No mere storm, but a goddamn tsunami. He sniffed, hoping to smell that clean, clear tang of a morning after rain. But just the inside of his helmet and suit: sweat, body odor, and rancid breath.

Ben tried to stand and sat back down with a gasp. His entire back had the aching soreness of a fresh bruise. Certain, if he stripped off his suit, the whole length of his spine would be black, blue, and angry to touch. The headache came raging in then, like the sun's searing heat corkscrewing through his skull.

His stomach heaved again. He fought it, pushing against the acid flux, practically choking but keeping it down. No way did he want to smell bile in the helmet until the next Way Station. Didn't want to swim in it from chin down either. He had enough sloshing below in the suit, festering into warm human soup.

He groaned—half pain, half effort—and managed to haul onto his feet. Off-balance. Ben stuck his right hand out to steady himself on the wall but slipped on the surface. Stumbling, head screaming, back flaring, instinctively throwing his left hand out to catch himself on the other wall. Falling, knowing the glass was too far to save him—

But it did. His left hand hit the opposite wall. Kept his balance. He spit in frustration, spattering the front of his visor and dripping into his beard. Blood pounding in his head, making him wince.

"Fuck."

Ben hauled himself to stand up straight. Left hand on the wall, he stretched his right arm to get the kinks out. Feel a bit more alive.

But his right hand hit the other wall. He jerked it back, fearful. That couldn't be. The tunnel wasn't big enough to touch both sides at the same time. Tentative, he reached out again. Touched both at once.

The tunnel was smaller.

"What . . . what the hell. That can't be right."

But it was. He was staring right at it—*palming* it. Claustrophobia tickled his spine like he could physically feel the walls pressing close. Any moment the wall would force itself closer still, constricting. The bile was teasing his gullet again, but this time he didn't think he could stop from coming. Pushing, fighting—

But the stomach won. He fell back to hands and knees, body spasming with effort and rushing pain. He choked, coughed. Vomit spewed out his nose and mouth.

Clear liquid. Water, but with a salt tang. Ocean water.

"What in the . . . *fucking hell*." He spit again, not caring that it had nowhere to go. Teary eyes staring at the collected inch of water sitting in the helmet face. How could salt water get *inside* his mouth? "That . . . that's not possible."

Nothing in the last fifty miles has been possible. The talking crab, the storm, the shrinking walls.

"Just need to relax. There's always an explanation. *FUCKING RELAX.*" He spun in place. First things first. "Where am I? Where's next—"

The next bulkhead was nowhere in sight. No gleaming eye. No wall. Just endless tunnel.

Ben started walking, not caring what direction he went, just needing to move. Trying to close some distance, trying to will the next bulkhead to come into view. He needed to know where he was. There was something ahead on the right-side wall. A light junction box and the hatch above it. The mile marker would be stenciled there. *Good.* He hobbled the rest of the distance, limping and listening to his suit *slosh.*

It wasn't just the walls pressing in, but the ceiling too. He could run his hand across it. Could grip the hatch without even stretching, and on its face—

"Mile 631."

But that . . . that couldn't be. It was—

"Impossible?"

Yesterday he'd been in the low 600s. 603 or 604, somewhere near there. Before the storm. There was no way he could've cleared thirty miles in that time. Gone through—*opened*—so many bulkheads without remembering a single one.

What could he remember? The colossal wave crashing. Hurtling through space like the tunnel had been turned upside down. Falling. Falling for a while. He should've hit a bulkhead—*many.* No, he'd just been tossed through the sky like a jumper from a ledge. Then, what . . .

"Black. It all went black."

He shook his head, brain-jostling headache rearing. *Impossible, yes.* Had there even been a storm? The tunnel was no worse for wear. Nothing nearby in the ocean gave any sign. But it had to. Impossible. IMPOSSIBLE. Everything was unraveling. How? How could it all . . . how?

Light. He needed light, like revealing more of the ocean would pare away the *wrongness* here. He would find evidence of the storm, of the churning sea, and everything would make sense again. He opened the housing and pushed the button.

Nothing happened.

He pushed again, hearing it *click* and depress back. Still nothing. That . . . shouldn't happen. He hadn't triggered this junction yet, this was *supposed* to work.

Ben punched the button again. Frantic now. Forgetting for a moment about the storm and sea, needing to know that this small piece of autonomy was still available to him. Here and in the coming miles.

Punch. Punch. Punch.

Still nothing.

"No . . . no, no."

He paced the perimeter of the box. Staring at it. He'd have to wait, that was all. It must be cycling, needing to recharge or reignite or *something*. So he walked, back and forth, counting all the while. An eternity in waiting. The ocean around him seeming to grow darker as he did. Like ink.

He couldn't wait anymore. Ben stretched a trembling hand toward the button, one final time.

"Please . . ." He hiccuped. "I need this."

Pushed the button. *Click.*

Nothing. No light, no ocean. Not even an echo.

Ben dropped to his knees. Laughed once. Twice. And cried.

MILE 640 | DRIFT

He scratched at the sides of his suit but couldn't relieve the itching. He rubbed at one spot, then another, then another, could feel his now-long nails scraping hard against the insides of the suit's glove lining, but found no respite. He gnashed his teeth as he walked, beating the prickly limbs with closed fists all the while feeling those overgrown nails sink into and sting his palm, but could do no good otherwise. Teasing him. Even the simple act of walking irritated his sides, feeling like fire ants were crawling over and under his skin. Unbearable.

Use the shiv. Now. Use it.

"Yes, *yes!*" He ripped the PVC shiv from its makeshift sheath. Twisted the point at his right hip, free palm on the handle top, ready to plunge through the layers to reach his skin, pull apart the protective sleeve so he might scratch and scratch and scratch.

Stopped. Mind clearing. Horrified. "Fuck. What am I doing?"

He sheathed the knife, quickly and with shaking hands. Aware he was sweating, despite the cold. How close he believed he'd been to exposing himself to the vacuum that would make his eyes pop like overcooked eggs.

"Can't get so wound up. It's just the water in your suit—understand the cause and move past it."

Ben had taken to lying on his back and lifting his feet against the wall each morning, maneuvering his hips to juggle the ankle-deep water from one suit leg to the other. He needed to make sure each foot wasn't submerged for longer than a day. Barely six inches of water, but he was certain even that little could turn deadly given enough time. He was thankful to not be wearing socks in the suit. He had no medical expertise to speak of, but could imagine well enough what would happen if his feet soaked for too long. Festering past the pruning stage and into the putrefaction, with raisin-like bumps on his toes sinking to become deep furrows of skin. Blood and pus oozing out, all gangrenous and smelling like sour meat.

Not just his feet either. Whenever he sloshed the water around, it would coat his ass, lower back, and legs. If he pulled back his secondskin suit, there was sure to be angry red pustules like chicken pox all over his skin. Oozing, crusting, ripping open again as he beat, tore, and rent.

Ben caught himself scratching again.

"If this tunnel won't drive me mad. This. Fucking. Itching. *Will!*"

He jumped up and down, grimly grinning. Hoping the blood flow would be enough to distract. He focused on the impact of his boots on the floor. *Boomboomboom.* Letting the dull ache reverberate from heel to shoulder.

"Focus there. Focus, focus. Wrap your mind around it. Get to the bulkhead. Not so far away now." Jump. Walk. Jump. "Get there . . . get there and you can grind your arms against the pipes . . . the walls. Your own personal back scratcher. Fix that itch."

But tell himself all he wanted that the bulkhead was getting closer . . . deep down he knew it wasn't. Mile 640 was miles and miles. The gleaming eye of the lock was dead ahead, but no matter how much he walked, jumped, ran—

scratched, can't forget scratched

—the doors simply wouldn't get any closer. Silently mocking him from afar. *That* he wouldn't focus on though, another route to madness. There were so many now, he couldn't keep track of them all. Brain octopus Holden Fontaine SGO tunneltunneltunnel. Focus on one thing at a time, that's all he needed. That'd be just fine. Stay right, stay rigid, stay golden.

"Not so far now. *Just breathe.* That's the key."

Couldn't though, could he? Not with the itching. Not with the never-ending corridor. Try and fool himself all he wanted but the truth sat right there with him. Always. Just beyond the shadows, waiting for its time in the light. He needed to scream. Fill the helmet and drown out anything that might try a mental coup. Maybe he'd scream hard enough to rip those spider-web cracks open. Take back the *power* in his own voice. Or was the one inside his head more powerful still? The one that delighted in being the devil on his shoulders. Taunting, seeding doubt. Scream. Just need to scream and scream.

Music drifted down the tunnel.

He stopped, head cocking and ears perking like a dog. Music in the tunnel? That couldn't be. Not since he smashed Ellie's iPod miles and miles back.

Yet there it was. Strings. Cello and violin, played under an expert's hand. Loud, now soft, swelling and simpering. Clear as if played by a full orchestra only feet away. Not tinny through a speaker, but pristine. Filling the ever-encroaching walls with crisp echoes. A somehow familiar song, classical, done by one of the greats, if Ben had taken the time to learn their names—Beethoven, Bach, Mozart—the suite titles, overtures or whatever.

"That can't be real."

He twisted his still-cocked head, right ear propped up and craning like a makeshift antenna. The itching gone from his mind now. Was it coming from behind? Drifting across the spaces as a whisper, tempting Ben.

Could be a trap. Something drawing you closer. Honey to the ambush.

He'd follow, he didn't care. It was music again. *Music.* How far back was it since he'd lost his connection to music? Since that iPod had been reduced to pulverized bits of plastic and circuitry? Too long. Much, much too long.

"Humans need songs like they need water, right?" Ben whispered.

To stir the soul. Arouse long-hidden memories. Ben didn't care if it was a trap. He was alone. Already trapped and alone for miles.

Truly alone? Or—

"No, alone! Just me. Only me—" Ben stumbled. The cold pumping into him again.

He was ready for another nightmare, the churning imagination never quite quiet. What would it be this time? A mad hunter with a Bowie knife and a squid's face who wouldn't stop to consider whether Ben could breathe as he sliced open his suit. Or Fontaine, aiming a SGO-branded pistol, blasting Ben's cracked faceplate clean off, then standing over as Ben tried to crawl to the bulkhead, unloading the rest of his clip through the fractured plate and into his skull, saying "*You stole my lottery.*"

But he hadn't expected the child. Not again.

Standing thirty feet back, an eerily similar tableau of the first time he'd seen it. But this time, it was alone and not bloated. Nor was it surrounded by flames as in Ben's dream, yet charred by them. Haloed with singes and scars. Wisps of dark hair stuck to its cheeks and small freckles formed constellations on his sun-kissed face. *His.* It was a little boy, he could see that now. Looking so much like . . . like Ben, yet not at all. Frightened.

Ben reached a hand toward the boy but took a step back at the same time. Tantalized yet terrified. And now . . . now the music was coming in again. Swelling louder and louder.

The child took a step forward. Two. His navy shorts suddenly lit with the living fire, blackening. Charring. Dripping wet onto the floor in sticky, syrupy patches. His face and arms swelling, ballooning as his pores absorbed seawater, turning tiny limbs to cartoonish, gouty appendages. Water and fire hissing as they met.

Still dozens of feet away, Ben was afraid. Like he'd done the child wrong and it had returned for retribution. Ben imagined those hands gripping his stomach and twisting, wringing terror out his gut like a wet and dirty sponge.

"Please, don't. Don't come any closer," Ben said.

Back beyond the boy, the runner lights started guttering out. One by one, a marching darkness came their way. With each fading light, Ben could see shapes filling the empty spaces. People. One first, then three. A dozen. All facing toward him, the white of their eyes the last thing catching the blue white of the runners before the shadow took them, staring at him. A horde, waiting for the gloom to come so they could press forward, en masse.

Their voices joined the music. Accusatory, worried, angry, scared. Volume building with the darkness, gaining power. That unholy chorus, ready to swallow the boy in their ranks. Then Ben.

Now the climactic moment. The little boy stepping forward, opening his mouth.

Crescendo. They call this a crescendo.

Here was the boy's solo, the moment they'd all been waiting for. But out came a different voice, a woman's. Wordless. Mature and terrible.

Wailing.

Ben paled, slack-jawed. Wanting to wail too in a tribal screech of connected misery and mourning. To meld it with the little boy, to share the pain. But his voice seemed beyond reach, too inconsequential to summon here and now. The darkness was coming. These ghostly, melting horrors with their piercing eyes and distorted limbs would reach him, tear him apart.

Run. He had to get away. Get away before this sonic wave could cave in his head. Before the darkness swallowed him. But the boy. Would he leave him to be taken by the nightmare wave? He had to. It was Ben or the boy.

He fled, tripping over himself, unable to keep from staring as the shadows surged forward. Wanting to run back, save the kid from the evil that crept close by. But he couldn't, he could only save himse—

Ben smashed face first into the bulkhead door. The music cut off abruptly, just shy of its final note. The tunnel bubbling to silence.

He gripped the locking mechanism, hearing nothing but his own rasping, labored breath. His O2 clicking lower. Too low. Over. It was over, just like the first time. He'd look back and everything would be normal again. He twisted, looking over his shoulder.

The boy was still there, standing in utter silence as the flames rent skin and fat. His teeth slipping from melting gums to *tick-tack* on the floor. His bones shedding the blacked skin, exposing a tiny skeleton that teetered, unsupported, ready to collapse as the darkness rushed in. People. Dozens of faces now careening inward, reaching out. *Stretching.* Swallowed him and kept on coming.

Ben's hands couldn't stop shaking. *Prime, twist, pull.* Sweat dripped into his eyes. Stinging. Mingling with the tears. The door slid open with a wet *hiss.* He vaulted over the descending lip—

| BULKHEAD 640/641 |

Into the bulkhead. Somehow wanting to keep the doors open—
for the little boy? It's too late for him
—wanting to slam them closed just the same. Still the darkness came. He toggled it closed. Watched in horror as the dying lights tried to beat the shutting door. Wondering what would happen if they managed to make it. To breach his protective shell.

But the doors closed first, blocking the way. Ben slumped to the floor, disquiet creeping over him. Adrenaline and exhaustion battling for control, but he just sat. Unable to focus.

And scratched.

With nothing to distract, the itching got worse. No music, no miles to walk, no—*hallucinations, just say it*—to keep his mind busy. He argued with himself, wanting—*needing*—to get back on the road, but he wasn't ready yet. Not when the child could still be out there. He believed somehow the boy could move *past* him—both behind and ahead—just waiting for Ben to step free of the bulkhead's safety. So he stayed inside. Inside the bulkhead, inside his suit, inside his helmet. *Trapped trapped trapped.* He'd already strung up his hammock, then smashed the LCD screen for the hell of it, laughing as he did. All that was left was exhaustion, an inability to sleep, and the itch.

He was too wired, his mind racing. Couldn't push the image of that little boy away. The child with the bloated face, the wail. Psychiatrist Ashvin never said whether hallucinations repeated. That was, what, the third time he'd seen the child? He was getting closer every time. What would happen when the child reached him?

Itchitchitch.

Ben beat at his left leg. Hip. Thigh. Wishing he could just set fire to his skin. A distraction, he needed a distraction. He gripped the studded metal on the doors, climbing their copper-colored faces and began swinging from side to side. It made him feel like a monkey, even considered hooting a bit to regress himself down the genetic chain. Anything so he wouldn't think about the boy, the need to scratch. Play. Have a little fun. *Try and relax.*

He swung a foot toward the next rung. *Smashed* his knee instead. Dropped three feet to the floor below, right heel hitting too soon, followed by a jolt up the knee. Gasped at the pain and watched as his O2 clicked lower again. **Oxygen Reserve: 19%.**

"*Fucking . . .*" Breathe. Just breathe. He looked up at the walls. "Knee should've had plenty of room there. It always has, in the other bulkheads."

It looked different though, didn't it? *Slimmer.* The hammock hung a bit looser, far too much slack. The oceanlight glass maybe half an inch thinner. The distance between the walls too. Two and a half feet between at a glance instead of three. Maybe less.

The bulkheads are getting smaller. Just like the tunnel. Like everything else.

The violins came again. Piquing into action on the other side of the bulkhead. But now . . . now Ben *knew* they weren't real. Just another delusion. Everything just figments of his imagination. He needed to push back or be lost. Those violins were simply the soundtrack of this scene. The realization that his sleeping space was shrinking. Maybe they would bring the boy back.

Instead, they roused memories. Ben and Ellie having a picnic in Shoreditch Park, escaping the glare of rare London sun in the shadow of an art installation shaped like a great iron button. Him struggling to open a wine bottle without the corkscrew he'd left back at their flat, her staring at a pair of children chasing each other in the fresh cut grass. The children's giggling laughter pulling a sad smile to Ellie's face.

Ben didn't need her words to know the thoughts. The longing.

"Nope! Nope, nope." He brought the bulkhead back to bear. Shaking the memories off, speaking louder to drown out the violins. "Focus on the problem here: a shrinking bulkhead. Not *collapsing* or smashing inward like a compactor. But just . . ."

Smaller. Yes. They'd been a uniform three feet until here, now less. He nodded, pleased to wrap his mind around a simple problem. His mind wasn't lost, the stakes were simply changing.

The implication wormed in. Smaller. No doubt 641 would be smaller still . . . then 642, 643. What if the bulkheads get smaller and smaller until there was nothing left? Just unbroken, never-ending tunnel. Would the tube itself grow smaller? Force him to walk hunched? Doubled over? What would happen in the Belly? Would he be *crawling* by then? How could a *train* possibly get through?

The violins grew as they had before, back when he'd been in the tunnel. Different now, tinny and discordant.

"Don't you want one?" She turned her eyes up to him. Those bright eyes, the shadow moving away so sunlight sliced through her left eyebrow.

"A drink? Absolutely. What do you think I'm trying to do here?" The cork was stubborn. Wasn't he supposed to be an engineer—shouldn't he be able to figure out a solution for a problem like this? Unless of course, he was only *playing* at being an engineer. Good for one, maybe two good ideas before grasping at straws and riding coattails.

Ben was about ready to smash the bottle.

She nodded back to the kids, chasing after a pigeon. "Just watch them. They're so . . . carefree. Happy."

The pigeon retreated in flight and the children squealed. A boy and a girl.

Ben turned away, back to the problem at hand. "The world's on fire, El. Cyberwar, nationalism, climate going to shit. It'd be cruel to have kids now." He glanced her way. Fleeting. Gauging.

Ellie, always so tough and self-assured, looked fragile. Lost. She bit her lip, and a cloud passed over the sun.

Ben stretched his arms between the bulkhead to measure. *Yes, shrinking.* He paced the confines. Vertically. Then horizontally. What would he do? What *could* he do? Nothing. He had to keep going, always going, there was no other option. He needed to reach the Belly, needed to reach Holden, needed to reach 781, despite how much the confines might cave. First, the next Way Station. Nine miles away—but how far would nine bulkheads actually be? Supplies were running low, it would have to be soon.

Someone's doing this to you, aren't they? The violins, the shrinking bulkhead, the madness. Someone doesn't want you to succeed.

"Who? Why? What could they possibly gain?"

But that nugget of doubt peeked its ugly little head out, coiled its way around his brain. The violins swelling. Grating. Ben was pacing now, an animal in his cage. Anger flooding bile into his throat. Filling his mind with horrid, violent thoughts. *They.*

Has Fontaine been lying to you all along? About the past scavenger? Maybe SGO wants you as a puppet. A no one. Break you. Break you down. Break you until you're nothing while they watch you stumble and pace, anxious. A loser.

In the park, the wine bottle slithered in his hands, battling him. The more he squeezed, the more it moved. Sweat beaded on his upper lip.

"Stop that. You're always saying that." Ellie sat up, but didn't face him. "The world's not on fire. Even if it was, don't we . . . don't we have a duty to keep trying? As people? You can't let fear beat out the possibility of something beautiful." She wouldn't take her eyes off the kids.

The bottle twisted and Ben jammed a finger. He shook it out, trying to not let the pain get to him. Trying to focus here, on the bottle, on Ellie, not thinking about *all the other things* on his plate he needed to get done. Deadlines, approvals, interviews, reports—each piling higher and higher while he wasted his time wrestling a wine bottle in a park. Needing to be away. Needing to *work*.

Ben hoped she'd look at him again, away from the kids. Give him that smile, that light. Reassure him. *Settle* him. But he knew there'd be no turning her away from this topic. There was solidity in her voice. Her "time to talk" voice, earnest and not budging. Vulnerable too, sure, but only because it was something she truly wanted.

A baby.

But Ben . . . he didn't think he could do it. Not now, not even for her. Couldn't risk bringing a child into this world. It wasn't safe, not yet. Maybe if more people stepped up, if more people sacrificed their time, their bodies, their *happiness*, and put in the work. "*Be the Change You Want to See*," and all that nonsense. Then, maybe then, it would be okay. But until then, there was too much evil in the world. Too much apathy and contempt and ugliness, all of it compounding. Stacking like sores and scars until the weight became leaden anchors that would drown the whole of humanity.

"Besides, I don't want to be scared of *what if*," Ellie said. "I want *what could be*. Don't you?"

Nearby, the children ran for another group of pigeons, tiny chubby legs pumping furiously. Steaming their curiosity. Smiling, laughing, squealing.

The bottle slipped in his hand, bottom striking an errant rock. Shattering in the grass.

"*SHUT UP!*"

The violins ground to a stop as if the strings snapped. His breathing slowed. Ben realized he'd been clenching his arms, pumping fists as he paced, grinding his teeth too. He eased, unclenched. SGO wasn't out to get him or break him. They were coming for him.

Ben shook his head. Enough. Enough conspiracy theories. Enough memory. Enough . . . just enough. He felt tired. Finally tired, his mind having enough. Sleep. Maybe he could sleep.

No light came down in the oceanlight as he climbed back up into his hammock. The suit water sloshed and settled under his back. He lay, staring upward. No violins now, discordant or otherwise. Only echoes, the music of children's laughter, stuttering into shocked silence.

Absently, his hand traveled to his arms, his legs. Scratched.

MILE 645 | PANIC

It wasn't the beeping that woke him up, but his own appalling smell. The always rancid, stale odor of his breath, his damp musk of body odor, his putrefying, jungle rot flesh far within the suit. He was certain the line for his urine collector was leaking. More flavor for the Ben stew. If he made the mistake of sleeping sideways, it washed back on him. Stuck in his beard, his hair. Water, piss, vomit. The smell was ungodly.

He didn't care. He just wanted to sleep, but his suit was screaming at him. The miles were killing him. His nightmares were unrelenting. The hot spots on his toes where soggy blisters had once formed now had engulfed both feet. Not athlete's foot, but an unbearable heat like his soles had been smeared with lava.

"Kraka-toes," Ben chuckled. Rolled over. The stew sloshed. The beeping continued.

He blinked. Couldn't just be at Mile 645. No. No had to be closer. Must've already passed the Way Station. Had to have. That was the beeping. Warning him. Turn. Turn around.

A warning blazed across the HUD. **Oxygen Reserve: 12%.**

That got him to sit up, groaning. Low. Dangerously low. Getting lower. He had to get to the Way Station. Five miles, that was it.

But he was so tired. So . . . goddamn tired. Let him sleep. He'd feel better if he slept a little more.

MILE 649 | EDGE

Ben stumbled. Limped. His knees were getting weaker, grinding like loose gravel in the joint with each step. He wanted to stop. To rest. To breathe deep. But if he stopped, there'd be no getting back up. He wouldn't make it to Way Station 05. He wouldn't reach safety.

The helmet continued its incessant beeping: **Oxygen Reserve: 08%**.

Something might catch him if he stopped. Before he suffocated. The octopus or the demons or the little boy. For so long he'd thought nothing could touch him here in the tunnel. Secure and surrounded by unyielding glass. No. Hell no. Anything could *reach* him, he knew that now. There wasn't safety in the tunnel. The storm had taught him that. The monsters had. His fragile, Swiss-cheese mind had.

No matter, just one more mile and he would be okay. Way Station 05. That would be his haven. He felt it with every fiber of his being. What else could explain why this final mile was dropping away faster than all the others. Calling to him.

And Holden. She'd be there, waiting for him, splayed out on the bed. He'd walk in to find her sleeping peacefully. Her eyes would flutter open as he pulled the cracked helmet off, then she'd help him remove his sopping clothes. She wouldn't mind the dampness of his body, or the smell. She would run a hot shower for him. Steaming. She'd watch as he scrubbed himself down, as he closed his eyes and let the water rejuvenate and baptize him. A new man. When he opened his eyes, she'd be close. Running her hands along his torso, exploring. She'd kiss his neck, his scrabble-beard cheek, his lips.

When Ben looked again, it would be Ellie. Here with him. Under the sea and six hundred and fifty miles from shore. She'd be there and all would be okay. Forgiven.

His hands fumbled with his helmet. Already tugging at the clasps. Any of them, all of them. Preparing. Almost there. Just about there.

". . . eckenridge?"

The dream dropped away like cut strings. His hand going from helmet to side, the shiv coming out. Someone behind him? The shadows stalking again. The discordant violins mimicking speech.

"Leave me aloooone," Ben said, drawing out the vowels. He was slurring like a drunk these past few days. Couldn't tell why.

"Ben Breckenridge. Do you copy?"

He stared down the long way back. Another voice from a dream. Another dream that couldn't be. Speaking that name in a rote, bored sameness. Ben thumbed the relay.

". . . Fontaine?"

"Superhero? That really you? Hell boy, where have you been!"

Ben swallowed. That . . . that was Fontaine. Over the relay. A hallucination. If he answered, was he accepting the delusion as truth? Like acknowledging an imaginary friend. Could be trouble. Still. It'd be rude not to answer. Where had he been?

"Walking."

The Ear laughed from miles and miles off. The sound of it was a jolt to Ben's diaphragm, a five-finger-death-punch. It'd killed him. How could Fontaine be laughing?

"Well thank all the creatures of the fucking sea for that. SGO's been trying to get a hold of your next of kin, but me, I saw the look in your eye. Knew you'd be back. Cut from sterner stuff. I said, 'good old Ben Breck will be your guy. No worries at all.' Now here you are, cracking jokes."

Jokes. Cracking jokes. Ha-ha. Ben wondered how he could hear Fontaine now. What had changed? His right hand groped the relay switch.

Aren't you happy about this? Or is this an intrusion—

Ben gripped the helmet like it was his true head, shaking. Enough. *Enough.* Scraggly mustache strands clung to his upper lip and he tried licking them away, worrying at them like a sore in the mouth. Waited. Waited to see if the hallucination would fade.

"Breck?" Fontaine's voice was crystal clear. Not a hint of static. *"Still there?"*

"Fontaine . . . where-where the fuck have *you* been?"

"I'd ask you the same thing. Been trying to hail you for weeks. Couldn't get through—eggheads here were saying there was no explanation other than your relay bein' off, that, or . . . y'know how these guys always assume the worst. I've had that Ashvin guy bout ready to rip my ear off. Keeps talking about cons and fucking domestic terrorism. Guys really been grindin' the last of my gears. Doesn't matter now, you're here. Jesus Christ, don't know how happy I am to hear you."

Course you are. This means you haven't killed someone. How's it feel? Guilt like that is liable to drive some people absolutely batshit.

"Well what's happening down there, superhero? Give me a report!"

"I . . . I . . ." Ben nodded. Okay. Okay. Take it easy, take it slow. "Fontaine, is that really you?"

"Yeah! Course it is. Who else would it be?"

"The octopus." Whispered. Not too loud.

"The what? Breck . . . easy now, son. Come this far, don't tell me you're getting funny. C'mon now, made of sterner stuff, right?"

Ben clamped his eyes. Nodded. Smacked the side of his head and fought back the tears. "Right. Right." Sniffed. "Sterner stuff."

"Good. What marker are you at?"

He looked around to get his bearings. Knew where he was but wanted to be sure. Ahead, the bulkhead, to the side, a boxed protuberance. Way Station 05. "Uh, mile six . . . 649."

"Right on the edge of the Belly, eh? You've been moving pretty quick, coming up on that finish line. Almost hate to tell you the good news."

Ben could feel the tears squeezing out. A familiar voice. The Ear's gruff baritone dripping in his ears like sweet nectar. Hearing it was like that first shower, transformative and cleansing. It might be enough to save him . . . if only he wasn't so scared of it. Of what might be coming next.

For the first time in dozens of miles, Ben let himself glance left, outside the tunnel. There. The twisting shadow. Still there. Still keeping pace. Ben's tired eyes snapped back forward.

Just get to the Way Station.

"Breckenridge?"

"Yeahyeah. I'm here. What . . . what good news?"

"We got through! Drilled through the door and ripped that sucker down. One hell of an operation. Almost like these things are designed not to

be broken through." Fontaine chuckled, low. Ben could hear the relief in the Ear's voice. Like a weight—
all that water just makes my spine fucking tingle.
—had been eased off. Things finally going the way they'd been intended. "*That was a joke. Not a very good one, I know. Good to laugh now and then, right?*"
Laugh. The laugh. He heard it down the long miles. That startled, shocked laugh. Now though, it sounded different. Mocking him. *All this way . . . for what?*
"*Breck, did you hear me? We broke through! We're coming to get you!*"
"Yeah, no, I heard you. I-I-I . . ." Ben shook his head again. Feeling some comfort in the pain he got from the headache. It helped to clear his thoughts. He needed a clear head—a new panic was rising now. He started searching the tunnel. "Fontaine, you can't send a train to get me. I'm walking the tunnel. I'll . . . I'll fucking explode!"
A million pieces strewn across a million steps. What will they find? Bits of my bone like crab shells? Teeth?
"*Hey, hey. Calm down. No one is going to explode. We couldn't send a train if we wanted. We're gonna get something down for you though, even if we need to roll a truck in or ride a dolly. We're coming. Hell, you're right near the goal, you might find your escape there anyway, right?*"
His goal, his escape. Yes. *How right you are, my dear Fontaine. You can't come yet.*
"Right. Yeah." Ben's voice quiet and far away. Thinking.
"*Superhero . . . buddy,*" he was calm. Wary. "*You doing okay? Are you, uh, injured or something?*"
Or something. Yeah. Definitely or something. He was injured. Mentally, physically. A mass of a revolting, rotten flesh. Limping along, trying not scream until his vocal cords shred and spewed from his mouth like afterbirth. Now . . . now they were going to ruin everything. He was *so* close now.
"Fontaine, another one of the bulkhead doors is stuck tight. It was damaged when a section flooded. It won't open, I tried."
The Ear cursed. "*You sure? I'm looking at our map, we don't have any sections lit up here. No red and no black. Showing all green topside.*"
"Nope. It's stuck, I'm telling you. Deep in too, around Mile 550 or so, if I remember right. Probably be too dangerous for anyone to attempt."

"*Ben . . . I don't want to ask, but I've gotta. You sure you didn't* think *you saw it?*"

Ben scoffed. Tried to spit, not caring it would stick to his faceplate, but he didn't have enough saliva. Suddenly parched. "No. No, I was *there*. It was, um, near the flooded tunnel, but-but before the storm. It was stuck. I don't think it was the octo—" He paused. Took a shuddering breath. He knew how he must sound. Solid. He needed to be solid. "Fontaine. There's a stuck door. Trust me."

A pause on the relay. Then one of Fontaine's grunts and the squeal of the swivel chair. "*Okay, Breck. We'll look into it. Got some original SGO contractors here now, so we know a quick way through the bulkhead doors. A nice sweet spot. But listen . . . I'm hearing you buddy, you don't sound good—*"

Yeah, no SHIT.

"*—but it's going to be fine.* You're *going to be fine. You're right on top of 05, maybe you should get in and relax. Wait out the storm. You know, our original plan.*"

Storm. Wait out THE STORM.

"No!" Who was Fontaine to tell him to relax? But . . . he needed to be rational. At least *sound* it. He sounded nuts and it would all come undone then. They'd swoop in and straitjacket him before he could reach 781. That *couldn't* happen. Sane speech could save him. "No, I'll keep moving. It'll do my head some good. Keep it clear."

"*Okay . . . okay good.*"

The telltale glow from the lock at 650 was just ahead. Close now. A neon buoy, minutes away. The finish line. Ben let himself chuckle too, but it choked him. Sobs trying to squeeze out.

"Fontaine . . . I'm . . . I'm really sorry that I did this to you."

"*Hey now, nothing to be sorry for. Tunnel just went bad. It's me that should be sorry . . . shouldn't let you go down there alone. Worried too much about my bottom line. It's not your fault.*"

But it was. Fontaine didn't understand. Not really, not like he should. Or would. Ben could have him go on forever being bemused at the weird circumstances that got them here. But Ben just had to push a little further, that one piece that shouldn't have been tugged.

"You . . . you ever figure out what happened?"

"*Yeah, damndest thing. That whole black lock thing was a 'master code.' No way to bypass it unless you knew the code too. Ashvin managed to track down one of the original architects so if we come across another, hopefully he'll know what to do."*

There it was. The final piece. "One of the original architects. Really."

"*Weird, right?*" Then a long pause. "*Doesn't matter at this point, really. What's that phrase? All good that ends well?*"

Ben opened his mouth to speak but couldn't. Now was the time. No turning back. Time to do what needed to be done.

"Don't bother sending anyone, Fontaine."

"*What? You think that's best, superhero?*"

Prime. Twist. Pull. The doors to 649/650 hissed open.

"Course it's best. It's what needs to be done. You can't stop me now."

| BULKHEAD 649/650 |

Ben beelined for the LCD screen and booted it up.
"*Superhero . . . what are you talking about?*"
He should tell Fontaine. This is where the hero—
villain
—reveals his grand plan, all those hidden details that fit *Ben's* puzzle. No more lying, just the journey. He should apologize for misleading Fontaine. Now, before it all unraveled, before the cavalry arrived and ruined everything.

"I'm going to find Holden, then we're going to reach Mile 781. It's time the truth came out," Ben said.

"*I . . .* what? *What the fuck are you talking about?*" That jocularity in Fontaine's voice was gone. Anger was coming back, gaining more control. "*Who's Holden?*"

"She's still alive, she's still down here. I know because I talked to her. She's in a bad way, but she'll live."

Ben navigated down to the bottom of the LCD screen, to that orange broken pixel. Tapped it, triggering the hidden dialogue screen.

Enter Password. His fingers danced across the keyboard. Accepted, in. The original, simple menu listing disappeared, replaced by a second screen that was infinitely more complex. A place he shouldn't have been able to access. Ben bypassed a few set menus, navigating until he reached the one he wanted. Typed a corresponding command sequence.

"*We never had a scavenger named Holden,*" Fontaine said.

Ben froze, finger hovering over the Enter key. "What?"

"Yeah, our last scavenger was a guy named Ramirez. Bucked out saying he wanted to get away from the ghosts down there. Hightailed it to the West Coast."

Ghosts in the tunnel. Horrors following. *Are you being followed?* Yes, every day. But they weren't going to catch up. Not this time.

"I heard Holden, I *talked* to her. Don't try and confuse me, it's not going to work. I'm getting to 781. I'm getting Ellie out of here and you can't stop me."

He punched Enter.

At the far end of Mile 649, the bulkhead lock light cycled color, switching from blue-white, to red, then disappeared altogether. The floor runners wavered, blinked, and switched off. The entirety of Mile 649 going dark as the doors to Ben's bulkhead shut, sealing him in. The lock shifted and shut down. Turning black.

Just as he'd done back at Mile 83.

"The . . . the fuck did you do? All of Mile 649 is dark. It's," Fontaine's shocked voice getting louder. Trying to be heard over a steady beeping back in New York. "*What did you do, Breckenridge?!*"

"What I had to, Fontaine. I'm sorry, I really am." Quieter. "But it's time to fix it."

"Breckenridge? BRECK—"

Ben switched his comms relay to **OFF**, hearing that steady dead line. He gripped the LCD screen with both hands and ripped it off the wall, severing its power.

No time to dawdle, the timeline was accelerated. Already Fontaine and SGO would be scrambling to figure out what he'd done and how. Who he was. With SGO contractors on hand, they'd manage to get through the dead mile, but with luck Ben would be long gone by then.

The beeping in his helmet suddenly grew more incessant as his helmet ticked over: **Oxygen Reserve: 05%**. He needed to get into the Way Station, replenish his O2 supply, and get back on the road. Nearly to the final stage.

But when he turned toward the Way Station, Ben stopped cold. His eyes disbelieving, blood in his veins turning to sludge.

"No . . . *NO!*"

The door to Way Station 05 was welded shut.

ADMIT

Ellie found him pacing the living room of their London flat, his presence foreign and strange in the space after so long an absence.

She'd come to expect the silence of their apartment, the late-night apologetic texts, and the subsequent lonely dinners. Ellie couldn't remember when she started turning the television on to fill the silence—an act she'd abhorred, associating it with people who couldn't be alone with their thoughts. But now it was always on, replaying the same shows for the companionship of familiar voices.

Ellie didn't regret moving to England with Ben, not quite yet, but the sentiment was growing. Sitting at the table, listening to the TV but never watching, her boredom would turn to doubt, then uncertainty and self-blame, and finally, to crushing loneliness. She missed the comfort of home: the eccentricities of her flag-dappled neighborhood, the spontaneous chaos of her brothers roughhousing, the low moan of freight trains rumbling in the distance. Despite her attempts, London had never become a home to her, and she suspected it never would be.

Home had been Ben and the life they'd planned to build together. But as the months marched on and the solitary nights grew cold, as she forgot the shape of his body in bed or the tang of his aftershave, as she tried, cried, and questioned, she felt that future slipping away too.

Now he was here, filling the flat with the warmth of his footsteps. For a moment she forgot to close the door, the groceries keeping her from rushing up the stairs and throwing her arms around him. Preventing the skin-to-skin contact she so desperately yearned for.

But she paused. Seeing the odd way his limbs squeezed and retracted as he walked. The hiss-whisper of manic mutterings. The teeth grinding.

"You're home," Ellie said, willing some lightness in her tone even as every muscle in her body tensed.

Ben twisted and she had to keep herself from recoiling. It wasn't the splotchy, picked-over complexion that shocked her, or how quickly his hair had receded to a stark widow's peak streaked with silver at thirty-two. It was his eyes and their desperate mania. His mouth opening and closing like a fish sucking at air, not sure how to proceed.

Ellie made her way up the stairs into the living room. Slow and sure, as if trying not to frighten a skittish animal.

"I didn't think you'd be here tonight. I only picked up enough dinner for one. But you can have mine." She laughed, setting the groceries down. "You're here. It's really you." She moved to him, smoothed down his hair like trying to right a crooked picture frame. She could smell him, his breath and aura gone sour. "I bet you've been surviving on microwave dinners and gallons of coffee, huh?"

She felt tears rising and rushed into Ben so he wouldn't see. Throwing her arms around him, feeling that frame whose firm muscles were giving way to fat. Squeezed tight.

"I'm so glad you're home," she said.

Ben's throat creaked. His Adam's apple rose and fell. "You're having an affair."

Ellie's eyes flashed open. It wasn't a question, but a statement. "What?"

"Teddy. You're *fucking* him, aren't you?"

She backed away, watching in a dazed, distracted way as he picked up the laptop—*her* laptop—from off the table and waved it in her face. That hyper jerking infecting his limbs again.

"I've seen the messages between you two. Meeting up for coffee. Exchanging calendars. Talking about dodging 'him.' ME!" Ben's face couldn't seem to decide which way it wanted to go: collapse into tears or snarl in vindication.

Ellie stared, dumbfounded. Never mind the invasion of privacy or lack of trust. She *saw* him now for the first time in a while. The gradual unhinging that had developed over weeks and months.

"I should've known. Should've *fucking* known!" He was pacing again, barely looking at her as he railed on. "All his sly looks—all yours.

I could always see what those looks were. Pity. Loathing. Overly critical, overly analytical of the imposter. Biting into me." A barking, scoff of a laugh. "Always looking to hurt me."

"I'm not cheating," Ellie said. Her voice low. Gaining momentum. She needed to bring him back from the edge. Now before it was too late. "We're *worried* about you! Both of us! We've been trying to figure out how to talk to you."

Ben threw his hands up. She knew he wasn't listening again, but she had to try. *Had to.* Feeling an inevitability here. An ending.

"You're never around anymore. You barely sleep. Teddy says you've been sleeping beneath your desk, getting obsessed with your looks, fixating on hitting your deadline. Saying . . . strange things. Your-your weird whisperings. Your teeth grinding. Can't you hear it? You're doing it now!" But he wasn't listening. Of course not. "He's afraid you're on the edge of a nervous breakdown. We both are."

"Teddy is just *jealous!*" Ben screamed.

Now Ellie did step back. Wincing, willing herself to stand despite the whole of her body telling her to retreat. Could this be the moment her husband took that fateful step and turned violent? She'd promised herself long ago, when that night came to her childhood home and she watched her mom collapse in tears, that Ellie would never be the battered wife, meekly absorbing one blow and then the other. She'd fight back or leave. Or both.

But now, the power of her own mind and fathomless love for this man in front of her, changed things. It frightened her to think she might allow a single hit. One. Maybe that'd be enough. Enough to snap him back from the brink. See the error of his ways and become *Ben* again.

No. That's how it would begin, not how it'd end.

"Always jealous!" Ben was continuing. "He doesn't see my vision. Doesn't see this is my one shot. Now, right when we're so close to the end. My work is going to change the world! My name is going to stand the test of time, don't you see it? Don't any of you see that? And Teddy wants to pull the plug. Well, we can't. We *won't*. I don't care how he tries to justify it—it's *sabotage*, pure and simple. And you. *You* won't stop me either. I don't care if you are sleeping with him, no one will stop me. NO ONE!"

He was in her face. His breath hot and musty, almost like urine. His skin yellow and sickly, the sort of face you saw in a beggar on the street and turned away from, not wanting it to infect you too.

And it broke Ellie's heart seeing how far he'd fallen. The man who'd gone canoeing with her down a river, helped her climb out of her own fears. The man who'd whispered with so much earnest and endearing naivete about wanting to change the world by building bridges instead of walls.

This man, who was pushing her away. Pushing everyone away. Had been for months and months.

"Listen to me." Ellie took his face in her hands. Her voice firm. "You lost sight of why you're doing this. It was never about you, or your name. You wanted to *help*."

Ellie saw his gaze shift, focusing.

"You've been so busy trying to become a great man, you forgot how to be one."

Those familiar words, said so innocuously but laden with enough history and weight to be hideous. The exact thing she knew would cut him. Ellie watched him stutter. Stop. The clouds pulling away from his eyes, showing lucid Ben again. Thoughtful. Hurt.

"I . . . I'm." He turned away from her. Shamed. Practically fleeing to the corner for time-out. Face in hand. "I'm sorry. I'm so sorry."

Ellie walked to him, hearing the floorboards creak beneath her feet. Footsteps firm. She wouldn't comfort him, wouldn't let this pattern repeat. Knowing the glass had shattered and couldn't be mended again as she slowly put her arms around him. What's done was done.

"I think you need help. I really do."

He closed his eyes, and Ellie could see him hearing the truth. "I . . . I know. I do." A long, shuddering breath. Ben turned around. Looked to her, tired and on the brink of tears. "I'll get help. Right now, I . . . I just need my light to guide me back." He touched her forehead with his.

He collapsed into her and the tears came. Relief and release. Ellie knew they would shift into a pantomime of normalcy now. Eat sparingly and talk of frivolous things. Later they'd fall into bed and even have sex, fumbling for the reassurance of intimacy. And in the morning, he'd try and talk to her about this argument, like he always did. Patch things up. Say it was a momentarily lapse of control, never to happen again. Like Ellie's dad always said.

At one time, she would've sworn she and Ben had great communication, but that was just more false light. A hope to bounce back, for things to change. But how could they now? Accusations of cheating. Broken privacy and trust. Unhinged aggression. More than just red flags, but those bridges they'd built burning to ash.

Her Tarzan held her, and Ellie knew Ben longed for the clarity of the morning. The sun, the light. He'd be convincing himself he had mastery over anxiety in this moment—that he understood it and could overcome. But Ellie knew better, was already preparing for the moment she knew it would start over. When she'd be woken up in the middle of the night.

Listening to the sound of grinding teeth.

| BULKHEAD 649/650, STATIC |

Ben beat the door. Over. And over. And over. Feet and fists hitting the steel, ringing his swan song. It was either attack or examine the situation. Admit the point of finality. Without a resupply, without the ability to turn around, he was dead. Dead. He wasn't ready to face it. Not yet. It would come, but for now he simply raged and tried to kick the door in.

His already tired feet pulsed with each blow. His already shattered knuckles ground to finer dust. His already raw throat tore to shredded strands, fogging his helmet. *Nonononono.*

"OPEN UP! OPEN!" Then as his yelling grew coarse, as his vocal chords stripped to nothing: "*PLEASE!*"

He slipped—a booted stomp sliding on the smooth surface. Momentum hurling his bruised ribs to careen off the steel. His roar cut off, dissolving to hiccuping sobs as he crumpled. He tasted the saline salt on his tongue flecked with bloody iron. His entire body pulsing with flared pain. He forced trembling breaths to settle.

His O2 meter clicked. **Oxygen Reserve: 04%.**

Get a grip. Assess the situation.

He'd sabotaged himself. Shut down the past mile then destroyed the screen so he couldn't fix it. Appropriate and deserved.

"Wouldn't have mattered if I could. Four percent is a death sentence. I'm going to suffocate."

But you have to try. That or die down here. What about the plan?

"Fuck the plan. If I'm going to die, better to do it right here. Just . . . slip off. Go to sleep."

What about Ellie?

"Doesn't matter." Ben bit back another sob. "It's too late. It's been too late for a long time."

Now, the despair sinking its claws deeper than ever before, the tears finally came. Not a weeping, but a soul-tugging, exhausted crying. Hopeless. The entire endeavor, only to give up now. An unceremonious end, one hundred and thirty miles from the goal.

Color flared across his closed eyelids. A flash of brightness like when the jellyfish had come, yet somehow different. Warm.

Dazed, Ben opened his eyes and saw a golden shaft of light before him. A single beam of sunlight, shimmering with an aquatic haze. He put his hand out and felt the warmth tickle his palm, spreading hot tendrils across his fingers. Ben craned his neck.

There was a curtain of golden light high above. An undulating, ethereal cloud, shapeless and pure. As he watched, it spread. Overtaking the oceanlight, filling out its edges but not passing through. A rectangle of iridescent gold. Like a door.

Ben could reach that door. Could claw his way up and out of this bulkhead, this tunnel. Reach the sunlight above.

The curtain flared, swelled. A shape in the window-door. A silhouette.

Ben needed to reach that shape, to reach *her*. He didn't need to strain anymore, but simply float. Suddenly doggie paddling through the air. Untethered, weightless, drifting high to the ceiling. He stretched to touch through the glass, to grasp that light, to feel it warm him, fill him, buoy him. Just *there*. It was a challenge, yes. An endurance test like he could never imagine. But the reward would be everything.

And somewhere both far away and immediately in his ear, he heard a voice. Crystal clear, playful yet firm, the words honeyed.

"Ben . . . get up, Ben."

He snapped back. Ben wasn't touching the ceiling, just reaching up from his seat on the ground. There was no golden doorway above, no silhouette. Never had been. Just his mind playing memories like snowy channels on a blank screen. His hands wove through empty space, nothing beyond and above but shifting blue ocean.

Nothing, except the shaft of light. Weak. It no longer fell on him, but across the bulkhead. Highlighting a glint of silver within the bronze. A rucksack, buried deep in the piping as though shoved into a hiding place. And spilling out of its folded mouth: silver tubes, their nozzles resting on the grating. O2 canisters.

He stepped forward. Shaking. Bent down, hoping beyond hope, upended the bag. Three tubes. Ben picked up the first one and plugged it in to his secondary air slot. The helmet *beepbeep*ed. Empty. He chucked it away. The second canister, slotted in. *Beepbeep.* The third. His hands shaking, waiting for the final bit of hope to choke out, to render him into a blithering fool. He punched the third canister in.

The red HUD cleared. The number upticked slowly. Stopped. **Oxygen Reserve: 14%**.

Ben laughed, squeezing his eyes shut then reopened, expecting another delusion that quickly disappeared. But the number stayed. Fourteen percent.

He looked back up at the oceanlight. The beam of golden light was already fading, the warmth disappearing, leaving just the cold of the bulkhead. He was certain the rucksack hadn't been there before but wouldn't ask how it had gotten there, left by who or what. There was a phrase he remembered from the old-school hikers he'd met, a fervent belief regurgitated through tall tales. A sort of magic on trails, a fey force bound to keep hikers alive, arriving the moment they were most needed. *The Trail will provide.* These canisters weren't trail magic to Ben, but fate. A small boost to see him through, to finish what he'd started.

"Fourteen percent . . ." he whispered, smiling through to the ocean above. "Thank you."

Ben pulled himself off the ground. His face was wet from tears and sweat, body tender from tips to toes, but he could stand. He could walk. He could *try.*

He examined the door to Way Station 05. Welded shut all around. Smoothly done. A professional, precise job. The rivets and lines done with a practiced, yet shaky hand. Determined. Not a chance in hell to pull it back open unless he had a welding torch himself to carve through. There was evidence of someone trying to do the same to the bulkhead doors. The beginning of rugged spray of heat, like a scar on the metal.

"Like someone was trying to seal themselves in . . ."

Remember when SGO wouldn't give you tools? What sort of salvage crew isn't allowed to take tools?

"This wasn't SGO. Holden. Holden did this."

Holden doesn't exist.

Fontaine had said she didn't exist, but Ben had talked to her. And here . . . here was clear evidence that someone had preceded him. Holden, or at the very least, another tech. Maybe the station had sprung a leak, or caved in, or . . .

Something needed to be locked out, or in.

Ben took a step back, the doorway emanating menace. Images haunting his mind. Beady black eyes. Fins and tentacles. No, the Way Station was closed to him. Best to leave it be.

Inventory check. Fourteen percent of O2, with luck, could *just* get him to the next Way Station. He'd have to be careful, breathe slowly. Rations were a different story. He'd have to parcel them out. He'd be hungry but if he was smart, he'd have enough to get him halfway . . . that was it. Water he had plenty of.

The suit was another story. There was no question that the refuse liners were leaking, he could smell the piss dribbling into his suit to mix with the Ben stew. His feet were numb now, telling him what he already knew: jungle rot would take his feet if he couldn't clean and dry them soon. And his helmet . . . one trip, one good hit, and the faceplate would shatter.

He could almost laugh at his terrible state, but fatigue bowled in instead. His body was a massive, decomposing sore. It all seemed so . . . futile. Prolonging the inevitable.

"I've got a chance . . . that's all that matters. And I'm going to make it." One last push.

He looked at the door to Way Station 05. So many problems solved if he could just get through. Ten feet away.

"Holden, you better hope you're not real. Because if I find you, I'll rip off your helmet and see what it means to have your blood boil."

That only left the way forward. Mile 650. More than the bulkhead, he could sense a presence forward. A . . . sinister feeling. Ben spoke its name in defiance, showing that he wouldn't be intimidated or afraid.

"The Belly."

But he was afraid. This entire pilgrimage, there'd been one thing he learned to fear above all: the darkness and shadow. Light had been his saving grace, the only thing holding back the horrors. But with the Belly out of power, he'd have to face his fear.

Just you. Alone in the dark.

Ben shrugged off all the extra bits from his rucksack: the hammock, pens, a few odds and ends. He wouldn't need them, could cover more ground without the extra weight, so he left them beneath the Way Station's door like an offering. *May the gods of the Deep—Poseidon, Neptune, Octo—give me safe passage.* He pressed his head to the door, wondering if he ought to at least rest before continuing on. Gather his strength, go out with a clear head. But he'd never have a clear head, not anymore, and his air was growing thin.

Instead, he turned to the bulkhead for Mile 650 and cycled the lock, watching as the doors hissed and slid open. He steeled his fragile mind and took a shuddering breath before stepping into the gathering dark.

One foot. Then the other.

MILE 664 | THE BELLY

Ben was too tired to notice when he finally entered the Belly.

There was no grand threshold to pass. No sign or icy premonitions to tell him that he'd crossed the tunnel's equivalent of the River Styx. Wasn't even another bulkhead. Just one mile bleeding into another. The only mark being the sudden absence of light. No lock lights, no floor runners, only his helmet beam to pierce the gloom. Boots squelching into inky night, enveloping him like a dark blanket.

Ben was too exhausted, too broken, whispering his mantra to keep forward and keep heart. *Just breathe.* One foot forward, then the next. His eyes fluttering open and closed, sleepwalking, ever onward.

Into shadow.

PART FOUR
THE BELLY

MILE 671 | REASON

"B*en?*"
 Ben woke in darkness so profound he couldn't see his hand right in front of his face. Cold too. All the heat sapped out, causing him to involuntarily shiver. Teeth chattering. He was certain that if he could see, his breath would come out as dense vapor, fogging the helmet glass.
 "Hey, Ben Breckenridge. You there?"
 He pushed himself up, arms almost too weak to do that small a task. He could feel how thin he'd become, the suit hanging baggy now, his hunger insatiable. He hated waking up, disoriented, never truly remembering how he got there. Having to piece his journey backward to find the whole picture. Remembered wandering, exhausted. Swaying. He must've slumped at some point, face down on the tunnel floor. *But why was it so dark?* The floor runners were off.
 Ben clicked his headlamp on, watching the thin penlight play across the walls in a laser-tight arc. The tunnel was smaller than ever before, the ceiling brushing the top of his helmet as he stood. He shivered again, this time not from the cold.
 "Holden."
 "There you are. Was beginning to think I'd . . . doesn't matter. How far are you now? I'm getting restless. And itchy. Thirsty too . . . hungry. Everything."
 Ben reached for the comms toggle but stopped himself. Not wanting to know if it was on or off. Bliss in ignorance. "You're not real, Holden. Stay off my relay."
 A laugh from over the comm. *"If only you were in my head. Can't tell you how much hearing you say that puts us in the same boat. Tell you the*

truth, it makes me trust you a little bit." More laughter. Tinged with a sort of madness. "*Really though. How far? You in the Belly yet?*"

"N—" He paused, realizing. The darkness coming to full relief. The cold. Oh yes. He was in the Belly all right. "Why is it so much colder in here?"

"*That's how He wants it.*"

"Who wants it?"

Silence from the tech. Ben knew it wasn't because of a lost connection. Holden didn't want to speak the name out loud. Like a kid staring in the mirror saying Bloody Mary thirteen times, hoping the ghost would come out and visit her summoner. No one ever said what Bloody Mary would do to you if she came.

"Holden. Who wants it like that?"

"*Him. The octopus.*"

Ben skittered to the corner, closer to the floor. Whispered back. "You've seen it too?"

"*I saw it first. I wanted to trap Him when I flooded that tunnel . . . they can squeeze into really tight spaces you know. No bones. A little manhole like that hatch? Nothing to Him. Push right on through, tentacles and all.*"

Ben remembered the feel of the tentacle wrapping around his wrist. Thinking back, something that large could've pulled him out easily. Or come in to play, nothing Ben could do to stop him. The octopus had been testing him.

Or playing with you.

"*I think the water around the tunnel is His home, but the Belly . . . that's where He thrives. All the shadows and dark . . . It's His domain. Octopuses are smarter than we give 'em credit for. Big brain, long memory.*" She went quiet again and Ben felt the walls tightening. He remembered Fontaine talking about octopuses. Smarter than dogs. "*We never should have come here. This is His punishment.*"

Click

click

clickclickclick.

Ben whipped his headlight behind him. The tunnel was empty. Of course it was. It wasn't in here with him. Ben turned the beam out toward the glass. *He'd be out there.* The light caught nothing to either side, and he let that be enough. Convinced not to look *up.* Where he *knew* something would be watching him.

"How long have you been down here, Holden?" He lilted his voice a bit higher. A bit firmer. Trying to convince himself and whoever was listening that he wasn't as scared as he was.

"*Shhhh! Keep your voice low. I think He follows by sound. Not sure about that . . . but it's worked okay for me. Once He starts following you, it's almost impossible to shake Him loose. Why do you think I haven't been calling? Silence. Silence is key.*"

"I thought it was because your batteries are low?"

Silence again.

"Holden . . . who are you? Really?"

"*Told you, I'm the tech. I fix things.*"

Those words tickled. Ben was sure he'd heard them before. Or had he said them? Recently too . . .

"Like you fixed the door to Way Station 05?"

A more prolonged silence this time. Deliberate.

"Fontaine told me there was no tech named Holden."

"*Who told you my name in the first place?*"

Ben opened his mouth. Paused. Had Fontaine told him her name, or did he read it on the wall first? He didn't like second-guessing himself. Not down here. Again, he wondered what would be different if he hadn't walked this long way alone. What would be the same.

"*Are you coming or not, Breckenridge?*" Then in a voice distinctly Ellie's: "I need you."

Ben pushed back onto his feet, careful of the low ceiling. Made sure he was pointed in the right direction, the helmet's light slicing into the far darkness. A lighthouse beam leading to—not warning from—the safety of shore.

"What choice do I have?"

MILE 680 | LICORICE

The Belly was not the tunnel, but something wholly different. Disturbing and wrong. An alien presence pervaded the still air and heightened all sound so every footfall and drip of water were as loud as rifle reports. There were no bulkheads, no lock lights way off ahead, just the dark road.

"It's like walking through a mausoleum," he whispered, inching along step by shaking step.

He wanted to shout and curse, to break the frigid gloom, but dared not. Fear of rousing—what? *Him?* Something. Did he believe Holden that the octopus's stranglehold was down here? That the long shadow not only continued to stalk him, but somehow *controlled* the Belly?

"Not fucking likely."

Why not? It's been following since the very beginning. Playing with you. And now you're speaking in soft whispers. Furtive. Like a mouse running from house to house. You know what IT is. Look for it. Go ahead.

"I don't need to look. Just walk. Eyes on the prize." But no matter how hard he tried, the octopus was never far from his mind.

The Belly had the feel of a cave system. Dripping water somewhere far away like runoff from a stalactite. The walls pressing further and further in. Tight on his shoulders, his chest. Pretty soon, he wouldn't have room to move. He'd be squeezing down tunnels and chutes. No more of the spaciousness he'd felt when first stepping into Mile 1.

"How long ago was that now?"

A lifetime. A whole continent's breadth away.

He'd been so light then, so cocky. Remembering the bravado in which he'd told Fontaine. "Tight spaces never really bothered me," and laughing when he thought of Ellie's aversion to claustrophobic movies and activities. But now . . . now he felt it. That constant, unwavering fear of the walls closing in. The struggling to breathe. He had to remind himself his O2 was low—11 percent now and dropping—otherwise he'd panic. Hyperventilate and burn through what little oxygen he had. Anxiety giving way to a slow death.

What did Ellie always say about tight spaces?

"She could feel a mountain pressing on her back. She'd had dreams since she was a teenager of pulling herself through a crawl space in a house wavering in a storm. Going inch by inch, one shaking forearm at a time, struggling to breathe. Always terrified a lightning strike would come when she was halfway through, and—"

Boom. Collapse.

"Right on top. Squeezing her insides until she popped like an overripe peach. 'All sticky juices,' she said."

Think you'd pop too?

As if in answer, the tunnel swayed. Abrupt. Not violent, but with the suggestion of it. Ben tensed, putting both arms up to secure himself, like it was a doorway to protect from an earthquake. Eyes bulging, heart jackhammering.

"Relax . . . just a current."

Or the wake of something huge.

Ben dropped his arms but kept a single hand on the wall, looking for comfort in its rigidity. Turned his helmet so the light could peer out. If he could see something—*not Him*—it might be some comfort that he wasn't alone. But the darkness outside was impenetrable. Solid as concrete. A wall of black ice.

"Maybe I'm not even in water at all . . . but ice. A sea of ice."

He could feel the cold, slimy slickness of it through his gloves. Like a melting ice cube. He pulled his hand back and smoke drifted off his palm. Inky vapors. A conjurer's trick. He extended his tongue out, licking the air in the small spaces of his helmet. Wanting to taste the vapors, the ice, the wall. He knew he couldn't, not past the barrier of his crumbling glass plate or the flat, dead air. Yet somehow . . . he *could* taste it. The glove, the walls, like—

"Black licorice. Licor-*ice*" Ben said. Licked again and smiled. Awed. "Like Good & Plenty. Grandma's candy."

A sound slipped between his teeth. A giggle. Like a little kid's. He clamped a gloved hand over his "mouth." Slapping his faceplate.

Took a step back.

"Easy, buddy. Easy."

Ellie always hated black licorice. Said even if you built a castle out of it, she'd never visit. Didn't she?

"Yeah, she did—NO! Stop. Fuck, Ben. Stop talking to yourself. Stop."

You've been doing it for miles . . . and miles . . . and miles. Embrace it . . . we should be working together now.

Ben wouldn't respond. Not again. He took his hand from the wall. Set his shoulders. Walked. Determined.

"It's only the isolation. Your nerves."

Gonna say it again? Aren't you sick of saying it all the time?

"Breathe. Just breathe."

Another shudder. In. Out. In. The black licorice taste stayed on his tongue.

MILE 68B | CHARGES

Ben was learning, his senses becoming hyperaware and fixating on everything around him. The rotted carrion stench of his body. The subtle tweak of his grinding joints. The tiny pinpricks of light that would suddenly appear like will-o'-the-wisps in the near distance.

But his hearing . . . hearing most of all. The dark magnified all sounds: Ben's own ragged breathing, his uneven, shuffling gait. Most of all . . . he could hear *the other*. Following him. For—*miles?*—he convinced himself it was merely his imagination transforming every drip of water on the floor. A pitter-patter squelch. But there was no denying it now. Something was following. More and more . . . he recognized the sound. Footsteps.

It's the child.

Ben nodded, cognizant that the boy was close. That it wasn't just his acute senses, but that this little demon dogging his steps was catching up.

And what happens when he reaches you?

"Nothing. He's—"

The sound of his own voice made him jump. Hurl and press himself against the curve of the wall. The other's footsteps paused. Ben listened. *Listened.*

The child started again.

"He's only a hallucination. He can't hurt me," Ben whispered. Walking. The footsteps behind him too. "Keep moving. Faster now."

And if it gets narrower ... smaller? If you have to crawl? What's to stop it from pulling you backward?

Ben was hunched now. Enough to make walking in his bulky suit agony on his back, pressure pushing on his neck. He really was spelunking now, down in the cave. Conscious of hundreds of thousands of tons of water pressing above him. He wasn't even sure how far down in the water he was, what day it was, what mile marker he was at. All he had was his suit and the light on his helmet.

Drip ... Drip drip.

Don't look, keep going, don't look. His beam cantered in the gloom ahead, cutting through. His eyes always watching the small dust particles drifting in the beam. Like snow.

Or ash.

Drip ... drip DRIP DRIP

It was close. Too close now. Needed to look. Now. Do it now.

Ben put a hand to the wall so he wouldn't be turned around. Whipped backward. But his light sliced over empty tunnel, nothing else. Just shadows and darkness. No one there. But he'd *heard* it.

Something brushed past, ruffling his suit leg.

Ben yelped. Twisted his head back around, frantically scouring the near dark. Nothing. Nothing at all. Nothing by his feet, not even a sign that his pants had been touched. But something *had* touched him. His light roved, feeling so unsubstantial against this hidden threat. He was being toyed with.

There was something on the floor. Something he hadn't seen before. Footprints. A child's footprints.

Ben heard himself hyperventilating from a long way off. As he fell to his knees on the cold, cold floor. As he touched the footprints with a shaking hand and watched as his fingers smeared fresh mud. As he crawled on hands and knees, following the footprints where they ran off, farther and farther into the Belly.

"Hello! Is someone here?"

Echoes and echoes.

"HELLO?"

Silence. Deep, profound. Then ... farther ahead, so quiet as to be inarticulate. Growing.

"Be ... my everlasting light ..."

Ben's throat hitched. Unconsciously, his hand went to his heart. An intense depression and fear stole over his chest. Chilled his very core. He knew that voice, and somehow didn't. He couldn't move, felt lashed to the floor.

"I can't . . . I can't go forward."

You have to. You don't have a choice.

"My star . . . now the night has come . . ."

His and Ellie's song but distorted with the wrong words and cadence. Coming from a child's mouth. He knew that voice, but not how, other than terrible discomfort it gave him. Yet, he was proud to hear the song. Despite the terror. It was getting closer.

Move. You need to move.

A light pierced the gloom ahead. A needle of white, bobbing along with the melody, arcing back and forth. Ben didn't want to be caught by that light. Didn't want it to see him. Still, he couldn't move.

"Guiding me, when the sun is gone . . . when the sun is gone . . . when the sun is gone."

Repeating now, uncanny. The exact same inflection. A broken record made flesh.

"Stop . . ." He whispered. Gained traction. Volume. "Please . . . *STOP!*"

"The sun is gone . . . the sun is g—"

Then stuttered. Stopped. The light hovered in the air. Frozen. Waiting . . . waiting . . . *moving*. Sweeping left, then right. Then

Falling on Ben. On his face. So bright, he raised his eyes to guard against the glare. Whispers bloomed from everywhere and nowhere. Dozens of voices, coming from all sides. Rising like a tide. Whispers that cut like knives.

"There he is."

"The great man."

"The visionary."

Muddling and dissolving to that single word.

"Visionary visionary visionary."

"STOP!" Ben screamed.

As quickly as they came, the voices cut off. Like they'd never been there in the first place. The light remained, but now fell to his chest, just above his heart. Weighing it like some Egyptian god. Falling again to the floor, light pooling five feet away.

Ben's forehead beaded with sweat. He was happy the light was gone, but terrified of what would happen next. He felt dirty. Skin riven with ugly fluid, twitching with dread and guilt.

"They're all waiting for you." A distorted whisper. Not the child anymore. A new voice. "Say the word."

Ben was shaking his head. He wouldn't. He tried to open his mouth to speak, but it was like a dream. Try as he might, nothing came out but choked groans.

The other light flicked suddenly. Tiny shadows passing before the beam. Tinkling scratched across the floor surface like strewn gravel. Tumbling into the pool of light. Ivory flecked with red.

Bloody teeth.

"Ben?" The voice changed. No longer distorted, but hysterical with fear. "Ben. Please, Ben, *stop. Don't.*"

Ben stepped back. Horrified.

"*BEN!*"

The child *screamed*. Both lights went out.

Ben tripped over himself in the sudden darkness. Fell. Fled backward, running full tilt, pinballing off the wall, not caring for his O2, the slippery floor, or his direction. Get away. He needed to get away. Away from the voice, the child, away from a headache that was building and building with each stomp of his boots, searing his dark world white.

There was something edging his terror. Recognition. A question that needed answered, but he wouldn't find it now.

He was running blind in an utter absence of light. He tripped again, his ankle twisting. Pain like a dry ice burn crumpled his foot beneath him, and Ben fell to hands and knees. Sprawled out. Crawled as quickly as he could. Distance. Needing distance. The water in his suit sloshed up to his chin. Cold. So cold. He'd get hyperthermia. Any time now. He could hear ice crystals forming on his helmet.

No. Those are tears. Tapping your helmet.

Yes. Tears. Why? From terror or the insurmountable sadness that was creeping over him? *Breaking* over him? He collapsed. Couldn't crawl any farther. But now. He'd—

Have to turn. Have to turn and

"FACE IT!"

He did, falling onto his back and staring into the wall of darkness. Blind. Ready to be consumed, ripped and rent apart. Watching. Listening.

Nothing there. No light, no sound. No child, no voice. Only impenetrable darkness.

"They were there." His whole face was shivering. "Something was there. I saw something there."

What'd you see? A person? A child . . . down here?

"Teeth."

Laughter. *Inside his skull.*

"I'll fucking . . . I'll fucking show you." *Me.*

Ben shrugged his pack off. Fumbled at the pockets with his numb, dumb hands, searching for the glow sticks he knew would be in there. Needing light like he needed water or air. Anything to beat back the impenetrable dark. The skulking shadows tugging at his clothing with tiny hands.

"Where are they? Where where where?"

Something fell out onto the floor. He could feel the small pack of cigar-shaped lights. Here. Here they were. He'd get his light now, he'd be able to see.

An explosion came. Not the flashlight beam or glow sticks, but something else. *Outside* the tunnel. Bright and agonizing white. A puff and then gone again like artillery flak.

Ben turned just as a second one went off, to the right. Another. Another. Depth charges.

Not sounding with their characteristic, deadened *boom*. But the metal-curtain slam and whine of camera shutters.

Ka-schuuk. Ka-schuuk.

The depth charges lit the ocean outside with brilliance for split seconds. Concussive bursts rocking the tunnel. Bombs bursting in the dark. Flashbulbs blinding. Beautiful at first, then overwhelming. All with that unsettling sound.

Ka-schuuk. Ka-schuuk. Ka-schuuk. Ka-SCHUUK!

They burst all over. Falling stars and exploding suns. Stabbing his eyes, chopping his eardrums. But why? Why now? Why here? What could possibly—

Out in the darkness, shapes drifted among the blasts. Debris. Illuminated for a moment, then gone again. Shredded bits of steel siding and exposed wire, mold-mottled headrests, split baggage racks. The nose of a lead train car.

And behind it all, the octopus loomed. Grown to titanic proportions, its eyes malevolent and hateful, piercing down at Ben as the depth charges exploded like deadly fireworks in the undersea sky. Its tentacles flurried past the detritus, gripped the tube. Its maw opened.

The voice. The child. *Screaming.*

Ben fled, directionless, farther and farther into the dark. Screaming too.

MILE 6-92 | T

Miles later, after the slamming of his footsteps had drowned out all other sounds, after his helmet light—mercifully—flickered back to life, after he was just making certain he could gather his wits and face the Belly again, Ben came to a dead end.

His light found it first, the beam inexplicably stopping short and hitting a wall. Ben trudged forward, reasoning its was simply his eyes suffering from the trickery of the dark, another mirage from the never-ending abyss. That or the first bulkhead in days. *Relief.* A chance to sit and eat. To sleep.

But now, closer, he could see it wasn't a bulkhead. No steel doors, no glowing eye of a lock. Just a blank, glass wall. He refused to believe it, not until he touched it, not until it firmly said *no* to him.

Shuffling, he closed the distance. Throat constricting, tension rising. Stood before it. Put his hand out. Firm, just like the walls, the ceiling. Steel glass and the black ocean beyond.

"This . . . shouldn't be here."

It wasn't possible. There couldn't be a dead end here—or *anywhere*. The blueprints didn't have any variation: all one single line. There were still miles and miles and bulkheads and Way Stations to go from here to London. If a train came this way, it would crunch and fold like an empty can. No passing Go, no collecting two hundred fucking dollars. Just pulverized metal and bones, smashed here or strewn out across the Atlantic.

"You *shouldn't* be here!"

He was trapped. Nowhere to go. Screaming at a wall. The area around him pitch, stark black. He couldn't turn around. There was no way he could've taken a wrong turn. It was *one* path. ONE way.

Ben wanted to hurl himself against the wall. That was how he approached the impossible down here, right? Beat the wall until his fists were red and raw, until his feet ran out of steam and he collapsed to the ground. But he couldn't, not this time. Instead, he just put his back to the wall and slumped. Staring down the long miles he'd just walked.

What could he do now? He couldn't go back, it wasn't an option. He needed resupply, needed the next Way Station. Needed Mile 781. He'd run out of food, the hunger scraping a hole in his stomach. Making him lightheaded, jumbling his thoughts. Only water now. Oxygen at 7 percent.

He grunted. Coughed. Almost relieved to reach an end, finally. Stop pretending there was an alternative. Push away the part of him that urged him to stand. To fight and run backward if need be. There had to be something. *Something* to do. Knowing it was no use, not with 7 percent and the lack of will. His head bobbed. Tired. So tired—

Tap . . . Taptaptap . . . tap tap.

"Just let me DIE!"

Tap . . . Taptaptap . . .

The SOS. Holden. Not coming from the way he'd come, but from—

The left. Ben turned his head and his headlamp pierced through darkness. Not striking the opposite wall but continuing forward into open air. The route banked hard left. A perfect ninety degrees.

Another tunnel.

Ben pushed to his feet, unsteady. Thrust a hand out into the open air, again needing to be certain with his own senses. No resistance. He ran a palm against the split seam in the wall—a seam that shouldn't exist. It was machine perfect, not a last-minute solder like the last Way Station. It was constructed this way.

"It's—

Don't say "not possible." Don't say it.

"It's . . ." Ben swallowed the words. "How is a train supposed to get through this? It's too sharp a turn. It wouldn't work. It—"

Tap . . . Taptaptap . . . tap tap.

Again. Coming from behind.

Ben turned. Horrified. A possibility coming into his head that was . . . nonsense. Pure and simple. There couldn't be—wouldn't be. But it was. Staring him in the face as another never-ending chasm. Another tunnel.

He had arrived at a T-intersection.

Ben stumbled. Knees popping, threatening to spill him. Head whipping between both openings, the enormity of the situation *just* slipping from his grasp. Another hallucination, it had to be. A waking nightmare.

But you've touched it. You've seen it. Real. Three ways.

Ben thumbed the relay. "Holden . . ." Silence. "Holden please tell me you're there. I need some help." His voice cracked as he spoke. From what, he didn't have time to think. This . . . *trick* of the light was taking all his attention. Taking everything in him to realize. It wasn't a trick. His oxygen reserve: 6 percent.

Everything is a choice. Now which do you choose?

"I don't . . . choices can be dangerous."

Doesn't matter. You're running out of air and out of time.

Ben shone his light left and right, hoping to see some shape in the far gloom. Something that might point him in a direction to test and try. He scanned for footprints on the floor, or dust marks, or water stains—something, anything. Both stretching off in the same fog. Both cold and quiet. Identical.

"Hello?" His muffled voice went out, echoes dying almost immediately. The air damp.

Ben stepped toward the left-hand tunnel. Stopped. Not liking the way it *felt*.

"But what if that's the right way? What if I'm supposed to go that way?"

Another step. A quick twist around.

"What if the *right* way is the *right* way?"

A giggle started in his mouth. Morphed. Became a strangled, animal cry. He turned on the wall again.

"YOU'RE NOT SUPPOSED TO BE HERE!"

What happens if you go the wrong way?

He was endlessly walking into the ocean. Never to reach shore. SGO never said anything about a T-intersection. What if there were no more Way Stations? No more rations or O2? No pneumatics?

"The pneumatics! They'll show the right way."

His headlamp jumped across the ceiling, trying to locate the delivery tubes. The inky shadows swirled, obscuring, but yes . . . *yes*. The pneumatic was there. Ben hobbled along the line, following it to the split and . . .

It separated into two parts, branching in both directions.

"*FUCK!* Okay . . . okayokayokay. Choices. Need to make a choice." He whined. "I can't. I just . . . I can't do it."

The shiv was in his hand now, and Ben stared at it. Eyes widening. "Maybe *I* don't need to make the choice. Leave it up to chance." He set the blade on the ground, right at the branching paths. "Like spin the bottle."

He gripped the handle between thumb and two fingers. Spun. The blade stuttered and stopped, its peeling tape grip catching on the floor. Ben scooped it up and smoothed the sticky bits out. Tried again, the blade spinning freely on the steel top. Slowing, slowing, stopping to point—

Backward.

Ben grunted a laugh. Tried to wipe the sweat from his brow and punched the side of his head instead. Took the blade handle between his fingers again.

"Try this again. Round and round we go. Where we stop, nobody knows." Spun.

The blade twisted round a third time, skittering just off direct center with the force of his push. His headlamp reflected off the piping "blade."

Spin. Light. Spin. Light.

Pulling Ben's eyes ever closer. Hypnotic. Slowing, slowing, slowing. Stopped. He followed the blade's direction.

The right branch.

"That's it. The die's been cast."

He sheathed the shiv, quickly stepped toward the right tunnel, not giving himself time to think. To doubt. Paused. Looked backward one last time. Uncertain. Grinding his teeth. Shook his head.

Commit. Need to commit.

"Right is right. Right is right."

A new mantra. A new theory to test.

"Right is right . . . *right?*"

The tunnel gave no answer.

MILE 7CE | RIGHT IS RIGHT

There wasn't just one T-intersection, but many. After the first came a second. Then a third. A fourth. He came to expect them after a mile (?) or two. Even came to count on them. Once, Ben experimented by taking the left branch, but panic forced him to about-face. A physical compulsion that was almost painful. The right branch felt instantly better.

"Right is right. Right is right."

What if it's not?

"It is. It has to be."

Ben assumed after enough rights he'd loop back to where he started, but the tunnel just kept on and on. He lost his concept of distance. Rationally he knew SGO had carefully parceled out each prefab section: a mile, a bulkhead, then the next. Wash, rinse, repeat. But not in the Belly. Oh, no no no. Down here, in the pressing dark, it was all coming undone. There were no mile markers. No bulkheads. No reprieve. No sleep.

He didn't panic. Not when he met his first four-way intersection (and took the right fork). Or when the tunnel began to twist, sloping sideways, forcing him to walk with one foot on the "floor" and one on the "wall."

But his dwindling supplies were worrisome. His hunger all-consuming, his water tasting stale, his O2 meter seeming to drop by the hour.

"And SGO coming. Not far behind now. Maybe they'll even take a train down. All *a-choo-choo*ing down the flue. The train's a'comin!"

Would it be an unmanned kamikaze train, or one packed with suited SGO jackboots? Would they see his grinning face as they barreled toward him at two hundred miles per hour, or just his sticky insides as he splattered across the windshield?

"No, no. It only takes three screws to cause a disaster," Ben tittered. Swallowed. "They hit me, they'll be pulverized too. My bones carving through train and passenger alike."

Then the flames, the water, and just teeth left behind.

"One big happy family."

He was so lonely. No Fontaine. No Holden. No Ellie. Of course no Ellie.

But Ben laughed more often now. Couldn't really say why. He knew the sign of madness even as it spilled out of his mouth. Unchecked impulse, powerless to stop. He supposed it ought to be a positive thing—laughing and grinning as he descended. But the sound was just . . . *off.*

"That's the scariest thing, down here," the tunnel whispered. "The idea of losing your mind."

"Too true, too true," Ben responded, adjusting now as the tunnel twisted more, so his foot touched the "ceiling."

MILE P0B1 | GARDEN

There was light ahead. Unnatural in a tunnel under the sea, but the most natural anywhere else. It wasn't the return of slow-blooming morning in the water, or the floor runners reigniting. But sunlight. *True* sunlight.

Ben made the next turn, the corkscrewing tunnel righting itself so he trod on what he guessed was originally floor. Found himself walking across lush green grass. The tunnel lit with the familiar, yet disconcerting, sunlight. A garden. Bursting with color from azaleas, orchids, and sunflowers.

Ben slowed, feeling sensations that almost brought the tears back. Everything feeling intimate and real, as if he wasn't wearing the suit: warmth seeping into his skin, alighting on his head, and turning his thinning hair hot; the drag of the grass beneath his foot, tickling his soles and the undersides of his toes; the touch of fragile petals and stems between his bare fingers. He inhaled and the stench of sweat and damp flesh was gone, replaced by the soul-affirming scent of flowers.

He recognized this garden, a small oasis tucked just behind their bench along the canal. How many times had they wandered through here, swaying from one too many pints, or carrying groceries home on a lazy Sunday? How many picnics shared looking over the small bay? How many times had he kissed Ellie's shoulders and neck, inhaling her heady mix of perfume and hair conditioner, wishing their flat—their bed—was a few minutes' walk nearer?

It was different, down here under the sea. No wrought iron fence shielding the garden from the road behind, so the garden spread out endlessly in every direction. No overflowing rubbish bins or small tugboats anchored in the canal. No other people. The gravel path was gone, leaving only the greenery, the canal, the sun, and the distant call of birds.

And humming. Someone was humming farther up, just beyond the tree. A figure in the distance, sitting on a bench. *Their* bench.

Ben went forward slowly, not wanting to break this waking dream. He could recognize the tilt of her head, every detail screaming, threatening to buckle his straining legs. The blue-and-white polka-dot sundress she religiously wore on the first day of spring. The black leather backpack, scuffed, worn, and repaired more times than it was worth, leaning against a bench leg. The rose-gold heirloom necklace she never took off, even in the shower. She was humming a familiar tune. Beautiful yet melancholy. Leonard Cohen's "Dance Me to the End of Love."

"Ellie."

There was a metallic croak in his voice, seeming wrong and broken in this place. She didn't move, just sat humming and swaying.

This had been it. That moment beside the water, their talk. That last sunny day when he'd seen her eyes. The lack in them.

Ben reached forward. Terrified to break this dream but wanting to see her face. *Needing* it like he needed more air. Convinced that if he could see her face, he could change the outcome of what was to come. One last chance to fight. He could take her hand in his, tell her he would grow, that he could conquer the anxiety and be less selfish. That he was stronger. For himself and for her.

He touched her back. Fingers grasping a firm shoulder gone marble hard. But Ellie kept on humming. No longer swaying.

"Ellie?"

Ben gently pulled to turn her around, but she was stuck firm. Immobile. Why wouldn't she move? He was here. Right *here*.

Their voices tickled in his memory, as they had so many times. Played over, time and time again. For years. A wound carved deep. As much a part of him as blood and sinew.

Ben... I can't help you. Not if you can't help yourself. It hurts too much to watch you self-destruct.

Ellie, come on. We're right at the finish line. I know I haven't... I haven't been the best husband lately, but don't say anything just yet. It'll be different once everything is over and done with. You'll see, I can change. I'm sure I can.

You can't, you've tried. You're fine for a moment, but then it's always right back to what it was. You've always been more in love with your work than me. I need my husband, not a visionary. You can't change. I know that now.

Ben pulled at her shoulder. He had to stop her now, before those final words came tumbling out. Have her face him. If she turned to him, he could change the words, change the world. But first, he needed to see her face. Now more than ever.

His anger, becoming shorter and shorter as the miles lengthened, rose in him. Knowing what came next. The part of the memory that reduced him to a quivering mess, punctuated sleepless nights, and . . . everything else. All of it.

Ellie. I'm about to show the world what I can do. What I'm capable of. I'm going to be a pioneer! I'm going to change the world!

Ben . . . I want that for you, I really do. But I don't think there's room for me in that vision. I'm sorry. I . . . I can't do this anymore.

Ellie. I need my light by my side. Please come. I need you there.

You're not listening, Ben. You're stealing my light, not sharing it. And I can't keep waiting for you to change. Not now. Not anymore. I love you, Ben. But it's over.

Ben yanked her shoulder. Remembering the profound, almost physical pain of her walking away. The utter despair. Staring until she disappeared. His stumbling through the garden, across the canal crowded with people. Wandering along the water, shocked, realizing what he'd done and why. Wanting to jump and drown. Sink away and never come back. He remembered collapsing, falling face forward, and the sudden cold. Swallowing, swallowing all of it. Wanting to be a lead weight at the bottom to join the rusted bikes and shards of broken bottles.

Instead, he'd woke to gray dawn. A hospital room. Teddy smiling and ruffling his hair. Talking about delaying their project for recovery time, but Ben refusing. They'd come too far and he was ready for greatness.

Then, after they let him go home, he remembered returning to his and Ellie's flat. Empty. Colorless and quiet. And after, fleeing back to the States, unable to stay in the city where he'd pushed her away. Hoping maybe to find her, to rekindle what they'd lost, but disappearing into the work with a zealot's fervor instead.

"Ellie!"

Ben put both hands on her now, shoulder and arm, and tugged. *Needin*g her to turn, to face him, feeling something break off between his fingers. Discolored blood. No—not blood. Rust. Caked on and flaking. Ben pulled harder. He could feel her giving in now, leaning toward him. The humming had stopped. Why had he pushed her away? Why? *Whywhywhy?* Ben wrenched backward so Ellie twisted.

And saw a featureless face. Not Ellie's but something metal and mechanical. A steel gray visage. As he watched, it peeled from scalp to chin, the whole of her cheeks opening to a yawning black-hole center.

That suddenly spewed seawater.

Ben was hurled backward—head striking the tunnel wall. His vision slipping to unequivocal dark. The sun gone. The trees, the flowers, the grass, flaring and burning bright with star-fire intensity, then fading. Swallowed by shadow. Darkness. Just the sound of his own breath, the smell of his rank, decaying body.

His head spun, afterimages dancing across his eyelids as the anguish came—so deep and profound it was etched in his bones. The memory had been so vivid its absence hurt all the more.

"*Breckenridge, what are you doing?*" Holden's voice. Panicked.

Ben opened his eyes. No garden, no sun, just the tunnel, the Belly. Ellie hadn't sat in front of him, he hadn't been pulling on her shoulder. No . . . he saw now, the tunnel had twisted so the ceiling had become the wall. He'd been turning the wheel-lock for the mid-mile hatch. Not all the way but enough so ocean-spray was geysering in. He was sitting in an inch of buildup on the floor, the hatch creaking more and more to open.

"*Breckenridge!*"

"I'm here, I'm here," Ben said, his voice groggy. Without the nonexistent sun, he could truly feel how cold he actually was. Almost numb. Teeth chattering uncontrollably.

"*What's happening? Is there a rupture?*"

He could hear an alarm, screaming. The tunnel was compromised. Did it almost sound like humming . . . faintly in the distance?

Close it. Close it now.

Ben hurled himself against the hatch. Watched rust cake off and crumble as he hit the cap with the full weight of his body.

A deeper shadow moved past the glass, so infinitely large its passage caused the corridor to vibrate. Its wake pushing more water against the hatch, forcing it more open.

Ben fought the resisting hatch. Its long-rusted hinge groaned but wouldn't budge. He was worn down. Exhausted, hungry, and heartbroken. At the edge of his limits, prepared to let the water claim him.

You can do it. You feel that numbness in your fingers? Your body freezing? That's oblivion creeping in. Embrace and fade, or fight.

He'd touched her, hadn't he? Real, if only for a moment. The thought alone spreading a flickering warmth in his chest. He'd been at their bench. He'd heard her humming.

Let that give you an edge. Use it. Now. FIGHT!

"ELLIE!"

Ben hurled himself against the hatch. Feet slipping and struggling to find purchase on the floor. Screaming an animal, tortured scream.

The hatch closed with a heavy, decisive *thunk*. Ben spun the locking wheel with the heels of his palms, fingers not cooperating. Then splashed back to the ground and the freezing water.

And sobbed in the gathering dark. Knowing how different it could've been, if not for one afternoon. One conversation on a bench beside a canal.

"*Ben!*" Holden's voice cut in, over his relay. Did she hear? Had his relay been activated? "*What section are you in?*"

"Please, Holden . . . not now. I just . . . leave me in peace."

The darkness had returned. No color, no warmth. Just him and his headlamp holding back impenetrable night.

"*I* heard *that alarm, Breckenridge.*"

That made him pause.

"Over the relay?"

"*No. I heard it down the tunnel.*"

"Well . . . how far?"

"*Close enough.*"

There was hope in her voice. Elation. He could hear disbelief in there. A promise of something she hadn't reckoned to get again. Something he recognized now. Hope.

"*It was faint . . . but I heard it. Jesus Christ. You might actually get here.*"

MILE #B1< | HOLDEN

"How much farther? Can you hear me?"

Ben limped down the tunnel, knocking on the wall, not caring that his helmet flashed red, screaming at him to take it slower. He was eating up his oxygen too quick: 5 percent and dropping. He was going to burn through his whole supply in minutes at this pace. But it didn't matter. She was close now. She could hear him. He wouldn't be alone anymore.

"Something. I can hear something. Not far."

An answering bang on the walls. Not SOS anymore but just a constant *bangbangbang*. Frantic. Echoing from farther down the corkscrewing tunnel.

"Yes! I can hear you! I'm coming!"

He limped faster. Pulse screaming, limbs burning as he pushed. Farther. Just a little farther now. Sweat cascading down his body, trapped in his suit. He couldn't even imagine the state Holden was in. What would she think of him? Would she—

Ben tripped. Fell flat onto his face, his helmet's faceplate bouncing violently off the floor.

He froze. Staring at the spiderweb cracks. Spreading by inches. Creaking along the glass, engulfing the entire right side of his vision. It was going to shatter.

It can't, not right here. Not when I'm so close!

He didn't breathe, didn't move. Watching, staring. Entire world focused on the faceplate, the cracks, the agonizing crawl . . .

. . . but the glass held.

Ben hauled himself back to his feet. Grinning. Laughing maniacally. Still had a bit of luck left in him. Even now. His O2 dropped another percentage. **Oxygen Reserve: 4%.**

He came to another dead end. But instead of an intersection or branching paths, there was an open hatch in the floor. A ladder descending deeper into the darkness. He paused. Questioning whether to go forward.

Bangbangbang!

"Holden?" Ben said. Swallowing. "Are you down there?"

Bangbangbang!

That was enough of an answer for him. Carefully at first, then with growing speed, he dropped down the shaft. His sense of direction had become so skewed, he wasn't even sure if this shaft went *down*, but he somehow knew this was a descent. Deeper into the Belly.

"I'm coming!"

Too fast. His foot slipped off a rung, and he was falling. Dropping for what seemed like forever but could've only been fifteen feet. His back hit first, the empty O2 canister in his primary line snapping its nozzle, the last bits of residual pressure bursting out the top in a puff of blue-white air. Ben gagged as the trapped, soupy water washed up to his neck and beard and flipped himself over. He whipped the canister off his back like it was liable to explode, grunting. Turned around.

To find a substation deep in the belly of the ocean.

A wide, rectangular room not surrounded by glass, but fully enclosed in steel siding. Banks of computer stations and swivel chairs bent beneath dark monitors covered with a patina of dust.

He knew this room, had been here countless times before. Once recently. And before that . . . the last time. Ben's eyes settled on the massive wall-sized monitor running along the southern wall, humming with electricity. The map of the tunnel with its prefab sections blinking red and green lights, but no Belly in blue.

"The control room."

Ben shook his head, squeezed his eyes shut, hoping that when he opened them again, the hallucination would fade. But his newfound luck wasn't that good—the room was still there when he opened his eyes, unchanged. He couldn't be in the control room, that was back in New York. That's not what had drawn him this way.

Or is it?

"Holden. I'm here for Holden."

BANG BANG! Right on cue.

"Holden!"

He ran forward. Loose papers were strewn about the ground at his feet, dust kicking up in the light of the monitor's bluish haze.

BANG BANG!

Lights were pulsing to life in his wake, first blinking then blazing. Voices too. Voices without bodies, spawned from the air. Like the electricity, like the banging. Familiar.

<Bulkheads green. Tethers through quadrants six and eight seeing movement.>

<Weather settings wavering.>

<Hey, Nick! Maiden voyage!>

A round of clapping hammered his ears. Tears tipped down his cheeks in fat, unchecked droplets. He punched the side of his helmet again, wanting the garbled voices to dissolve into mush, become unintelligible, to *not* bring him back. But the voices remained. Smells too. Sweat-hot anticipation, stale coffee, and the odd cigarette.

<Passengers all buckled in and accounted for. Awaiting go-ahead.>

<Storm's escalating again. Hold for sign-off.>

Pandora's box was opening, but instead of hinges, it was his skull splitting down the center, unleashing ghosts of monitor trills and rote voices over speakers. He pushed it all away, wouldn't get lost.

His blood was up, daydreaming of what might happen when he met Holden, purposefully clinging to the hope that everything around him would disappear. Holden the tunnel technician, not . . . not the other. He'd find her injured, sitting beneath the monitor—no. No monitors, but the tunnel wall, as regular as all the rest. She'd be wounded, and Ben Breckenridge would sit beside her. The lone hero. Ready to carry her out safely. He wouldn't let her down. Wouldn't let anyone down again. Not himself not Ellie. *Nonono*, not Ellie. *Holden.* Ellie was—

BANG BANG!

"I'm here!"

Ben turned the corner, right on top of the sound. The center of the room. Best seat in the house, the place of honor. Exactly where he'd stood when Fontaine gave him the briefing two months ago. Turning to find—

Holden, sitting upright in a chair. No ruptured suit or broken helmet—no diving outfit at all. She wore a mix of smart civilian and start-up branding: khaki pants and a green polo that seemed a bit tomboyish on Holden's thin frame. She turned to face him. A sandy, pitted complexion flush from nerves, sharp chin, and heavy-lidded eyes. A black-foam headset sat perched atop dark hair that had been pulled into a messy ponytail. She was biting her lip, just as in the picture he'd found in Way Station 01.

"Storms escalating still. The tethers are holding for now, but it's . . . it's really fucking dodgy. Personally, Nick, I'd recommend a delay to launch." Holden's smile turned hopeful, the curses falling naturally from her mouth. "I know that's not what you want to hear, but you always told me to give it to you straight, right? Well . . ." She shrugged, handed him a slip of paper.

They weren't alone. The station was filled with people. Their shirts emblazoned with the **STEEL GLASS OCEAN** logo, headsets hanging round their ears. Someone had low music playing. Classical music, swelling strings and piano. The excitement was palpable, all the techs were pretending to stare up at the monitor, but furtively glancing his way. Waiting for Ben's word.

Ben took the paper in one hand, holding a pen in the other. **SIGN-OFF TO LAUNCH PROTCOL: SAFETY CONCERNS**. Beneath, terse sentences outlining the issues. A list of problems associated with a growing tropical storm.

"We need a decision, can't launch before sign-off on both ends of the line. Dr. Reed says conditions on his side are fine, but he's wary. He'll follow your lead," Holden said, nervously worrying at her hair. "Choice is yours. If you sign, we go."

Subconsciously, Ben knew the room was holding its breath. That a PR rep had a camera trained on him at this very moment and the press was waiting just outside the door. Everyone waiting for a single stroke of ink to spark history.

Without Ellie, it was all he had left.

Ben looked up, hearing his own words without opening his mouth. "Want to be a visionary? It starts here." He looked at Holden. "Tell Dr. Reed to sign off. It'd take an act of God to derail this train."

The pen scratched a name, a camera shuttered.

A cheer went up through the station. A flurry of motion as technicians set to, preparing for launch. Ben's hands shook almost imperceptibly, noticed only by him. And Holden. Her gaze lingering for a moment too long. Judging.

"Starting countdown," she said, turning to the screen. "Launch in ten . . . nine . . ."

<Here we go!>

<Gimme eyes, people!>

The tunnel blueprint minimized to the wall screen's bottom, replaced suddenly with a live feed from the train platform, then jumping inside the train itself. Inside, train attendants in deep blues and whites finished safety demonstrations. Passengers tugged at their seatbelts, grinning and posing for photos.

Lightning shot through Ben's skull. Remembrance like echoes. He wanted to look away, but he couldn't. Had to see it through again to the end. It was why he was here.

"Six . . . five . . . four . . ."

Despite the hazy feed, the faces of the passengers were shocking in their clarity. Every wrinkle, stray hair, and imperfection as sharp as a snapshot. Ben knew those faces. Every single one.

He could stop this. Stop it now. Rip up the paper in hand, slam the emergency stop. But he couldn't. It was too late. Eight years too late.

"Two . . . one . . . *launch*."

The main bulkhead doors whined open. The train—*The Odyssey*—pushed through at a lazy, lazy pace, belying the speeds it would reach as it ratcheted up farther down. It slipped into the tunnel darkness and blinked from view.

The control room erupted into cheers. *Houston, we have liftoff.* The people all around pumping fists and hugging one another, ecstasy infectious. Ben realized with a cold dread that their faces were blank. Featureless as if scrubbed clean. All save—

Holden. "Here we go . . . here we go." Eyes rapt on the progress heading on her computer. Her tone not exuberance and joy, but apprehension. Fear. She knew. She'd always known.

Ben was split into two parts. Both overwrought, overtired, and overcritical of everything happening. One, glowing and confident. The other, horrified and powerless.

The train gone, the monitor bank switched back to a grid of live feeds—train interior, weather satellite, platform, and more—set beneath the massive tunnel layout which now sported a new color passing across the various sections. A gray-black line—the train. Colors danced in sequences as bulkheads opened and closed: blue, green, gray-black, green, blue. The train rocketing through, momentum pushing it farther and faster.

A minute passed. Two. Five. An eternity slipping away in the snap of a finger. Nothing but the hum of soft speech and the screech of the classical music nearby. He wanted to tell them all *shut the fuck up* and to turn off the music so it wouldn't haunt him later. To punch toggles and mash buttons. To curse until his voice was hoarse and it all faded back into blind nightmare. Make them all see—

A bell rang. Soft enough that it wouldn't be heard if you weren't looking for it. Alerting a single computer. Holden's. Followed by another, much louder than the first. Then another. A klaxon pierced through the room and error codes flashed on *every* screen. A red strobe woke and whirled from the far wall.

<Something's wrong. What is that?>

<Experiencing extreme turbulence onboard.>

<Guys, the storm fried my instruments!>

<Someone give me status! Status now!>

"Oh, God. It's happened," Holden turned around again. Limbs stiffened with an inability to do anything. Watching him do that same. "Nick?"

Ben opened his mouth, pointed at the feed showing the train's interior. Said the word now and eight years back.

"Rupture."

The wall screen went to a live satellite image showing the eye of the storm, its tempest center sweeping above the tunnel only a hundred miles off the East Coast, punching the water around it up and down. Not the graceful back and forth rocking of the sea, but a violent churning.

The image shifted to a submersible feed, stationed somewhere along the train's route like a spectator at a marathon. The camera tracked what looked like the train as it blurred past, looking like a rollercoaster spiraling along an uneven track, spilling sparks and continuing to pick up more and more speed.

"Inside!" Holden yelled. Authority covering fear. "Show me inside."

No. No, don't show it. Two minds, the same voice. He had to. He had to see. There was no stopping it. The screen sizzled with static. Jumped, showed the interior.

Chaos. A three-point tear had ripped across the train's ceiling like a monster's claw, punched through and pulled back, shedding debris, loose items, and hair up and out into the tunnel. No sound came from the feed, that was probably for the best.

All the passengers were choking. Straining at purpling necks and unforgiving seatbelts, as the air sucked out the cabin through that terrible puncture. Some made it free of their seats. A train attendant rocked back and forth like she was taking punches from a boxer. Everyone else couldn't do anything but struggle. Choke. Jostle in their seats in an unforgiving, killing wind.

Ben was aware of the technicians around him trying to stop the train, pulling at his arm and screaming for him to *do something*, but he couldn't move. It was everything he could do to not pass out. And stare. Stare until his eyes fell to the last passenger row. Focused on a woman just visible between two headrests. Looking so . . . frightened. And alone.

Smoke rapidly filled the screen. Smoke that shouldn't be there, spelling certain catastrophe. It was coming now. Blessedly. Only a moment away. The woman looked up, eyes falling directly on the camera.

A spark spit into view. Two. A split-second flash of white, but already the world changed. A burst of light, then an uncoiling inferno, red as burst capillaries, tore through the train. Engulfing. The feed hazed with static. Cut out.

Holden screamed. The control room went utterly silent.

And Ben *laughed*. A single, short bark.

He never knew why. Shock warps the mind the moment it hits, but even that could never comfort him in the low moments of night. Couldn't save him from the self-loathing of laughing while *The Odyssey* burned. The horror and revulsion in the eyes of Holden and the technicians.

An act of God.

Ben howled. The present Ben. Wailing at the monitor, at the tiny black dot now stuck at Mile 781 on the screen. His knees buckled and he crumpled, burying his face in his hands. Sobbing as the well of memory refreshed and he imagined all of them stuck, confused, and choking all over again. Begging for a final release but met by flames instead.

MILE 780 | BRECKENRIDGE

He didn't know how long he was on that cold floor. An eternity on his knees. He'd stay there until the sea dried if he could. Until his air went. Until SGO came down looking for Fontaine's mistake of a scavenger only to find a grinning, emaciated corpse kneeling in the control room near the center of the Belly, lulled by a siren song from a long-lost technician.

Ben knew none of this was real, like the corkscrewing tunnel or talking crab. The control room was back in New York, Holden wasn't here. Yet when he looked up, there she was, frozen at that point of perfect remembrance. The revulsion, the horror. All around too, those featureless faces. Everything, immobile. Ice-still in the ocean—the tunnel's—embrace.

"I could've listened. I should've. I knew better," Ben said. Staring at Holden.

Holden didn't speak, just stared back.

"I'm not asking you to forgive me. I don't deserve it." He shook his head. Exhaled a fragile, unsteady breath. "I'm a monster. I'm the ghost haunting this tunnel."

She wouldn't respond, not to admonish or agree. Because she was just another hallucination spawned from a damaged mind. Born from him. Ben reached for his comms relay, switched it from **Off** to **On**.

"*—ckenridge. Come in, Breckenridge. This is Steel Glass Ocean, New York. Do you copy?*" Fontaine's voice, clear as cut glass. Exhausted. It sounded like he'd been repeating himself for a while now. "*This is Steel Glass Ocean . . .*"

Ben forced himself up to his feet. Walked the few feet to Holden, stared in those horrified eyes. All around, the scene was dissolving away. Snowy ash, drifting and falling as dust.

He put a hand on Holden's rigid shoulder.

"I'm sorry, Holden. I really am."

Holden—the real Holden—was dead. Had been for years. A victim of *The Odyssey* disaster fallout, unable to cope with what she'd seen and been a party to. After the inquiry and the trial, Holden moved back to her parents' home in San Francisco, looking for solace in therapy and grief counseling. When that proved insufficient, she hopped off the Golden Gate Bridge on the second anniversary of the crash. Another death added to the tally.

"Ben Breckenridge. Come in, Breckenridge. This is Steel Glass Ocean."

He looked down the long tunnel. Not the control room, but the tunnel. Simple and straight. What it had been the entire time. There was the pinprick of blue white, the weakly gleaming eye of the next mile's lock at low power. He swallowed hard. Mile 781. Beckoning to him. Calling. His goal, the end.

What could be done, would be done there. He walked.

"Fontaine."

A pause on the far side. A stutter.

"*God-loving Christ. Breckenridge? Where the* fuck *you been?*" Behind Fontaine's admonition, Ben could hear the low rumble of voices. A dozen people peppering the background.

"Walking."

Fontaine didn't laugh this time. Ben could feel his seething anger as he hissed low as to not be heard. "*You really put your foot in it, you know that? Slapped my neck on the rail line next to you too. I had a perfectly good system going here, then you had to pull the fucking rug out. You know how much trouble you've caused me? The fucking feds are here. The goddamn* FEDERAL *agents.*"

Ben was barely listening, the words and curses flowing over and around like an errant breeze. Inside, his subconscious was inching awake. He couldn't be stopped. Eyes and feet forward.

Nearby, he could feel them, rather than see: the shadows, shifting. Coming alive. If he looked behind, the horrors would be following him. Watching him go. And beside—

BOOM. BOOM BOOM.

Outside, the octopus was back.

"*HEY. Fucking superhero?*"

"Yeah . . . yeah, I'm here."

An exasperated huff. "*I looked into you, buddy. Too much fuss happening 'round here for a simple scavenger. Know what I found? There is no Ben Breckenridge. No social security, no W2s, no goddamn digital footprint at all. The man doesn't exist.*"

Fontaine paused, waiting for Ben to give in. Let it all pour out. But Ben didn't, only kept walking.

"*Well? Got anything to say?*"

"You were wrong about *The Odyssey*."

"*What?*"

"It wasn't just three loose screws that caused the crash. There was a storm. Small enough to escape a great deal of scrutiny, but big enough to jostle the train off alignment. Made the hull scrape along the ceiling." Ben tripped over his feet but stayed steadily walking forward. "An 'act of God.'"

Another long Fontaine pause. "*Who are you, really?*"

"My name's Nicholas Moore. I built this," And, as a whisper, "I'm here to fix things."

"*Mr. Fontaine, what's goin—*"

"*Sh— the, uh, goddamn scavenger, sir. I—*"

A voice from farther in the room. Fontaine's plaintive, caught red-handed fumbling, then silence. The absent hum of a muted microphone.

Ben walked on, undeterred. Willing and wanting to reach the bulkhead but fearing it. Fearing it like nothing else before. It was time now. Seconds passed. A minute. He turned. Watched the octopus inch along, not interfering but never leaving.

The microphone switched back on. Feedback.

"*Hey, Nick.*"

"Teddy."

Theodore "Teddy" Reed's familiar voice creaked now like well-worn leather. His North London accent was stronger than it'd been the last time Ben heard it, thousands of miles away and a lifetime removed. Ben imagined the etched wrinkles on the old, easy face. Graying temples and a burst vein nose from one too many drinks, trying to forget.

"*How far did you get this time, partner?*"

"780."

"Just there."

"Yeah. Just here."

Teddy spoke away from the microphone. *"Mile 780. Send a crew would you, Mr. Fontaine? And push auxiliary power to the surrounding area."* A muttering in the background—Fontaine, cowed and embarrassed. *"Everyone else, could you all give us a moment please?"*

"Dr. Reed . . ." Someone said.

"Please . . . just a few minutes."

Footsteps and voices melted away into the background.

Ahead of Ben, the subdued gleam of next mile's lock light flared as the auxiliary power arrived and stoked it to life.

"Haven't gotten a moment's peace from the vultures since Ashvin called. You went and caused a good many problems this time, my friend. Trespassing, falsifying employment records." There was a smile in the old man's voice, that same old ease. Teddy was always good for some mischief. *"Sure it's got one hell of a story."*

"Sure," Ben said absently.

"You going in?"

"It's why I'm here."

"Right. Of course."

A grunt from Teddy. The squeal of a chair. Exactly the same, yet somehow different from Fontaine's. Exhaustion rather than laziness.

"You know, you've tried this before. This'll be attempt number three," Teddy said. *"First time . . . was about two years after. Nearly made it all the way too, but you eventually had a mental break. Talking about ghosts and monsters. Used a welding torch to try and seal yourself in a bulkhead like a coffin. Had the Way Station door closed and was starting on the bulkheads before we caught up.*

"Second time wasn't long after that, but we were quicker to grab you. You hit a section of flooded tunnel that freaked you out, and you couldn't cross through. You tried to kill yourself instead. Went into a Way Station and cut your stomach open. There was . . . a lot of blood. I was pretty sure you weren't gonna make it."

There it was. The puzzle pieces falling together as memories bubbled back to the surface, repeating like corrupted data:

The first time. Flooding the tunnel so no one from New York could follow and stop him. Running out of potable water and deciding the bulkhead would be his tomb. He could recall soldering the Way Station door and contemplating turning the flame on himself before a submersible "rescue" crew arrived and pulled him out.

The second time. Reaching the blocked tunnel, terrified to swim through. Ransacking the Way Station, being low and desperate, slicing his stomach open with jagged metal. The blood, spurting then oozing. The SGO blacksuits rushing in.

He touched a hand to his stomach. The scar. He remembered it all. And that remembering was more than scratching at an old wound. It was reopening a chasm where his heart used to be, filled now with sharp and suffocating things.

"*I . . . I had you committed after that.*" Teddy sighed, deep and horrible. "*I'm sorry, Nick . . . I . . . You were a liability to yourself. I just wanted you safe. I missed my friend.*"

"It's okay, Teddy," Ben said. "Really. You were doing what's best."

Silence for a moment, and Ben knew Teddy was contemplating what they'd lost. The price for their ambition. Like he did. Ben felt that loss, could sense it in the smallness of Teddy's voice. That ease of his loss.

"When did you decide to dismantle the tunnel?"

"*Last year. Finally got the go-ahead from Congress—it's officially no longer a crime scene. I was going to tell you once deconstruction started so you couldn't stop it as part owner. Didn't want* this *to happen again. But I figured you were safe in the home. Imagine my surprise when I call over and hear you'd been released.*" Teddy laughed. "*Never could sit still, could you? Should've known the tunnel would bring you back.*"

The lock light loomed closer, and near it. A shape. A figure in the shadow.

"*Care to explain this name?*"

"What?"

"*Your name. You change it every time. I always thought it was your way of getting past security and scrutiny, but I know better now. First time you went down it was . . . what, Rigby, I think. Like the conductor. The second time*"—and here Teddy's voice got smaller still—"*you called yourself Holden.*"

"Because I want to escape my name. Don't deserve it . . . don't want it." Ben swallowed. "Breckenridge is her maiden name."

"*Yeah . . . yeah, I know. Best for last, I guess. What about 'Ben'?*"

The figure coalesced: the little boy he'd seen all through the tunnel. He watched Ben draw closer, then turn away. Walked *through* the bulkhead door. Into 781.

"It's what she wanted to name a boy if we ever had one."

"Ah . . . Jesus. Nick . . ."

The silence again. The sadness. Ben walked on. His oxygen ticked. **Oxygen Reserve: 3%.** Nearly there.

"I could've stopped the train, Teddy. I *should've* stopped it. They warned us about the storm . . . but I was so . . . *certain*. So eager to be some visionary. Build something to stand the test of time . . . to do *good*." He choked. "It was my fault."

"*It wasn't your fault*." Teddy had said this before. "*It was a freak accident. Pure and simple. You saw the reports, the investigators called it an—*"

"Act of God."

Ben paused. Turned. Behind him were the horrors that had haunted him. Silhouettes of people. Waiting. Watching. He continued on.

"Is that why you buried the official report for me, Teddy? Why we didn't disclose the storm warning to the presidential inquiry, or the sign-off orders to launch?" He swallowed hard again. "Everything . . . for what? It wasn't an act of God. It was just . . . vanity and pride. And now they're all dead."

Teddy went silent for a long time and Ben realized he was still doing it. Still being selfish, thinking only of himself. Teddy had lost too. Had to watch the disaster unfold at *The Odyssey*'s finish line in London, then pick up the pieces when his partner shattered over and over again.

"*Even if you hadn't insisted we launch, I would have signed off anyway. We couldn't have stopped it. All that pressure, all those people. The investors, the press . . . It was inevitable.*"

All those people.

"*We had to . . . we had to. I'm sorry I put the burden of that final decision on you. I really am. But the choice would've been the same.*" Teddy's voice was worn, beaten down. Ben felt he could sense the man better now, form a picture of the friend he'd shared a joint with in Grant Park. Shared a vision with. "*We're all grieving, Nick. Eight years on and it still hurts, but you can't keep doing this. Trying to atone for a crime you didn't commit through this . . . self-imposed solitary confinement.*"

Ben opened the door to bulkhead 780/781 and stepped inside the threshold, closed it behind.

"*It's a sickness, coming back to this place. Keeping yourself from moving on. This tunnel . . . it's a comfort to you.*"

"I know." Ben wished he could see Teddy, to look him in the eye. He put a hand on the lock to 781. "Last time, Teddy. I promise."

"*Nick.*" Teddy's voice was thick. Falling to a whisper. Both of them knowing. "*Please. Don't do this. You don't have to.*"

"I do." He hardened his resolve. "For her."

"*Nick—*"

"Goodbye, Teddy."

"*Nick, don—*"

Ben toggled the relay and Teddy disappeared.

BOOM! BOOM BOOM!

The tunnel heaved, trying to toss Ben to the floor, but he held onto the bulkhead lock.

The octopus was above him, its huge eyes boring down through the oceanlight. Tentacles warped and wrapped around the glass, gripping and flexing. Ready to rip it from its bearings, to get to *him*. It was a threat, *Don't go forward.*

Ben wouldn't be stopped now. His O2 dropped another percentage: 2 percent. Enough. It would have to be enough.

Prime. Twist.

Breathe. Just breathe.

Pull.

MILE 781

Beyond the bulkhead door stood a wall of water, suspended in air. Pure blue and bright.

Ben put his hand through but didn't feel the resistance as it should've been. His glove was bone dry when pulled back. He stepped in.

It wasn't the tunnel, but the train interior. Submerged. A long row of white walls, gray seats, and accents in blue. Chairs like molded movie seats set in two rows by four, then two, then four again. Each seat occupied with a corpse.

Ben didn't look at their faces but walked down the row, head down like a penitent. Not wanting to see the eyes of those he passed. They weren't featureless like the technicians in the control room—each passenger was perfectly rendered from memory. They were the horrors in the tunnel, his ghosts. Their eyes livid white and terrified, their skin blackened and crisped. He knew them, better than his own face these days. He'd lived with them every night for the past eight years, both in their burned state and before. He could describe them in perfect detail.

The grandmother with the bright lipstick and coifed hair, her vein-wrought hands gripping the armrests tight while her grandson clutched at her blouse with two plump fists.

The train attendant with the wine-colored birthmark beside her left ear, unbuckled and floating listlessly through the air. A wide cut on her forehead where she'd hit the ceiling, her heels drifting down the aisle just beside her.

The businessman with the scuffed leather suitcase, sitting calmly in his seat as if good manners would be enough to see him safely through. Staring at his phone with mute appeal, at an image that was always too blurry to make out.

The tourists with their matching Palisades Country Club hats, the bald man in the Hawaiian shirt trying to pry open his window, the impossibly blond teenagers clinging to one another with both arms. Everyone and more in stark relief, one full train car out of ten.

None of them mattered though, not in this moment. They'd have their time later, as they always did. Ben made his way to the car's extreme rear, to the sole single seat settled against the far wall. To—

The woman Ben had seen on the live camera feed. Those eyes peeking out from between the two chairs, the false light turning her auburn hair red. Glowing like the sun. All alone.

Ellie.

She was here. Right in front of him. Separated by years, and miles, and the empty fullness of life. Ben went to his knees, putting his arms around her waist. He could touch her. Feel her skin beneath his fingers. He tried to kiss her hands, but the helmet was in the way. He was desperate to touch her with his naked hand. It was all he needed now in the world. All he had ever needed. He put his hands on his helmet clasp, his finger twitching. Not fast enough.

BOOM.

Somewhere nearby, something rattled the fabric of the world. The octopus, furious. Still coming. Still desperate with rage.

Ben turned to look, and found himself outside the train, on the platform in New York. Crowded with people—press, influencers, and simple passengers. All smiling, all doomed. The din they made was incredible and jarring.

The little boy stood before him. An island of calm in the chaotic sea of unloading and boarding, everyone in a hurry for the main event. But the child just stared at Ben, waiting for him to notice, then slowly backed away and disappeared into the crowd.

Ben gave chase, catching glimpses of the boy as he pressed farther toward the far end of the train before losing him just before the very last car. He paused, craning to look over the tops of milling heads, trying to spot the boy.

And saw Ellie instead, standing beside the train. Waiting expectantly. Her face all glee and excitement.

Ben pushed forward, the child forgotten, needing to reach Ellie and stop her from boarding. But the hordes of people and press were between them. He was struggling again as he had against the flood of bloated corpses in his nightmares. Swimming but never moving an inch. Always a moment from drowning, flailing to reach just a little farther.

The conductor approached Ellie and the two of them spoke, but Ben was too far away to hear. The conductor's mustache broadened with a laugh and Ellie flushed with a pleased but embarrassed smile.

She placed a protective hand over her belly.

Ben was so close now, jostling toward the sleek bullet-car, but seeing Ellie's rubbing her stomach, he slowed. Swallowed again by that knowledge. That earthshaking happiness, followed quickly by the lowing, fathomless grief.

The little boy was standing there, watching him. Something—someone—that could have been but would never be. Standing in for all the possibilities that may have come to pass if things had been different. If *he* had been different. A life unlived. The child looked so much like Ben. Like Ellie.

The conductor offered Ellie a hand onto the train. This time Ben could read his lips, as he had so many times before, pouring over grainy security camera footage: "*Come on quick, wouldn't want to ruin the surprise.*"

Ellie turned in place, one last scan across the crowd, looking for him, knowing he'd planned to be on the maiden voyage. But the past Ben—*Nick*—was off in the control room, no longer planning to join the passengers. Unable to return to London, to face that city where he'd lost her. Unaware she was boarding the train. Gripping a piece of paper and signing his soul away and her death warrant.

"*ELLIE!*"

It was no use. She couldn't see or hear him. Finally, smiling mischievously, she took the conductor's hand, and boarded.

She'd come here wanting to support him. Honoring that fateful last request to be a part of his grand moment, knowing how much this meant to him. Despite how terrible he'd been, Ellie wanted this to be the greatest day of his life, surprising him with her presence, and an unexpected gift.

Ben wanted to scream. *Don't let it leave! ELLIE! I'm RIGHT here!* Instead, he watched his wife board the train, surrounded by strangers, but alone. Alone, except for their son just stirring in her womb.

BOOM. BOOM BOOM.

The world shook and Ben was back in the water. In the train. There were no open seats, so he sat on the ground beside Ellie, holding her around the waist. He rested his head in her lap and sobbed.

"I'm here now, Ellie. I'm not going anywhere."

His O2 clicked down. 1 percent.

"Here to the end."

This was it. The long road and its inevitable finish. Right here, exactly where he wanted to be. His plan and his penance.

Ben would let that final percent of O2 click away, then he would drift off. He'd find her and they'd be together again. They would watch their son quicken in her womb, then grow, and be happy beneath the sun, the stars, and back again. Everyone, the three of them, the passengers, they'd all be well again. That would be the end. The end for Ben Breckenridge. For Nicholas Moore. He was ready. He was tired. Just so . . . so tired.

"Hey, Tarzan."

That voice. Heard so often he couldn't believe it was real. Not anymore, not down here. He wished he wouldn't look, but he had to. To see . . . to *see.*

Ellie hadn't moved. She stared on ahead, unseeing. But she *had* spoken. Ben squeezed closer to her waist. "I'm here. I'm right here."

"It's time." Her lips didn't move. Those perfect lips. But it was her voice. He would know it in life. In death. Know it anywhere. "It's time to let go."

He shook his head. "No, I can't. I should've been there. I should've been less selfish. Tried harder. I should have been a better man. I should've been there for you." He gasped ragged gulps of air. "You were what made me a great man . . . I can't do it without you."

And as he said it, the water disappeared from the train. The lights hummed awake. All around the passengers were returned to the fullness of life. Bright and excited, as they'd been in the end. The grandmother, the train attendant the businessman—all looking to him. Grateful he'd come to see them off.

"You can," Ellie said.

She was looking down at him, not with the empty stare of death, but with life and light shining through her eyes. His everlasting light.

"Just breathe . . . and let me go."

She leaned forward. Touched her forehead to his. Skin to skin. Kissed him. Soft. So very soft. Melting him.

Then he was in the tunnel. On his knees. No water and no train, just the tunnel as it had been for hundreds of miles. Same as ever, save a scar in the glass ceiling where SGO had cut in eight years ago to remove the debris, *the bodies*, and sealed it back up. That jagged wound, the only remaining sign that this had once been a tomb. Now, just another prefab section in thousands.

Ellie was gone.

"No. *No*," Ben moaned, feeling so cold. He scrambled like a madman looking for something lost. He couldn't let it go. Couldn't let *her* go. He wasn't ready, not yet, not now. They'd destroy the tunnel, and he'd have nothing. Not his grief, not his guilt, not his purpose.

Ben wailed. Let the anguish wash over. To pour from his eyes. To drown him. To fill that aching chasm deep inside. Wanting to die too. Wanting to die in that train, with everyone. To finally give in.

But they'd all looked at him. Acknowledged him there, in the end. For the journey he'd gone through. The suffering to make it right. It wasn't forgiveness exactly, but perhaps . . . somehow, they might finally be able to find a sort of peace.

BOOM. BOOM BOOM.

Ben raised his eyes, saw the octopus above. The shadow. *His* shadow.

"I see you now . . ." Ben cried, feeling the spittle run down his cheek. "I know what you are."

Staring up, Ben saw himself in the reflection off the steel glass. Those eyes he'd seen seven hundred and eighty-one miles ago. No longer a wild animal's and no longer caged. Broken, yes, but ready to accept. Maybe . . . ready to be free.

Let me go.

Ben rose to his feet, looked away from his reflection, and took in the tunnel. Soaking it in. Heaving a wet, strained breath.

Knowing what he had to do.

HIM

Way Station 06's computer flickered into life. Ben cycled past the main scrawl to the broken pixel and the hidden menus. The key master's secret operations for special occasions. Like when he'd set a timed master lock to seal him in Bulkhead 83/84 or shut down Mile 649.

PASSWORD REQUIRED flashed on the screen and his fingers danced of their own free will.

0-8-0-5-e-v-e-r-l-a-s-t

The day he'd met Ellie, their song.

The indicator went red, then green. Unlocked.

He pushed past door override codes, to commands, then emergency sequencing. A flurry of buttons punched before he lost the nerve, each press felt like another piece of him stripping away, laying bare. Writing and arranging a new action, ready to execute when ordered.

Ben plundered the Way Station, grabbing a new roll of duct tape and a dive computer from the emergency stores, then pulled an O2 canister from the station's care package, spilling rations onto the ground as he veered for the door. He paused before heading back out onto the road, looking at the Way Station and the bulkhead. Neither looking comfortable, but functional. Constricting.

"You're right, Teddy . . . solitary confinement. It's been a prison from the very start," Ben said, no trace of a grin—mad or otherwise. Wondering if he'd done his time.

BOOM BOOM.

Ben moved back into 781, heading toward the mid-mile mark. He plastered his helmet with duct tape, going over the new cracks and creases. Twice. Three times. Then around any seams he thought might be dodgy, just to be safe. He plugged in the O2 canister and watched the reading jump from 1 percent to 33 percent. Finally, he strapped the diving computer to his wrist.

He didn't realize he was crying until the tears tapped onto the faceplate. Questioning if he had the nerve, if this was the right decision. If he'd ever truly be free of the never-ending cycle of war with his own mind, battling and never winning. Always drowning. Reverting him to a terrified, weak animal.

"Not anymore." He looked up, past the mid-mile hatch. "You hear me? Not anymore."

The shadow loomed. A tentacle falling nearby. Dark eyes staring down through the glass. Fear prickled Ben's spine. This was what he wanted. Right? No. It was what he needed.

He unclipped the pouch at the suit's belt and pulled the hidden treasure from its folds. His wedding ring. Looking out of place in this hostile, cold place. Unremarkable. But in truth, it was the most remarkable thing he'd ever possess. That last piece of her.

"Ellie . . . I . . . *I* can do it."

Ben placed the ring on the tunnel floor. Without looking away, he opened the junction box and punched the button. Flares burst into the water, illuminating the ocean, revealing the waiting octopus. Ben put his foot atop the junction box and hoisted himself up to the ladder, climbing rung over rung until his body became nearly parallel to the ground. He gripped the locking wheel in his hand. Twisted.

And pulled the mid-mile hatch open.

It peeled backward, hurling Ben to the floor as water flooded the chamber. Ankle-deep before he could get himself back to his feet, force building faster than he could've imagined. Chest high now. Getting higher. Higher. Over his head. Now, fully submerged.

A tentacle slithered in through the hatch. Then another. The octopus *squeezed* its way into the tunnel, its entire gargantuan body contracting then filling the space, looking almost comical if it wasn't so utterly horrifying. It twisted, turning to look with those abyssal eyes at Ben.

Ben returned the stare, seeing a calculation there. He backed up, breath heaving, watching two tentacles stretching his way. Waiting for the python wrap and squeeze, the rending and ripping apart. His fear so profound as to be paralytic, but he faced it. Pushed against it. Stood his ground.

The attack never came. The octopus's gaze remained, its tentacles wavering in the rushing water. And in those eyes, Ben saw no malevolence at all, but empathy. Kinship.

He felt the shadows of his mind peel away, a new understanding solidifying in their place. Reshaping Ben's journey, and the creature before him: no stalking, murderous force, but a companion in the long and lonely dark. Not trying to suffocate Ben or to harm him, but to save him from this place.

From himself.

Ben reached forward, wanting to touch the octopus. To make certain with his own hand and know *this* at least was real. No delusion.

Instead, his fingers groped for the keypad on the hatch and punched in the new sequence.

A piercing trill rippled through the chamber. The hatch didn't close or the water empty, instead the tunnel doors on either side of the mile opened. Water gurgling out and spreading, falling into the bulkheads, then into Miles 780 and 782. But it wouldn't stop there. Ben's operation had tricked the system into thinking a train was preparing to be launched, causing the miles and miles of bulkheads to open, lock lights spinning under a master code, the entire expanse of tunnel ready to accept the damning deluge.

The octopus kept its gaze steady, but its tentacles wavered and tensed, feeling the change in environment. Its intelligent eyes rising, its mantle shifting. Questioning.

"Go."

The great eyes focused. Unfocused. And the octopus floated away, closing the distance to the opening bulkhead door in moments and wrenching it fully open. Moving quickly. Tentacles gripping, ripping, and tearing, carving a path. Destroying as it went.

Ben swung his hands to either side of the open hatch, feeling the push and pull of suction. He gave one last look down the long mile, then to the floor where he'd left her ring. He thought he could see a glint of gold down there, resisting the whirlpool. He could drop down, pick it back up, hold onto the last remembrance. Instead, he fought against the crush of water.

Moving up and out of the tunnel.

THE DEEP

The Atlantic was utterly still and silent. All Ben wanted to do was float, ceaselessly, to the top.

But he couldn't. He needed to decompress first, or he'd get the bends. Nitrogen would settle beneath his skull, expand to air pockets, and decimate what was left of his brain. He'd be floating to the top as a corpse. Maybe that would be for the best.

He'd have to wait. Reach seventy-five feet up, then hold for five minutes. Slow. Slow going. Never ascending faster than the bubbles. He stared at the dive computer, watching the ascent as the feet ticked away.

174 feet . . . 173 . . . 172.

Ben tried hard not to think about all that water, the horrible, all-consuming fear of drowning making his spine tingle like nothing else had. He needed a distraction and quick—so he fixated on the helmet's plate. Listening to the minute cracks as the glass strained against the pressure. Surprised it hadn't buckled yet. This was suicide, absolute madness, but there were no other options.

The helmet's going to crack. It's going to crack, the water's going to rush in, and I'm going to drown. Pulled back down.

111 . . . 110 . . . 109 . . .

Ben pushed the panic away. He had the air to burn and hyperventilate, but it wouldn't help. No . . . he couldn't drown. Not here and not now. He *wouldn't*.

Water bubbled through a seam. Another. The faceplate leaking as the spiderweb cracks inched across his vision, threatening to cave at the slightest wrong breath. So much pressure, he could feel it across the whole of his body, ears popping.

77 . . . 76 . . . 75 feet.

Ben stopped his ascent and set the dive computer to count backward. Five minutes.

Five whole minutes with nothing to do but be afraid, to feel that familiar crawling sensation over his scalp. The leaking, the water. *Drowning. It would be so easy.* In the tunnel he'd been safe, but here . . . everything was different.

Open water. Darkness. The deep in its purest form. Nothing but endless, pure blue. Pressing against him. Warning him. Readying to embrace him and pull him down to its bosom. Pulverize his bones and suck every last bubble from his lungs.

Ben could fear the unknown and uncertain, or he could overcome. Despite the leaks, despite the terror. Sometimes, you have to do the thing you're scared of.

He twisted, turned his body, and looked *down.*

The tunnel stretched across the ocean farther than he could see in two directions. A snake uncoiling its way across a shadowed backdrop. From above it looked so simple, unthreatening. Beautiful even. His Wonder, there to behold.

And as he watched, the tunnel began to sink. Filling with water and slowly drifting down . . . farther and farther. The many tethers that kept it from floating upward now chained it in place as every nook and crevice flooded.

His life's work. His own shadow and shackles, plummeting into an unknown world to become a new home for the creatures of the deep. Never to be seen again.

Ben closed his eyes. A final, wordless goodbye. Letting go.

Just breathe.

Like she taught you, but you learned. All you now. Alone. Breathe. That's it.

Live.

The crawling on his scalp dissipated. The bottomless pit in his stomach found surface. His panic receded. The dive computer trilled in the close water. *0:00.* Five minutes up, time to surface. He reopened his eyes.

And his faceplate shattered. Water flooded into his face and down into his suit, weighing him down like an anchor.

Ben tore at the suit, gloves too stubby for the clasps and zippers. The panic returning, terror reasserting itself. The suit was dragging him back down. Determined to rejoin the tunnel. Back into the maw of the beast.

He wrenched at unyielding buckles, writhing as salt threatened to fill his lungs. As the sky drifted further away.

Ben couldn't panic. If he panicked, he died.

The shiv.

He yanked it from his belt, slicing away. Legs first, then arms, not caring to watch as shreds of blue-black tech flapped away to the inky depths. No surgeon's careful cutting, but a hacking and tearing, catching skin but rending suit most of all. Soon, he felt weightless, unencumbered for the first time in months.

But with no helmet, no suit, there was no oxygen. The fear of drowning was no longer a simple phobia but a reality. He wasn't safe yet.

Darkness was closing in as he kicked. Air. He needed air. Now. His strokes were erratic, pulling at the water. Steady. Up. Faster. Following golden shafts slicing from above.

He was too far. He'd never make it. He couldn't. He would drown before he saw the sun again.

Kick. Control.

One more. One more.

Shadows. Edging his vision.

One m . . .

THE BLUE DESERT

The light was blinding as he broke the surface.
    Gasping, floundering, then inhaling deep. Air. Real air. His cracked helmet bobbed beside him in the calm sea, and Ben rested his head on the duct-taped edges. Exhausted beyond words, waiting for his vision to adjust.
    Sunlight. He turned his face skyward and smiled, feeling warmth seep into his frigid bones. Burn his pale skin. He resolved, then and there, to chase the sun wherever he could and be nourished by it. If he lived.
    The ocean stretched out as far as his eyes could see, unbroken to the horizon. The blue desert. Seven hundred and eighty-one miles from land. After being trapped in the tunnel for so long, the sudden enormity of open water was terrifying. Possibilities limitless. He would have to formulate a plan. Decide on the next course of action before panic overtook and treading water was no longer enough.
    Or, he could relax. No longer a desperate man haunted, watched, or shackled. He was alone. Just him and the open sky. At peace. Whole and free.
    Just breathe. He did it now, lungs feeling raw and misused but finally right. Laughed. Truly laughed until there was nothing left.
    Ben Breckenridge tucked the helmet under his arm as a buoy. He didn't point toward land, toward rescue or certainty. Instead he lay back, floating on the current. Content to close his eyes, listening to the ebb and flow of the waves.
    And enjoy the sun.

ACKNOWLEDGMENTS

The creation of a novel is an odyssey, and the journey of *The Darkest Deep* was no exception. Without the support of several people, this book would never have seen the light of day, and I am thankful to have them in my life.

Of the many people I owe a debt of gratitude, chief among them would be its champion: my incredible agent Pam Gruber at the Highline Literary Collective. Thank you for pulling my story from the slush pile and believing in it for long, quiet years.

A great thank you to the fine folks at Podium Publishing, especially Brian Skulnik, Stephanie Beard, Taylor Bryon, Nicole Passage, Nicole Antos, Gina White, and Annie Stone.

Thank you to the unbelievable team at WME, including Nicole Weinroth, Carolina Beltran, and Perry Weitzner whose excitement for this book is infectious.

Thank you to my editor, Wes Miller, who helped refine a funky writing style, and who insisted I see the worthiness of octopi over whales.

Of course, the greatest thanks to my family—Sarah, James, Peter, and my parents, Paul and Ann. Your support, understanding, and love are as important to me as oxygen. Thank you, dad, for instilling in me a love of the written word, and mom for your unending encouragement.

My deepest gratitude to Candy and Bo Hirsch, who gave me a safe space to write this book, a healthy amount of uplifting when I needed it, and an unhealthy number of hamburgers every Tuesday.

Thank you to Kenny Langer, Will Lentz, Beau Rawlins, and Ethan Moore, who have kept the forge of my imagination burning red hot for years, and whose laughter will keep my engine running for many campaigns to follow.

Thank you to Matthew Lee Murphy, who listened to the very first incoherent pitch of this novel nearly a decade ago while wandering through Borders bookstore, and all the many pitches thereafter.

A deep thanks to the many writers' groups that I have been a part of, but especially to the Busboys and the (Zoom) Cave Dwellers—with special recognition due to Josh Durst-Weisman, Nick Owen, and Maja Olsen. Companionship and criticism are needful things for a writer, and you all made me a better one with each note and cut word.

A massive thanks to Chris "Prime" Bowen, who has read every draft and every page I've churned out. I'm not sure what special astronomical alchemy brought our brains together, but I thank fate, luck, and charm that we did every time I stare at a blank page. I wouldn't be half the man I am today without your sage advice.

And finally, thank you to my everlasting light, my wife Hayley. What I said on our wedding day still holds true: I don't have the words. A simple, whole-hearted *I love you* will have to do.

Chris Butera
September 2024

ABOUT THE AUTHOR

Chris Butera received his MA in creative writing and publishing from City, University of London, where he was a graduate with distinction. His short stories have been featured in Fireside and Near-Future Fictions. He wrote the story for the first two seasons of Contiloe Pictures' *Taj: Divided by Blood* and currently serves as the comic and prose editor for *Conan the Barbarian*. Butera lives in Los Angeles with his wife and two dogs.

Podium

THE PLOT THICKENS
follow us on our socials

 podiumentertainment.com
 @podiumentertainment
 /podiumentertainment
 @podium_ent
 @podiumentertainment